Murder at the Dacha

MURDER
AT THE
DACHA

ALEXEI BAYER

Russian Life
BOOKS

ISBN 978-1-880100-81-3

Library of Congress Control Number: 2013935580

Russian Information Services, Inc.
PO Box 567
Montpelier, VT 05601-0567
www.russianlife.com
orders@russianlife.com
phone 802-234-1956

Cover photograph: Andreiuc88 (dreamstime.com).
Cover design: Vanessa Maynard

CAST OF CHARACTERS

Main Characters

Sr. Lt. Pavel Matyushkin – detective, Criminal Investigations

Antonina (Tosya) Ivanovna Tolkunova – his girlfriend

Sevka – her son

Daniel Frezin ("Freak") – career criminal

Sr. Lt. Lenny Urumov – friend and colleague of Matyushkin

Lt. Col. Ashot Modestovich Martirosyan ("Budyonny") – Matyushkin's boss in Criminal Investigations

Col. Vladislav Mironovich Nakazov – State Security officer

Anton Pavlovich Polishchuk – Director, Mikoyan Meat Processing Plant

Anna Panteleyevna Polishchuk – his wife

Lyuda Polishchuk – their daughter

Hera (Herman) Gnatyuk – Polishchuk's driver

Natasha Polyakova – Polishchuk's secretary

Other Characters, in Alphabetical Order

Arkady Matveyevich Brunevsky – fixer

Della – Budyonny's secretary

Sasha Gregoriev – medical expert, Criminal Investigations

Zhorik – driver, Moscow Criminal Investigations

Maj. Karbyshev – internal investigator at Senya Pavlov's labor camp

Aunt Ksenia – Uncle Nikolai's wife

Grandma Masha – Tosya's neighbor

Uncle Nikolai – peasant, friend of Matyushkin

August Karlovich Nuremberger – consignment shop appraiser

Senya Pavlov – inmate, Lyuda Polishchuk's ex–boyfriend, convicted as an associate of Rokotov and Frezin

Mrs. Pavlov – Senya Pavlov's mother

Praskovia – concierge at the Polishchuks' apartment building

Raisa – Lenny's wife

Victor Rastorguyev – thief, Ryzhikov's stepfather

Ian Rokotov – black currency trader, convicted and executed for his crimes in 1960

Jr. Lt. Ryumin – Criminal Investigations, Moscow Region, Zapekayev's second-in-command

Peter Ryzhikov – small-time thief, Rastorguyev's stepson

San Vasilich – local drunk, Matyushkin's neighbor

Shamil – Brunetsky's bodyguard

Vitaly Arkadevich Tyatkin – Polishchuk's neighbor

Victor – driver, Moscow Criminal Investigations

Yevdokia Filippovna – Matyushkin's neighbor

Cpt. Zapekayev – Criminal Investigations, Moscow Region

SEPTEMBER 1962

ONE

Coincidences happen all the time. They set in motion other coincidences, which then intersect and twine about one another to form the fabric of life. The incident on the train wouldn't have happened at all, or would have happened differently, if Misha the mechanic had fixed my war-booty Zundapp a few days earlier.

My Zundapp had been in the shop for several weeks. Misha had done his best to explain what was wrong. He poked at the disassembled engine, strewn on oil-sodden newsprint, and mumbled something about the fuel pump, the rifling on the cylinders, and the air-fuel blend in the carburetor. Having thoroughly confused me, he extinguished my last ray of hope, declaring that I should not expect my bike back before the November holidays.

The basic problem was that domestic spare parts don't fit Nazi bikes. Any number of tinkers could, no doubt, fit it with something meant for a Ural or an I-Zh, or maybe even for a Czech-made Java – even though Java spares were themselves worth their weight in gold – and the Zundapp might run reasonably well. But the tinkers had no illusions about their abilities and admitted freely that their solution was at best a last resort.

Misha said he knew a man at the flea market, a collector of various machines captured from the Germans during the war, who could

apparently get authentic German parts. When this might happen
– and, more importantly, how much it would set me back – were
questions that went unanswered. Misha shrugged and walked away.

Meanwhile, the nights were getting colder. In the morning, out in
front of our apartment building, frost glistened along the edges of the
yellowed grass. Since early September I had stopped going to work
in shirtsleeves. If we wanted to spend a day by the river, there was no
time to waste.

"What do you think, Antonina Ivanovna," I asked Tosya, using her
full name and patronymic, all respectable-like. "Should we try to go
or not?"

"Let's go, of course, Uncle Pavel," Sevka exclaimed.

In the summer, when Tosya and I visited Sevka on a Parents' Day
at his Young Pioneers' Camp, I had promised him I would take him
fishing on the Oka, where I knew of a really great spot.

"Do you really want to go?"

"Of course I do. You promised in June."

"I know I did. But we'd have to go by public transport, because my
bike is still in the shop. It'll take us two hours just to get there."

I was talking to Sevka, but I kept looking at his mother. She would
be the one to decide.

"So what?" said Sevka. "The train is just as good."

"We'll need to set off early."

"But you promised," Sevka whined.

"That I did, but it may just not work out."

Tosya listened and frowned. She didn't want to give up her Sunday
morning sleep-in, but she also felt sorry for Sevka. During the school
year, he never gets out of town. He spends Sundays hanging out with
his buddies in city lots, climbing fences and tearing his school uniform
on rusty nails.

I waited for Tosya to decide. Sevka stared at her with eyes full of
hope.

"Come on, Mom. Please."

Tosya pondered the issue, then jerked her head decisively. Once she makes a decision, it's always final. It's no use arguing with her.

"Forget your bike, Matyushkin," she said. "We'll go by train."

Sunday began thick with morning fog as I bundled them up and marched them out across the courtyard. They looked like two zombies in the white mist, and I kept shaking Sevka by the collar of his windbreaker to make sure he wouldn't fall asleep on his feet. During the train ride to Serpukhov, Tosya stared straight ahead, glassy-eyed. Sevka nodded off the moment he sat down.

But by eight o'clock, when we got off the local bus at the other end, the fall day had cleared. We got lucky with the weather, catching the peak of a brief Indian summer. I was actually glad that we didn't have my Zundapp. It was such a pleasure to walk through the bosk of young pine trees and along the collective farm field, to follow a slippery narrow path through the alluvial pasture along the river.

"Look around," I told them. "That's why they call it Golden Fall. Smell the fresh air, Sevka. Keep on breathing, Tosya. Take a deep breath. One-two. In-out. Fill your lungs."

By then, Sevka and Tosya were sufficiently awake to start breathing. What else could they do but breathe? They were living beings, after all.

"Wow," I continued, gushing lyrical. "Living in the city, you never get to see anything like this. No nature, nothing."

We skirted the village, walking through a pasture of tall, sweet-smelling clover and gasped as we came out onto the low bank of the Oka. The morning air was brisk and almost frosty, but the river held the warmth of the previous day, and its smooth, reflective surface was shrouded in translucent vapor. The sky was blue and gold, and the woods on the high bank opposite were gold and red. It was like a painting hanging in the Tretyakov Gallery, only better. The fir trees were black brushstrokes amid a purple blur of maples, birches and aspens, standing like the honor guard in a funeral procession for a four-star general or a member of the Politburo.

To the left lay the city of Serpukhov, looking majestic from a distance with its old bell towers falling into ruin and its factory chimneys belching clouds of grey smoke.

I may not be as good at describing nature as Lermontov or even Pushkin. I'm just a criminal investigations detective. But it doesn't mean that I love it any less than they did.

And I also love Tosya.

I looked at her and smiled. Such a beauty. She dresses so nicely, so neat and elegant, yet at the same time practical.

"What are you staring at, Matyushkin?"

"Nothing. Just feasting my eyes on you."

I laughed.

"You're a fool, Matyushkin," she said gruffly. But there was tenderness in her voice and she smiled.

Sevka was eager to start fishing. That's because fish bite better in the morning, he said, offering his learned opinion.

Tosya and I piled our bags up next to Sevka and went for a walk. Sevka, like any fisherman worthy of the name, had eyes for nothing but his float. My backpack and Tosya's purse could have been stolen from under his nose, he wouldn't have been aware of it. Fortunately, there was no one around.

We got to higher ground, where the path was dry and firm, and began walking to the village.

At first glance, Zyatkovo was a perfectly ordinary village of three-dozen homesteads, even though it used to be a lot bigger. The log houses were ramshackle and listing, with peeling paint and neglected facades. Roofs had been patched with mismatched slate tiles and picket fences around meager vegetable patches leaned this way and that, their missing sections haphazardly replaced with barricades of rusty bed frames, carcasses of old bicycles and other household detritus. Chickens rooted in overgrown gutters along the main street, among rotted logs and sections of old sewer pipes. The country store, a large room smelling of kerosene and laundry soap, was in the back of a red brick building, which had whitewashed columns in the front and also housed the collective farm office.

But the place was famous in Russian history. A writer who also came to the Oka to fish, had told me once that the town was mentioned in the earliest chronicles. Recounting this to Tosya, I couldn't remember what century the fellow had said that was, but surely it was a very long time ago. There used to be an iron ore mine in the region, dug into the side of a tall mountain during the reign of Ivan the Terrible. The village church, even though it had been shut down after the Revolution, was also a historic monument, dedicated to Saints Boris and Gleb. Saints, like police patrolmen, apparently preferred to travel in pairs.

We stood around for a few minutes, staring at the church. Over the years, the building had sunk into the ground at least two feet. The front entrance was not in use, and the churchyard was overgrown with weeds and nettles tall enough to almost entirely conceal the collective farm machinery dumped here years ago. The way in was through a small metal door on the side of the building. Elderberry bushes grew in the steel carcasses that remained of the onion domes and in the arches of the bell tower. A flock of jackdaws circled over the building, cawing angrily. The windows were covered with plywood.

Tosya didn't like the church. It gave her the creeps.

Uncle Nikolai and his wife Aunt Ksenia lived in a house across the street.

"This is Antonina Ivanovna Tolkunova," I said, introducing Tosya formally. "And this is Uncle Nikolai."

As is customary in the country, Uncle Nikolai rose early, even on Sundays. Then, for the rest of the day, he did little except sit on a wooden bench in front of his house.

Uncle Nikolai studied us at length and shook his head doubtfully, as though he didn't entirely approve of our appearance. Then, he looked away and declared reluctantly, "Good morning to you, comrade copper. Sit down. Take a load off your feet, as long as you've come to visit."

We sat next to him and Aunt Ksenia brought us two glasses of fresh milk.

Aunt Ksenia was glad to see us. Uncle Nikolai was too, but he didn't like to show it.

"What is she?" asked Aunt Ksenia, pointing at Tosya and smiling mischievously.

"What do you mean, what?" I asked in mock surprise. "She's a bookkeeper. She works at the famous Tryokhgorka Textile Plant, the largest in the country."

"Don't make me laugh, Pavel," said Aunt Ksenia, laughing. "Why should I give a damn where she works? I want you to tell me what she is to you."

I hesitated, while Aunt Ksenia gave Tosya a wink, as if to say: "Let's see what answer he comes up with."

I gave it some thought, blushed and blurted out, "A fiancée, I suppose. I mean most likely."

The two of them burst out laughing like they were crazy, and kept at it for a long time.

Uncle Nikolai, meanwhile, sat stone-faced, staring at something far beyond the Oka, ignoring our conversation. That was his attitude: when the silly sex laugh, it's no business for a man to pay them any mind.

As we descended the steep slope toward the river, I took Tosya by the hand, my excuse being that I was trying to help her down a slippery path, and, once we got to flat ground, I pulled her suddenly toward me and kissed her on the lips.

Tosya is tall for a woman, and very strong. There is nothing soft or tender about her, especially when you first meet her. But whenever I kiss her lips they become like the petals of a field poppy. They are large, too, like an enormous flower in bloom. When we kiss in the dark, there is no need for me to search for her lips. I just keep kissing her, and wherever I kiss her, her mouth is always there, wide open and receptive.

"Come on, Matyushkin," said Tosya, pushing me away. "You and your nonsense. What if Sevka turned around and saw us? What would he think?"

"First of all, he wouldn't turn around in a million years. Don't you see he's busy fishing? But even if he did turn around, what of it? He'd see his Mom kissing Pavel Matyushkin. I bet he's already kissed every girl in his class."

"Don't bet on it, Matyushkin. I'll knock such thoughts out of him if I find out that it's true."

Something had made Tosya angry with me. Or perhaps she only pretended to be angry. As we walked along the river, she sneered a few times and finally said, derisively, "A fiancée my foot."

Later, when we took out our lunch and placed it on the brown bedspread we had brought from home, Uncle Nikolai came down the slope, limping slightly, and joined our small picnic. Tosya had made a kind of potato salad from boiled potatoes, chopped scallions and sliced tomatoes dressed with sunflower oil. She had also packed hard-boiled eggs, with small brown triangles of eggshell still clinging to their bluish sides. Tosya is not a good cook, but when she puts her mind to boiling potatoes or chopping vegetables, she always makes a big batch. Plus, in the country, the air makes everything taste better; any food that's fresh and plentiful will do.

Uncle Nikolai had no interest in our boiled eggs or potatoes. What he had come down to the river for was the quarter liter bottle of vodka that I had stuck into my backpack in the morning, in case we got too cold by the river and needed something to warm us up. Uncle Nikolai had a sixth sense that should be studied by learned professors at the Academy of Medical Sciences; it seemed to signal him whenever a bottle of vodka was about to be cracked open anywhere along the banks of the Oka within a distance of a kilometer. It never failed: whenever you started to pour, you would see Uncle Nikolai's gaunt figure limping toward you over the crest of the hill.

Sevka was given no vodka since he was a minor, and Tosya accepted a symbolic thimbleful. Uncle Nikolai and I quickly emptied our glasses and I refilled them.

"Where is that two-wheeled stinker of yours?" Uncle Nikolai asked, referring to my Zundapp.

"My stinker broke down," I said. "It won't be ready until November. Just in time to garage it for winter."

"I see," observed Uncle Nikolai. "Hitler kaput."

He lifted his glass and went on:

"No big deal, I say. Public transportation is safer and more convenient. Let's drink to public transportation, Pavel."

We clinked glasses and knocked them back.

"So," he said, concealing his disappointment when we finished the bottle and it turned out that I didn't have another. "Should I get the boat ready? Will you be taking a boat ride?"

"If you please, Uncle Nikolai," I replied.

While we were still fresh, we rowed against the current. The Oka flows strong and we went no more than three hundred meters before all three of us grew tired and gave up. We tossed the oars to the bottom of the boat and let it drift. But then we got very far very quickly, all the way downstream to the Serpukhov rail bridge. Tosya and Sevka pleaded complete exhaustion, which left me to get us back upriver.

In the late afternoon we played a game of soccer on an even patch high enough to be dry and not too densely covered with cow dung. We marked two goals, one was my backpack and Tosya's purse, the other was Tosya's jacket and the bucket Sevka had brought to hold his catch. The two of them were one team, I was the other.

Tosya, despite being a woman, is an excellent soccer player, better than most men. She can hit the goal from any distance, shooting with both feet like Streltsov, Russia's greatest star. She can pass, too, serving the ball to Sevka into open space behind my back. They scored on me a dozen times, making me sweat and gasp for air.

"Don't take it too hard, Uncle Pavel," said Sevka when we were done. "We were two against one."

Tosya was less charitable.

"I don't know about you sometimes, Matyushkin" she said shaking her head. "You're not as good as I would have thought. Getting blown out like this by a woman and a kid."

"Where did you get to be so good at soccer?" I asked her.

I had to pause between words, to get some air into my lungs.

"Come on, Matyushkin. I grew up at an orphanage, remember? You get to be good at lots of things, growing up at an orphanage."

Other people who had been in an orphanage were likely to hide it. It's nothing to be proud of. But Tosya, on the contrary, was always the first to mention it. Nor was Sevka ever embarrassed for his mother. He was proud of his Mom and her great soccer skills. They had beaten such a big strong guy.

Darkness comes early in mid-September. By six o'clock the daylight dims and the cold air begins to move in from the fields. We sat for a few more minutes in the thickening twilight, watching the sunset die beyond the village and the sky darken across the river, over the distant woods and the city of Serpukhov.

"I'm sorry I didn't catch anything," said Sevka. "The fishing was real lousy today. Such bad luck."

"Maybe next time," said his mother. "You'll bring us here again, won't you, Matyushkin?"

"Will you, Uncle Pavel?"

I nodded in the dark. Of course I would.

By the time we started back for the city, night had fallen.

Uncle Nikolai offered to accompany us as far as the paved road. He walked between Tosya and me, leading a woman's bicycle by the handlebars. A light on its steering column lit the uneven path's puddles, potholes and protruding tree roots, and it made the fields on either side of the path darker, larger and even a bit threatening. Uncle Nikolai's bike left us almost no room and we clung to the edge of the path, stepping on the soft, dew-washed grass.

Sevka walked a few paces ahead of us and the semicircle of light bounced off the back of his head and his dark sweater.

Uncle Nikolai broke the silence.

"Hey, Pavel," he said. "I wanted to ask you something. I mean, what's his name? You know. The writer?"

"What about him?"

"The one who kept telling us, you know, all that crap about Zyatkovo."

"Sure," I said. "The one who told us that Zyatkovo was mentioned in the old chronicles. Of course I remember him."

"That's right. Him."

Uncle Nikolai was silent for a long time.

"What about him?" I asked at last. "Was it all a pack of lies? I just told the whole story to Tosya."

Uncle Nikolai sighed.

"He's no writer," he said at last.

"I see. What is he?"

"A cop like you."

"How do you know?"

"I have my sources," he replied evasively.

We walked in silence, hypnotized by the bouncing beam of the bike light. The front wheel was deflated and the rubber, catching on the metal mud guard, squeaked at every turn.

"The *kolkhoz* chairman said so the other day," Uncle Nikolai resumed. "That he's a big cheese over at the cop department. If he doesn't like something, he could make chopped meat out of all of us here in Zyatkovo. Even wipe Zyatkovo off the face of the earth. In fact, they are already starting to do it, he and the other big cheese coppers. Right here, next to us, they're going to build a nucular redactor."

"They're going to build what?"

"A nucular speriment, they say," Uncle Nikolai explained. "The biggest in the world. Maybe you've heard them mention it over at your cop department?"

"I haven't. Not at my cop department."

"Then maybe you know the writer? If he is such a big cheese in your line of work?"

"No," I shrugged. "I never met him. Only here, on the Oka, I mean. In the city, we've got so many coppers, you wouldn't believe your eyes."

"Sure," said Uncle Nikolai. "There's any number of you bloodsuckers in the city."

There was another silence.

"Maybe he lied to us, our chairman," Uncle Nikolai said. "It wouldn't be the first time."

"God knows, Uncle Nikolai," I said. "We've got plenty of bosses and big cheeses. It's hard to know who your own bosses are, and then there are other people's bosses and their bosses, too. You can lose your mind trying to meet them all."

It's true, the writer had never told me his name. "I'm pretty sure you have read some of my work," he had said. "But the real writer has to be modest. The proof of a writer's worth is in his writing, not his name. A writer, as somebody once said, is an engineer of human souls. If you met a civil engineer, you wouldn't ask his name. You would want to know what bridges he built, or what factories. An engineer may be a lot more useful to society than all the writers put together."

Looking back on it, it was a pretty convoluted explanation for not giving me his name.

"If he were such a big cheese that he could wipe Zyatkovo off the face of the earth, Pavel, don't you think you'd know who he is?" Uncle Nikolai insisted.

"I don't know," I shrugged. "Nor do I care whether he is a real writer or not. But I wouldn't worry about Zyatkovo. No one is big enough to wipe out Zyatkovo. It's been around for centuries and was even mentioned in the chronicles. It will go on."

"And what if it isn't so old?" Uncle Nikolai asked thoughtfully. "What if the writer was lying about that, too? Just as he lied about being a writer."

Perhaps he was a writer, who knows, I thought. The military jeep he drove didn't have police department tags. Car tags tend to register in my head automatically, it's an occupational necessity. On the other hand, such military jeeps were for official use only and weren't sold to civilians.

"I don't know whether he's a writer or what," said Uncle Nikolai as though reading my mind. "All I know is that he makes the fish bite something awesome."

There was a touch of envy in his voice.

We had reached the paved road and stopped under the shelter of the bus stop. A light bulb glowed in the ceiling. Uncle Nikolai's bike light went out when the bike was not in motion. The road was empty and the crowns of the tall pine trees on either side of the road closed in above our heads. The wind picked up, rustling the dry leaves and toying with a faded May Day poster on the bulletin board.

"I had no luck," Sevka complained. "I didn't get a single bite all day. Otherwise I could've caught lots of fish and Mom would have made us fish soup."

Uncle Nikolai patted Sevka's hair, recently cut for the school year, smacked him lightly on the back of his head and said, looking at Tosya, "A nice kid. He's got a practical bent, thinking about providing food for his Mom."

Uncle Nikolai's words pleased Tosya. She was strict with Sevka, but deep down she was very proud of him.

"What about you, Uncle Nikolai? Do you and Aunt Ksenia have kids?"

I shoved an elbow into Tosya's ribs, but it was too late.

"Us?" asked Uncle Nikolai as though he was carefully weighing an answer. "Kids? We did have kids once, my dear girl."

Having not entered their house, Tosya had no way of knowing that, in the far right-hand corner where in the old days peasants used to place their icons, there now hung two out-of-focus black and white portraits in identical homemade frames. Two passport photos crudely enlarged at some studio in Serpukhov. Two village lads looking neither like Uncle Nikolai nor like Aunt Ksenia but a lot like each other, thanks to their frozen, bulging eyes, the khaki caps resting angularly on freshly shaven skulls, and the discolored, standard-issue fatigues of Red Army privates.

"We did have kids once," Uncle Nikolai repeated, suddenly speaking as though he were explaining a complex task to a not-too-bright apprentice. "My youngest, Semyon, got drafted the day he turned eighteen. Eighteen years of age, time to go into the infantry. And a month later his mother got a letter from the infantry. In so many words, dear Polyksenia Ilyinishna, the heroic battle for the city of Stalingrad, your son is a hero, and some such crap. A standard letter they send everybody in such cases. As to my eldest, Yegor Nikolayevich, he managed to get through the entire war without a scratch. From the battle of Moscow to Budapest. Then he went missing. The devil knows what happened to him. We waited and waited for him to come back but he never did."

"I'm sorry, Uncle Nikolai," said Tosya softly.

"We had a girl, too," added Uncle Nikolai. "Anna by name, I think. She died too, but earlier. In thirty-five."

"I'm very sorry," Tosya repeated, crestfallen.

"No big deal, dear girl. Keep on asking if you want to know. It's all the same now. You can't bring them back."

Uncle Nikolai took another of my cigarettes, twisted it between his thumb and index finger, tore off the filter and lit up. On the back of his right hand, at the root of the thumb, there was a dark-blue tattoo of an anchor.

An awkward silence fell over our small group. To dispel it, I asked Uncle Nikolai whether he thought I was a big cheese copper too. Would I have been able to raze Zyatkovo to the ground, if I wanted to?

I was kidding, but Uncle Nikolai took the question seriously. He answered it after a long pause, during which he apparently gave it a great deal of thought.

"You might not be a big cheese, Pavel, but you're a copper all the same. Every copper wants to be a boss. Whether big or small it don't matter, but you must boss people around. You might be a nice guy deep down, I can't tell. Don't be mad at me. I reckon that if you didn't want to boss people around and show off how high and mighty you are, why on earth would you want to be a copper?"

I didn't have time to reply. Suddenly, a bus rounded the corner, fixed its headlights on the bus stop and began to barrel toward us at great speed.

I tossed aside an unfinished cigarette and ran to the edge of the road, waving my hands. The bus came to a stop and opened its front door. I helped Sevka up, to make sure he didn't dawdle and waste the driver's time. Tosya pushed me aside and hopped onto the bus landing, despite her heavy boots.

"See you around, Uncle Nikolai," I shouted. "Thanks for everything."

"See you," replied Uncle Nikolai, waving.

From the back window of the moving bus we saw him push his bicycle forward to gain momentum, throw his leg over the seat and move out of the circle of light illuminating the bus stop. Then, in the darkness, his bike light switched on. It flickered among the trees until the bus followed the turn of the road and Uncle Nikolai swung out of sight.

"How embarrassing," Tosya said. "You should have warned me about his boys. It must have upset him terribly."

"Probably not," I shrugged. "He's used to it."

"Did they have any medals?" asked Sevka.

"I don't know," I said. "The older one might have gotten some."

"And the younger?"

"I don't think so. He didn't have time to do anything they award medals for."

TWO

Having left Serpukhov half-empty, the train gradually filled up with Muscovites returning to the city after Sunday outings to their dachas. At the frequent suburban stops, new passengers, dressed in heavy raincoats and compost-splattered rubber boots, brought in the brisk September air and the sharp smell of late summer apples. They carried knit bags full of loose beets and potatoes, bunches of scallions, jars of raspberry preserves, and pickled cabbage.

Grandmothers rushed in as soon the doors opened, pushing their lackadaisical grandchildren forward, urging them to grab the remaining empty seats.

We sat in a row on a hard wooden bench. Sevka had nodded off by the window, resting his head on his mother's shoulder. The country air and outdoor activities had worn him out. I got up every few minutes to assist the fresh crop of grandmothers, hoisting their bags onto a rack above Sevka's head.

Soon the car was full and I let an older woman have my seat. She held a gorgeous bouquet of yellow dahlias and red and white gladioli in one hand and a bag of large cauliflowers in another. I headed to the landing to smoke a cigarette.

"May I come with you, Uncle Pavel?" Sevka asked, suddenly waking and hopping from his seat.

"Be careful out there," Tosya shouted after him as we headed toward the end of the car.

Tosya is always worried about Sevka and doesn't trust me to watch over him properly. Since he's not my flesh and blood, I simply can't be expected to care about him.

Tosya slid along the bench toward the window, making room for the older woman's husband. He was overweight and short of breath, and as he squeezed in next to his wife, she immediately plopped the cauliflowers and the bouquet onto his lap.

On the landing, the wind swirled, blowing acrid cigarette smoke out through a missing windowpane.

A kid with a grim face came toward me.

"Hey, buddy, got a cigarette?"

He was no more than seventeen and his windbreaker had a hole in the shoulder. I had noticed him and his two companions when they got on the train. Stopping at the door, they had surveyed the passengers and positioned themselves on the landing.

I shook two cigarettes out of the pack, one for myself and one for the kid.

"Give me two, will you?" he snapped, attempting even as he spoke to snatch a third cigarette from my packet with his dirty fingernails. "There are three of us here."

"I've only got two left," I replied sharply, moving the packet out of his reach.

The kid gave me a long, unfriendly look but decided not to pick a fight. A wise decision.

Sevka and I found a place to lean against the wall and absorb the bumps as the wheels bounced rhythmically beneath us. The train was moving fast. An unlocked door rattled somewhere between two cars. The three kids took turns taking drags on my cigarette, each spitting on the floor after exhaling. I didn't like them. They were the sort of juvenile delinquents capable of any sort of nastiness. In short, hooligans.

"You shouldn't have given up your seat," I said to Sevka. "It's much warmer in the car."

He shook his head.

"Mom would've made me get up sooner or later. Too many oldsters standing around."

"True enough," I agreed.

The train stopped and the landing momentarily filled with people squeezing past us with their bags. Somebody accidentally bumped one of the hooligans. He cursed at the offender and punched him in the back.

"Watch your mouth," I said. "Don't you see there's a school kid over here?"

"Mind your own business."

It got even colder after the doors had been opened, and a sharp draft blew through the landing. Sevka shivered.

"Go back to your Mom," I said. "Tell her to give you a sweater. If you catch a cold out here and end up missing school, she'll wring my neck."

Sevka went back into the car and I turned to the hoodlum in the torn windbreaker, clearly their leader, in case he intended on picking a fight, after all. He still didn't, and neither did I. It's not my job to improve young people's manners.

I finished my cigarette and threw it out the window. The kids finished theirs, too, and dropped it on the floor, where it rolled back and forth amid the spit and litter, giving off red sparks each time it hit the wall.

"Uncle Pavel, come quickly."

Pulling apart the sliding doors, Sevka burst out onto the landing.

"Mom told me to get you. There's a fight. Lots of shouting. Some guy has been bothering a woman."

Sevka was slurring his words with excitement. He turned and, not waiting for me, began pushing his way back through the crowd. The people were packed tightly in the aisle, blocking my view. They were all watching something very exciting taking place at the other end of the car.

At just that moment, a tall man in a long tweed overcoat stood up. His back was turned and I couldn't make out his face. He was facing a middle-aged woman. She wore a pink cardigan, its home-knit fabric stretching over her ample bosom in long diagonal folds. She was plump and short, her head barely as high as the man's shoulder. But her hands rested defiantly on her hips and her double chin was thrust forward, her posture suggesting that she was not going to take anything from anyone. Things had clearly gone pretty far between the two of them.

"What kind of behavior is this?" she screamed, stabbing the air with an index finger. "Harassing a young woman like this! On a suburban train no less!"

She had become red in the face and her eyes gleamed. A lock of hennaed hair burst out from under her kerchief.

"Shut up," said the man.

His voice was weary and soft, but the words were distinctly audible in the sudden silence that had overtaken the car. He had the air of someone who had been holding things in for a long time.

"What do you mean?" shrieked the woman. "This good-for-nothing has been harassing women in plain daylight, and no one has dared say anything. I've got a car full of witnesses."

Night had fallen and outside it was thick and black. A train, gliding at speed back toward Serpukhov, met us in the opposite direction, yellow light glowing from its windows.

"A drunk," opined a woman next to me.

"No way," declared a man. "A thug. A jailbird, for sure. I can spot them from a mile away."

As though to confirm the man's assertion, the tall man leaned over the woman in the pink cardigan and said, "Shut your mouth or I'll wring your neck."

The woman momentarily got choked up but then immediately recovered.

"Did you hear that?" she shrieked, turning to rally the other passengers. "He threatened me. You all heard it. Somebody do something about it. Why are you standing still, men?"

"Somebody should call the police," a voice said reluctantly.

The tall man had been sitting by the window, across from a young woman who appeared to be the cause of the commotion. Yet she was ignoring the intense argument going on over her head as though it had nothing to do with her. She wore a fashionable nylon headscarf with large blue polka dots, obviously imported, that cast a shadow over her face. The light of the passing train flitted across her sharp cheekbones.

The other passengers sitting on the same bench kept to themselves. They clearly did not want to get involved. I also decided to stay out of it for now and to let events unfold at their natural pace. The tall man may have been bad news, but the woman in the pink cardigan looked more than capable of taking care of herself. Nevertheless, moving slowly sideways, I edged up the aisle, which seemed to have become strangely less crowded, and positioned myself between the tall man and the nearest exit.

While the pink cardigan shrieked and gestured, appealing to her fellow passengers, I had plenty of time to study her adversary.

He was a character, no doubt about that. His clothes were worn and old-fashioned, and his tweed overcoat had at one time belonged to a heavy-set man. But he wore them neatly, and with great care. His boots had been recently waxed and polished, even though they were now splattered with mud. His hair was short and his cheeks were clean-shaven. I couldn't easily tell his age. He had a young, energetic, intense face that became even more intense when he got angry, but it was also tinged with grey and deeply lined, showing signs of exposure to the elements and, at the same time, a lack of fresh air – a combination most frequently encountered among those who have done time in labor camps.

He clearly didn't relish being the center of attention. He would have paid dearly to make the pink cardigan shut up. His attempt to scare her had backfired, eliciting a never-ending torrent of invectives.

Finally, he gave up and started to edge out to the aisle, not worrying too much whether he stepped on other passengers' feet or bags. Once in the aisle, he glanced back – not at the still-shrieking pink cardigan, but at the younger woman by the window. He gave her what seemed a contrite look and headed toward the exit.

I stood in the aisle, blocking his way. He stopped very close to me – a little too close for comfort.

"Come on, asshole," he said in the same soft, weary voice. "Get out of the way."

I was starting to get used to being insulted on this train. I remained silent and didn't move.

"What the fuck, man? Are you deaf?"

"No," I replied. "My hearing has always been very good."

"What's your problem then?"

When his voice rose, it got higher-pitched, suddenly taking on the hysterical tone of a career criminal.

I shrugged, as if to say that I wasn't quite sure myself.

"Very well then, " he said. "You've asked for it."

He calmed down just as quickly as he had worked himself up. He looked like he had made a decision. He had had enough talk and was going to start acting. His right hand slipped into the pocket of his overcoat and came out again, empty but for a gleaming millimeter of straight razor squeezed between his thumb and forefinger.

The pink cardigan was surprisingly observant. This time she didn't shriek, but threw up her hands and whispered, "Oh my God. There's going to be a murder."

I don't think he was going to slash me right then and there, with so many people present. His intention was to frighten me enough to get me out of his way, and to encourage others on the train to stay out of it. But I have an aversion for straight razors. I've seen what damage they can do a person's face and neck. I shielded myself with my left arm, just in case, jumped as high as I could – he had an inch or two on me – and, throwing my head back and then bringing it sharply forward, head-butted him in the face. I felt a slight resistance just before his septal cartilage gave way, and then my forehead hit soft tissue. Something cracked, making a dull, sickening sound.

He sagged, blood streaming from his face, flooding his mouth and chin and dribbling down his shirt and onto his tweed overcoat in a narrow red rivulet. It gathered at his feet in a rapidly spreading dark puddle.

"Oh, my God," the pink cardigan said again. "They're going to kill each other. Men, comrades, what are you doing, sitting around like this? Get a move on!"

At last the men and comrades came to life. Several jumped up from their seats and rushed at the tall man, who was now sitting on the floor, his back against a bench. I pulled the razor from his grasp and, just as I did, a heavy-set citizen fell on top of him, pressing him down with the weight of his body and speaking hoarsely into his ear, "You goddamn thug, you'd better watch out."

"Get the police," shouted another passenger from his seat. "Let the cops deal with him."

I pushed the heavy-set citizen off the man and told the others to stop kicking him.

"I'm the police," I announced. "I'm Senior Lieutenant Pavel Matyushkin, Moscow Criminal Investigations. Do we have any witnesses?"

I pointed to the heavy-set citizen.

"You for instance? Are you a witness?"

"Yes, of course," the pink cardigan butted in, not waiting to be called. "I saw everything, Comrade Officer. When it started. I saw how he pulled a knife on you. He scared me so badly, I'm still sweating. Such a nice-looking young woman, too. The moment she got on the train, he sat down right across from her and started harassing her. A sex maniac, I'm sure. She'll tell you it's true. Won't you, my dear?"

She turned to where the young woman in a polka dot headscarf had been sitting. But her seat was now empty. At the other end of the car, the sliding doors slid shut.

"I see," I said, trying to catch sight of the female figure. Other heads turned after her, too. All I could see was the polka dot headscarf bobbing up and down as she moved into the next car.

"Never mind," I said, shaking my head and turning to the problem at hand. "We'll be getting off at the next stop. Somebody will need to help me pull our friend from the car. I don't think we should let him walk on his own. Please, comrades, no punching or kicking. We're Soviet citizens, after all, not Americans. We don't kick a man when he's down."

I finished up quickly at the police station in tiny Pokrovskaya. The pink cardigan and the heavy-set passenger both got off the train with us, then made and signed their statements. A local cop said he'd drive them to the first metro stop in the city. The perpetrator, who by then had come to, was to spend the night in lockup, possibly to be followed by a few additional nights, if they decided to slap him with a 15-day administrative detention for possession of a straight razor.

Sevka, Tosya and I returned to the station to wait for the next train.

It was going to be a long wait. Pokrovskaya was a small village being swallowed up by the spreading metropolis. Several suburban trains rushed past on their way to Moscow without slowing down.

The wind had picked up, chasing shapeless clouds over the black, moonless sky. An accordion played behind the tall fence around the station and discordant female voices broke into a song about a sailor on leave to his hometown. The lyrics warned the local beauties to stay away from him, and Tosya, who sat on a platform bench next to me, elbowed me gently in the ribs.

"Look at our senior lieutenant here," she said to Sevka in mock admiration. "A real hero. Caught a dangerous criminal, didn't he?"

Sevka sat at the other end of the bench holding his fishing rod. Poor guy, he was tired and sleepy, shivering and jerking his head now and again to stay awake. He started and asked, "Why didn't you punch him, Uncle Pavel? Just to make sure he got the message?"

"Punch who?" I asked.

"The dangerous criminal."

"He was already down."

"So what?"

"Should I have punched him while he was out for the count?"

"Why not? I would. He's a dangerous criminal. I would have really socked him one in the eye."

"I think you're getting carried away," I said. "Socking a person in the eye should be an extreme measure. Otherwise, it's counterproductive."

Sevka said nothing, but he seemed skeptical. Never mind, I thought. He'll get it when he gets older.

But, truth be told, even though on principle I don't approve of fighting, I actually like it. In fact, I've always liked it, ever since I was a kid much smaller than Sevka. In the factory shanties, where I lived with my mom and little sister, we kids used to fight constantly. The first time Kostya Trebushev called me out to go across the rail tracks I was no more than five or six. I remember being so scared, I thought I'd wet myself. Trebushev was older and had started school that year.

He punched me first, the moment we were round the corner and out of sight of any grown-ups. He didn't waste time on trash talk the way other kids did, psyching themselves up for a fight. I hadn't expected a punch and I caught it squarely on the nose. Blood dripped down the front of my white shirt. I remember thinking that Mom would give it to me for ruining a brand-new shirt. I felt no pain, and my fear suddenly disappeared, replaced by a strange excitement, exhilaration almost. I suddenly had an overwhelming desire to beat the crap out of Trebushev, even though I didn't know how to punch properly. I just made a fist and shoved it into Trebushev, but after that my hands took on a life of their own, pummeling poor Trebushev until he turned and ran off crying.

An overnight express flew by the forlorn Pokrovskaya at full speed, sounding a whistle, its wheels rattling down the tracks. It was headed south, to the Crimea or Sevastopol, to the warm southern sea. Its windows shone with bright electric light; you could see families getting ready for the night in the sleeper cars, and groups of unshaven men in undershirts playing cards and drinking tea in third class. The restaurant car glided past our hungry eyes, exhibiting the starched splendor of its snow-white tablecloths. Couples were dining, clinking champagne flutes and dipping tiny spoons into bowls of ice cream.

Their warmth and comfort made us even more miserable. The accordion behind the fence continued voicing melancholy tunes, and the chorus kept singing, sounding increasingly drunk and maudlin.

"Is this train ever gonna come?" Sevka asked in a whine.

"Don't you start," his mother responded sharply. "Just be patient. We're all waiting and nobody's complaining."

Tosya could be quite hard on Sevka sometimes.

Moscow's Kursk Station was nearly empty when we finally arrived, long after midnight. In the main hall, three figures loitered around a newspaper kiosk. I recognized them as the juvenile delinquents from the Serpukhov train. When they spotted me, they swiftly turned away, as if on cue, pretending to read the headlines plastered on the insides of the darkened kiosk windows.

The few transit passengers lying on benches in the main hall did not trust the hooligans either. A Central Asian man in a skullcap, grey suit, and dirty white shirt, frowned and noisily pulled his plywood suitcase closer.

THREE

It was the middle of the night when we got home. It was all Sevka could do to stand up after a day in the country and our subsequent misadventures, so Tosya went up to put him to bed. I whispered to her that I'd be waiting for her by the door of my apartment, so that she wouldn't have to ring the bell and disturb the neighbors.

She squeezed my arm above the elbow, by way of a promise.

By the time I finally walked her home, the day had started to dawn. We'd been awake for twenty-four hours. I felt sorry for her. She didn't get to catch up on her sleep on Sunday and would have to get up for work in a few hours.

The weather had gotten worse. The wind had brought in dark, heavy clouds and the grey September daylight had trouble getting through. The day promised to be overcast and wet. It started drizzling.

We had been lucky with the weather, I thought, as I jogged across an empty courtyard back to my apartment building, scowling under the raindrops. I got home, took off my wet clothes and towelled myself dry. I changed the sheets and covered my bed with the brown bedspread we had taken with us to the Oka. It still smelled sweetly of grass and autumn sunshine. It didn't make much sense to go to bed. I put on a fresh shirt and headed for work.

As expected, Monday was boring and grey. All day I was half asleep at my desk, clearing up old files. Nothing much happened, except the clouds got thicker and the rain turned colder and nastier, setting in for a long spell.

Not expecting much to be happening on Tuesday, either, I slept in, which turned out to be a mistake.

"What a shirker," said Lenny, my office mate, partner and friend, when he saw me.

Lenny Urumov was the world's greatest shirker and proud of it.

"Some working habits you have, Comrade Matyushkin, showing up for work at a quarter to eleven," he continued when I didn't respond. "Budyonny has been looking for you since early this morning and he's getting impatient. 'Where the devil is Senior Lieutenant Matyushkin?' he keeps asking me. 'Why on earth is he not at his desk? I want to see him right away.' In short, Budyonny told me to tell you, when you finally deigned to show up for work, to go and see him in his office."

Urumov was very good at imitating our boss' Armenian accent, even if he tended to exaggerate it for comic effect.

"Budyonny" is our boss, Lieutenant Colonel Ashot Modestovich Martirosyan. We probably have bigger bosses higher up, but Urumov and I never raise our heads so high. His subordinates call him Budyonny behind his back because of his long, luxurious moustache, one that, by some estimates, is even longer than the world famous moustache that was worn by hero and Red Cavalry Commander Semyon Mikhailovich Budyonny.

I tossed down my raincoat, which was dripping rainwater over my and Urumov's desks, piled everything up on my chair and ran to the door.

"I see," said Urumov as I squeezed by his chair. "So you've decided to pay a little visit to your boss, after all?"

To my surprise, Budyonny didn't start by yelling at me and didn't even mention my coming to work late. He seemed to be in the best possible mood.

"Thattaboy," he declared as I came into his office, winking at me. "Some performance on Sunday night."

I clicked my heels and stood at attention.

"In the service of the Soviet Union, Comrade Lieutenant Colonel," I responded smartly.

To be frank, I had no idea what he was talking about. True, I always do pretty well with Tosya – quite well, if I say so myself. We can really get things going, when we put our minds to it, and my body was still aching from our last bout of lovemaking. I've noticed that when there is love, the lovemaking is always great, and when there isn't, it gets boring pretty quickly. The problem was, first, that my superiors at Criminal Investigations had no way of knowing about my heroics and, second, even if they had, why on earth should they care about it and express their approval.

"At ease," Budyonny commanded, waving his hand as if to indicate that he was not interested in formalities.

I stood at ease and shifted my weight from one foot to the other. Neither of us said anything for several moments.

"Anyway," Budyonny said, at last breaking the silence. "How do you manage it? Do me a favor, share your secret with your colleagues."

"I do my best, Comrade Lieutenant Colonel," I said cautiously, playing for time.

"The weird thing is that I don't see you trying very hard," Budyonny said. "But it doesn't matter. Results speak for themselves."

I said nothing, waiting for him to continue.

"Actually, I don't care how you do it. All I know is that whatever you do with your Sundays, whether you get drunk like all normal people or go visit your mother-in-law or what have you, you also managed to catch a dangerous recidivist along the way."

Recidivist is a hard word to say, especially for somebody for whom Russian is not their native tongue. Budyonny spent quite some time getting his tongue around it, but still botched it in the end.

At least now I knew what he was talking about. This being Tuesday, the incident on the train out of Serpukhov had already slipped my mind.

There's so many scum riding on suburban trains, it'd be impossible to keep them all in your memory.

"Really?" I asked stupidly. "Did they get an identity check?"

Budyonny nodded. "They did. Very much so."

"And he turned out to be a dangerous recidivist?"

Budyonny nodded again.

"I haven't been told anything about it, Comrade Lieutenant Colonel."

Budyonny snorted and shook his head. He was getting excited, which always made his accent stronger.

"Wow," he said. "He is a true recidivist. You really don't know?"

I shrugged.

"His name Daniel Mikhailovich Frezin. Aka 'Freak.' A record as long as my arm."

"That's wonderful," I said. "I'm glad he's behind bars again. All's well that ends well."

"Nothing has ended yet. No need to rush to judgement. It has only just started. I want you do go to Podolsk, Moscow Region. There's a certain, what's his name, Captain Zapekayev there. I want you to look in on his interrogation. You made the arrest, so you're entitled to see how it turns out. I don't want them to get all the glory. By the way, what have you been working on?"

I shrugged.

"A routine case, Comrade Lieutenant Colonel. Apartment thefts. Breaking and entering. A bunch of very similar cases, the same people at work."

"Excellent. Pass it on to your partner, what's his name? Umanov? I mean Senior Lieutenant Urumov, of course. I want you to shift your attention to that fellow Freak."

"Is he wanted for something? Is he a suspect in a case?"

"Not that I know of. Not yet, at least. He's just got out, after paying his debt to society, as they say. He was dispatched to Belgorod, to live with his stepmother. What he was doing on a suburban train from Serpukhov is anybody's guess."

"He was harassing a woman, Comrade Lieutenant Colonel."

"Don't you get smart with me," Budyonny barked. "We've got plenty of smart asses around here without you joining them. You have to go to Podolsk now, this minute. Zapekayev has been having his fun with your Frezin since early this morning, ever since they figured out who he is. They've already contacted the police in Belgorod."

I stood at attention once again.

"I'll be ready, Comrade Lieutenant Colonel."

"By the way," Budyonny added before I went out. "If Zapekayev gets difficult, don't stand on ceremony. Tell him you are there on my orders. Call me right away if you have any problems. Understood?"

FOUR

Actually, I didn't get it at all. It wasn't clear to me why my presence in Podolsk, at the questioning of a minor thug, was so urgent. Nevertheless, after I finished explaining to Urumov where I stood on the apartment break-ins and what was in which folder, I went to look for our departmental driver, Victor, who as usual was biding his time in the windowless smoking room on our floor, and the two of us drove to Podolsk. Victor drove like a bat out of hell, which was his usual rate of speed when there was no traffic, and that was how I got there before the final curtain.

This proved to be exciting, if you go in for that kind of thing. I'm an old hand at interrogations, and I'm familiar with the methods of my Moscow Region colleagues, but what I saw was a little too dramatic even for me.

The room, under a low-slung, vaulted ceiling, was dark and airless. Thick iron bars covered the windows. The local jail had been built in Peter the Great's time and little seemed to have changed in two hundred years.

Near the door stood a small metal desk and several chairs. Captain Zapekayev, from the local criminal police, was squeezed behind the desk. He wore a full police uniform with two medal ribbons on his grey jacket and jodhpurs tucked into his polished leather boots. He was chain-smoking Kazbek cigarettes, squashing their cardboard filters into a bronze inkstand decorated with a bust of Leo Tolstoy, then immediately lighting another. A ledger with handwritten entries lay on the desk in front of Zapekayev. It was – I could tell right away – the Moscow Region police log.

At the edge of the desk sat a very young, very blond cop. He was taking notes – writing everything down as diligently as a grammar school student – in a lined notebook. He was using a thick fountain pen, but it was giving him trouble. Every now and then he had to stop and, cursing, shake the ink off the tip of the pen and onto the floor.

At the other end of the room, close to the window, stood Junior Lieutenant Ryumin, one of Zapekayev's subordinates.

All three were short and skinny. Their police uniforms hung baggily and untidily on their frames. It made them look more like civilians than police officers.

The fourth man in the room was my friend from Sunday night, looking much the worse for wear. His face showed two days' of stubble and a bandage was plastered across the bridge of his nose, black with dried blood. A large purple bruise spread around his nose, onto his sharply delineated cheekbones.

A bruise is a good thing, the doctors claim. It means that the patient is getting better.

Next to him stood a grey metal stool from the same set as the desk and the chairs. Apparently no one had offered Frezin a seat, and he stood next to the stool, easily a head taller than the tallest of the three cops. His hands dangled in front of him, held together by a pair of shiny steel handcuffs. We had received a shipment of identical handcuffs a few months ago, complete with the stamped inscription "Made in the German Democratic Republic."

"I'm not interrupting anything, am I?" I asked politely as I pulled the door open.

"Here already?" Captain Zapekayev exclaimed, his words dripping with sarcasm. "You guys move quickly up there in the big city. God forbid you leave us alone and mind your own business. Naturally, we country bumpkins are sure to make a mess of things without you looking over our shoulders."

Both he and his colleagues glared at me. And Frezin of course had no reason to be glad to see me, either.

I positioned myself against the wall, behind the blond kid's back.

"Ignore him," said Zapekayev. "Let's continue."

The proceedings resumed.

"The night of September 10th?" Zapekayev asked the prisoner after consulting the log in front of him. "Where were you? Grand larceny at the country store of the collective farm Path to Communism, near Serpukhov. Address, Pushkin Street 6. Can you account for your whereabouts that night?"

Frezin's face expressed exaggerated disbelief.

"Sure," he said, shrugging. "I was in Belgorod. At my stepmother's place."

"Will she be able to confirm it?"

"She will," Frezin affirmed, confident.

"No problem," said Zapekayev, turning the page. "How about this one? The evening of September 12. Approximately ten thirty at night? We have here a mugging of pensioner Ivan Orekhov occurring on First of May Street in the village of Ramenki. According to the victim, the mugger used a knife to threaten him, but it might have been a straight razor, because it was dark at 10:30 at night and the pensioner was shaken by the experience, which could have certainly affected his perception."

Frezin shrugged.

"I told you already a million times," he said in a monotone, as though repeating something he had memorized. "I bought a third-class ticket from Belgorod to Moscow in order to find a buddy of mine who knew of a job opening at a factory. In Serpukhov, I got out of the train to buy myself something to eat, then missed my train. I took a suburban train and rode without a ticket. What's the punishment for unticketed travel? You gonna shoot me?"

"We might," said Zapekayev. "We just might."

Zapekayev took a drag of his cigarette. The blond kid didn't smoke. He was too busy. Taking notes was hard work. Ryumin was also busy. He was staring at Frezin like a python trying to hypnotize a rabbit.

The blond kid cursed, unscrewed the plastic cover of his fountain pen and squeezed the ink pump a few times.

"Very well, then," Zapekayev continued after a short pause. "What about Serpukhov? On September 13, at approximately six in the afternoon—"

"Say, comrade police officer," Frezin casually interrupted. His eyes suddenly brightened and his face grew younger. "Maybe you could find a few crimes and misdemeanors on the railroad? Like maybe somebody took an unauthorized piss between cars on the night of August 31? It's more your speed."

Ryumin took two quick steps toward Frezin, but Zapekayev held up his hand.

"Hold on," he said. "There'll be plenty of time for that."

Ryumin restrained himself with considerable effort, stopping very close to the prisoner.

"Tell me, my friend" Zapekayev said, addressing Frezin in a suspiciously friendly tone of voice, "which of these crimes we should hang on you. Do you wanna choose one yourself or let us make the selection for you?"

Frezin shrugged.

"Don't be shy. You can pick more than one. Actually, I would like you to."

"May I ask a question?" I said.

The three pairs of unfriendly eyes shifted silently to me. Then, after a prolonged pause Zapekayev said, drawing out his words sarcastically, "Go ahead, Comrade Senior Lieutenant. Ask away. Make yourself useful."

Then, he added softly, under his breath: "Goddamn Sherlock Holmes."

"On Sunday, the day you took the train to Moscow," I said, ignoring Zapekayev's insult. "What time was it when you missed the train in Serpukhov?"

"I don't remember," Frezin replied cautiously.

"He was never in Serpukhov," Zapekayev laughed, lighting yet another cigarette. "Do you think we didn't check?"

"All the better," I said. "Then tell me what you did that day. Everything from the beginning."

"What do you mean?"Frezin asked.

"Just tell me everything you did on Sunday," I replied. "Start with when you got up, presumably very early in order to catch a train to Moscow, what you had for breakfast if you did have breakfast, what time you caught the train for Moscow, who was on the train with you, and so on. Give me as many details as you can remember. And, of course, don't forget to tell us who the young woman on the suburban train out of Serpukhov was and why you decided to bother her."

It was a fairly innocuous question, and one he should have been able to answer. All I wanted to do was to shift the interrogation in a different direction, to keep Zapekayev from trying to frame him for crimes he had obviously not committed. But the mischievous spark was suddenly gone from his eyes and his body grew tense with rage. It was a genuine jailhouse rage, frightening to behold. It sprung to life somewhere near the pit of his stomach and convulsed his body like a wave, causing him to painfully twist his mouth and clench his fists. He leaned forward, the whites of his eyes turning bloodshot, and shouted in my face, "Fuck you, pig. You want to hang this one on me, do you? Don't even fucking try."

His outburst finally gave Ryumin the opening he had been waiting for. Everything happened in a flash. Ryumin took one last step toward Frezin and struck him in the face with the edge of his palm. The blow caught Frezin on his broken nose along the line of the soiled bandage.

Frezin gasped but managed to suppress a howl of pain before it could leave his throat. He spun around, describing a full circle, and as he turned to face us again he swung his handcuffed hands at Ryumin's temple. The shiny East German handcuffs flashed through the air like a dagger.

The blow was swift and extremely accurate. Ryumin's head jerked one way while his body flew across the room in the other direction, limp as a rag doll. Frezin threw himself on top of Ryumin, pinning him to the floor.

Zapekayev, who had just taken a drag from his cigarette, was seized by a coughing fit. The blond kid's mouth fell open . He had not been on the force long, and had yet to see a suspect beat up on a police officer, rather than the other way around. I was the closest to them, but also didn't react fast enough. By the time I joined the action, Frezin was sitting solidly astride Ryumin's lifeless body.

Frezin had no intention of continuing to beat Ryumin. Instead, he wiggled himself forward until he was practically sitting on Ryumin's head. Ryumin came to and opened his eyes only to see the prisoner's padded trousers hanging over his face.

Frezin thrust his pelvis into his face and said softly, "Open it up, faggot. Take it in."

I don't know how far things would have gone, but I wasn't going to stand there waiting for the outcome. I threw my right arm around Frezin's neck and began to pull him off Ryumin. Frezin tried to twist out of my grasp, shaking his head and sending a semicircular jet of blood around the room. By then Zapekayev had reached us, followed closely behind by the blond kid, who had tossed his large notebook and temperamental pen onto the floor.

Working together, and assisted by Ryumin, who had recovered enough to push from below, we managed to pull Frezin away and onto the floor. He yelled obscenities at Ryumin, spraying his face with blood. Ryumin yelled back at him, matching his vocabulary word for word.

Finally, Zapekayev pulled Frezin's handcuffed hands up, over, and behind his head, allowing us to push him to the wall. Despite the pain from his twisted arms, Frezin still managed to kick at Ryumin's face, but this time Ryumin was more alert. He caught Frezin's foot and began twisting it. Then he jumped to his feet and, not bothering to dust himself off or wipe Frezin's blood from his face, he closed on the prisoner, who was being kicked by the other two.

"Out of my way," he shouted, breathing hard and pushing the blond kid aside. "Let me have a go at him."

I moved to the window and stood with my back to them. The bottom half of the window pane showed several coats of white oil paint, one on top of the other. Under all the thick layers, a three-letter curse word had been scratched into the glass long ago and was still perfectly legible. The day outside, whatever could be seen of it through the barred window, was overcast and dark. In the room behind me there were the sounds of heavy blows, cursing, groans, and the panting of my Moscow Region colleagues.

"Very well then," I said after a while. "I'm leaving. The proceedings will continue in the morgue."

I didn't expect an answer, but Captain Zapekayev interrupted his labor of love long enough to wipe sweat from his brow and respond, "Take it easy, Sherlock."

"I'll be back," I said, "if you plan to conduct any more interrogations. It's always a pleasure to watch you work."

It took us a lot longer to get back to the city. Victor steered with one hand and gesticulated with the other. Continuing the conversation we had started on the way out, he described the move a Spartak forward had made against a Dinamo halfback, or something along those lines.

Victor's words went in one ear and out the other. The rain was falling monotonously onto the road. An line of trucks snaked its way into Moscow, and our little official Moskvich felt squeezed between their mud-splattered sides. Condensation made the windows opaque and I rolled mine down a quarter of an inch to get some raw fall air. After the smoke-filled room of the Podolsk prison, my lungs needed airing out. Something else needed airing out, too, the part of the chest cavity where, old wives used to say, our immortal soul resides in its earthly abode. Mine had collected too much dirt during my visit to Podolsk.

It was nearly four in the afternoon when we finally returned to Petrovka. The staff cafeteria was closed, but Urumov had a friend at a greasy little restaurant on the Boulevard Ring, tucked into the dark basement behind a fish store. Her name was Katya. Even though they too had stopped serving lunch, Katya let us in and brought us two *prix fixe* lunches. Urumov had useful friends like Katya all over the city.

"Zapekayev is a character, of course," Lenny declared once I finished telling him about my adventures in Podolsk. He spoke with his mouth full, chewing on the bluish meat patty that had been served atop a bed of overboiled noodles.

"You're not kidding," I agreed.

Urumov ate systematically and in large quantities. Having finished his food, he moved aside the ceramic vase with the droopy yellow mum that was sitting in the middle of the table and stared avidly at my plate. I didn't have much of an appetite and was just picking at my meat patty with my fork.

"Are you going to eat that?" he asked.

I wasn't hungry, and the meat patties weren't going to rouse anyone's appetite. But Lenny's gluttony was annoying.

"Yes, I am," I replied, pulling my plate closer.

He sighed, fished the last piece of rye bread from the straw basket between us and began to spread it with a thick layer of mustard.

"You know, of course," I said slowly, "that at the labor camp it's the gluttons who succumb first. The ones who never have enough no matter how much they eat."

"In short," concluded Urumov, chewing on his bread-and-mustard. "Your visit to our colleagues was an abject failure. You can take back your stinking apartment break-ins."

"I will," I said readily. "I'll take them back soon. But you keep them one more day. I want to double-check something, just to make sure. Plus, it would be great if you brought a fresh eye to the files. Perhaps I missed something."

Lenny shrugged.

"I doubt it very much," he said. "Not because you're such a great detective, but because those break-ins are as ordinary as a donkey's ass."

I didn't get the metaphor, but he didn't care. He finished his dessert, which was, as usual in that restaurant, a cup of viscous, starchy, pink wild berry drink. Then he reached across the table for my cigarettes.

FIVE

Wednesday was also a busy day. A little too busy for my taste.

In the morning, before going to work, I stopped by the shop to ask if there was any news on my Zundapp.

Misha said he thought he had found the part, although not through the first guy at the flea market. Some new guy claimed to have it and Misha only needed to find time to go see him and make sure it was the right one. If it was, he would start installing it.

"You can come and pick it up later today."

"Later today?" I asked, astounded, convinced that I had misheard him.

"Or you can wait till next week, I don't care," Misha replied, turning away and climbing under an old Pobeda suspended on a hydraulic lift.

At work, where I arrived on time, I took the elevator down from the main floor to the central archive of active cases in the criminal investigations system. I found Daniel Frezin's file surprisingly quickly. It was thick and gave plenty of food for thought.

Frezin was born in Belgorod, where his father's widow was still living and where he had been sent after his release from jail. His own mother died early, his father was a drunk and had two minor convictions, to match his two official marriages. Frezin was a high school dropout who got in trouble with the law at an early age, mainly for fighting and petty hooliganism. At the end of the 1940s he spent a year at a correctional facility for underage offenders and then, the moment he reached the legal age of 16, got three more years as a member of a gang specializing in stealing luggage at the Belgorod train station. Frezin served his sentence in Gorky and was freed early, but was promptly arrested again for violating Article 144B of the old Penal Code – grand larceny committed by two or more persons forming a criminal association. Once more, Frezin was lucky and came out the very next year, this time thanks to a nationwide amnesty.

In other words, my new friend had a habit of committing crimes, getting caught and going to jail – but also serving little time and getting out early for one reason or another.

After that, he stayed out for four whole years. When he finally got in trouble, it was on a completely different matter.

His new indictment was part of the well-known Rokotov case, that was both extensive and politically important. People gossiped about it in queues at Moscow shops and *Izvestia* even ran a series of articles about it, first in the form of hints and insinuations, and then openly and in great detail.

It was a highly unusual case, involving illegal currency transactions with foreigners. Since all currency transactions between individuals are illegal, and a Soviet citizen is not allowed to hold any foreign currency, what those people did was a crime in and of itself. But the stunning thing in this case was the amount of money involved, amounts that, to an ordinary Soviet citizen like myself, seemed like something out of a book about American millionaires. At least three hundred members of the clandestine organization were put on trial. Three of their leaders, including Ian Rokotov, who gave the case its name, were executed. Anyone in any way connected with the gang got lengthy sentences in high-security correctional facilities reserved for hardened criminals.

So you would expect that Frezin, given his colorful past, would have attracted particular attention from prosecutors. He was all the more unusual in this case, because most of the other members of the Rokotov gang had no police record or, at most, had been booked for selling American LPs in front of record stores. They were Moscow kids from prosperous families attending good colleges and universities. Certainly none were career criminals like Frezin.

At one point, one of the arrested kids started to talk to the investigators about Frezin, but no actual testimonies made their way into Frezin's file. This suggested that they had been the work of the investigators' own imagination and in the end had to be thrown out. In fact, judging by the laughably short sentence Frezin got at trial, they couldn't make anything stick. Most likely he had absolutely nothing to do with the case and simply happened to be in the wrong place at the wrong time.

I shrugged and continued reading.

Still, it was very strange. I'm no rookie in Criminal Investigations and I know that men with a past like Frezin's don't usually quietly slip out of high profile cases. If they do, it means they are escaping through some back door. In other words, prosecutors have their reasons to keep them out.

On the other hand, this time he served his full two-year sentence. According to camp administrators' reports, his behavior during incarceration was as bad as could have been expected. He socialized with hard-core criminals who rejected rehabilitation, frequently refused to work, and barely avoided getting slapped with an additional sentence while in jail.

Frezin got out only recently, in mid-summer, and was sent to Belgorod, where he had to share his father's apartment with his stepmother. (His father had died while Frezin was in jail.) His parole officer had yet to submit his first report, which is as expected, given how little time had passed, but the absence of any new information meant that Frezin had not missed any of his compulsory appointments at his local police station.

The mug shot in the file, full face and profile, matched Frezin's curriculum vitae. It showed him with head shaved, grim-faced and hard to recognize. A list of tattoos, piercings and scars was also enclosed.

After I finished working through this informative sheaf of documents, my lungs now filled with a vacuum cleaner's allotment of dust, I left without stopping in at my office. Yesterday's rain had stopped, the skies had cleared, and the unpaved path cutting through the boulevard lay covered with fallen leaves. Hopping over puddles and sliding on the wet clay, I walked briskly to Trubnaya Square, where the A tram makes a sharp turn on its way to Mary's Wood. I got off a couple of stops beyond the Garden Ring, at the Durov Menagerie. There began a skein of crooked side streets and alleyways stretching toward Meshchanskaya Lane. The houses in this neighborhood were old, squat and made of wood, with village-style ornaments framing the windows. The gardens behind the high wooden fences were thick with tall trees and shrubbery, concealing from the prying eyes of strangers whatever might be going on inside the houses. As a matter of fact, if you didn't know your way around, it was best to stay away.

Leading away from a side street – so inconspicuously that it could have been missed between two tall fences and a pigeon coop – was a narrow blind alley. The paved surface turned into cobblestones and soon ended at a solid steel gate. The gate was painted blue and sported a large lock, along with the sign: "Beware of Attack Dog."

Barking began the moment I touched the bell button. I did not hear the bell. If it did ring, its sound was entombed somewhere beyond the fence. I waited for a long time, even though I thought I saw a curtain move in the far window of the one-story building behind the fence. At last, a voice on the other side quieted the dog. There was the rattling of a heavy chain and a short, dark kid opened the gate.

"What do you what?" he asked tersely.

"Arkady Matveyevich at home?" I responded.

"Get in."

I squeezed through the crack he made for me in the gate and found myself in the leaf-strewn front yard.

The kid promptly closed and barred the gate behind me.

"Name?" he asked.

"Matyushkin," I replied, matching his laconic manner.

He nodded.

"Wait here."

Leaving me in the yard, to be watched over by the large German shepherd, which growled softly inside its dog house, he walked up the steps and disappeared inside the house. A brand-new, motorized cart – made for disabled war veterans – stood under a canvas-topped carport in the corner.

"Come in," said the kid, sticking his head out the door.

He stood aside reluctantly, letting me enter, and shut and relocked the door the moment I was through it.

The living room was unexpectedly large, spacious, and expensively furnished with heavy, antique furniture. A spinet stood against the wall, topped by a bronze candelabra that was covered with drips of congealed wax. A large bookcase, overflowing with well-thumbed volumes, rested on sturdy dragon clawfeet. It seemed to be buckling under the weight of the books, driving its twisted talons into the thick nap of the Persian rug that covered the parquet floor.

I don't know much about paintings, but I could tell that the ones hanging on the walls were foreign. The first was a double portrait; a lady in a shiny satin dress, with a pearl necklace around her neck, leaned on the arm of a gentleman who was wearing a tall, old-fashioned starched collar and had a top hat perched atop his bald skull. The woman's dress and pearls, as well as the evening coat worn by her companion, had been painted with great care, but the faces were done in a slapdash manner, as though the artist had become bored and decided to complete it as quickly as possible. The subjects' faces blushed an unnaturally bright shade of pink.

That painting was bad enough, but the one hanging next to it was worse. It had a thick, gilded frame, yet seemed to have been painted by a small child. I couldn't figure out what it was. At first I thought it was another portrait, but while the eyes were relatively easy to locate, the nose and the ears were nowhere to be seen. There also seemed to be a pair of bare breasts painted on the side, but I couldn't be sure. In other words, a waste of a perfectly good frame.

Arkady Matveyevich had placed his huge, hairy forearms on the table and sat staring at me. He wore his salt-and-pepper beard long and the thick curls of his hair, which framed a large bald spot on the top of his head, were also long, greying and wiry. He was a large man and gave the impression of being strong, rather than just heavy. The impression didn't disappear when he pushed back from the table and sent the old mechanical wheelchair in which he sat rolling toward the middle of the room. The empty legs of his soft wool trousers had been carefully folded and tucked beneath his stumps. The chair's tires left deep ruts on the rug as they rolled across it.

"Cheers," he said, offering a familiar greeting. "You'll forgive me if I don't shake your hand."

"Good day to you, Arkady Matveyevich," I replied as courteously as I could. "I'm glad to see you in good health."

"I won't get up," Arkady Matveyevich continued. "Nor am I going to ask you to sit down."

"Don't worry about me," I assured him and smiled politely at his joke. "I'll stand. Thank God I can."

"Enough joking," the invalid said sharply. "State your business and be gone, chop-chop."

"I've got a question for you, Arkady Matveyevich."

"Then get on with it, man. Don't beat around the bush."

"I want to get some information. Daniel Frezin, also known as Freak. What do you know about him?"

Arkady Matveyevich gave it some thought. He was doing some careful calculations in his head. He was a good actor – he had to be in his line of work. If he hadn't wanted to show me that he was doing calculations, he wouldn't have.

What he was calculating came down to this: He, Arkady Matveyevich Brunetsky, owed me a small favor. It was a matter of something I had once done to help him. Of course he would never have dreamt of refusing to pay it back. On the contrary, he would have gladly done it a long time ago, but the problem was that, until then, I had not asked for repayment. I was waiting for a rainy day. You never know when you might need the help of such an important person.

Brunevsky was calculating whether his debt to me was large enough to provide the requested information. And, at the same time, he had to make sure that I noticed the complex calculations involved, so that if he decided to share his information with me, I would know that his debt had been repaid in full.

"Freak, you say?" he said after a while. "A circus freak perhaps? One of those who perform at country fairs?"

Apparently, the information I had requested was too valuable in comparison to the size of his debt.

"I wonder," I said, hiding my disappointment. "If he did in fact perform at a circus, they might want to contact the understudy. The thing is, I recently arrested him."

"Really? Where?"

"On a suburban train."

"That's a surprise," Arkady Matveyevich exclaimed. "What happened? Have you been demoted to train cop?"

"It happened by accident. I was coming home from a fishing trip."

For all his teasing, I could tell he was interested.

"I see," Arkady Matveyevich said. "You were driven by professional instinct. Once a hound, always a hound. Grab and hold on, etcetera. Like my Duska."

I smiled.

"Something like that."

Duska was probably the German shepherd tied up in the yard. I didn't mind Brunevsky mocking me. He wouldn't have kidded around if he didn't have an interest in the conversation. I was keeping up my end of things and staying cheerful.

"What was Freak doing there? Picking pockets?"

"Not really," I replied. "He was harassing a woman."

That really did take him by surprise. He couldn't quite hide it.

"Come on," he said. "Tell me more."

I told him what happened on Sunday on the Serpukhov train. I also mentioned Frezin being framed by Regional Criminal Investigations for crimes he hadn't committed.

"Probably breaking and entering or a mugging, but they might come up with something more serious. He's a good candidate to pin a bunch of unsolved crimes on, and, more to the point, he nearly raped one their cops during the interrogation," I concluded.

"Shamil," Arkady Matveyevich said to the kid who had been standing behind me with a bored look on his face, guarding the locked door. "Go to the kitchen and put on the kettle. It's almost time for lunch. I'm not asking you to stay," he added, turning to me, "don't be offended."

Once we were alone, Arkady Matveyevich sat in silence for a long time. Finally, he asked me thoughtfully, "Do you play chess?"

"Not really," I replied, wondering what he was driving at. "I took one or two lessons in my time at the Young Pioneers' palace."

He nodded.

"In chess, the king is like me. Good for nothing. Who knows, maybe he too got his legs blown off by a German landmine. The point is that all the king can do is hobble around the board. It can't take other pieces because it lacks mobility. But the king is very important. It's the most important piece on the board. The pawn is even less mobile than the king, but it isn't important either. It's next to worthless."

"I see," I said tersely.

I knew now that he was pulling my leg.

"But there is one exception," Brunevsky added. "A pawn can sometimes hobble all the way down to the end of the board. Then, watch out. Not only have you got a new queen, but it's operating behind enemy lines."

He sighed, placed his hairy arms on the tires and, rolling his chair toward the corner, turned it sharply around. It was time for lunch. My audience was over.

At the entrance to our Petrovka 38 headquarters, by the heavy doors in front of the security desk, I ran into Lenny. I was entering the building and he was coming out.

"I've been looking all over for you," Lenny said, not breaking his stride. "Let's go."

"Where?" I asked.

Urumov had a reputation for never being in a rush.

"Come along," he said quickly. "Another burglary. The call has just come in."

Barely managing to keep pace, I followed him through the wrought-iron gate. Lenny's Moskvich, the 401 hatchback model that is no longer in production, was parked at the curb. Looking important, he rounded it and got behind the wheel.

Lenny was a fanatical car lover and reveled in mocking my Zundapp and sidecar. In his opinion, the future belonged to motorcars, and not to three-wheeled toys.

"Who gives a hoot about fresh air and panoramic views?" he always said. "You can't argue with the self-evident fact that the level of comfort provided by the automobile is vastly superior."

If truth be told, however, the level of comfort provided by Lenny's Moskvich leaves a lot to be desired. To begin with, even I, hardly a fat man, found it tight to squeeze in next to Lenny, and, even at just 5' 11", my head presses against the hard top.

In addition, Lenny had a habit of shifting gears jerkily, under the mistaken impression that it made him seem like a race car driver. In reality, it only made the engine hiccup and the Moskvich leap and skip.

What is more, his 401 spent even more time in the shop than my ancient war-booty Zundapp.

"Where are we going?" I asked after Lenny had elbowed me in the ribs twice and put the car into third.

"Not far. Sadovaya 15, apartment 66."

I waited, expecting him to continue. But he kept silent, breathing hard and concentrating on steering.

"Maybe you'll be so kind as to fill me on the details?" I asked at last. "A few juicy ones, perhaps?"

He brushed my question aside.

"Later. Don't you see I'm driving? The traffic in Moscow is simply insane."

I shrugged. The four lanes of Petrovka stretched wide in front of us. The street was mostly empty, except for a Volga taxi that was about to pull out of a side street and a bus that was braking at a red light beyond the Hermitage public gardens.

At the light, Urumov relented.

"Anyway," he said. "The lady leaves in the morning to go shopping. She comes back in the afternoon to find that there has been a robbery in her apartment. This is all I know. Nothing about what was taken, how or why. We'll find out once we get there."

We passed Samoteka and reached the Forum Cinema in no time. There, Lenny made a theatrical, broad U-turn across the entire width of the Garden Ring, pulling up in front of a beige apartment building.

The building was solidly built and respectable, its high balconies supported by columns. On one side hung a giant poster promoting the services of the State Insurance agency in life and property insurance. We climbed out of Lenny's matchbox and he carefully locked both doors: first his and then, walking all the way around the car, mine.

I simply had to comment on that. "Good job," I said sarcastically. "An excellent example from a Criminal Investigations officer of how to trust one's fellow citizens. A great way to put the general public at ease about the crime situation in the city."

For once, Urumov couldn't think of a comeback. He just nodded and hurried toward the entrance in the left wing of the apartment building.

"Whom are we visiting today, young men?" the concierge asked.

"Criminal Investigations," Urumov replied curtly. He had gotten a few feet ahead of me.

"No. 66 is on what floor?"

Suddenly, the concierge began to scream, "Oh, my Lord. Can you believe what's going on? That Polishchuk woman is roaring at me like a wild beast. 'You, Praskovia, are either asleep on the job or else doing your knitting. Why they pay you is beyond me. You let all kinds of scum come and go.' But I had nothing to do with it. You should tell her it's not my fault. All I know is that three men came in this morning. Young and nice looking, like you. They looked like ordinary house painters, I swear to God. Wearing what painters always wear and they even had those hats on, the ones they make from folded newspaper to keep paint from getting in their hair. But otherwise all covered with paint, head to toe. They even had a huge bucket of paint, it took two of them to carry it. They weren't even going to the Polishchuks' place, they said, but to No. 65. To the Vetoshins, that is. Then, less than half an hour later they came down again, still with their bucket. 'The woman don't like the color,' they said. I told them I knew all about her. 'Vetoshina is a finicky one,' I told them. 'Worse even than that Polishchuk woman.' Ilya Fomich, our local patrolman, says those three might have been the burglars. He says they never even went to the Vetoshins but headed straight for the Polishchuks. What was I supposed to do? How could I have known they weren't for real? It's your job to tell thieves from house painters, not mine"

The door of No. 66 on the fifth floor was ajar. Lenny adjusted his sweater while I straightened his collar, which had managed to stand up straight during the car ride. Then we rang the door bell. "Criminal Investigations," Lenny announced into the door's purple leather upholstery.

"Oh, my. Finally, here they are," a cranky voice responded from inside the apartment. "How long does one have to wait for our local Pinkerton agents to show up? I suppose I should thank you for bothering to come at all. Should I serve you some tea and cookies?"

The owner of the voice stood in the middle of the living room. She was a fairly tall woman, nicely dressed and wearing diamonds in her ears and gold rings on her fingers. She was no longer young, but her good looks hadn't yet faded. A middle-aged cop sat at the desk and, bending low over his work, was assembling the list of stolen property. He seemed unhappy.

In addition to those two, the living room contained a huge guy in his mid-twenties, wearing a brand-new leather jacket and a pair of slippers.

"Thank you, we've just had lunch," Urumov replied, ignoring her sarcasm.

She glared at him.

"I'd like to see some identification, please," she demanded, switching to cold formality.

I handed her my Criminal Investigations ID, a red leather-bound booklet with a gold sword, shield and wreath of oak leafs embossed on its cover. While Lenny searched for his, patting every pocket in turn, the woman glanced at my name and rank and handed the booklet back to me with an unpleasant nod. When Lenny finally found his, she held on to it for a long time, staring suspiciously at his picture and checking it against the original.

"Well, Comrades," she summarized, her sarcasm returning. "You can get on with your work. Our local talent is having a bit of trouble getting anywhere on his own. Not enough brain power, I fear."

The grey-haired policeman stared into his report and only bent his head lower.

Urumov and I looked around, taking in the premises. The furniture was modern, made of light-colored maple and imported from Czechoslovakia. Such furniture was currently all the rage. Every surface in the room was densely lined with statuettes, paperweights, porcelain vases and other trash. The walls were covered with plates with different floral patterns painted on them. Opposite the window, lit by a special museum light, hung a large, good quality oil portrait of Nikita Sergeyevich Khrushchev. Alongside it was another portrait, of our hostess standing next to a pig-faced middle-aged gentleman in jacket and tie. I have no idea whether the artist had tried to flatter the pig-faced gentleman, but he clearly didn't want to have any problems with the lady. He didn't make her look exactly like the movie star Lyubov Orlova, but the resemblance was striking.

"Good," I said dryly. "Please tell us what happened."

"What's there to tell?" replied the woman indignantly. "Hera and I went out to do some shopping. He drove me to a couple of stores and to the farmers' market, where I bought some things. When we got back, we found this. It's an outrage. You can't leave your house even in the daytime anymore. Should I be sitting here all day, guarding my property?"

I turned to the cop. "Fill us in on the details, please. I didn't notice any signs of a forced entry. We'll have to get forensics in here, of course."

"What's the point?" the cop responded reluctantly. "There was no forced entry. They were dressed as house painters and they must have had a key. There were three of them. That's how they got past the concierge. They used the paint bucket to carry the loot."

"We know all that," said Urumov. "But we'll have to question the witness some more."

"Who's the witness?" the woman asked in surprise.

"The concierge," Urumov replied over his shoulder.

"And a fine witness she is, I'm sure" she sneered. "I bet you'll get a lot of useful information out of her. If all your hopes rest with that witness, I can kiss my things goodbye. They were, by the way, all paid for with honest money. Money earned through hard work on behalf of our Motherland."

"Who resides in this apartment?" Urumov asked, ignoring her comments. "Let's start from the beginning. First name, last name, place of work."

"Why? Is it relevant to your investigation? We are, after all, victims, not criminals."

"Yes," I put in my two cents. "Absolutely necessary."

Urumov pulled out a notebook from his jacket pocket and got ready. The woman looked doubtfully at him and, especially, at his notebook. Indeed, it was dog-eared and shabby, covered with doodles and brown streaks from where tea had been spilled on it. Lenny might have been a slob, but he was actually a very bright slob.

"My name is Anna Panteleyevna Polishchuk," the woman declared. "I am a housewife. My daughter, Lyudmila Antonovna Polishchuk, resides with us on this property. She recently turned twenty-one, we just had a birthday party for her. She is a student. She studies at the Maurice Thorez Foreign Language Institute, where she's just started her fourth year. In the morning, Lyuda went to school and, while I was getting ready, Hera drove her there by car, before he took me shopping."

Urumov patiently recorded all this in his notebook.

"As to my husband," the woman went on. "His name is Anton Pavlovich Polishchuk and he is currently at our dacha. He is Lyuda's father. He was supposed to come back last night, and his office has already called us three times this morning looking for him. Apparently, something has kept him at the dacha. By the way, Anton Pavlovich had a sense we might be robbed. He said to me: 'Anya, if something goes wrong, don't call the police before you let me know.' It's strange, how he had a premonition that something like this might happen. He knows people in high places. Hera, have you tried reaching Anton Pavlovich?"

"A hundred times," the guy in a leather jacket replied sullenly. "It's always the same. Either a busy signal or no answer."

"Here we go," the woman declared. "See? That's the management office of the dacha cooperative for you. No one takes responsibility for anything any more. For two straight days, either the line is busy or else it's like they've fallen off the face of the earth. I'm going to give that Tyatkin fellow a piece of my mind, I swear. We're in hysterics here, looking for Anton Pavlovich, and they just couldn't care less. Hera and I decided to call you, anyway, because we couldn't reach Anton Pavlovich. Even though he had told me to let him know first. Isn't that right, Hera?"

The giant mumbled something that could be taken as assent.

"And your husband," asked Urumov. "What does he do for a living? I don't have anything except his name."

The woman paused meaningfully and then answered softly, yet clearly, enunciating every syllable. It was a lot like the final scene in Gogol's play, when the true Inspector General is announced.

"My husband, Anton Pavlovich Polishchuk," said the woman. "Is Director General at the Mikoyan Meat Processing Plant."

Her words were followed by a stunned silence. The head of the Mikoyan Meat Processing Plant was probably the most important man in Moscow. After Nikita Sergeyevich Khrushchev.

The woman looked at Urumov and me triumphantly, relishing the effect she had produced. She ignored the local cop. Apparently, this was old news to him.

"Are there any other families living in the apartment?" Urumov asked, after he had partially regained control of his senses.

"What are you talking about, man? What other families? There are no communal apartments in the entire building, only private ones. Four rooms each, by the way."

"I see," said Urumov. "Let me see the list of stolen property, officer. I can see that Nikita Sergeyevich's portrait has not been taken. Unless there was a second one, of course."

"Don't play the clown," the woman said sternly. "What are you, a police detective or a buffoon?"

"Right," said Urumov, pulling the list toward himself and glancing at it. "I see. Nothing special here..."

"What do you mean, nothing special?" started the woman.

"Oh, I'm sorry," said Urumov. "I was just thinking out loud. What about cash, jewelry, your daughter's property? Did you check it? Is everything intact?"

Apparently, in her confusion after discovering the robbery, this simple thought had not entered the woman's head. Saying nothing, she got up and went down the hall, striking the parquet floor loudly with her high heels.

She was gone for a long time.

Urumov sat, drumming a tattoo on his notebook with a pencil. Then, as though he had just become aware of the slipper-shod giant's presence in the corner of the living room, he asked, "What's your connection to the victims?"

"I'm Hera," replied the guy. "I'm the chauffeur."

"Hera is short for what?" Urumov asked. "Heracles?"

"What? I don't know what you're talking about," said the big guy in surprise. "My name is Herman. Herman Vasiliyevich Gnatyuk."

"I see," said Lenny and wrote down this important information in his notebook. "What kind of chauffeur? Private, or working for the Meat Processing Plant?"

Instead of replying, Gnatyuk stared at something above Lenny's head. He looked as though he had just seen a ghost. I followed his stare, and Urumov also turned his head.

Mrs. Polishchuk stood in the doorway. She had come in silently, her heels no longer making any noise on the floor. Her face was deadly pale.

"All our things will be recovered," she said softly, almost in a whisper. "Every last one of them. You have no idea what kind of connections Anton Pavlovich has. Everything will be recovered. As to the bastards who did this, who dared... They'll be squashed like so many bugs. Hera, let's go. This minute, let's go to the dacha. Let's go get Anton Pavlovich."

SIX

Lenny and I were in a foul mood by the time we left the Polishchuks' apartment.

"Well, my friend," he said. "I'm afraid you're back with your burglaries, and this particular one is not going to make your job any easier. You'll need to get to the bottom of it very soon. Think of it, the head of the Mikoyan Meat Processing Plant. We're dealing with high-level nomenklatura here."

I nodded, saying nothing.

"Did you find out anything about that Frezin character?" he asked.

"Only that a pawn can sometimes make its way across the entire chess board and turn into a queen. That's the only difference between a pawn and a king, apparently, except that the king is the most important piece in chess."

Urumov dropped me off at the repair shop and waited for me to make sure I in fact got my Zundapp before he drove off. It was a kind thing to do and for that his reward was witnessing a minor miracle, one of those that do not often happen in our everyday life. My Zundapp was truly fixed and in fact returned to me on the date and at the time promised.

It ran like new. Actually, I didn't know how it ran when it was new, thank God, but riding it now felt great. In my joy, I even forgot to wave

goodbye to Urumov, riding off, literally, into the sunset. I circled half
the city on the inside loop of the boulevard, speeding through Red
Square, past GUM department store and across the Stone Bridge to
Ordynka. I would have liked to ride some more, but it was getting late.
I crossed back to my side of the river, and ten minutes later brought
my softly purring baby to a stop in my courtyard. I had a special
parking place for it under my windows, where I could keep an eye on
it. Winking at the bust of Lenin enclosed behind a metal fence and
half-hidden by acacia trees in the middle of the courtyard, I hurried
upstairs. Tosya and I had plans to catch a movie. The Uran cinema on
Sretenka was showing *Amphibian Man*.

Tosya loved going to the movies as if she were a little girl. She loved
watching the film, but she also loved all the perks that went with going
to the movies, the 19-kopek ice cream in a waffle cup, the orange soda
at the concession stand, and the singer and her jazz trio in the lobby
of the Uran cinema, swinging her hips workmanlike and singing the
insanely hot tune from the film:

We would, we would, we would, we'd all go to the bottom of the sea...
There we'd, there we'd, there we'd drink wine freely...

Tosya had been nagging me to take her to see *Amphibian Man* for
a long time. Everyone had been humming the tune and her friends at
the textile factory had been talking her ear off about it, retelling the
story and warning her that she'd fall in love with the star.

I don't care much for movies. Movies are not like soccer, where you
never know what will happen next. But I like going to the movies with
Tosya. Because it makes me happy to see how happy it makes her.

Afterwards, we walked through the dark city, along the boulevard
where streetlamps shone brightly and the piercing autumn wind chased
leaves along empty paths and ruffled fading mums in flowerbeds. On
benches in the shadows under old poplar trees, couples pressed hard
against one another, either from an excess of tenderness or to ward off
the cold wind. In the windows of the old Russia House, which took up

almost an entire side of Sretensky Boulevard, orange cloth lampshades glowed. The lights reflected in Tosya's eyes, which still shone with a flame of their own from the well of emotions she had experienced at the Uran.

We walked slowly, deliberately and in silence. We said goodbye at the entrance to her building. It was almost midnight and we both had an early morning ahead. Besides, her Sevka had been on his own all evening. The neighbors could never be relied on to check on him properly, to make sure he had warmed up his supper and finished his homework.

I gave Tosya a kiss and she responded with a hot, passionate one, like the girl in *Amphibian Man*, even though I had the ordinary smoke-damaged lungs of a Criminal Investigations cop, and not the gills of a shark like the pretty boy in the movie.

I had almost reached my own building across the courtyard when I heard quick footsteps behind me.

"Matyushkin," Tosya said in a dramatic whisper. "I want to go to your place."

I have to admit that movies are sometimes useful. Especially love stories.

To keep quiet, we didn't take the elevator, but climbed the stairs to my fourth floor apartment. With such contingencies in mind, I had long ago oiled my front door, all of its locks, hinges and other metal parts, so that Tosya and I could come and go at night without making a sound. Silently, like Native Americans somewhere in the State of Illinois, we snuck into my room, leaving the hall light off and finding our way by touch.

I had barely had time to close the door before Tosya began pulling my clothes off, starting with my pants and not even bothering about my raincoat. In the state she was in, it was not easy to undo a fly. But without unbuttoning it, it's no use trying to pull one's pants off, even though I wear them loose, contrary to current fashion.

Then came a knock on the door.

"Pavel, are you there?" asked my neighbor, Yevdokia Filippovna.

I kept quiet, but she put her mouth to the keyhole and whispered:

"They've been trying to reach you. They've called at least five times already."

When she makes love, Tosya becomes oblivious to everything around her. She becomes deaf and shuts herself off from the world. She's like that at the movies, too – the building could catch fire or the roof might collapse, but she would see nothing but the screen in front of her.

I pushed her aside gently, slid out of her arms and pulled up my pants.

"What is wrong, Matyushkin?" Tosya asked.

I clamped my hand over her mouth and asked Yevdokia Filippovna through the door:

"What did they want?"

"How would I know?" Yevdokia Filippovna replied. "They didn't tell me."

"Who called at least?" I asked, opening the door just a crack.

She shrugged again and was about to give me her usual reply, something like "Why don't you ask an easier question?" but at that moment the phone began to ring, sounding harsh and intrusive in the dark hallway.

"See?" she said. "Here they go again."

The insistent ringing finally brought Tosya back to reality and she let me go. I quickly adjusted my pants, to make sure I could go into the common area without embarrassment, and rushed to the phone. The reason for my hurry was not that they might hang up – whoever was calling clearly had no thought of quitting – but because lights were coming on, one by one, under my neighbors' doors and the close air of the communal apartment was becoming charged with anger.

"Hello," I whispered. "Senior Lieutenant Pavel Matyushkin speaking."

"Yeah, sure," came a grim reply.

The voice was familiar but I couldn't place it. Especially since Tosya's caresses were still throbbing in my ears.

"Who is this?"

"Who is this?" echoed the receiver. "It's Junior Lieutenant Ryumin. Moscow Region Police."

He was the last person I would have expected to call me at home.

"Home at long last, Sherlock?" Ryumin said while I was gathering my wits. "Visiting the ladies? You're lucky, buddy. Meanwhile, we've had some curious developments."

He whistled.

"I can imagine," I said. "I've had plenty of developments on my end, too. Like, I've got bigger fish to fry here than trying to frame a thug on a suburban train. Besides, I might be evicted if you keep calling me this late."

"Don't worry. If you get evicted, you could shack up with one of the ladies you've been seeing. As to this case, I doubt you've ever seen bigger fish than this one. How do you think I got your number? That's right, from your boss, the lieutenant colonel with the long moustache. He wants you to get your ass over here right away. You'll get to see some of your friends."

"What friends?"

I wasn't getting it. Was he drunk? He seemed to be in a suspiciously good mood.

"It'll be a nice little surprise."

"Where am I supposed to go?"

"Where are you supposed to go? You know the Vesna dacha settlement, along the Kursk railway line? No? Find it on a map. We'll be there. Waiting for you with bated breath."

That settled it. I was almost certain that he had had one too many and was playing telephone pranks late at night.

"What's going on, Ryumin?" I asked sternly.

"What's going on? You really want to know?"

This manner of his, repeating everything I said, was starting to get on my nerves. I said nothing and waited for him to answer.

"We've got a murder on our hands," Ryumin finally said. "Anton Pavlovich Polishchuk. Ring a bell?"

While he was giving me directions to Vesna, I tucked my shirt into my pants and smoothed my hair with the palm of my hand. Almost at a run, I got Tosya to her door and climbed onto my Zundapp. It had been fixed just in time.

The Zundapp purred contentedly when I gave it gas, like it was raring to go. Beyond the Ring Road the air got fresher and the cold wind began to pierce through the leather jacket and threadbare sweater I was wearing. Now and again large trucks on their way to Moscow flashed their brights at me from out of the complete darkness. Thin suburban copses seemed like dense virgin forests, hugging the road and reaching out with their scraggly limbs. The road passed through sleepy villages with ramshackle houses, and when I shot past seemingly deserted settlements, I could hear, over the hum of the engine and the sound of wind rushing past my ears, the baying of local curs. In one village, I nearly crashed into a harvester left standing in the middle of the road. I managed to swerve onto the oncoming lane at the last moment. The wheel under my sidecar lifted and spun in the air, then plopped heavily back onto the concrete.

I drove fast, but the trip still took close to an hour. By the time I got to Vesna, it was the middle of the night. I got lost briefly in the dacha settlement, coming up against the gate of a Young Pioneers' camp that had been boarded up for winter, then suddenly found the right dacha.

It was the only one in the neighborhood with any lights on, and all of its windows were brightly lit. Five cars were lined up in front of the gate: two beat-up police cruisers, an old military jeep with a patched canvas top, a Pobeda that belonged to our office, and a brand new, shiny Volga. In the flash of my headlight I saw that the Volga's windshield was covered by a layer of fallen leaves. More leaves lay on its hood, half-concealing the nickel-plated hood ornament of a leaping buck. The Volga must have been standing there a long time.

The sodden clay in front of the gate had been churned up by many feet, and deep tire tracks led through the gate toward the house. The gate was tall, twice the height of an average man. Next to it was a door with a mailbox nailed to it. The door was propped open with a log.

Our office Pobeda was idling and Victor was fast asleep at the wheel, curled up in the warmth of the cabin.

"The big man here?" I asked him, tapping on his window.

Victor's left cheek, with yesterday's stubble pushing through, was pressed against the windowpane. A cigarette hanging from the corner of his mouth had gone out.

"Should've left a long time ago," he said, rolling down the window and staring at me with sleep-encrusted eyes. "I've been keeping the car warm."

"Do you know what's going on in there?"

"Premeditated," he said, yawning. "Strangulation. They used the line from his fishing rod. Forensics is on the scene, as you can see."

He jerked his head toward the parked jeep.

"What about the body? Gone?"

Victor nodded.

The house stood in the back of a large property surrounded by tall lilac bushes. In the summer, the lilacs must be dense enough to conceal the house almost entirely. But now they had already shed most of their leaves and, looking from the footpath through the tangle of bare limbs, I had an unobstructed view into the house. At the door, I ran into my boss, Budyonny.

"Finally," he said in greeting.

"I wasn't at home," I began. "I came as soon as Junior Lieutenant Ryumin—"

He dismissed my protestations with a wave of a hand.

"Don't worry about it," he said. "Walk me to the car."

We walked back to the gate, sliding on the wet clay. The bright light from the windows didn't reach this far and the darkness under the pine trees was total. We almost tripped over a pile of slate tiles, thrown haphazardly onto the grass. Budyonny cursed.

"Well," he said. "Bad business."

"This morning, comrade Lieutenant Colonel, the Polishchuks' Moscow apartment was robbed. Urumov and I were going to submit a report first thing tomorrow."

Budyonny shrugged impatiently.

"I know about it. Do you see what we have here? It's a crime involving a member of the nomenklatura. I've got a call from the ministry already. Actually, two ministries. One from Interior, and another from Food Processing. They'll be sending someone down from State Security to supervise the investigation."

I nodded.

"It happens now and again, Comrade Lieutenant Colonel. Even big bosses get murdered."

"Sure. But if we don't get to the bottom of it quickly, they're going to reassign the case away from us. It would definitely be embarrassing, but I don't know what to wish for. Perhaps it would be better if it were reassigned?"

He thought it over.

"Okay, Matyushkin," he said after a while. "I've been thinking out loud, that's all. Don't mind me. I'm going home. Please give it your best, okay? I'm counting on your – I don't even know what I'm counting on more – your professional expertise or your dumb luck."

The Pobeda drove off, after spinning its back wheels in the mud for a few seconds. I waited until its red taillights melted into the distance, then turned and headed back toward the brightly lit house.

A figure was silhouetted on the glassed-in terrace. At first, I didn't recognize Mrs. Polishchuk. A dramatic change had come over her since earlier in the day. She seemed to have lost weight or shrunk. She reclined in a rocking chair under a thick lampshade. She raised her head with difficulty, turned a puffy face toward me and nodded toward the door of the house.

I slowed down as I passed her. I knew I ought to say something, to express my condolences, but I couldn't think of the right words. I had done it so many times in my career, but could never avoid the feeling that I was saying something wooden, awkward or artificial. Something superfluous.

The forensics team was busy in the front room, collecting fingerprints from armchairs and crawling all over the runner spread atop the floorboards. They swept the floor with their tiny brushes and pushed piles of dust onto tiny dustpans, gathering it into numbered bags. Stas, the team's gawky photographer, kept pointing his large reporter's lens here and there and working the flash. Grigoriev, the medical expert, stood by the kitchen stove absorbed in his thoughts, smoking.

The house was very cold. The wood-burning stove was unlit, even though someone had carefully stacked a dozen birch logs in front of it. The house smelled of mold, stale wood smoke and something less pleasant, perhaps of a dead body.

"Where are they?" I asked by way of greeting.

"Down the hall," replied Grigoriev. "The dead man's study."

From the terrace came a few sniffs and the sound of weeping.

My old friends Zapekayev and Ryumin were sitting on a leather couch in the study. Hera the chauffeur towered in front of them. I came in and stood by the door.

"What?" asked Hera throwing me an unfriendly glance. "Should I start from the beginning all over again?"

It didn't appear to be an official interrogation, or at least no one was writing anything down. But pressure was clearly being applied. Hera was breathing hard and sweating.

"Why not?" said Zapekayev with a note of irony in his voice. "Why don't you start from the beginning all over again? It'll do a world of good to you and to us. We'll all make sure there are no inconsistencies. And Comrade Senior Lieutenant Sherlock Holmes will get to hear your story, too."

Actually, there wasn't a lot to hear, especially since I knew the beginning. On Monday afternoon Polishchuk was supposed to call and let Hera know when to come to Vesna to pick him up. He never did. On Tuesday morning there were repeated calls for Polishchuk from the meat processing plant. They had scheduled some kind of a meeting, requiring Polishchuk's presence.

The wife, Anna Panteleyevna – or rather, the widow – wasn't worried at first. Her husband might have forgotten all about the meeting. His position was high enough that meetings at the plant were important only inasmuch as he graced them with his presence. He never came back from the dacha for a meeting unless it was a meeting with ministry officials, but such meetings were held at the Ministry, not at the plant.

Nevertheless, before she went shopping, Anna Panteleyevna told Hera to call the management office at the dacha cooperative. Despite Anna Panteleyevna's considerable outrage, they still had no private line at the dacha and the phone company always found all sorts of reasons why they couldn't install it. Hera made a call, but the line was busy or there was no answer. Either way, he didn't reach anyone and he and Anna Panteleyevna went out.

When they returned home in the early afternoon, they found that the Polishchuks' apartment had been robbed. Anna Panteleyevna started calling her husband herself and thereafter tried the dacha cooperative office regularly, every five or ten minutes. Hera could not think exactly how many times she had dialed the number, but he assumed it had been less than ten or fifteen.

"Are you sure it wasn't twenty?" Zapekayev asked.

"Could very well be," agreed Hera good-naturedly. "She was swearing like a cobbler."

Unable to reach the office, at around three o'clock in the afternoon Anna Panteleyevna told Hera to drive her to Vesna. Along the way, they had a little mishap. Their Volga had a flat tire. As a result, when they finally reached the dacha on a spare, it was completely dark.

The lights in the house were off. The front gate was closed but not barred. At that moment, for no reason at all, Anna Panteleyevna started to panic.

"When we got to the gate, I was going to wait outside, like I always do. They never invite me in unless they have something for me to carry to the car. But now the mistress said, 'Hera, I'd rather you come along.'"

The door had been slammed shut, not locked the usual way, with two turns of the key.

"How do you know?" I intruded. "Was it you who unlocked the door?"

"No," replied Hera reluctantly. "The mistress did. She said: 'Anton Pavlovich has probably gone for a walk. The door is merely slammed shut, not locked. Thank God. I was terribly worried there for a moment.'"

"Very well. Go on."

"I've told them everything already. Twice. How we came into the house and how we saw the master right away."

"Where did you see him?" I asked.

"Comrade officers saw where, before they took him away. Right here in his study. He was lying in the middle of the room, on the rug. Spread-eagle, with a bloated stomach. Even when he was alive, the master was a big guy, but now he was just huge. He looked like he was going to pop. And his tongue was hanging to the side, purple, like he had had it painted."

He shuddered.

"And your mistress?" asked Zapekayev. "What did she do?"

"Nothing, of course. At first she began to scream like any woman would. 'Hera, do something about it. Help him. Don't stand there like a statue, move. Lift Anton Pavlovich, can't you see he's not feeling well? Get him some water.' But the master was already hard and cold. Like he was made of rubber. I couldn't lift him at all. Then I noticed a black line on his throat. The mistress also saw it and began hugging him. 'Tosha, my love. What have they done to you?' she kept shouting. But then she got a grip on herself. And of course the master had started to smell pretty bad by then. The smell almost made me puke."

"You say you spotted the body right away," said Zapekayev. "But the study is nowhere near the front door. To reach it you had to go down the hall."

"The mistress at first called out to him, in case he was still in the house. Then we went around looking for him."

"By the way," Ryumin finally joined in. "Why do you constantly call them 'master' and 'mistress'? We kicked out the masters forty years ago. Besides, officially you work for the meat processing plant, don't you? That's who pays your salary, right? So your *master* is not the late Polishchuk but the working people of this country. Because the meat processing plant is the property of the people."

"Okay, the boss," Hera corrected himself.

"Did you touch anything in the house?" I asked. "When you went to call the police, or while you were here waiting for the cops to arrive?"

"I don't think so," Hera replied after a moment's reflection. "Although who the hell knows. We wanted to move the master – I mean the boss – to the couch, but we couldn't even lift him. He was heavy even when he was alive. In the old days, he would have too much to drink and nod off in the passenger seat on the way home. I couldn't even pull him out of the car and had to shake him to get him to wake up."

Zapekayev put an end to his reminiscences.

"Okay. We get it. You can go now. Wait on the terrace."

"I'm sorry," I interjected. "I have another question if you don't mind."

"Go ahead, Sherlock," Zapekayev said. For some reason, he was in a generous mood.

"What do you want?" Hera asked, becoming apprehensive.

"Your boss, Polishchuk, did he often stay at the dacha on his own?"

Hera thought it over.

"Sometimes he did, I suppose, especially in winter. I'd bring him here and leave him on his own. His daughter also came here on her own. In the summer, the whole family stays here together."

"Did he ever stay behind at the dacha? I mean not returning when he was supposed to?"

"Not really," said Hera. "I can't think of any such time."

There were many curious things about this, but I didn't want to get too deep into questioning Hera with Zapekayev and Ryumin looking over my shoulder. I decided to change the line of attack.

"What was Polishchuk wearing when you found him?"

"Comrade officers saw him," said Hera, looking at Zapekayev and Ryumin. "We didn't change him."

"Answer the question," Zapekayev shouted, while Ryumin, who had kept his boy-sized fists in the pockets of his jodhpurs, took them out deliberately and rested them on his knees.

"Very well, then. Striped pajama bottoms and a yellow undershirt. That was what he usually wore around the house. He could go a week without changing his clothes. The stove keeps this place pretty warm."

"Are you done?" Zapekayev asked impatiently.

"Pretty much," I replied. "Another minute, if I may."

The two cops exchanged a significant stare. Zapekayev made a face to show mock respect for me, the local Sherlock Holmes. Like I was hard at work and the only thing missing was my magnifying glass.

"When were you here last?"

I didn't have any particular line of questioning. Just fishing for something.

"Two days ago," Hera replied promptly. "Sunday morning, to be exact. I came over to take the mistress and her daughter home. I mean Anna Panteleyevna. That was the last time."

"They were here all together over the weekend? And Polishchuk stayed behind?"

"That's right."

"Did he say why he was staying?"

Hera shook his head: "Not to me, no."

I could have gone on in this vein forever, but Zapekayev stopped me.

"All right. Enough. What's the point of wasting everyone's time?"

"Go wait for us on the terrace," he told Hera. "And send in the widow."

SEVEN

A moment later, loud, energetic footsteps came from the hall outside, the door opened and instead of Mrs. Polishchuk, we were joined by a short, sturdy figure of about forty-five in a colonel's uniform with the distinctive red trim of State Security. Zapekayev and Ryumin grabbed their peaked hats from the coffee table and stood at attention. I also got up and fixed my eyes on the newcomer.

"Colonel Nakazov," he introduced himself. "Call me Vladislav Mironovich. I have been detailed to you from the Committee on State Security, to provide you with whatever assistance you might need. As you know, comrades, it is a very important case. Comrade Polishchuk was a high-level official. You can well imagine that we on Lubyanka Square are taking this case extremely seriously. We must identify all the perpetrators of this vile misdeed. We must also uncover the true aim of this crime. In other words, was it an ordinary crime or something far more serious?"

"In what sense, Comrade Colonel?" I asked.

Nakazov looked straight at me, ignoring Zapekayev and Ryumin.

"In the most direct sense possible, Comrade Senior Lieutenant. When a Soviet official is murdered, we must always keep in mind that such a crime may have been committed not by a common criminal, but by someone in pursuit of a more devious political aim. We must not forget that we remain encircled by our enemies, that we're living in a constantly tightening ring of hatred. Our foreign enemies have accomplices on the inside. There are plenty of vermin still hiding in various nooks and crannies. We have not yet smoked all of them out."

Nakazov sighed.

"I'm telling you this to clarify the situation," he went on. "I'm not going to interfere with your work, you should know this from the outset. I believe we have top-notch criminal investigators on Petrovka Street. I'm just going to glance over your shoulder every now and again. Keep in mind that I can be of assistance, too. If you ever need anything at all, don't hesitate to ask."

He kept addressing me, not the other two, and he now ended on a particularly warm note:

"Of course, it is a distinct pleasure to work with an old acquaintance, a fellow fisherman from the Oka. Our tastes are similar. We both love Russian nature, the Oka and fishing. In short, I expect the two of us to get along very well."

"I immediately recognized you," I said. "Except on the Oka you told me you were a writer. And I believed you."

"Ha-ha," the colonel laughed happily, winking at Zapekayev and Ryumin. "I'm an old conspirator, tried and true. Did you really think I would tell you I was with State Security? I would've scared away all your fish."

He laughed at his own joke and Zapekayev and Ryumin joined in.

"You don't mind if I address you informally, with '*ty*'?" he asked. "I don't like to stand on ceremony. After all, we're old buddies."

"Of course not, Comrade Colonel. No problem."

"Very well, then. Continue with whatever you were doing, comrades. Ignore me. I'll sit over there in the corner."

However, to ignore him completely was not an option. Mainly because the widow, the moment she entered her late husband's study, immediately rushed over to him.

"Vladislav Mironovich, my dear," she cried. "Look what's happened to us. First they cleaned out our apartment, took Lyuda's jewels, even the emerald earrings you gave her for her birthday. And now look at what they've done to Anton Pavlovich."

"Anya, my darling Anya," Nakazov said, trying to calm her down. He rose and held her hands. For a second I thought she might drop on her hands and knees before him, turning the scene into a farce.

The colonel was apparently worried about the same thing.

"Please, compose yourself, Anya," he said. "I see that you're distressed. I see that you're beside yourself with grief. But you must not fall to pieces. I give you my word that the perpetrators of this vile crime will be brought to justice."

"All our hopes rest with you, Vladislav Mironovich. Who will help us now, Lyuda and me? Poor girl, she doesn't even know about this. She has no idea that her dear Daddy..."

The widow broke down and began to cry again.

"Let's not, Anyechka. Let's not," Nakazov said even more sternly and urged her lightly toward the middle of the room.

"I'm an old friend of this family," he explained to me. "This is why this tragedy, this vile crime, is not only a matter of state security, but to some extent it is also my personal tragedy. Yet that will have no effect on the course of the investigation, you understand."

His calm demeanor helped steady Anna Panteleyevna's nerves. She wiped her eyes and sniffed and then sat heavily in a chair behind her husband's desk.

"Could you tell us, Mrs. Polishchuk, why your husband decided to stay behind at the dacha?" I asked, trying to speak as gently as possible. "Why he didn't return to the city with you on Sunday?"

Since Colonel Nakazov had let it be known that he clearly considered me responsible for the investigation, Captain Zapekayev no longer contested my right to ask questions. Even though the crime had occurred in Moscow Region, his territory. Both he and his junior lieutenant looked deflated. They shrank into the background, leaning against the wall.

Anna Panteleyevna snivelled.

"Anton Pavlovich had not been feeling well and had stayed at the dacha in order to improve his health. He had high blood pressure, a heart murmur, diabetes, a liver complaint, what have you. Nephritis, too. He worked hard his whole life. Literally, killing himself on the job. But I insisted that he take a week off. He needed rest, and fresh air was supposed to do him good. Last Tuesday I came here to be with him. It's no good for a man to be alone, especially if he's ill. No one to boil him water for tea or to cook his favorite cabbage soup. We have a maid, but in September she has her vacation. She goes back to her village. Which is why I came here myself. Turns out we spent our last days together here, Anton Pavlovich and I..."

She started to cry again and cried for a long time. Then she took out a wrinkled lace handkerchief, wiped her tears and blew her nose.

"Anya," Colonel Nakazov said finally. "Please get a grip."

The colonel's words again calmed her. Zapekayev and Ryumin kept silent. Their eyes were glued to Nakazov.

"Yes," said the widow, also looking at Nakazov and addressing him, even though I was the one asking the questions. "On Thursday, Lyuda joined us, our dear daughter. She too saw her Daddy for the last time. He simply adored her, poor thing..."

She glanced apprehensively at Nakazov, who was frowning back at her, and managed to restrain her tears.

"While Anton Pavlovich was staying here, he arranged for some men to patch the roof. But the men here are all completely unreliable drunks. They never showed up last week. They promised to come on Monday. Lyuda had classes, and I decided to return to the city with her. He stayed behind to wait for the workers. Could it be the workers who did this to him, Vladislav Mironovich? They are such drunks."

"Anya," said Nakazov. "Let's wait until comrade senior lieutenant sorts this out."

"I was just making a suggestion. I have no idea what to think. It's so horrible."

I continued with my questions.

"Mrs. Polishchuk, please try to recall exactly what time you left here on Sunday."

"It was early. Around ten in the morning. I remember asking Anton Pavlovich why he had told Hera to come get us so early. He told me that he had an errand for Hera to run in the afternoon, after he drove us to the city. It was a beautiful day and we could have stayed a bit longer."

"One more question, if I may. Did you happen to see a pile of firewood by the stove? Do you recall whether it was there on Sunday morning when you left?"

For some reason, the question made the widow very angry.

"Vladislav Mironovich, why does he keep asking me such nonsense? He should be catching the criminals, the murderers who are walking around free after what they have done to Anton Pavlovich. He's wasting time."

"Anya, my dear," replied Nakazov. "Comrade senior lieutenant knows what he's doing. If he is asking you a question, you should answer it and not worry about anything. If I see that he is not getting anywhere, I'll find a replacement for him."

I gave Nakazov a quick glance, but decided to ignore his statement.

"There was no firewood," Anna Panteleyevna stated firmly. "I'm sure of it because in the morning, when I got the fire going to make sure Anton Pavlovich didn't get cold, I used the last logs. I wanted to ask Hera to bring some more from the woodshed, but I forgot. I thought of it only when we were already in the car, on our way to Moscow. I even complained to Hera that I had forgotten to ask him to get firewood for Anton Pavlovich. It's so hard for him. He has a weak heart."

"And yet now, there is a neat little stack over there," I said. "Could he have brought it in by himself?"

Anna Panteleyevna smiled at me through tears and her face suddenly became young and pretty. Not so long ago, she must have been a very attractive woman.

"I doubt it very much," she said, still smiling. "Anton was a huge slob. He would never have brought more than two or three logs at a time. Nor would he have stacked them up so neatly. He would have dropped everything on the floor and let it lie there as it fell. Just look at his desk. It's complete chaos. Yet I had tidied it up before we left on Sunday."

Further questioning elicited no new information. Everything she said confirmed her driver's testimony and fit the picture of the previous day that I had started to form. After calling the office repeatedly and getting no answer, they decided to drive to the dacha. Lenny and I were in her apartment when that decision had been made. Once they arrived, they found Polishchuk dead in his study. End of story.

Nakazov walked Anna Panteleyevna back to the terrace and, when he returned, asked me a little guiltily, "Do you mind if I review the testimony of everyone you have spoken with? And debrief your forensics experts while I'm at it? I take my job as a supervisor of this investigation seriously."

Naturally, he didn't expect me to mind, and was already holding a notebook and a gold fountain pen at the ready. But I did like it that he asked my permission, underlining for the Moscow region cops that I was the one in charge.

While he talked to Hera in the study, I went around the house. The work in the kitchen was complete and the forensics team had spread out around the premises. Fingerprints were being collected upstairs, in the four second-floor bedrooms, which had thick down comforters and huge peasant pillows on every bed. Stas's flash was going off somewhere, illuminating the corridors like the lightning of a distant electric storm.

A serving tray stood on the kitchen table, holding two china cups, a tea kettle, cookies in a small straw basket, and a spoonful of cherry preserves in a small dish.

"Have they already taken fingerprints here?" I asked Stas as he came down the stairs.

He nodded absently while fixing a light over the tray and preparing to take a picture. It was as if he was photographing a still life.

"Wait a second."

I pulled out a handkerchief and removed the cover from the tea kettle. It was full of cold, almost black liquid. I checked the level of fuel in the kerosene burner. All the kerosene had burned out.

Anna Panteleyevna sat on the terrace with the same vacant expression on her face as when I first arrived. A small, neatly dressed man now sat silently by her side. His eyes were closed and he seemed to be napping.

"May I have a word?"

He started, opened his eyes and stared at me, trying to figure out who I was.

"Senior Lieutenant Matyushkin," I said. "Moscow City Criminal Investigations."

"Oh, Petrovka," he said appreciatively, then fell silent.

"And you are?"

"Oh, yes, of course," he exclaimed hastily. "Everybody knows me here, so that I forget to introduce myself when I meet new people. My name is Tyatkin. Vitaly Arkadevich Tyatkin. I'm the chairman of the dacha cooperative and I live nearby, the third cottage to the right. Fifteen years I've lived here already. I'm retired, you see. Widowed, not a party member, never been abroad, no relatives in foreign countries. As you might say, an exemplary Soviet citizen. Do you happen to have a cigarette on you, young man?"

I took out my pack of Red Presnya.

"Be my guest."

I pulled one out for myself, but didn't light it.

"Let's go outside," I suggested. "We're bothering Anna Panteleyevna."

She heard her name and came to life.

"You can smoke here, comrades," she said in a weak, dramatic voice. "Nothing bothers me anymore."

"We had better go out to the garden, anyway," I said, helping Tyatkin up and nudging him toward the door.

As we walked toward the gate, I stumbled on the pile of slate tiles. It had gotten cold outside, almost frosty. But I enjoyed the fresh air. The dacha had been very stuffy and I could not get used to the unpleasant smell.

"It's a nice place," I said. "Do you live here year round?"

"I do, comrade investigator. All winter long and all summer, too. I look after people's properties and sit at the office. I don't draw salary, mind you, and the pension only goes so far."

"You've got the only working telephone in the settlement? The one they used to call the police?"

"It's not mine, comrade investigator. I mean not mine personally. The telephone is at the office, which is at the other end of the dacha settlement. Sometimes, when you need to make an urgent phone call, you've gotta run there like your house is on fire. Like this evening, for instance."

"Is it the Meat Processing Plant's cooperative?" I asked.

"What? Meat Processing Plant? Are you kidding? It was built in the 1930s, specially for heroic Soviet flyers. The flyers are all pretty much gone now. Some got shot down by the Fritzes during the war, others crashed on their own and the rest..."

He broke off and gave me an apprehensive glance.

"Were you an airman?" I asked, surprised.

"No, sir. To be an airman you need to be made of a different kind of stuff. I surely don't have what it takes. I got this place from my sister. Her husband was a famous test pilot, Grishaninov by name. You might have heard of him. He was awarded two Hero of the Soviet Union stars. No? Don't know him? Anyway, it doesn't matter. He's long dead now, but before the war he flew all the way to North America. From Moscow to Chicago without landing even once. It was a great sensation at the time, and all the newspapers around the world wrote about him on their front pages. He was a good-looking fellow and could sure hold his liquor. The women were his weakness. My poor sister, God rest her soul, had a lot of trouble with him on that account. And my God, how the women loved him back! I remember one story, all of Moscow talked about it for months..."

The old man came alive and looked ready to go on in this vein for a long time. I cut him off promptly, "The Polishchuks are recent arrivals then?" I asked.

The old man grew serious.

"They bought their dacha about five years ago, if I remember correctly. It's a good place, as you can see for yourself. Except they keep changing everything around there."

"What do you mean?"

"They redid the house when they first bought it, and they keep making improvements all the time. Every time I come into their house, something is always different. They either buy new furniture or shift their old furniture around. Like today, for instance, at the dead man's study..."

I was going to question him about this some more, but I heard my name being called from the terrace. Nakazov had finished interrogating Hera and now wanted to see Tyatkin.

EIGHT

At home, where I stopped off to change out of a wet shirt and, standing over a stove in the communal kitchen to shove a hastily scrambled egg into my mouth, I put on my full police uniform. The investigation of the Polishchuk murder was turning into quite a high-profile affair and some big wig from the Ministry of Internal Affairs, the Committee for State Security or some other agency could be expected to demand that I come to report at any moment.

Also, before going to work, I wanted to see Tosya. Despite the early hour, Grandma Masha Yegoriyevna had taken up her usual observation post under the metal awning at the entrance to Tosya's building.

"You're late," she said.

She was ancient, at least sixty-five years old and maybe older, and everyone called her Grandma Masha or Yegoriyevna. She was Tosya's seventh floor neighbor.

"Your sweetheart left for work," she reported. "But not Sevka. Puttering about upstairs, as usual."

She sighed.

"It must be hard for a woman to raise a boy on her own."

"No doubt, Grandma Masha," I promptly agreed.

Yegoriyevna was already dressed for winter, wearing a man's overcoat with a faded dog-fur collar sewn onto it for warmth. A length of string was tied around her waist and a wool shawl was wrapped around her shoulders, making her look packaged, as though ready for shipment to some northern land. The shawl and the coarse black fabric of her coat were covered with yellow triangles of fallen birch leaves.

"Why don't you marry her, Pavel?"

"I'd be glad to, Grandma Masha."

"That's right. Because tongues are wagging about the two of you all around the building. Don't kid yourself, folks have noticed. It's no good."

"Not at all, Grandma Masha."

"What are you waiting for, then?"

"We're going to get married," I assured her.

But deep down I wasn't so certain. There was no point of trying to explain to Yegoriyevna that Tosya is a difficult and conflicted person and that getting her to agree to anything so intimate as marriage is no easy task.

"You're a good man," she said approvingly. "Who cares that she has a child, God knows by whom? She's not a bad sort. I know what I'm talking about. I've been her neighbor for seven years."

"You don't need to convince me, Grandma Masha. I mean, I'm—"

I hesitated for a moment.

"I'm in love with her," I concluded hastily.

"Marry her, then."

"I will, Grandma Masha. I certainly will. But not right now. Some other time. Now I've gotta get to work."

Yegoriyevna nodded and declared, "You'll probably be able to exchange your rooms for two in the same apartment. This way Sevka could have a room of his own, if he decides to get married."

I was leaving the courtyard when, glancing back, I saw Sevka coming out the front door. He was wearing his mother's winter coat, altered to fit him, and a grey peaked cap. In his hand, he held a shapeless, ink-blotted briefcase Tosya and I had bought him at the flea market. It was getting late, so I merely waved to him. He waved back.

"I should take him to a soccer match," I said to myself, crossing the street to where I had left my Zundapp half an hour before. "The season is almost over, and we haven't been to a single game."

Just as the day before, I ran into Lenny at the entrance of the Criminal Investigations building, but this time we were both moving in the same direction. At my suggestion, we took the stairs and, as succinctly as I could, I told him what happened overnight. Lenny listened in silence, especially since climbing the three floors to our office was making him wheeze.

"Well, my friend," I concluded. "You'll have to pick up the burden of those unsolved apartment robberies. Except the one in the Polishchuks' apartment, of course."

"I see a meteoric rise through the ranks," Lenny observed gloomily as we reached our landing. "Keep wearing your uniform, and before long you'll move into Budyonny's office. And, speaking of the devil..."

Della, Budyonny's secretary, stood on the landing, smoking a cigarette and leaning elegantly against the wall. Her feet, wrapped in tall, laced-up boots that were made in Poland, were twisted tightly around one another.

"Ciao," Lenny greeted her.

Despite being married and the father of two beautiful daughters, Lenny was friendly with Della. Truth be told, Lenny was a big-time womanizer. If he liked a woman, he knew how to get into her good graces. He liked lots of women. Actually, he never met a woman he didn't like. But he seemed to like Della more than most.

Della gave him a charming smile, and then grew serious as she turned to me.

"Good day, Pavel," she said.

She and I were on more formal terms.

"Comrade Lieutenant Colonel wants to see you," she said.

"I'll be in his office in a moment," I replied. "I'll just take off my raincoat."

"Oh no," Della said hastily, putting out her cigarette in the roots of a dusty ficus plant, where cigarette butts lay twisted like grey worms. "He wants to see you right away. He specifically told me to intercept you on the stairs or at the elevator."

Lenny gave me a meaningful look as I hurried off to see the boss, leaving the two of them alone on the landing.

I entered Budyonny's office and saluted him in accordance with regulations, which was required when wearing a police uniform. He lifted his eyes, gave me a quick glance and went back to his papers. It was a bad omen, and the fact that he remained silent for so long was another, even worse sign.

"I've questioned the witnesses, Comrade Lieutenant Colonel," I reported.

Budyonny nodded, to indicate that he was aware of this.

I stood at attention. Silence once again settled over the office.

Budyonny's office was large enough that it could have belonged to an officer of much higher rank, to a general perhaps. It was located on the street side of our massive building, on the three-story high, open balustrade designed in imitation of some Ancient Roman palace. The window opened onto the bell tower of a rickety old church with a rusty onion dome. The church had long since been converted into a carpentry shop.

Standing at attention, I felt a cool drop of sweat roll down my spine. Budyonny liked to keep his office hot, but it was the tension in the room that was getting unbearable.

"You've disappointed me, Senior Lieutenant," Budyonny said at last. "There is no beating around the bush. You've disappointed me."

"In what way, Comrade Lieutenant Colonel?"

"In the way that I asked you last night to do me a favor. I practically begged you, Senior Lieutenant, like one human being to another."

I waited to see where he was going with this. I also noted that his Armenian accent was getting stronger – yet another bad sign.

"Did I ask you to do me a favor or not?" he insisted. "Answer me."

"What kind of favor, Comrade Lieutenant Colonel?"

"There we go. You don't even remember. What was the point of me asking you, Senior Lieutenant?"

I didn't know what to say. He was speaking in charades.

"I asked you last night to do everything possible to solve the murder of Comrade Polishchuk, and to do so before those villains from the Moscow Region office solved it. Have you forgotten so soon? Is your memory as short as a hen's?"

"No, sir," I replied cautiously. "I mean, I certainly remember our conversation."

"And?"

"I have not solved it since last night. By the time we were done at the Polishchuks' dacha, I only had time to stop at home and put on my uniform before coming to work. Is there a problem?"

"Of course there's a problem, Matyushkin," Budyonny said, his exasperation growing. "Those Moscow Region cheaters, they got there ahead of you."

My jaw dropped.

"What do you mean they got there ahead of me? It's impossible. They were at the Polishchuks' dacha with me the whole time."

"Go to hell," said Budyonny. "The point is they solved comrade Polishchuk's murder and you didn't."

"Just like that?"

"Indeed, just like that."

"What you're saying is that in the last three hours they were able to find the killer and take him into custody?"

"Spare me your sarcasm, Matyushkin. I would have kept my mouth shut if I were you. Yes, that's exactly what happened. They found the killer, but the irony of it is that they didn't have to take him into custody. You'd already done it for them, but while arresting him you completely missed the most important aspect of the case. Even though it had been staring you in the face all along."

Budyonny shook his head.

"Colonel Nakazov from State Security was pretty clear about it. 'Senior Lieutenant Matyushkin may be a decent professional and I personally like him very much,' he said to me, 'but he dropped the ball as far as the Polishchuk case is concerned.'"

Budyonny raised a finger to emphasize the point.

"You made a huge mistake. You missed a crucial piece of evidence, and if it weren't for Captain Zapekayev from Moscow Region Criminal Investigations, the killer might have been set free. I had to admit to Nakazov that we on Petrovka are not up to snuff when it comes to important political cases, especially ones like the Polishchuk murder. This may have serious consequences for our entire department, not just for you personally, Senior Lieutenant."

I could not believe my ears. I must have looked like a complete idiot, because Budyonny stopped, stared at me and quickly asked, "What's the matter with you? You've got no answer to this?"

"Comrade Lieutenant Colonel, if I understand you correctly, it's Daniel Frezin they're talking about. The guy I arrested on Sunday on a suburban train."

"One and the same," Budyonny admitted.

"And he's the one they intend to charge with the Polishchuk murder, is that right?"

"Good man," said Budyonny sarcastically. "You may not be as slow-witted as you look."

"Well, then everything is crystal clear. The moment he laid his hands on Frezin, Zapekayev started looking for a suitable crime to frame him with. He even offered him a choice: breaking and entering, assault, mugging, anything you want. A shameless bunch, those Moscow Region detectives. Frezin should have picked what they offered him at the start, because the murder of a nomenklatura official is a more serious offense."

Budyonny took a sip from the mug of tea on his desk and shook his head.

"Nakazov is under pressure from his superiors to solve this murder," I continued. "I don't know whether he believes Zapekayev or is just going along. Frezin is a convenient scapegoat. He's a career criminal and a burglar. No one is going to look into this case too deeply if he's charged with Polishchuk's murder."

"You have a very strange logic, Matyushkin," Budyonny said. "Especially for a detective. If a police detective – even a nasty piece of work like Captain Zapekayev – were trying to frame a career criminal for a crime he hadn't committed, does it absolve him of any other crime he could have actually committed? That Freak of yours, he could have committed a murder before he got on that train. Why else do you think he left Belgorod, violating the terms of his release?"

"He said he was looking for a job," I said. "I don't necessarily believe him, and I'm sure the moment he got out of prison he started looking for some way to get in trouble with the law again. But it's too much of a coincidence, isn't it? Nakazov is looking for a murderer, and, presto, the murderer is found in a Podolsk jail. Far too easy."

"Maybe," Budyonny admitted. "But then what to do with the piece of evidence Zapekayev found? Nakazov is convinced it closes the case."

I shrugged.

"I have no idea."

"You see," said Budyonny. "You have no idea. Go visit your friend Zapekayev, then, and find out. By the way, Freak has been moved from Podolsk. He's a suspect in a capital case now, so he's at Butyrka prison, in the city. Solitary confinement, a special guard, the works."

He went back to his papers, which meant that our conversation was over, but as I saluted him and turned to go, he added, "Keep in mind, Matyushkin, that Captain Zapekayev is now in charge of the Polishchuk investigation. You're out. Your job is to solve those apartment break-ins you've been spending so much time on. And get on with it, will you?"

I stopped at my office to chat with Lenny. In a matter of hours, I had been put in charge of a high-profile investigation and then ignominiously dismissed.

"It's a mess," Lenny said, although I wasn't clear whether he was referring to the murder investigation, my falling out of favor with Budyonny, or both. "If there is a crucial piece of evidence in this case,

I bet it was planted by Zapekayev. Even so, there is nothing you can do about it. It's up to Nakazov to decide whether he believes in Frezin's guilt or not. If he approves Zapekayev's version, they'll make short work of it."

I nodded.

"What do you think of the burglary in the Polishchuks' apartment," I asked. "It must be linked to the murder."

"We don't know that," Lenny replied. "It seems different from your other cases. There wasn't much valuable stuff taken in any of them. On the other hand, the other apartments didn't have any valuable stuff, so they took what they could find."

"Say, Lenny," I said, "you're not working on anything important now, right?"

"That's debatable," said Lenny. "But go on."

"Maybe you could look into the Polishchuk family. Their daughter, for instance. I can only imagine what she's like, growing up in that family. You get along with all sorts of women, and for this social class you're irresistible. I'm sure she has an interesting circle of friends, like restaurant goers, fashionable young people, underground businessmen and gamblers who hang around the racing track."

"Wheeler-dealers," Urumov added.

"Right."

"Okay," said Urumov. "I'll give it a try. Especially since, according to you, I never work on anything important."

NINE

Things developed pretty much as expected after my talk to Budyonny.

Naturally, I was removed from the Polishchuk murder case and returned to my burglaries, which I hadn't actually had time to forget about in the course of the twenty-four hours or so that they were under Urumov's care. The Polishchuk break-in was separated into a case all its own, not directly connected to the murder, since, according to the official version, by the time the apartment was burglarized, the murderer, Daniel Frezin, was in police custody. But it was not a free-standing case either. Neither fish nor fowl, in other words.

It was none of my concern, Budyonny said. The Polishchuk break-in was being investigated personally by Colonel Nakazov, who, in the murder case, was acting merely as an overseer of what Zapekayev and his crew were doing.

The more I thought about it, the more I became convinced that those responsible for my break-ins had nothing whatsoever to do with the Polishchuks'.

The ones I had been investigating were crude, straightforward affairs. True, the first robbery they committed, where they robbed the well-known furrier Blimenkrantz' apartment, was cleverly executed and they got plenty of loot. But it went downhill from there. After that, one theft was a lot like the next: the thieves broke through the door or climbed in through the balcony if it wasn't too high. The victims were ordinary people of limited means, so that the list of missing property was the usual litany of everyday items: sweaters, skirts and jackets. In one place, they got away with a portable radio, in another with a sewing machine.

But the Polishchuk burglary was of an entirely different caliber. They had the key, they used a disguise, and they tricked a suspicious concierge. Above all, the thieves had known that there was expensive jewelry in the apartment, and a lot of it, and they had to be able to fence it once they laid their hands on it.

I did as I was told. The next morning I rode my Zundapp to Butyrka to meet with Captain Zapekayev. I was actually curious about the damning piece of evidence that he had so conveniently found. A button from Frezin's overcoat on the floor of Polishchuk's study? An engraved gold cigarette case presented to Anton Pavlovich by the collective of the Meat Processing Plant on the occasion of his fiftieth birthday that Frezin hid in the folds of his overcoat? A hook from Polishchuk's fishing gear that lodged in the seat of Frezin's pants?

The damning evidence turned out to be a small piece of paper. Or rather, a dirty, half-torn envelope with the address of the Polishchuks' dacha printed on it in a semi-literate, labored hand.

"You guys missed it when you searched him at the police station," Zapekayev announced. "I'd expect this from a bunch of patrolmen at a sleepy station on the outskirts of the city. But not from you, a big city Sherlock Holmes. Of course, at the time you all had no way of knowing that a murder had been committed. Still, you should've been more thorough. When I searched his belongings, this thing turned up immediately."

His face brimmed with pride.

"See how it's done, Sherlock?" he added. "We have our methods, too."

"That search you did," I asked. "Why did you decide to do it? And when?"

Zapekayev gave me a suspicious look.

"After I got back from Vesna. It must have been around four in the morning. Why?"

I shrugged.

"Don't you think it was an unusual time to search a prisoner? Especially one you had no reason to suspect of having anything to do with this particular murder?"

He pondered my question.

"Let's just say it was a hunch. A pretty lucky one, wouldn't you agree?"

"Sure," I said. "A pretty lucky one. Congratulations. Good work."

I turned to leave and Zapekayev looked relieved. Just before going through the door, I turned to him and asked:

"When you searched Polishchuk's body, did you happen to find the keys to his Moscow apartment?"

"No," Zapekayev shook his head. "I don't think so. Everything he had in his pockets is in my report. Why?"

"Were there apartment keys at the dacha?"

"I don't think so."

"Don't you think it's strange?" I asked innocently.

This made Zapekayev mad.

"Hey, Sherlock Holmes," he said. "Why don't you quit fishing around? We have our murderer and the case is basically closed. You might as well admit that we beat you to it and go home."

"Don't forget who served up Frezin on a platter," I replied. "Signed, sealed, delivered. All you needed was a nice frame, and he was ready to hang on the wall. Or, rather, stood up against the wall to be shot. "

I reported to Budyonny on the results of my visit to Butyrka, leaving out the specifics of my pissing match with Zapekayev, and after that the Polishchuks disappeared from my life – for good, so I thought. The only thing was that Urumov had taken my request to work on the dead man's daughter too seriously. After the father's funeral, he waited a few days for things to settle down and looked her up at the Foreign

Languages Institute, apologizing for disturbing her at such a time and saying that he needed to ask her a few questions related to the burglary of her apartment. Having inserted the thin end of the wedge, he had no difficulty getting closer. He went on working on her even after I told him I was no longer interested in the case. And, since I was no longer interested in the case, he wasn't in any hurry to report to me on his results.

Meanwhile, Frezin was moved from Butyrka back to Moscow Region, this time to the town of Odintsovo. He was being held incommunicado and there, in that bucolic suburban setting, Zapekayev, Ryumin and whoever else they had on their team were busy building a case of premeditated murder with intent to commit robbery.

The thought of how they were going to charge Frezin with the theft of jewels from Sukharevka did enter my mind every now and then, but I spent no time worrying about it. It was none of my business. There was, perhaps, a reason why Colonel Nakazov put himself in charge of investigating the break-in. I had no doubt that Zapekayev and Ryumin knew what they were doing and could create an appropriate sequence of events to satisfy everyone. After all, what came first, the murder or the break-in, was as unimportant as the chicken-or-egg quandary. Who cares?

I did feel a bit sorry for Frezin. It was bad luck he traveled to Moscow on that Sunday afternoon train. God knows why he decided to chat up the young woman wearing the fashionable head scarf with large, blue polka dots. It was bad luck that the woman in the pink sweater sitting next to him was eager to stick her nose into other people's business and had a penchant for making scenes in public. And, finally, it was bad luck that I was riding in the same car. If it weren't for all those coincidences, Frezin would have been back in Belgorod, paying regular visits to his local police station to confirm his presence in the city and figuring out how to make some easy money without doing honest work.

A very smart pawn can hobble its way across the chessboard, all eight squares of it, moving the only way it is allowed, forward, one square at a time. It can even survive the intersecting risks of the chess game long enough to become a Queen. But these rules obtain only in a board game. In the larger world, there is a different set of rules. A stronger force could upset the board and unsettle all the players' clever strategies. This is particularly easy to do if the game is played away from the public eye, behind the impenetrably thick walls of the Odintsovo detention center.

A few weeks passed.

One day we were sitting around the dining table at Tosya's. We were having some potatoes that Tosya, in her usual abundance, had fried with mushrooms and onions. Urumov had contributed a smoked eel, a can of crab meat with a foreign label, a paper cup of red caviar, and a bottle of vodka. The vodka was Russian, but the label was in English and the bottle had a twist-off cap, which could be used to reclose it after it had been opened. That was a novel conceit, because it was highly unlikely that, if a vodka bottle were tapped, it would not be finished in a single sitting. Urumov also brought two chocolate-glazed cottage cheese snacks, one each for Tosya and Sevka. But he had either sat on them or placed something heavy on them, because they had lost their shape; the chocolate glaze was cracked and peeling. Still, they were rare delicacies and Tosya refused to eat hers, saving it for Sevka's breakfast.

"This is what I have found out," Lenny said while chewing his fried potatoes. "In her first year at the Foreign Languages Institute, Lyuda Polishchuk had a classmate, a kid named Senya Pavlov. Pavlov came from a good family, his parents were educated folks, and he was a good student. He was particularly good at English, which he spoke as well as the Hound of the Baskervilles. He was a minor member of the infamous Rokotov gang, a real small fry."

"The Rokotov case," I explained to Tosya, "was what Daniel Frezin went to jail for. The gang specialized in buying hard currency from foreigners, which is illegal, of course."

Tosya nodded, but it was clear that she didn't know what we were talking about.

"The Pavlov kid never bought any hard currency," Urumov said. "Others did, perhaps, but not him. It was a complicated network and they had an extensive supply chain, going from guys who bought currency in the street and reaching up to the head of the operation, Ian Rokotov. There were at least five layers between the street traders and the boss, and each layer knew only one person on the level above them."

"What makes you say that Pavlov didn't buy any currency?" I asked.

"He didn't. That's the whole point. Lyuda claims that Pavlov knew Rokotov, that the two of them got to be friends, or rather acquaintances, because they both liked jazz. But Pavlov never even suspected that Rokotov was a crime boss or that he was the head of a huge black market operation. Every once in a while, Rokotov would ask Pavlov for a favor. Innocuous stuff, like taking a useful foreigner to the Bolshoi or the Tretyakov Gallery. Pavlov was a smart kid, very presentable and he could chat with foreigners about lots of things in English. Everything above board. A few times, Pavlov even took Lyuda along, especially if Rokotov paid for him to take a foreigner to a fancy restaurant. Eventually, of course, Pavlov figured out that he was doing something fishy, especially once Rokotov began paying him a fee for those outings."

Urumov paused and stabbed his fork into a marinated mushroom. He slipped the slimy thing into a narrow opening between his full lips, where it was methodically masticated, then swallowed. Urumov ate efficiently, even chewing small, soft things like marinated mushrooms. He, like the Pavlov kid he was describing, had come from a well-off family. In such families, eating was serious business. One didn't devour everything in sight at lightning speed, the way Sevka or I did. Even now, despite having to survive on the meager salary of a Criminal Investigations detective, Urumov lived comfortably. His wife Raisa knew how to make things cozy, even though the four of them – she, Lenny and their two small daughters – shared a single room in a communal apartment. Their room was always pleasant to visit.

"There goes another mushroom," Lenny declared.

"Keep talking," I said.

I didn't want him to get too relaxed and lose his train of thought. But my concern was misplaced. He was eager to continue.

"Anyway, even though he was, as I said, a naive kid and had no police record at the time of his arrest, and even though he was well down the list of accomplices ranked by guilt or involvement, he got eight years in a labor camp."

"What are you trying to say?" I asked.

"Only that," Urumov replied, his voice now sounding like a particularly pedantic schoolmarm, "it is a bit of a surprise that Daniel Frezin, a career criminal with a record as long as my arm, got just two years of jail time at the same trial."

"That surprised me too, about Frezin," I said after thinking it over. "But Pavlov may have been given a longer sentence precisely because he spent so much time hanging out with foreigners. Don't forget that State Security was in charge of the case and their views on what constitutes a serious crime are rather different from ours. Most black market currency dealers had little contact with foreign tourists, and it was just a commercial transaction for them. Pavlov, on the other hand, spent a lot of time with foreigners and had lots of conversations. State Security spends all its time trying to keep Soviet citizens away from foreigners. He might have gotten an even longer sentence if they had charged him with anti-Soviet activities."

"I doubt it. Eight years is a very long time, even for anti-Soviet activities."

I wanted to argue with him, but Tosya interrupted me.

"I still don't understand what this is all about. Who's Rokotov?"

"I don't know all the details," I began. "It was investigated by State Security. As far as I can tell—"

Urumov had already downed a shot or two of vodka – after initially refusing alcohol, explaining that he was driving – and butted in with great enthusiasm. He had a strong penchant for educating and explaining.

"Are you kidding?" he exclaimed, fixing Tosya with his shining dark eyes. "It was all over the papers two years ago. Surely you can't have forgotten."

"I have," Tosya confessed.

"Then listen up. Ian Rokotov was the biggest black market dealer in currency and gold the world has ever known. Or at least the Soviet Union. He traded mostly with foreigners, of course, because they are the ones who have the foreign currency. He didn't do any trading himself, but built up an extensive organization. The lowest level were street buyers, the ones who hung around Intourist hotels where only foreign tourists are allowed to stay. Another group were the dealers. They did business with students at military academies, mostly Arabs from the Middle East and Indochina. Then there were those who worked with regular suppliers, such as foreign journalists or members of Western communist parties, who don't have any restrictions on how often they can visit the Soviet Union and who live here for months on end."

"How come they weren't caught?" Tosya asked.

"They had a very clever structure. The gang was broken up into cells that were in no way connected to each other and didn't even know of the others' existence. Everyone dealt only with the head of their cell, who then kicked the loot up to the next level, and so on. If a cell were busted, it could be sealed off and did not take down the entire organization. It's how submarines are built. They are divided into sections, so that if a section takes on water, it can be sealed off and the boat can continue safely to port."

"It should also be added," I said, "that Rokotov was an informer, snitching on his comrades to the Economic Crimes Unit. It was a good way for him to clear out deadwood and to keep the law off his back. That's something no submarine has."

"That's right," Lenny conceded. He didn't like to be interrupted.

"Come on, go on," Tosya pleaded. "How come they got caught, despite their submarine structure?"

Lenny didn't say anything.

"If you don't know the answer, I'll take it from here," I said.

"No way," Urumov responded promptly. "Of course I know the answer. Here's what happened. One day, Comrade Khrushchev was visiting some capitalist country, and while he was there he began complaining about the untidy appearance and nasty behavior of the local kids. Since everything Comrade Khrushchev knew about Soviet youth came from watching physical culture parades on Red Square from atop Lenin's Mausoleum, he thought our kids were very different. But somebody over there decided to set him straight and noted with a pleasant smile that few capitals in the world had as many black marketeers and illegal currency traders as Moscow."

Urumov hastily poured more vodka into our glasses, and he and I emptied them.

"Nikita Sergeyevich didn't like what he had heard and he didn't forget it. When he got back home, he wanted to know if there was any truth in what he had been told. There was – and in fact things were even worse. He demanded an end to illegal activities around hard currency hotels and to black market currency trading. He assigned the Committee for State Security the task of cleaning up Moscow, stressing the importance of this effort. State Security went about it their usual way, catching small fry and trying to move up the ladder to catch the ringleaders. They put away a fair number of street-level dealers, but they didn't seem to get anywhere. The masterminds were still at large and they had no idea who they were. Eventually, however, they changed their approach and started investigating the case from the top down, which was more successful. Once they identified Rokotov and his top-level lieutenants, it turned out to be a huge organization dealing in millions of rubles. It had even set up affiliates in other Soviet cities, including Leningrad, Riga and Kiev."

"Did they go to jail for a long time?" Tosya asked.

Urumov rubbed his hands in anticipation.

"The sentencing in this case ended up being a saga in its own right. At first, they got the highest sentence provided for by law. It so happened that, under the old Penal Code, the longest sentence was eight years."

"That's all?" Tosya asked.

"That's exactly how comrade Khrushchev felt. When he heard about the sentences, he flew into a rage. Such terrible crimes, such enormous amounts of currency traded, such damage to the socialist economy and to Soviet prestige abroad, and this catalogue of offenses merited a lousy eight-year sentence? 'That's far too little, comrades,' he declared. 'In the old days, we used to shoot people for stealing a pair of underwear at a village store.' He insisted on a new trial, which was duly held and this time the gang leaders got fifteen years each. Still, Nikita Sergeyevich wasn't happy. He called together his ministers and said: 'I want a stiffer sentence.' They protested that a stiffer sentence would mean a death penalty and that, in any case, it would be illegal. 'Fine,' said Comrade Khrushchev. 'You're right, comrades. We need a law that provides harsher penalties for this kind of speculation and economic counterrevolution. I'll get the Supreme Soviet to vote on it right away.' Then Nikita Sergeyevich summoned the chairman of the Supreme Court and told him: 'Here is a new law, you can now put Rokotov and the other two gang leaders in front of a firing squad.' The Supreme Court gave in to the inevitable and passed three death sentences. After that, of course, there was an international spat, but by then the three gang leaders were already dead and buried."

"Oh, my God," Tosya exclaimed. "Why was there an international spat? The foreigners didn't like it that their currency was involved?"

"You don't get it?"

Lenny looked around, as though trying to ascertain that no strangers were within earshot. He leaned over the table and whispered dramatically: "In civilized countries, no law can be applied retroactively. It's a fundamental principle of jurisprudence, even in this country. If you commit a crime, you have to be tried based on the laws that were in force at the time when the crime was committed, regardless of what new laws the government has come up with in the meantime."

To give him his due, Urumov, although only a police detective like myself, knew not only all kinds of laws, but understood the legal principles involved as well as any trained lawyer.

"A firing squad," said Tosya. "They must have been very young, the three of them. Was there really a lot of money involved?"

"At the trial, overall currency transactions were estimated at five million rubles."

"Oh, my God," Tosya exclaimed. "That's like a year's turnover at our textile plant. So much money. Where did he keep it?"

"The guys who were involved in Rokotov's arrest say that he used to have a special suitcase with some kind of tricky American locks that couldn't be picked. He kept it checked at different train stations around the city, and that was where he kept his money."

"Really?" Tosya giggled incredulously. "Such a huge organization, three hundred members, cells all over the country, three top guys get death sentences, and all the profits fit into a suitcase? A bit of a stretch, isn't it, Urumov?"

Lenny started to respond, throwing his hands up in the air by way of a start, but at that moment Sevka came into the room. He had been playing in the courtyard all evening. It had turned dark outside and it was time for him to have his supper and finish his homework.

"Wow," he exclaimed, spotting an exotic vodka bottle on the table. "Don't throw it away when you're done, Uncle Pavel. I need it for my collection. Where is it from?"

"Uncle Lenny got it," I said.

"I mean what country?"

"It's ours, sonny," replied Urumov. "Soviet-made. Don't you see the three Russian knights on the label?"

"Check this out, too, Sevka," I said, pointing at the part that spelled "Russian Vodka" in English. "You've been taking English at school. You should be able to read it."

Sevka stared at the label, moving his lips silently.

"Come on, Sevka," Lenny said, cheering him on. "Show us how smart you are."

"Don't bother him, Urumov," Tosya said. She was nervous and wanted Sevka to do well.

Finally, Sevka said: "The first word is something about Russia. But I can't figure out the other one. It has a couple of letters in the Latin alphabet that we haven't learned yet."

"Oh, my God," exclaimed Urumov. "That's modern education for you. The kid is almost eleven – how old are you, Sevka, by the way? – and he can't recognize the word vodka. Even though it's in a foreign language."

Sevka was embarrassed, but not for long.

"Where did you get it?" he asked Lenny.

"None of your business," replied Lenny and winked at me. "It was a gift from a friend."

Ever since Lenny started working on Polishchuk's daughter, he had been showing up at work with various rare delicacies and consumer goods.

Tosya glanced at Lenny, then looked away and said, "You're bad news, Urumov. A real bastard. Your poor Raisa. I swear, if you were my guy, I would've killed you for chasing after every skirt the way you do."

"You wouldn't have, Tosya," said Urumov.

"Why not?"

"I wouldn't have been chasing after every skirt, Tosya, if I were your guy."

"Sure," Tosya replied. "I believe you."

Urumov was very pleased with himself. He sneered, puckered his lips and extended his white chubby hand toward her.

"No, seriously. If I were your guy, Tosya, I would love you alone and no one else besides."

That was my cue. I smacked Urumov's outstretched hand and said, "The real reason why you wouldn't kill this bastard, Tosya, is because you won't get the opportunity. If he even so much as thinks of making a move on you, I'll cut off that thing he chases after skirts with."

It was a joke, of course, but not entirely. It wasn't a good idea for Urumov to harbor any illusions as far as Tosya was concerned.

Sevka, who was still standing alongside the dining table, doing everything he could to delay his dinner and thus his homework, guffawed loudly. Tosya blushed and shouted, "Shut up, Matyushkin, you idiot. What are you doing, saying such things in front of a kid?"

We ended up not needing to recap the fancy vodka bottle, after all. Around midnight we left it, now empty and with the three Russian knights drooping sadly on its label, next to Sevka, who had fallen asleep on a folding loveseat despite the bright light in the room. Tosya tried to get Urumov to keep his voice down, but it was no use. He wanted to sing a duet with Tosya. Tosya, he insisted, had a heart-rending way of singing Russian songs, especially the one about two banks of a wide river that are destined never to come together.

"Cruel fate," Lenny sobbed, shedding drunken tears.

I should've been paying more attention, seeing that this sentimental song had suddenly become Urumov's favorite.

Had Urumov persuaded Tosya to sing along with him, regardless of the quality of her singing, her neighbors would have started to scream and pound on her walls, threatening to report her. But Tosya turned down Urumov's request and rather rudely forbade him from singing a solo. After that, we put Urumov into his coat, not without some difficulty, and walked him to the metro station at Kirov Gates, having convinced him to leave his Moskvich in the courtyard of our building.

When we reached the metro station, Urumov changed his mind and declared that he was going to walk home, which would save him five kopeks and help him sober up. Before heading off, he declared his undying love and admiration for Tosya and swore eternal friendship to me, urging us to love one another and to live in peace and accord. And, since we were his only friends in the whole world, our friendship imposed on us certain sacred obligations, such as staying awake and watching over his Moskvich, lest some hooligan in our neighborhood decided to damage it during the night.

"I'll hold you responsible," he said, wagging his finger at us. "I love that car."

Later, when Tosya and I lay side by side in my bed, she pressed her face into my shoulder and whispered, "Why do you care what happens to this Frezin character, Matyushkin? What does he have to do with you?"

"I don't want him to be executed for a crime he didn't commit," I said. "Colonel Nakazov doesn't seem to care whether it is the real killer who is brought to justice or whether somebody who had nothing to do with it takes the rap. He used to know Polishchuk and he's a friend of the family. Polishchuk's widow trusts him and believes everything he says. Whatever the real story, Frezin will be scapegoated."

"And what is it to you?"

"It's not justice, Tosya."

"I don't know, Matyushkin, what you mean by justice. Look at Rokotov. He was put in front of the firing squad and there was no justice in his case, either."

"Why do you say that?"

"Are you stupid, or what, Matyushkin? That story that Urumov was telling us, it stinks from a mile away."

"I don't think so, Tosya. Why?"

"Use your brain, Matyushkin. The leader of a huge gang with a suitcase in left luggage?"

I didn't argue. Whenever Tosya forms an opinion, there is no power on earth that can dislodge or alter it. All argument is useless.

"I would keep out of the Polishchuk case if I were you," she added.

TEN

I try to follow Tosya's advice in everything, including even my work. I believe that peace and accord between a man and a woman is based on this principle. That was why I put Polishchuk and Frezin out of my mind and turned to my direct responsibilities. I was spending far too much time on those burglaries and other cases were piling up.

I would have completely forgotten the whole mess if it weren't for Urumov. He was acting strangely. I kept waiting for him to finish up with the Polishchuk case and to give me a summary of what he had found out. Or, failing that, to at least complain what a spoiled, stuck-up brat Lyuda Polishchuk was. That is what he usually said when it came to women of this type.

However, time went by and Urumov kept showing up at work with various unusual things, like American cigarettes, a foreign cigarette lighter and, one time, a French men's fashion magazine that he studied assiduously at his desk during a lunch break. When he did refer to Lyuda Polishchuk, he did so rather airily and abstractly.

A week or two later, I got tired of waiting and asked him about her directly, without beating about the bush. To be on the safe side, I made it sound like a joke, but without the kind of ribbing that was usual in our banter. Urumov cut short my lame attempt at humor, raising his sad black eyes to look at me, shaking his head.

I could be excused for missing the signs of a coming earthquake. By then we had been working together for four years, and for three of that sharing the same office, a room that was long and narrow, like an eyeglass case and almost as small. Things were so cramped that whenever Lenny needed to get past me to his desk, he had to push me painfully against my desk to slide through.

During that time I had heard about so many women that I had long since lost count and, frankly, had stopped paying attention. Just the categories in which he divided his conquests were enough to make my head spin.

Take Della, Budyonny's secretary. Budyonny's secretaries didn't last long and Della was his fourth in four years. Budyonny's secretaries were so much Lenny's preserve that when Human Resources sent Della to Budyonny to be interviewed for the position, he stopped by the landing where we were all taking a smoking break and said to Urumov, "I can't make up my mind about the new secretary. How can I make a decision that would affect your life for the next year without getting any input from you? Maybe you should go take a look."

Budyonny was kidding, but as he stared at Lenny his eyes were dead serious and very angry. Despite this veiled threat, within two weeks Lenny and Della were fast friends.

Why anybody found Lenny attractive is beyond me. He was chubby and had a full, pink mouth and dark, curly hair, which was starting to thin on a catastrophic scale. He was never serious and constantly joking. Nevertheless, he was remarkably successful with women, and the quantity of fresh sausage and American cigarettes passing through his fingers suggested that Polishchuk's daughter was no exception to this rule.

Meanwhile, my own investigation into apartment break-ins was not going well and it kept me busy. Budyonny was looking over my shoulder and demanding results. Two more apartments were taken, in different neighborhoods, but over the same weekend. It was the same gang, judging from their habits.

Or rather, by lack of style. A true apartment burglar, a person who has made a name for himself and is respected both by his peers and the police, is not so hard to figure out. But no burglar worthy of the name would be bothered with this junk. Sure, minor hoods might branch out into apartments, but there are thousands of them in the city, and it would be impossible to track them all down. In a case like this you need not so much superior investigative skills as a bit of good luck. Perhaps someone spots the burglars and gives you an accurate description. Or, as it sometimes happens, a jacket or a sewing machine might surface at a consignment shop or a flea market. A thief, unless he's a complete idiot, would never take his loot to a consignment shop. But occasionally it happens that a thief sells something to someone who doesn't know the item is hot, and that third party takes it to the consignment shop. This is more likely with an amateur thief, which underscores the need for a competent fence.

But so far Lady Luck remained faithful to the robbers, which meant she was not being kind to me. That was going to change at some point, but all this was not easy to explain to Budyonny.

In short, I was deep in my investigation, doing leg work, visiting flea markets on Sundays, stopping at consignment shops during the week and so on. This is why, when a little while later Urumov came to work, shut the door of our office and began telling me something, his voice breaking with grief, I didn't immediately take it in.

"What was that again?" I asked.

"I'm leaving Raisa and the kids."

My jaw dropped and I sat in my chair thunderstruck, unable to say anything meaningful.

"Actually, I already have," Lenny added. "Last night. Threw a few things into the car and left."

"Wait a minute," I finally managed. "Why in the world would you want to do that?"

Urumov brushed the back of his hand against his face, turned away and stared out the window through the rain-splattered panes. The grey surface of the road glistened in the rain, and the ancient poplar trees in the Hermitage public garden across the street stretched their black limbs heavenward. The sky was low-hung, tattered and grey.

"You know," he said after a long silence. "Raisa and I have always gotten along. We were a good couple, despite everything. Even when I told her I was leaving she didn't make a scene. I think she understood. Even though it certainly isn't easy for her. And the girls are so little."

His two girls were indeed very little. One was Masha and the other, the little one, was Raisa. When Raisa was born, we were all surprised that he named her after her mother. In many families, boys are named after the father. Lenny laughed and said his Raisa was so perfect that he wanted to have two of them in the family.

"Raisa even helped me pack. I feel like such a swine."

Urumov patted his pockets for cigarettes, pulled out a pack of some unusual foreign brand, took one out and put it in his mouth. Then, he pulled it from between his lips.

"And I feel so bad for the girls," he said.

He crushed the cigarette between his fingers and threw it in the wastebasket.

"Give me one of your Red Presnyas, will you?"

He used his American lighter to light it and took a deep drag. He stood by the window smoking, even though Budyonny had banned smoking everywhere on the floor except on the landing and in a special smoking room next to it.

"Where are you going to stay?" I asked.

"What?"

Lenny was staring out the window and didn't hear me.

"Where are you going to stay?" I repeated. "You know, you're always welcome to stay with me. I've got a folding armchair, you can sleep on that.

Urumov brushed my suggestion aside.

"My brother has an apartment in the New Cheremushki neighborhood. He's a physicist and he works on some top secret project. Most of the time he lives elsewhere, where they do the experiments. I don't know anything about it, it's all a state secret. He got an apartment last year, but he never even bothered to furnish it. He's not married, or rather he's married to his particle collider."

That was typical Urumov. If there was something you needed, no matter what, Urumov always had a brother, an aunt, a second cousin twice removed, or at least a good friend who would either sell it to you or had a pretty good idea who would.

Predictably, in a city where housing was so scarce that even divorced couples had to go on sharing a room, Lenny would have a top-secret physicist brother with an apartment that he wasn't using.

"I'll stay there," said Lenny. "New Cheremushki is pretty far from the center, but it will do for the time being."

He fell silent again.

"Why all of a sudden did you decide to leave?"

Urumov turned away from the window and stared at me.

"What do you mean why? I told you: we're in love."

I must have missed that in the beginning.

"We who?" I asked.

"What do you mean who? Lyuda and me, of course."

"Lyuda, Polishchuk's daughter?" I asked in utter amazement. "Don't tell me you are in love with *her*?"

Urumov might not have been especially selective in his conquests and would flirt with almost any woman who crossed his path, from Masha's preschool teacher to Budyonny's secretaries. Yet he constantly repeated that a woman's looks matter a great deal. I had never seen Polishchuk's daughter, but, based on the pictures I had seen of her father – starting with the massive oil portrait hanging in their apartment and adding to that various official photographs – I had formed fairly strong expectations. It may not be kind to speak ill of the dead, but the man did have a piggish face, as if he had been fated to head up a meat processing plant. Anna Panteleyevna was still a rather good looking woman and may have been a real beauty in her time, but I didn't have much hope for their daughter. Plus, there was her upbringing to consider – the kind of family she came from, which was bound to make her pretty spoiled. A spoiled woman, as Lenny had told me many times, was his greatest turnoff.

"I thought you didn't like that sort of woman," I said.

"What do you mean? What kind?"

"I thought your favorite type were – what did you used to call them? – stars of the silent era."

"You mean good-looking ones?"

"Yes," I said hesitantly. "That's what I meant, I suppose."

"Are you kidding? She's an incredible beauty. Unreal. The most beautiful woman I have ever seen."

Lenny sighed.

"But it's not a question of looks," he continued. "I'm serious. Even if she weren't so beautiful, it wouldn't have mattered. I just can't live without her."

A few days passed and Urumov invited me to his new place.

New Cheremushki is located somewhere at the end of the world. It's an entire neighborhood of brand-new apartments built of prefab concrete. Functional to the point of brutality, the buildings are positioned in a rigid geometrical plan that must have derived its inspiration from labor camp barracks. The only difference is that I have never seen barracks that were five stories high.

The similarity to a camp was underscored by the fact that the streets marking the boundaries between the sections of five-story barracks had been laid out but not yet paved, leading to numerous potholes and puddles. But a line of sickly, foot-tall saplings stuck into the soggy clay hinted at an effort toward beautification. The saplings might one day grow into tall, shady linden or poplar trees, but for now they were a perfect symbol of the neighborhood as a work in progress.

Among all the identical buildings I found Lenny's easily enough and from a considerable distance, as his blue hatchback was parked next to the front door. There was no elevator, but the climb to the fifth floor was not difficult, as the ceilings in the new buildings were remarkably low.

The stairwell still smelled of whitewash and oil paint, but the lightbulb on the fifth floor landing had already burned out. After poking around the door frame in search of the bell, I gave up and knocked.

The door was opened by a young woman. Even in the dim light of the entryway it was clear that she was indeed remarkably good-looking. I had to make an effort not to stare. I find that I need a few moments to get used to a very beautiful woman when I first meet her. Not that I've seen many as beautiful as Lyuda Polishchuk.

Urumov introduced us officially, adding that I was the one who had caught Frezin.

"Mother and I are very grateful to you," she said softly, as a sad smile appeared on her lips.

I was touched by her smile, but it didn't prevent me from noting that, despite the absolute secrecy of this case while it was being investigated, Lyuda Polishchuk already knew that Daniel Frezin was a suspect in her father's murder.

I replied that I had made the arrest by accident and that, at the time, I didn't have any idea about her father's death. I added that Frezin had been linked to the murder by investigators from the Moscow Region police department, as well as by Colonel Nakazov of State Security, and that all the credit for solving the crime goes to them.

"He's so modest, my friend Pavel Matyushkin," Urumov said.

"Vladislav Mironovich is convinced that Frezin is the one who killed Daddy," Lyuda said, an icy note creeping suddenly into her voice.

"Apparently, you don't share his conviction," I observed.

"May I speak openly with you?"

She had grey eyes that exuded tenderness when she looked at me. No wonder she drove Lenny crazy. What I couldn't quite understand was what she saw in him.

"Of course you can, Lyudochka," Urumov exclaimed expansively. "It's as though you were talking to me. He and I have no secrets from each other."

Lyuda gave him a quick smile but kept looking at me, waiting for my answer.

I nodded: "Yes, of course."

"Everything Vladislav Mironovich tells us seems to fit together very neatly. Too neatly, I'm afraid. Especially since... I don't know whether you are aware of it, but Vladislav Mironovich and that man, Frezin, already know each other. Two years ago, Vladislav Mironovich was in charge of an investigation that led to Frezin being convicted. It was the notorious Rokotov case."

"Coincidences happen," I said cautiously.

I had no intention of sharing with her my own doubts about Frezin's guilt – or, for that matter, about the methods employed by my Moscow Region colleagues to tie him to a variety of other crimes before they had lit up on her father's murder.

"That's the thing," she objected hotly. "I'm afraid Vladislav Mironovich may have his own reasons for solving this case. I mean solving it personally."

"Yes, of course. I know that Colonel Nakazov and your father were friends."

"And not only that. Vladislav Mironovich was not just Daddy's friend. I have my own suspicions about Vladislav Mironovich..."

She broke off.

"What kind of suspicions?" I asked.

"You'll laugh," she seemed embarrassed. "I think he may be in love with me."

"What did you say?" shouted Urumov. "Who does he think he is?"

Lyuda ignored him and went on.

"I may be exaggerating, but a long time ago, when I was in eighth grade or so, he started to visit us more often. He would sit in the living room and talk to Daddy, but you could see that he was bored out of his mind. Only when I came into the room would he come alive. It was so obvious, almost deliberate, and I don't understand why Daddy never seemed to notice it. Even now I feel strange whenever Vladislav Mironovich looks at me. Don't get me wrong. He's a nice, charming man, he's witty and so on, but he scares me sometimes, the way he looks at me."

Urumov was seething.

"He's a dirty old goat."

Lyuda didn't even look at him and went on with her tale.

When she got a little older, sixteen or seventeen, and was still in high school, he drove her home a number of times. The first time she was walking home from school and Nakazov passed her in a car. He spotted her and offered her a ride. Then it started to happen regularly, every other week. The first ride might indeed have happened by chance, and he was in his official black Volga with a driver, but after that Lyuda suspected that he had deliberately waited for her. He would always be in his private car, a military jeep.

"Nor did he ever happen to be passing by when I was with my friends or—" she stammered and blushed, but concluded the sentence, "Or with a boy from my class."

Urumov gave her a strange look and turned away.

"The last time he stopped and offered me a ride, I suddenly got frightened," she went on. "It was in my final year. I got into his car but then, when he stopped at the light at Sretenka Gate, I jumped out and excused myself with some clumsy lie about having to go visit a classmate who was home sick. I think he understood."

Lyuda paused.

"There was that other time, when I was already in college. I had a few friends over, mostly from the Foreign Languages Institute. We were in my room, listening to jazz late into the night. Vladislav Mironovich was having dinner with my parents. He heard the music and knocked on my door. He was his usual witty self, and he charmed everyone, especially the girls. But you should have seen how he looked at the boys. Several days later he stopped by again to see my parents and said in an offhand manner that I should be more selective about the kind of young men I spent my time with. He said that if I was not sure, I should always ask him for advice."

"In other words," I said, "you think that Colonel Nakazov might want to solve your father's murder to impress you?"

"No, I'm probably wrong. Especially when you put it that way. I know it's impossible. A colonel at State Security would never charge a wrong man deliberately, would he? But, to be honest with you, I sometimes think that it's not impossible, after all. Vladislav Mironovich began this investigation with such zeal, and so quickly found the murderer, that I can't help being a little suspicious. When he comes to report on the progress of his investigation, he keeps looking at me the same way he used to before, when I was in high school."

Urumov liked this story less and less.

"He takes some liberties, this Nakazov fellow," he said angrily. "It's not 1937. Those guys at State Security can't go around doing this kind of stuff any longer, with the same kind of impunity."

"The worst thing is that Mother trusts him completely," added Lyuda. "He has some kind of supernatural power over her. Especially since Daddy was killed. She said to me recently: 'Lyuda, go kiss Vladislav Mironovich. He's been so kind to us, I don't know what we would've done without him.'"

"Sure," groaned Urumov.

"I don't know," I said dryly. "I don't have an opinion about this case. I'm no longer part of the investigation."

"Pavel is investigating different kinds of crimes," said Urumov. "He now specializes in apartment burglaries. By the way, what does your friend Nakazov think about the burglary at your place?"

"He's not my friend," protested Lyuda. "He is old enough to be my father. He's pushing fifty. I can't help thinking of *Dubrovsky* when I think of him. We read it in school, how Masha Troyekurova had to marry an old prince. It's terrible. If I were her, I'd take poison or something, rather than marry an old man."

"There was always an option of eloping with Dubrovsky," objected Urumov, revealing an impressive knowledge of the high school literature curriculum.

In the ensuing week, I visited them in New Cheremushki several times. Urumov kept inviting me because, except for me, no one knew about the two of them. Lyuda's family was in mourning, which was not a proper time to start love affairs. She was also scared of her mother and, possibly, Nakazov. Nakazov now found a pretext to visit them practically on a daily basis.

Urumov also had reasons to keep their relationship secret. Raisa had been understanding and helped him pack his suitcase when he moved out, but things would have likely taken a nastier turn had she known that he left her for a college student ten years younger than she was.

And, of course, Budyonny would not have been pleased with Lenny's new affair, especially one begun in the course of an official investigation. Budyonny liked Lenny, but a thing like this could have been the proverbial last straw.

In short, with the exception of Lyuda's frequent visits, Lenny lived like a hermit in his brother's apartment. Even his brother, who occasionally came to Moscow on business, knew nothing of Lyuda's existence. On the other hand, Lenny claimed that his brother, a typical scientist, would not have noticed Lyuda, even if he had run into her in his apartment. It is indeed amazing how one can get lost in a huge, crowded city. Lyuda came to see Urumov early in the morning before her classes started, and Urumov was now often late for work, which had never happened while he lived with Raisa. Budyonny started giving Lenny dirty looks. In fact, Urumov would have long since been taken to the woodshed were it not for Della, who defended him loyally.

Be that as it may, the tiger-yellow eyes of our lieutenant colonel shone with an evil light whenever they fell on Urumov. And on me, too, since Urumov and I shared an office. Being a native of the Caucasus, Budyonny probably saw me as a member of the Lenny clan, such that the mere fact of my existence made me fair game in any blood feud. Or maybe all Muscovites looked alike to a person from the Caucasus. Even though Urumov and I couldn't have looked more different.

Lyuda returned to New Cheremushki after school and sat at the kitchen table, reading her textbooks and taking notes. Or, opening a thick English dictionary and a book of idioms, she translated various texts, copying words she didn't know into a notebook. Every day at six o'clock sharp, Urumov shot from behind his desk and raced home in his Moskvich, where he spent hours watching her study, dripping with adoration.

Not surprisingly, I avoided visiting them too often. The apartment was poorly furnished and neither Lyuda nor Urumov were doing anything to remedy the situation. In general, the cozy feeling that Raisa knew how to create in their communal apartment was completely absent in Lenny's charmless New Cheremushki place. The presence of rare, quality sausage and American cigarettes did nothing to make up for the lack of hominess.

I've long noticed that beautiful women make poor housewives.

After my first visit, Lyuda and I no longer mentioned Frezin. One time, when Urumov asked me in her presence how I was getting on with my apartment burglaries, Lyuda suddenly blurted out that the baubles that had been taken from their apartment in September were not only very valuable but unique, priceless. Her parents had been giving them to her as birthday presents ever since she turned ten and she had quite a collection. But she had no idea how much they were worth until one day, in her first year of college, she took a pair of earrings to a pawn shop. At first the clerk wanted to have nothing to do with her and kept giving her suspicious looks. But when she insisted, he got the manager, who offered so much for the earrings that she got scared and ran away.

"Why did you need to pawn your jewels?" Urumov asked.

"I needed money."

"What for?"

"I had to raise a large sum," Lyuda said. "Daddy gave me the earrings as a high school graduation present."

She lowered her head and sighed, which she always did whenever she mentioned her father.

ELEVEN

Tall and, despite his thirty-plus years, slender, Lev Yashin paced the mouth of his goal – from one striped post to the other – like a caged lion. His visored hat was soaked with rain, his black jersey splattered with mud, and his huge goalkeeper gloves waterlogged. Even from the twenty-fifth row in Dinamo Stadium you could feel his red-hot anger.

Next to me, Sevka beamed with joy.

"Did you see it, Uncle Pavel?" he kept blabbering excitedly. "Voronin to Ivanov, and Ivanov tricked the defender so badly he flopped face down in a puddle, then passed it to Gusarov. Gusarov hugged the goal line and then returned the ball back to Ivanov, who was completely unguarded. All he had to do was to tap it into the goal. Did you like it?"

I didn't like it at all. Besides, not being blind, I too had just seen the play unfold before us.

We had barely had time to settle into our rain-drenched seats and spread my raincoat over our heads when Torpedo scored. I had to give it to them, it was a finely executed play. Dinamo, in their light-blue jerseys and extra-long, old-fashioned shorts, were shivering in the frigid rain as Torpedo's best players, wearing workmanlike black-and-white uniforms, put on a passing clinic, swiftly springing their top scorer, Ivanov, one-on-one with Lev Yashin. Yashin came out to cut the angle, but Ivanov calmly flipped the ball over him and it was 1-0.

Just like that, before the game was two minutes old.

Despite the weather, there were a fair number of spectators in the stands. On second thought, this was nothing out of the ordinary. A match between Dinamo and Torpedo is always exciting, regardless of the teams' positions in the standings. Dinamo wasn't doing well, and was stuck in the middle of the standings despite finishing first last year, and now Torpedo was on top. A win against Dinamo so late in the season would ease their path to the championship.

Dinamo is the Ministry of Internal Affairs' team. We all root for it at Petrovka. In fact, everyone in the police force roots for it, from the highest ranking general down to the rookie cop posted to direct traffic. Other uniformed services and law enforcement agencies also root for Dinamo, even foreign intelligence officers posted abroad.

More than anything else, Dinamo is what unites us and keeps us apart from the rest of the country.

But the kids, they like Torpedo. Torpedo is sponsored by Likhachev Automobile Plant. But that's beside the point. The kids love Torpedo because Torpedo is a great team. They were even greater before their young forward, Edward Streltsov, got in trouble with the law and went to jail. Sevka is a huge Torpedo fan.

Because of bad weather, Tosya had wanted to cancel our outing to the stadium, but Sevka wouldn't hear of it. So, since we were going no matter what, Tosya spent the morning making sure we were properly equipped. She packed hard-boiled eggs and a thermos full of hot tea. She prepared a bunch of sandwiches, buttering thick slices of bread and loading them with hunks of sausage. She instructed Sevka to put on two sweaters, because she was not interested in seeing him catch a cold right before the end of the quarter. When we were all ready and standing in the doorway about to depart, she made him change out of his worn sneakers and into a pair of rubber boots over warm woolen socks.

"Make sure you stay under the raincoat at all times," she instructed him, wagging a finger. "You too, Matyushkin, keep an eye on him. I rely on your relative sanity."

I had inherited my raincoat from my Dad. It's the kind of raincoat a patrolman on the beat can walk around in his entire shift in all kinds of weather. You can go through a monsoon in it, and if you open it up and spread it overhead, not a single drop of rain will fall on you.

Our seats were behind the goal line. They are the cheapest seats and, besides, I like watching the keeper during the game. I may be a Dinamo fan because it's our Ministry's team, but that's not the only reason. I have a huge amount of respect for Lev Yashin. I was smaller than Sevka when Yashin started playing, and back then the biggest rivalry in football was between Dinamo and the Red Army team. Everybody respected Yashin, even when he was a rookie. We all called him Lev Ivanovich, as if he were an old man.

I keep an eye on Yashin even when the ball is on the opponents' side of the field. I watch him as he gives instructions to his backs and organizes his defense. When you watch Yashin, you can see that a proper defense starts when your team is on the attack.

As the first half progressed, Yashin made a couple of incredible saves, stopping sure-fire scores aimed at the corners. Sevka could only grab his head in frustration. By halftime we would've been losing by three goals or more, were it not for Yashin.

The rain gradually tapered off, and the wind tore holes in the cloud cover, revealing stretches of blue sky and even a bit of tepid October sun. During half time we used an old T-shirt to dry the bench and spread out our feast, placing the hard-boiled eggs and sandwiches out on newspaper.

"Is it true, Uncle Pavel?" Sevka asked, chewing on the sandwich, "that one time the Soviet national team played the World All-Stars. We had Yashin in goal, of course, and they had a trained gorilla? The gorilla was so good, nobody could score on it."

I shrugged. "I don't know. It may well be true. I didn't see that match."

"Of course you didn't," said Sevka. "It took place in Brazil, in the middle of a jungle. The gorilla would have caught pneumonia and croaked in our climate. Anyway, we kept shooting at the goal the entire match and had all kinds of opportunities, but couldn't score. They played two halves but the score was still 0-0. They went into overtime and it was still the same. No score. Then, as the overtime was about to expire, we had a goal kick. Yashin kicked the ball from his own goal to theirs. It traveled the entire length of the field, struck the crossbar at the other end, rebounded against the back of the gorilla's head and slammed into the back of the net. The ref blew the whistle, game over. We won 1-0. Everybody ran out onto the field, the fans were going crazy, but the gorilla was still stretched on the ground. Turns out Yashin killed it on the spot.

I laughed.

"You don't believe it's true, Uncle Pavel?"

"I don't know, Sevka," I said patting him on the shoulder. "Maybe it is. Lots of strange stuff happens in life."

"Well, Uncle Pavel. If it weren't for Yashin, we could've been heading home by now."

"Are you bored?" I asked, kidding him.

"Of course not. What I'm saying is that the game could've been over by now. It could've been three-zip Torpedo."

"We may still get back into it. We're only down one goal , as far as I can see. What if Yashin kicks the ball, hits Kavazashvili in the head and Torpedo has to play without him?"

In the second half the weather continued to improve and the sun warmed things up. It dried up the stands, but the fields still bubbled with mud. The players had churned up the wet grass, erasing all the markings except for the sidelines, which still showed here and there in the sea of brown clay.

The slippery field played to Dinamo's advantage. Torpedo's center fielders were agile and graceful, like bullfighters, but they no longer could slice through our defensive positions. Dinamo, on the other hand, settled down and regrouped, and Yashin's brilliant goal tending gave them faith in themselves. They gradually recaptured the initiative and laid siege to the opponent's goal. By the middle of the second half we had tied the score and at the very end, when the sun had started to slide behind the Western bleachers, coloring the edges of the sky dark blue and pink, Chislenko leapt high over his minder and headed a perfect serve from the right flank into the net.

Naturally, Dinamo fans began hugging each other all around us, whereas Sevka and other Torpedo fans sprinkled around the stadium hung their heads. I had to turn away lest my joy become too obvious, adding to Sevka's misery.

After the final whistle, we walked to the exit in silence. Sevka walked with his head between his shoulders and was close to tears.

"You didn't deserve to win," he said at last. "It's not fair. We were better."

"You're right, Sevka. But these things can happen in sports. You can't just be better. You've got to be lucky sometimes, too."

"Dinamo is always lucky. We never have any luck. We play our hearts out, but in the end we always lose."

Getting out of the stadium wasn't easy. A huge crowd funneled into a narrow passage formed by two lines of mounted police leading to the Dinamo metro station and the trolley stops on Leningrad Avenue. We decided to wait them out and stopped at the concession stand. I got a bottle of orange soda and a cheese sandwich for Sevka. The sandwich, the last one in the display case, was a bit dry around the edges, but Sevka was a growing kid, so he was always starving.

"We'll go to a bandy match in winter. Dinamo beats everybody at bandy, there is never any question about that. Besides, there is no Torpedo bandy team. Speaking of winter, do you like skating?"

Sevka stared at me.

"I don't skate, Uncle Pavel."

"Are you kidding? Why not?"

"I've never had a pair of skates."

"And what about your Mom? She doesn't skate either?"

"Of course not. Where would she have learned? At the orphanage?"

"That's amazing," I said, shaking my head.

I made some mental calculations.

"You know what?," I said. "When I get paid next month, I'll buy you a pair of skates. Real hockey skates. Then, when it gets cold, I'll teach the two of you to skate. We'll go skating together at Clear Ponds."

The crowd had thinned out. The horses of the mounted police were getting restless and shifting impatiently beneath their riders, breaking the line.

"So, comrades? One more for the road," said a voice behind us. It sounded familiar.

"For the road, Comrade Colonel, sir," said another voice, which I also thought I recognized. "To victory."

Three men stood around the table. Colonel Nakazov was in civilian clothes, wearing a grey wool cap and a synthetic brown slicker known as a "Bologna," in a cut that was just becoming fashionable. His companions were Captain Zapekayev from Moscow Region Criminal Investigations and his second-in-command, Junior Lieutenant Ryumin. Each held an empty beer mug.

"I'll drink to that," said Nakazov, pouring vodka into the mugs from a silver flask.

He poured strictly according to rank: first for himself, then for Zapekayev and finally for Ryumin.

"I'll drink to that, too, Comrade Colonel," echoed Zapekayev.

Ryumin said nothing. All three were fairly loaded.

"To Victory!"

"To Victory, Comrade Colonel," Zapekayev echoed.

They drank.

Nakazov exhaled noisily after drinking. Zapekayev and Ryumin sniffed the sleeves of their police uniforms.

"Nice one," said Nakazov.

"Nice one indeed, Comrade Colonel," Zapekayev agreed.

Ryumin's face glowed with happiness. It must have been the first time he had drunk on an equal footing with such a high-ranking officer. He seemed ill at ease.

Colonel Nakazov raised his left hand a little unsteadily and stared at his gold watch as if he couldn't quite figure out what he was looking at.

"Soon," he began and hiccupped. "Soon, my driver is going to pick me up. But not just yet. Let's drink to Torpedo now. To how they choked."

He poured and they drank.

"Look who's here," Nakazov exclaimed suddenly. "In our midst, rubbing shoulders with us mortals."

He had just spotted us.

"Come join us, Senior Lieutenant." He waved his hand hospitably. "Come on over, join the collective. And bring your cup. We've been celebrating."

I went over and Sevka also joined us, albeit reluctantly.

"*We'll raise the first glass to victory,*" Nakazov sang, intoning the lyrics of a popular war song. He had a deep, pure baritone. "*We'll raise another to friends...* What a great song. Come on, dump out whatever you've got there. I'll pour you some vodka. Let's drink to good friends. And colleagues, of course."

I gulped down the rest of my warm orange soda and pushed my paper cup toward Nakazov. He poured. We drank.

"Is this your kid?" Nakazov asked, pointing at Sevka. "A big boy, too. He doesn't look much like you."

Before I could answer, Sevka replied, "I'm not his kid. I'm my Mom's. Uncle Pavel is a neighbor."

"A neighbor," Nakazov repeated, as if it was an important piece of information. He poured us more vodka. "I see. I guess he's a bit too old to be your son. Let's drink to victory."

We drank.

"A Dinamo fan?" Nakazov asked, still talking about Sevka.

"No, sir, Comrade Colonel. He roots for Torpedo."

"That's a big mistake," Nakazov said, shaking his head. "You, kid, had better start rooting for Dinamo. Dinamo represents the Organs of State Security, and the Organs are a force to be reckoned with. Our Motherland survives only because of her Organs. You start by rooting for Dinamo, and then we'll see maybe we'll get you to join the Organs of State Security when the time comes. But rooting for Dinamo comes first. One step at a time."

"I don't want to join the Organs," Sevka said. "I want to be a pilot. And I'll keep rooting for Torpedo."

"As you wish," Nakazov shrugged. "No one will make you root for Dinamo against your will, of course. What's new, Senior Lieutenant?"

"Nothing much, Comrade Colonel, sir. Working away, as usual."

"Very well. We, on the other hand, have been trying to crack your friend Freak for more than a month, me and your colleagues from Moscow Region. We're starting to make some progress with him. Am I right, Zapekayev?"

"Yes, sir, Comrade Colonel. Exactly right."

"You did a good job, Senior Lieutenant. Your assistance in solving this crime has been invaluable. Even though you stumbled upon Frezin by accident."

"In the service of the Motherland," I said, giving a regulation response.

"In case you catch someone like Frezin again," said Nakazov, "I hope you'll take them straight to Lubyanka. We'll know what to do with them… I'm kidding, of course."

Zapekayev and Ryumin giggled.

"Yes, sir, Comrade Colonel," I replied without cracking a smile. "May I ask you a question, sir?"

"At ease, Senior Lieutenant," Nakazov said becoming annoyed with my formality which was out of place at a stadium. "Relax. We're all having a drink. It's not a marching drill. Go ahead, ask away."

"You see, sir, I'm investigating several residential burglaries. Mostly unimportant crimes, none of which has anything to do with the burglary at the Polishchuks'. I wanted to ask you whether there has been any progress in finding the perpetrators of that crime."

Nakazov gave me a sharp look. I kept staring straight at him, my face the picture of innocence. Nakazov hesitated and then said, "Who cares about a few baubles? So what if a few pieces of jewelry went missing? We're investigating a crime of national importance, a murder of a key economic manager. You've got to see the big picture, Senior Lieutenant."

Ryumin laughed.

"The point is," I said. "All my burglaries seem to have been committed by the same people. Sooner or later we'll catch them. I thought it might be a good idea to question them about the Polishchuk burglary, as well? Who knows, they might have been involved in that, too."

Nakazov pondered my words.

"They might," he said. "They just might. Why not? It's not at all certain that the burglary at the Polishchuks' was committed by professionals or that it was in any way connected to Anton's murder. It could've been a coincidence. That's right, a coincidence. Why not? Do as you see fit, Senior Lieutenant, but make sure you keep me informed."

"I will," I said.

Nakazov wagged his finger:

"It's in your own interest. If you find those who burglarized the Polishchuks' apartment, I'll be sure to mention you to your superiors at the highest level. It could give your career a badly needed push. Is it a deal?"

"Yes, sir, Comrade Colonel."

"Not again, Senior Lieutenant. At ease, I said."

"Yes, sir."

An official black Volga pulled up to the concession stand. Nakazov gave us a general, perfunctory farewell. However, before leaving, he rolled down his window.

"Don't think you're smarter than anyone else, Senior Lieutenant," he said softly. "It's always the smartest people who make the dumbest mistakes."

Not waiting for a reply, he rolled the window up and the Volga started away from the curb.

"Take it easy," Zapekayev said, eyeing me derisively. He had heard Nakazov's final words and understood their meaning. He headed off, closely followed by Ryumin who, before taking leave, finished the last drops of vodka.

Sevka stared after them, scowling.

"We should go, too," I said. "Your Mom will get nervous if we're late."

TWELVE

The receiver crackled with Colonel Nakazov's mocking voice.

"Are you still asleep, Senior Lieutenant? I'm up, as you can see. The enemy never sleeps and we must keep our eyes open, too."

My neighbor Yevdokia Filippovna had been pounding on my door, and when I finally forced myself to wake up, she shouted through the keyhole, "A call for you. You should tell your colleagues not to phone so early. And not late at night, either."

I groped for my slippers and, wrapping myself in a blanket, headed out of my room.

At the far end of the communal hallway Yevdokia Filippovna slammed the door of her room angrily, making a sound like a gunshot.

"I need to speak to you," Nakazov said over the phone. "Could you brush your teeth and be ready on the double? Meet me by Kirov metro station? I'll pick you up on my way to work. Look for a black Volga."

He he gave me his license plate number and, while writing it down on the wall by the phone, I thought bitterly: "Now he'll be giving me a ride instead of Lyuda Polishchuk."

The morning air was dry and cold and the grass around the bust of Lenin in the garden was tinged white with frost. The metro station had just opened and the few early commuters, sleepy and irritated, made their way across the square to the entrance. At the tram stop in front of the one-story Turgenev Reading Library, a crowd of unshaven proletarians stormed an overflowing A tram.

At the other end of the square, behind the Kirov metro station, Clear Ponds Boulevard bristled with bare tree limbs, their red and yellow leaves carpeting the ground. The recently unveiled monument to the writer Alexander Griboyedov was ash colored against the grey dawn. The city was starting to smell of winter.

A Volga was idling its motor across from the monument. Nakazov sat in the passenger seat.

"Punctuality is the courtesy of kings, Senior Lieutenant," he said, leaning over his seat and unlocking the back door. "It took you twenty-two minutes to get ready. We're not monarchists, of course, but..."

"My fault, sir," I replied.

"You'll need to work on yourself, Senior Lieutenant. An officer must be punctual. Without punctuality we turn into weak-kneed civilians. Let's go," he said to the driver.

As I got into the back seat, I looked at my watch. Mine may not be a gold and mother-of-pearl Victory wristwatch like Nakazov's, but it keeps good time. Only fifteen minutes had passed since I hung up the receiver.

We rode in silence for several minutes, which was enough to get us through the empty streets to KGB headquarters on Lubyanka Square.

"Stop here, Grigory," said Nakazov.

The Volga stopped, nearly touching a steel gate on the side of the massive Lubyanka building. The gate was painted black and bore a large white "No Parking" inscription. It was guarded by two soldiers with Kalashnikovs slung across their backs and a lieutenant with a holstered pistol. The officer recognized Nakazov's driver and gave him a friendly nod. The entrance to Lubyanka had massive bronze handles and white curtains over the glass. Despite the early hour, the door opened and closed frequently, letting in young men in civilian clothes, with short military haircuts and a soldierly bearing.

"It's been a busy time for me, Senior Lieutenant," said Nakazov. "Besides, you know it's a hassle to get an outsider into our building. I hope you don't mind if we talk in the car. It won't take long. "

"I don't mind, Comrade Colonel."

"Very well then. What I wanted to tell you is that Daniel Frezin finally signed a confession. Just as we always thought, he broke into the Polishchuks' dacha, not realizing that the owner was at home. Frezin strangled Anton in his study. He had never met Anton, but knew about the dacha from another inmate, with whom he was doing time. The other inmate is serving a much longer sentence and isn't due to be released for a long time. He'll eventually get charged as well, but for now our first priority is to bring Anton's murderer to justice. I do not exclude the possibility that Frezin and his accomplice, the one who's still in jail, were somehow involved in the burglary at the Polishchuks' apartment, but I don't think we need to spend much time on that. Moscow Region detectives were the ones who solved this high-profile case. My contribution was modest and I prefer to keep a low profile, in any case. You, of course, will get full credit for apprehending Frezin, even if you didn't know about the Polishchuk murder at the time and missed a crucial piece of evidence when you searched Frezin."

While he talked, I was trying to puzzle this thing out, and in the end decided that the only thing for me to do was to take my hat off to Zapekayev and Ryumin for beating a confession out of Frezin in such a relatively short time.

"It's all well and good," continued Nakazov. "But we're still going to have a trial."

"Why's that?" I asked. "Didn't he confess?"

Nakazov gave me a quick look to make sure I wasn't poking fun of him, but I sat there with a straight face.

"Funny you should ask, Senior Lieutenant," Nakazov said, "but according to new rules it is no longer enough. In the old days, when I was a young and idealistic NKVD operative, a criminal could be sentenced based on his own admission of guilt. Justice was done promptly and efficiently, without pointless formalities and bureaucratic delays. Crime rates were low and there was no ideological unsteadiness. Everybody toed the Party line."

I nodded.

"I'm afraid you'll have to appear in court," Nakazov concluded. "You'll be a witness for the prosecution."

"Yes, of course, Comrade Colonel," I said.

Nakazov nodded.

"Good," he said. "You'll have to describe the circumstances of Frezin's arrest. That's pretty much all that will be required of you."

"And, as you recall, Senior Lieutenant Urumov and I also responded to the burglary at the Polishchuks' apartment."

Nakazov grimaced.

"No need to mention that. I mean, don't lie to the court, and answer whatever questions the judge, the prosecutor and, what do you call him, the lawyer for the defense ask you. But don't volunteer any information. Frezin has been charged with murder and he will be convicted for murder. Don't complicate matters. We'll deal with the burglary some other time, you can be sure about that."

"I got to the Polishchuks' dacha late, Comrade Colonel," I said. "Not much before you did. I don't know what I can say about it."

"There is no need to say anything about the investigation, either. No one will ask you about it. The court needs to hear from you about Frezin's arrest. Just tell them how he got on the train at the Vesna station and how he acted strangely and resisted arrest."

"Did he get on at Vesna?" I asked in surprise.

"Naturally. Where else?"

"I didn't notice."

"Come on," Nakazov said. "Of course he got on at Vesna. Didn't you say so yourself?"

"I didn't," I said. "It was dark outside. I wasn't paying attention."

Nakazov was starting to lose patience with me, but he restrained himself.

"I'm sure you'll refresh your memory by the time you testify. I've got to get to work. You know how to get back?"

We got out of the car. Nakazov pulled off his soft leather glove, shook my hand curtly and, not bothering to put the glove back on, stepped through the front door. The driver backed the Volga out of the driveway and parked it in the middle of the square, in a row of other official black Volgas. He locked all the doors and also entered the State Security building, using a side entrance.

A few days later I got a summons to appear in court in Podolsk, Moscow Region. The instructions were to present myself at 8 a.m. sharp at the court building and to show the summons to the guard. The address and directions were scribbled in light-blue ink and were barely legible, but on the back there was a long, detailed list of sanctions provided by law for those who ignore the summons, willfully damage or destroy it, or fail to appear on the date and time specified, except for the following documented reasons, etc.

Possible transgressions were so numerous and the sanctions so severe, that by the time I got halfway down the list I began to wonder whether it wasn't me who was on trial.

I did make an honest attempt to recall when exactly Frezin had boarded the Serpukhov train and even enlisted Tosya's help. She thought she recalled the moment when Frezin had entered the car, but the problem was that she wasn't familiar with the Serpukhov line enough to know which station stop it had been.

I was shown into a narrow, windowless room with walls painted a dull beige. I waited there for two and a half hours, contemplating the bottoms of my shoes in boredom. The furnishings in the room consisted of an uncomfortable metal chair and a wooden desk, topped with a decanter half-filled with yellowish liquid, and a stained glass.

Time tends to pass very slowly in narrow, windowless rooms.

The first thing I observed when I was at last called into the courtroom was that, contrary to my expectations, the defendant looked healthy and cheerful. As a dangerous recidivist presenting a risk of flight, he sat on a bench between two uniformed policemen, and two others sat behind him. Next to them sat his lawyer, a dashing young man with a carefree expression on his face. Frezin was dressed in a prison-issue suit and a white shirt that was a couple of sizes too small for him. It left his wrists bare halfway to his elbows. A fanciful jailhouse tattoo slithered from the back of his right hand and ran up underneath the fabric. Completing his attire was a narrow tie held around his neck by a rubber band. If it had been issued to him at the jail, then it must have been confiscated from one of those modish young men who imitated American dress styles and whom the Moscow Region police was in the habit of detaining whenever they ventured outside city limits.

Like a kid dressed up for a birthday party, Frezin occasionally pulled down the knot, causing the tie to snap back toward his prominent Adam's apple.

Frezin recognized me and nodded as if we were old acquaintances. All in all, he didn't act as if he was being tried for murder and could end up on death row. He kept turning his head and looking around the courtroom, examining the spectators with great curiosity. There weren't too many spectators, and if he was showing off in front of them, playing a hardened career criminal who didn't give a damn what he got, it was certainly was not a sellout.

I thought of the conversation I had had with crippled Arkady Matveyevich, when Brunevsky described Frezin, a.k.a. Freak as a circus freak performing at country fairs, and also as a pawn that had hobbled its way across the chess board to be transformed into a queen. Both descriptions seemed somehow fitting.

"Matyushkin, Pavel Vasiliyevich will appear as a witness for the prosecution," the clerk announced. "Confirm that you are Senior Lieutenant Matyushkin, comrade, a detective at Moscow Criminal Investigations?"

I confirmed that I was indeed me.

"Did you arrest Daniel Frezin?" the state prosecutor asked, rising from his bench.

"I did."

"Do you see Daniel Frezin in the courtroom?"

"I do," I said again, pointing to Frezin.

"Tell the court when and under what circumstances you made the arrest."

I began to speak in the low monotone that all policemen around the world employ when testifying in court. I gave the date and the approximate time, explained why I was on the train and indicated where I was when the quarrel in the car broke out. I then recounted the events in as much detail as I could remember.

The judge presided over her courtroom from a rectangular table covered with green baize. She was a heavy-set woman with an improbably tall beehive of blonde hair. On her face, at a similar distance from her nose, she had two brownish warts, their symmetrical positioning on her cheeks bringing to mind the possibility of being placed there on purpose, the way French aristocrats once faked beauty marks. All in all, she was an imposing and handsome woman.

She was deeply involved in reading an official-looking document lying on the green baize in front of her and seemed to be paying no attention to either me or the state prosecutor.

"Was there something unusual about Frezin when you arrested him?" the prosecutor continued.

"Not really," I replied.

"Did he seem to you to be nervous or upset?"

I shrugged. "Not particularly."

"Are you quite certain that this is the man you arrested?"

"I am," I replied.

"Can you point him out in the courtroom?"

Even though I was at a loss why we needed to go through this rigmarole yet again, I patiently pointed to Frezin. This time, Frezin got up and gave a buffoonish bow.

"At what point during the ride did the defendant board the train?" asked the state prosecutor.

"I don't know," I replied. "I didn't see him get on. After Serpukhov, the train took on passengers almost at every stop. It was Sunday night, and besides, it was the end of the dacha season."

"But you stated in your arrest report that you arrested Frezin after he had boarded the train at Vesna station," the state prosecutor said.

"I never did," I said firmly. "There must be some mistake."

Frezin's lawyer jumped up. "What do you mean you don't know where he got on? Didn't your report state it was at Vesna?" he shouted.

"I have not given you permission to speak," the judged said sharply, still not looking up from the document.

"I don't think so," I insisted. "I didn't see him get on. Besides, he was arrested two days before the body of Anton Polishchuk was found at his dacha at Vesna. It simply didn't matter at the time of his arrest where he got on the train."

"But now it does," said the lawyer, glancing apprehensively at the judge. She ignored him this time – but so did the prosecutor.

"In other words, you don't have any idea where Frezin boarded the train?" the prosecutor asked.

I admitted that I didn't.

"Then it is also possible that Frezin boarded the train at Vesna?"

"It is," I conceded. "It could have been any station after Serpukhov, wherever the train took on passengers."

"So what you mean is that my client could have boarded the train at some other station?" Frezin's lawyer again interjected.

Again, the judge let him speak. Or maybe she just wasn't paying attention.

I shrugged. "Sure. Why not?"

"But you didn't see him at Serpukhov?" the prosecutor asked.

"No, I did not."

The prosecutor finally dropped the issue of where Frezin had boarded the train and resumed questioning me about whether or not he had been nervous or upset, but not before the lawyer pointed out that the entire case hinged on the assumption that his client had been arrested after boarding the train at Vesna. I could see that the prosecutor was annoyed.

"I couldn't tell," I said. "He was rude and behaved aggressively. As I said, he started a quarrel with other passengers in the car."

"Was the defendant alone on the train? Did he have companions or accomplices?" the prosecutor asked.

"As far as I know, he was alone," I replied. "Except..."

The woman in the polka-dot scarf could have known Frezin before. That may have been the reason why she left in such a hurry. Why hadn't I thought of that before?

"Very well, thank you, comrade Senior Lieutenant," said the state prosecutor quickly. "You may go."

Suddenly, the judge intervened.

"One moment please. The witness was about to say something about an accomplice."

She turned to me.

"Were you about to say something?"

"I wanted to say that the quarrel with other passengers began when the defendant apparently tried to start a conversation with a woman sitting across from him on the train. He was being persistent and abusive. Other passengers intervened and tried to stop the defendant. The young woman could have known Frezin. They may very well have been travelling together."

"Who was the woman then?" the lawyer inquired. "Did you question her?"

"She got up and left while I was making the arrest. I was not able to identify her."

"In other words, you don't have any idea who she is."

"I don't," I admitted.

I tried to think of her face, but could remember nothing except for her polka-dotted headscarf. I had not paid much attention to her on the train. Only now did it occur to me that that had been a huge mistake.

"What a pity," the lawyer said, his words dripping with sarcasm. "Maybe she was my client's accomplice? Or she might have committed the murder at Vesna. Or else, she might have been my client's girlfriend, with whom he met in Serpukhov? So many possibilities, so little information."

The lawyer had a shrill, unpleasant voice.

I had to admit that he was right, however.

"It is the first time we hear of any woman being on the train who could confirm or deny the fact that my client boarded the train at Vesna," the lawyer continued, flushed with righteous indignation. "No young woman was mentioned anywhere in this case.

Silence fell over the courtroom. The prosecutor opened his mouth as though he was about to say something but changed his mind and turned toward the window.

"It is a shoddy investigation, comrades," the judge said, turning to the prosecutor. "Your work has been sloppy, evidence is circumstantial, at best, the charges are hanging by a thread. It seems that you have thrown the case together on the spur of the moment."

Her voice, unlike the lawyer's, was low, powerful and authoritative.

"Your witness is going back on what he wrote in his arrest report," the judge continued. "And with him retracting his testimony, you have not established even theoretically that the defendant could be placed at the scene of the crime. Now, all of a sudden, we have a potential new witness in the case who has completely fallen through the cracks in your investigation and who can't even be identified. Was she an innocent bystander who had no connection to the defendant? Or was she an accomplice?"

She glared at the prosecutor, who continued to stare out the window, and concluded ominously, "These are no idle questions, comrades."

"What's the goddamn point?" Frezin butted in. "What are you talking about? I don't get it. Why are you wasting your time on this monkey trial? I've confessed to everything. Go ahead, find me guilty as charged and choose the punishment that fits the crime, as they say."

"You have not been given permission to speak, defendant," the judge said. "As to you, Senior Lieutenant, I assume you have nothing more to add to your testimony. Correct? You may now leave."

As I went out, I glanced up. Anna Panteleyevna and Lyuda Polishchuk sat in the front row of the balcony, leaning on the plush upholstery of the balustrade. Next to them was Colonel Nakazov. They were alone on the balcony, sitting between tall slender columns. The area was closed to the public. Nakazov shook his head at me. He clearly wasn't pleased. It was, more or less, what I had expected.

Two new Volgas were parked near the entrance to the courthouse, one black and the other light-colored. Both were idling their engines. In the black one, Nakazov's driver Grigory was reading a sports paper. In the other Volga, the massive bulk of Hera the Giant occupied the driver's seat and then some. Hera was reading nothing and seemed bored out of his wits.

"You want me to drive you to the train station?" he asked when he saw me exit the courthouse.

I turned down his kind offer.

Della always knew all sorts of news and gossip that circulated not only around Criminal Investigations, but also throughout the entire network of the Ministry of Internal Affairs' departments and agencies. Sometimes I thought that Budyonny's old secretaries, who had subsequently spread throughout the Soviet justice system, kept in touch with one another and exchanged information, creating a kind of informal telegraph.

Several days later, Della came into my office. She wore a sad expression on her face, but she was positively bursting with something she wanted to share. But first, she started by telling me how sorry she was that my testimony at the Podolsk courthouse hadn't gone as well as could have been expected. I told her that it was not such a big deal, and decided to ignore the fact that she wasn't supposed to know that I had been a witness at the trial, much less that my testimony had gone poorly.

Having finished with these preliminaries, Della lowered her voice and made me swear that I would never, under any circumstances, share with anyone what she was about to disclose. When I assured her that her secret was safe with me, she told me that the judge, with her beehive hairdo, warts and deep voice, despite laying into the prosecution's shoddy work, had in the end found Frezin guilty as charged and sentenced him to death. Now the Presidium of the Supreme Court was reviewing the sentence, which was a mere formality and rarely resulted in any changes to the verdict. In a week or two Frezin would be executed.

For all his recidivist bravado, Frezin's sangfroid in court somehow didn't add up. There was too much looking around the courtroom, too much confidence, and even too much of a challenge when he looked at me during my testimony. It was as though he was trying to tell me: "Take care, Matyushkin. You'll see, I'll yet pay you back."

Then, at the end of that particular road, a brick wall and a firing squad.

Nor could I get over the woman in the polka-dot scarf. I kept trying to remember what she looked like, sitting across from Frezin, but for some reason different faces kept popping up in my head: Lyuda Polishchuk, her mother, or even Tosya.

I wasn't sorry about Frezin. Just a little taken aback.

THIRTEEN

"What are you thinking about, Matyushkin?" Tosya asked.

"Nothing," I said. "I mean, work actually."

About three years ago, while cutting grass along the Moscow-Volga River navigational canal, in a wooded section near the town of Khimki, a local collective farmer stumbled upon the body of a young woman. The dead woman was subsequently identified as a seventeen-year-old student at the local nursing school who had been reported missing several days before. She had been stabbed repeatedly and her body bore the marks of nasty sexual perversion. The case came to the attention of Moscow party bosses and quickly acquired ideological connotations.

This is not America, where such things are commonplace, law enforcement officials were told at the party headquarters. In the Soviet Union this is not supposed to happen, not within ten miles of Moscow. A team of detectives from Odintsovo, which had the reputation for being the best in Moscow Region, was assigned to the case and less than a week later arrested a suspect. His name was Kustanayev and at some point in the past he had done ten years for rape.

Kustanayev had since turned a corner, gotten married and had a child. For understandable reasons, he had concealed his checkered past from his wife and she, being young and naive in such matters, could never figure out why he hadn't officially registered in her apartment in

Khimki but had to have a residency permit in a town 100 kilometers outside Moscow, a usual restriction on released felons.

Kustanayev's wife gave him a solid alibi for the day of the murder, stating that in the morning he had been to the market with her and had helped her carry the groceries home. In the afternoon he had had a shot of vodka and taken a nap. Kustanayev's mother-in-law, who shared the apartment with the couple, had stayed at home from work that day and corroborated her daughter's testimony.

Kustanayev was let go, but, since investigators got no closer to solving the case, he was rearrested a few weeks later. His wife and mother-in-law had their eyes opened on the exact nature of Kustanayev's past transgressions, whereupon they were no longer certain that it had been the day of the murder when Kustanayev had accompanied his wife shopping. Meanwhile, Kustanayev was placed in a cell with a man specially imported from a labor camp. The cell mate first tried to worm his way into Kustanayev's confidence and get him to tell him about the crime, and, when that didn't work, began to beat him systematically in their cell, telling him to sign a confession.

After a few weeks of relentless pressure from interrogators during the day and brutal beatings at night, Kustanayev finally gave in and confessed to raping, killing and mutilating the nursing student, and was sentenced to be executed. He was duly put before the firing squad, and one month later the mutilated body of another student, bearing similar marks of sexual torture, cropped up outside Khimki.

Be that as it may, before they put him on trial, the Odintsovo detectives placed Kustanayev in the prison hospital, where he was fed a healthy diet of meat and potatoes, while doctors treated his cuts and bruises. Nevertheless, at his trial Kustanayev looked depressed and deflated, or, to put it in context, exactly the opposite of how Frezin looked at his.

But I wasn't going to worry about Frezin any more, simply because my own work suddenly took an important turn. There was at last a break in the case of the apartment burglaries I had been working on for so long.

I've mentioned before that I was prepared for the possibility of never catching the robbers. The more time that passed, the more I became convinced that I was dealing with unsophisticated but extremely lucky amateurs, possibly even out-of-towners who committed burglaries without any plan or system, not knowing what they would find once they entered an apartment. For some reason of their own, which I would then never find out, they might stop coming to Moscow as abruptly as they had started, making them impossible to catch. And if I did catch them, it would only be as a result of a lucky break, rather than of a professional investigation. I knew that, being amateurs, they would be busted because of some stupid mistake on their part. Which they were.

What I didn't expect was that they would be busted because of the Polishchuk job.

One of the consignment shops where I had left the list of missing items – patched-up jackets and old sewing machines – called me one day and asked me to come and see them without delay. August Karlovich Nuremberger, chief appraiser at the large Kuntsevo consignment shop, had a reputation around town as a skinflint and a sharp dealer, but also as an unsurpassed expert in second-hand clothing and antiques. His appraisals were always accurate and the sums he offered the owners were always the lowest in the range. He never haggled and he never added a single kopek to his originally quoted price.

Nuremberger took me into his cluttered office. He twisted two knobs on a large fireproof safe, stringing together a combination of Gothic letters and digits. When the massive metal door swung open, he reaching into its dark cavernous interior and pulled out a brooch. Tenderly, as though he was dealing with something extremely fragile, he placed it on the palm of his bony hand. His hand was shaking a little and his eyes, shining with a rapacious green light, remained fixed on the piece of jewelry until I took it from him and placed it on his junk-littered desk, the edge of which he had carefully cleared and dusted. When the brooch was put to rest on the desk, Nuremberger exhaled noisily, like a diver coming to the surface.

I had never seen such a precious object. The brooch contained five emeralds each the size of a large pea, selected so as to taper off in size gradually from largest to smallest. The variation in size was barely detectable to the naked eye, and all five were stones of exceptional clarity and depth of color. The emeralds were set in white gold and nestled against the background of dull mother of pearl, forming a green and gold pea pod that sparkled brightly in the light of Nuremberger's desk lamp.

"It's a work of art," August Karlovich crowed. "The stones are of the first order, But that's the least of it, you understand? My God, the workmanship is exquisite. Exquisite, there is no other word for it. If you have a few minutes, comrade detective, I could tell you a few stories about this little piece. Where such objects were made and when, and what crowned heads commissioned them."

"Thank you," I said coldly. "Some other time, perhaps."

"As you prefer, comrade detective. Of course, your primary concern is how much, am I not mistaken?"

"Yes," I said. "Let's start there."

"As you wish, comrade detective. But let me preface what I have to say with a short digression. I should explain that in our business we arrive at the price by means of comparison. We compare a given object to another, similar one that we have seen on the market. This is the only way to determine a price."

Nuremberger paused.

"And?" I urged him on.

"Based in this principle," Nuremberger said, "this object has no price. Because there are no other objects that can be compared to it."

This explained why good old August Karlovich had decided to call me about this piece of jewelry. If it were something less unique, more ordinary, cheaper, he would have probably purchased it with his own money and then resold it to a private client with a substantial markup, without going through the official channels of the consignment shop. This is the usual practice at state consignment shops, and even though there was risk involved, all appraisers did it. But this brooch was too unusual, especially in light of me showing up at his shop almost every week with a list of worthless old clothes. The sly old fox Nuremberger was afraid of being set up. You didn't survive in this business as long as August Karlovich had if you weren't extra careful. The temptation was no doubt huge, but a thing like this, if the deal went wrong, could have easily earned him a dozen years behind bars.

Since I clearly had known nothing about the brooch, August Karlovich was probably regretting that he had let a fantastic deal slip. He kept staring at it over my shoulder.

"It was brought in by a young man," he told me. "Nicely dressed, clean, carrying a briefcase and in general looking very much like a college student. Apparently, he and his mother inherited it from his grandmother. His mother wouldn't mind selling it, if they could get good money for it."

The first thing I did was to show the brooch to Anna Panteleyevna. She looked at it, wrinkling her brow in concentration, and shook her head.

"It certainly is beautiful," she said. "But I don't know much about jewelry. You should ask Lyuda. Her father, poor man, used to give her so many presents, I used to tell him he was spoiling her."

She sniffled and seemed ready to start crying, but held off.

"Anton Pavlovich earned good money. He didn't have anything to spend it on, except his one weakness, spoiling his daughter. He had a good nomenklatura salary. Plus, every year he earned a bonus, equal to one month's pay, and another special bonus from the Party, for meeting the plant's targets. Under Anton Pavlovich's management the plant didn't miss its target a single year. It always did the five-year plan in four years, if not three and a half. His superiors held him in a very high regard, especially Deputy Minister of the Food Processing Industry Vasily Nikanorovich Zotov. It was nice to have the recognition, but Anton Pavlovich used to say that he didn't care about the money. Except when it came to buying jewels for Lyuda."

Lyuda Polishchuk recognized the brooch right away and was clearly happy to see it. She even clapped her hands for joy, like a small child, which was kind of cute.

"It is my favorite piece. I'm so glad you were able to recover it."

She was still addressing me with the polite *vy*, even though Lenny kept pressing her to switch to the informal *ty*. I was in no hurry to get familiar with her. Lyuda Polishchuk was too good-looking for me to trust myself with her as far as *ty*.

"You see, you did it again," she said and a grateful smile lit up her face. "Mother and I are in your debt. You've done so much for our family."

I figured she was referring to Frezin's arrest. I nodded and said nothing. After the trial and the sentencing, we no longer discussed Frezin. I didn't know whether she still thought that Colonel Nakazov had been too eager to get Frezin convicted.

I think Lyuda thought that I was going to return the emerald peapod to her, but I took it away from her and replaced it in a special case that Forensics had given me to carry it around town.

"It's a piece of evidence, Lyudmila Antonovna," I said officially. "I hope you understand. It'll help us find the guys who robbed your apartment."

"Does that mean that I'll never get it back?"

"Of course not. When we catch the perpetrators and close the case, you'll certainly get it back."

"When will that be?"

"I don't know, Lyudmila Antonovna. We don't even have any suspects."

"I hope it's soon," she said. "It's my favorite brooch. It's so beautiful, isn't it?"

Her disappointment showed her face to its advantage. Actually, every emotion was becoming to her, even disappointment. But its extent was surprising, since she had once told us that she was not attached to her expensive baubles. I had the impression that, when it came to jewelry, she was accustomed to having her way.

I was not entirely candid with her. I expected the case to be wrapped up in a very short time. Indeed, two days later Nuremberger called me and whispered theatrically into the receiver:

"We have a visitor, comrade detective, if you know what I mean."

I did know what he meant.

"Keep him busy for half an hour," I said tersely, putting on my jacket as I held the receiver with my chin.

"I will. I have already told him that his beautiful brooch was sold and that all he needs is to pick up his money. One thousand rubles, I told him. He was very pleased. But because the sum is so large, I told him that we'll need to fill out some forms and that he'll need to sign them. If he only knew how much it's really worth. He's a milksop."

Neither one of our drivers was around, and even Lenny was out doing field work, so I couldn't avail myself of his Moskvich and his crazy driving. This meant that I had to travel to Kuntsevo by train.

Kuntsevo was only a ten-minute ride, but getting to the Belarus Station took time, and so did jogging half a kilometer once I got off the train. In all, the trip took close to an hour. I shortened my step before reaching the consignment shop and entered it having almost caught my breath. I spotted the visitor right away: a neatly dressed young man with a pale, nervous face. He glanced at me and shouted at the closed door bearing the plaque that spelled Bookkeeping.

"How much longer are you going to be? I've been waiting for an hour."

He was clearly angry and exasperated, but his voice lacked conviction.

The door opened and Nuremberger, wearing a wrinkled cotton suit and a red tie, peered out. When he saw me, he motioned the visitor to enter and gave me a wink behind his back. I came in behind him. Nuremberger shut the door and turned the key in the lock.

The visitor was a nice kid from Ryazan. His name was Peter Ryzhikov. He was a student at a vocational school, studying math. I'll spare you the description of the tearful scene that followed. Such scenes take place at police stations every day of the week. If we at

Criminal Investigations have any skill honed to absolute perfection, it is driving nice kids from vocational schools to tears. It would suffice to say that a quarter of an hour after my out-of-breath arrival he was wiping his tears with a grey, tobacco-speckled handkerchief handed to him by Nuremberger, who was himself nearly sniffling. In fact, the old man turned out to be far less stone-hearted than I had expected.

Peter's gang was laughably small. Just two of them, Peter and his stepfather. His stepfather's name was Victor Rastorguyev. Peter had known him pretty much since he was born, but he wasn't always his stepfather. Victor's first wife lived in the same apartment building as Peter, and when Victor lived with her he was known for selling loose cigarettes to underage kids at a substantial markup. Then Victor went to prison for a year, and when he was released his wife threw him out. So he moved into a room Peter shared with his mother.

"How come your Mom got involved with such loser?" I asked him. "And you too? Do you know what's going to happen to you now? You'll have to kiss mathematics goodbye for a few years."

Peter said nothing and went on crying, wiping away tears.

"Your only chance is to be completely honest with me, Petya. Sit down, stop crying and tell me everything about the robberies you committed."

I put a blank sheet of paper in front of him and handed him a stub of a pencil with a worn eraser, the only writing implement that Nuremberger was able to find in his messy office.

Peter was a smart kid. He mentioned all the burglaries, pretty much in the order they were committed. He remembered the first break-in, into the place owned by the furrier Blumenkrantz, and all the later ones, as well. He didn't know the addresses, but he had an excellent memory and a good head on his shoulders. He was clearly good at math: his ability to recall the prices they got for various items they sold would have done even August Karlovich proud.

It's always a pleasure to deal with intelligent people, even if they're criminals. I watched him fill up one sheet and handed him another.

However, when he got to mid-September, which was when the Polishchuks' apartment was robbed, Peter suddenly stalled. He didn't mention the Sukharevka place and claimed to have skipped a couple of trips to Moscow because he had to start the new school year. His memory also turned a bit fuzzy.

I waited for him to finish and then asked, as though I had just thought of it, "What about the brooch? Where did you get this?"

Peter sneered. "This one? We got it from a fence. We used to sell some of the stuff to a Georgian at Tishinka Market. Last time Victor went to sell the loot at Tishinka, he came back mad as hell. The Georgian took everything Victor brought, and gave him this instead of cash."

"I see," I said doubtfully. "I thought we agreed you were going to be honest with me."

"I am being honest, I swear."

Victor Rastorguyev, born in Ryazan in 1926, had jail stamped all over him. He didn't fight in the war, he never graduated from high school and flitted from one job to another – just enough not to be charged with parasitism. He drank heavily and when he was sent to jail he had been working as an unskilled laborer at the Ryazan Railway Car Plant. Jail taught him nothing useful, but when he came out, getting hired even at the Railway Car Plant became impossible.

That was both true and not. If he had any skills at all, he would've been able to find work. But now he wouldn't have to worry about employment for a while. For the next five-to-seven years he was guaranteed a bed, a roof over his head, and two meals a day at government expense.

Rastorguyev's plan for making a living by burglarizing apartments was simple. His assumption was that Moscow was a large and wealthy city, there were plenty of apartments to rob, and Muscovites were pretty rich. He made the first few trips on his own, without involving his stepson, but those were reconnaissance missions. He would walk the streets, hang out in courtyards and work out the plans for his burglaries. He targeted old houses scheduled for demolition or, on the contrary, brand-new apartment buildings where tenants hadn't had time to get to know one another yet. He preferred communal apartments with a large number of tenants but, if possible, few old women. Old women were stay-at-home types and, even when they did go out, they were prone to forgetting something at home and coming back when you least expected them.

"Wasn't just travelling to the city expensive?" I asked. "Where did you stay?"

"At the train station, where else? I slept in the waiting passengers' hall. Train tickets were expensive and there's no place to hide from the conductor if you travel without one."

"Not a very profitable business, is it?"

"Not terribly," he conceded. "But better than the Railway Car Plant."

"And what about jail? Is it also better than the Railway Car Plant?"

"You can always survive in jail. People there are more fun than working stiffs. The second time is easier, too. You earn respect, if you do time more than once."

"Maybe you're right," I shrugged. "Tell me all about it when you get out."

I spent a long time discussing the different burglaries with Rastorguyev as well. I was checking out Peter's stories, especially as far as the money they had gotten for their loot was concerned. That was important and questions would be asked about it at the trial. The list I had put together based on victims' reports was gradually being filled with figures. Interestingly, there had been several burglaries that had not been reported. Rastorguyev was sure that Muscovites were too rich to bother about a few things when they were taken from their apartments – or else they didn't want to attract the attention of the police.

While questioning Rastorguyev, I kept the emerald brooch, the cause of his downfall, on the corner of my desk. There was no need to hide it, but I also didn't want to mention it ahead of time.

Then, in the middle of some other, unrelated discussion, I asked bluntly, "Who gave you the Sukharevka address?"

Whenever I had asked him about other apartments, he didn't always remember them or didn't know the exact address, and would ask me to give their location relative to Three Stations Square, where he had been camping out. But when I mentioned Sukharevka, he seemed to know right away what I was talking about and clammed up. It was as if he and his stepson had agreed beforehand to deny everything related to the Polishchuks' apartment.

The emerald peapod, he said, had come to him from a Georgian at the Tishinka market in exchange for stolen goods, confirming the version I had already been given by Peter. No matter how hard I tried, he stuck to his story. An hour and a half later, I felt like wringing his neck.

"I was really pissed about it," he kept repeating. "I had a really bad feeling about this bauble. I must have had a premonition."

"Who the hell was this Georgian? Where did he come from? How do you know him?"

"I don't know him, that's the thing. He was a swarthy bastard, like all Georgians."

The first apartment they had burgled was that of Blumenkrantz the furrier. Quite by accident, they ended up with several expensive fur coats. A friend advised Rastorguyev to fence the loot in Moscow, since there was little demand for quality stuff in Ryazan and, anyway, such furs would be more conspicuous there.

At Tishinka, Rastorguyev approached a few secondhand merchants and they all sent him packing. No one was going to buy obviously hot merchandise from a stranger. But then an old woman told him to try his luck at a certain stall on the other side of the market.

Rastorguyev had to go behind the stalls and traverse a patch of deserted no man's land. It was there that he was intercepted by the Georgian.

"I had never seen him before, I swear," Rastorguyev said. "He asked me what I was selling, and at first I told him to get lost, because he didn't look like a serious customer. He didn't get offended, though. 'If you've got furs, I might take a look,' he said. Obviously he had been tipped off by someone that I had good stuff. He looked at the fur coats, checked out the stitching, sniffed at the fur with his big Georgian nose and offered me a pretty good sum."

"How much?"

"Seven hundred rubles for the lot. I was so happy I didn't even think of haggling. I had lots of furs and only now do I realize I could've asked for more. But that was our first job and I was still nervous. Then he told me that if I got something like that again, I should show it to him and he'd get me good money."

"Did he tell you how to find him?"

"No. Of course not. Guys like that have a way of finding you when they need something, not the other way around."

"No special way to contact him?"

Rastorguyev shook his head.

"Okay. Go on."

"There isn't much. We never got anything nice like that again. We kept taking lots of stuff, but nothing good. We would sell most of it to fences in Ryazan, even though at Tishinka we could've gotten more money. Once I had sold the furs to the Georgian, some of the second hand guys would buy stuff from us, but the Georgian didn't show up again. I figure he was only interested in nicer stuff."

"I see," I said. "How come he gave you the brooch then?"

"That was the strange thing. The last time we got lots of stuff, a bunch of old clothing, some household appliances – nothing valuable, though. I took it to Tishinka, pretty confident by then that I could fence it. But all of a sudden it was like the first time again. They all turned me down. No one even wanted to take a look, and they all stared at me as though they had never seen me before. Finally, there was an old Jew there I had gotten to know pretty well, and he sent me to a stall at the other end of the market. Just like the first time. The moment I got behind his stall, I spotted the Georgian. It was like he appeared out of thin air. I was glad to see him and he asked to see what

I had. I was sure he wouldn't touch it. But then he says, 'I'm gonna take it, except I've got no money on me right now.' 'What do you mean, no money?' I said. 'How are you gonna pay for it?' He goes: 'I can give you something better than money. Take this brooch. It's worth a lot. A lot more than you could get for this pile of crap you've managed to steal. You'll thank me for it, when you sell it.' I didn't want to take no brooch, and I said to him that the deal was off, but he turned nasty on me. I really had to take it after all, even though I didn't want nothing to do with it."

"You know," I said. "You're a funny guy. You didn't want to take it and you had a pretty good idea it was hot, and yet the first thing you do is go and take it to a consignment shop."

"I didn't," Rastorguyev objected heatedly. "It certainly wasn't the first thing I did with it. But what was I supposed to do? I showed it to a few jewelers, and everywhere it was the same thing. They were like 'Are you nuts?' I asked them: 'What if I break it up and sell you the stones and the gold separately?' 'Not on your life,' they said. 'You're crazy.' "

"Was that in Ryazan?"

"Are you kidding? In Ryazan there is only one place that sells jewelry, and if I had taken it there, they wouldn't even have turned me in to the cops. They would've skipped a step and called the ambulance."

Our conversation wasn't moving past this version of events and I was getting tired of it.

"Listen to me, Rastorguyev," I said at last. "You don't have to say anything now, just listen to me. This pretty thing was stolen from an apartment on Sukharevka Street on September 14 of this year. I don't know if it was a coincidence or not, but one day before that, the owner of that apartment was bumped off at his dacha. You might have noticed when you were robbing it that the apartment was pretty well decorated. The guy was a top-level, important government official. The investigation into his murder was supervised by a high-ranking officer of the Committee for State Security. A man named Daniel Frezin was convicted for the murder and sentenced to be executed. You can draw your own conclusions from these facts. Some State Security people still think the robbery in their apartment was connected with the murder of its owner and it was an act of political terrorism."

"What do you mean, terrorism?" Rastorguyev exclaimed, turning pale.

"Don't interrupt me, Rastorguyev. I know you have nothing to do with any terrorism."

"Of course I don't. I'm just a small-time apartment thief, that's all. It must have been the same guy who killed him. He must have robbed the apartment, too. And it probably was that Georgian guy."

"Don't interrupt me," I said. "It's clear that if you had anything to do with the robbery, you were most likely put up to it by someone else. If there is another person, Georgian or not, who gave you the address, you had better tell me about it now. Because if I pass this brooch to the guys from State Security, your future will become a lot dimmer than it already is. Give it a few moments' thought. That's my recommendation."

He started to swear that he had been telling me the truth, but I raised my hand to stop him and repeated that I wanted him to take his time. He nodded and took a minute or two to think it over. Then, he started to swear all over again.

"I don't know what I can do to make you believe me," he said, almost in tears. "Neither me nor Peter had anything to do with that apartment. We have not been there, we know nothing about it and it's the first time I've even heard that street name, Sukharevka."

I sighed and left the room.

FOURTEEN

Fall lasted a long time. Nature was in no hurry to transition into winter. At first, in mid-October, we had the usual frost in the mornings and even a dusting of snow, but by the Seventh of November – the Anniversary of the Revolution – the weather had turned unexpectedly warm. One Indian Summer day followed another and there was no end in sight to this astonishing streak.

After looking askance at Lenny and me for several weeks, Budyonny finally sprung a nasty surprise. Budyonny was born in the Caucasus, and people say a lot of stupid things about the Caucasus and its natives. In one view, the Caucasians, meaning real Caucasians, are supposed to be irascible to the point of insanity, losing not only their temper at the slightest provocation, but their mind, as well. They are capable of anything in a fit of rage. But, after blowing off steam violently, they cool off equally quickly. Let them scream and shout and wave their daggers about, because when they come to they never hold grudges and happily share a glass of wine with the person who, a minute ago, they were on the verge of murdering.

That's one view. The other is exactly the opposite. According to this version, the Caucasus is part of the inscrutable East, and the Caucasians tend to nurse every slight in the dark recesses of their souls, never revealing anything, but also never forgiving anything. Possessed of infinite patience, they wait for an opportune moment when their national dish, vengeance, cools to its serving temperature and the victim least expects an attack.

Then they stab you in the back.

I have no idea which is right. My own experience with Caucasians is inconclusive. Budyonny, it seems, combined both these character traits. He was quick to anger, never mincing words when he worked himself into a lather. At the same time, he was also fairly vengeful, and if he felt that you had crossed him in some way, he was sure to get back at you somehow. But I don't know whether it was due to his Armenian ethnicity or to some other circumstance. I find that all bosses are the same, they yell and scream and get you in the end. At least he didn't go overboard with the screaming.

Once I became aware that Budyonny's hooded, dark eyes were fixed on my back, and on Lenny's, too, I knew that trouble was brewing. Finally, just before the holiday, he called us into his office.

"You two have been delegated to march with our departmental banner on the Seventh of November," he said. "Both of you. It takes two to hold it, as you know."

We knew that only too well. Holding the banner is not the easy and joyful task it might appear from the sidewalk. To begin with, it required being up at the crack of dawn on a day when everyone else gets to sleep in, then travelling across town to an industrial suburb where Criminal Investigations keeps various unused stuff in a warehouse. Once there, we would ring the doorbell of a vast communal apartment to get Fatima, the warehouse manager. It was important to choose the right bell button and to press it the right number of times, because otherwise we ran the risk of waking up Fatima's quarrelsome neighbors. Having been assigned to hold the banner for the third year in a row, Urumov and I were friends with Fatima and had met her husband Rustam, the building's streetsweeper. On the two previous occasions we had heard all about their eldest son, who happened to be serving time at a high-security correctional facility.

The banner is a length of red fabric stretched between wooden poles with a slogan spelled out in gold letters. It's important to get the right banner, and not the one for May First Workers' Solidarity Day, which looks very similar, but is not appropriate for a Seventh of November rally. Lenny has no idea what either of the banners says. But I know enough to make sure we don't take the May First banner by mistake.

After that we have to get the banner back to Petrovka – on foot, because it is too big to fit into a tram or a bus and, besides, public transportation services are suspended on the morning of the march. The Hermitage Gardens across the street from our headquarters serves as the gathering point for all Criminal Investigations staffers chosen by Budyonny to attend the march. Since we're the ones with the banner, we have to be first to arrive, to provide the gathering point for our comrades in arms. As the others assembled, our task was to form them into a column and make sure they all had red flags and portraits of the founding fathers of Communism and the members of the Politburo.

Lenny tried to argue with Budyonny, but to no avail.

"Why, aren't you pleased?" Budyonny inquired in mock surprise. "It's an honor."

"That's what I'm trying to say," Lenny said, growing exasperated and ignoring the energetic signs I was making to him behind Budyonny's back. "We're not worthy of that honor, Ashot Modestovich, certainly not for three years in a row. Others might start grumbling. Let them march with the banner for a change."

"I don't care if they grumble or not, Urumov," Budyonny interrupted him. "Had they worked harder, the way the two of you have all year, they might have been marching in your place. Dismissed."

"Don't be upset, Uncle Pavel," said Sevka later that day when I saw him playing soccer in our sun-drenched courtyard. "Mom has also been delegated to march for her textile factory. Thirteen thousand employees at the plant, but they still have to have a representative from accounting. That's what Mom says."

"Why don't we take you along, Sevka?" I suggested in an ingratiating voice. "You'll meet real police detectives, ones who chase gangsters with real guns drawn. You'll be like a mascot for Criminal Investigations."

"No sale, Uncle Pavel," Sevka said. "I went with you last year, remember? You made me carry the banner. Once was enough."

"It's a great honor," I said, sounding a little like Budyonny.

"I'm going with Mom this time. There'll be lots of girls in her column."

"Are you starting to be interested in girls, Sevka?" I asked. "You should be doing your homework instead."

"I have no interest in girls, Uncle Pavel. At least not yet. They're boring to talk to. But I like the way they sing."

"I do too," I said. "They get very emotional."

When it comes to marching with the banner, the weather makes all the difference. Last year, the weather was rotten, it rained constantly, and the banner, soaked by the cold rain, weighed a ton. The wind howled overhead, threatening to rip it out of our hands; both of us got blisters and the poorly planed poles drove splinters into our palms. But this time the sky was clear, the sun shone brightly, and the air was as transparent as it can only be late in an Indian Summer, filled with the sweet smells of fall. The city, hung with red flags and red bunting and empty of traffic, looked nothing like our busy and chaotic Moscow, but more like some quiet, godforsaken provincial town in the North.

Down every side street and along the boulevards, where the ground was carpeted with layers of red and yellow leaves, at every distant intersection there was a column marching under fluttering red silk. The columns, streaking from the outskirts toward the center, were directed through the urban maze by the coordinated effort of leaders with red armbands. Great masses of people were shuffled and reshuffled along the way through smaller side streets and pressed into ever thickening streams on larger thoroughfares, melding mismatched representatives of various offices, colleges, ministries, research institutes, agencies and factories into one homogenous column. The chaotic motion of its parts was governed by some overarching higher logic hidden from us as we moved from street to street in an ever-swelling sea of humanity.

At Manezh Square, in front of the Kremlin, the cacophony of amateur music suddenly stopped, the accordions and the balalaikas were put aside and the impromptu singing fell silent. A single, unifying march blared from the loudspeakers, washing over the enormous crowd. The march stayed with us as we marched onto Red Square through a narrow passage on the side of the History Museum, loud and brazen and never missing a beat, the same for everyone.

We were all suddenly one, the faces around us had shed their individual features and became an abstraction: men, women, children, civilians, officers, athletes, retirees, workers, office personnel, citizens, comrades – the people. The leaders of the Party looking down upon us from a distance, standing atop the Mausoleum, were also identical, wearing identical grey overcoats and grey hats, their identical gloved hands waving synchronously.

This is how the Seventh of November march should be. The unity makes you realize what a huge country we live in. Your chest expands, you're overwhelmed with pride for your land and the departmental banner suddenly feels light in your hands. This is, after all, the main square of the nation. Your image – and the images of hundreds of thousands of marchers stomping in time to the heroic music, shoulder to shoulder, on the polished cobble stones – is beamed into every television across however many time zones there are, east to Vladivostok where a new day had already dawned, high up into the Pamir mountains, where the snow never melts and the shepherds are getting ready for winter, down into Central Asia, where they have never seen a television, and to the shores of the Baltic, which seem Western, foreign and hostile.

Move along. Raise high your banner, comrade. March. Don't smile.

On the other side of the river, the invisible hand suddenly stops directing us and the column crumbles into its tiny, constituent worker ants. Everyone is on his own again. Sure, the invisible hand is still there. If you happen to glance into a courtyard, you might glimpse a military truck with a camouflage canvas top, barely visible in the early November dusk and marked "Personnel." It is filled with men huddling on wooden benches, tightly gripping the barrels of their automatic rifles. It's Colonel Nakazov's people. No longer directing us, just making sure that nothing unexpected takes place.

After the rally everyone gathered in Tosya's room. By which I mean Tosya and Sevka, Lyuda Polishchuk, Lenny and me. We had all gone to the march. Tosya and Sevka were part of her Tryokhgorka Textiles delegation and Lyuda, along with other students from the Foreign Language Institute, had to attend the rally as well.

Lenny and I were late and bone-tired. By the time we arrived, Tosya had put out a platter with hastily sliced ham and a bowl of pickles, and had chilled a bottle of vodka for Lenny and me. Tosya was not very good at being a hostess. Lyuda was also useless from this point of view, but her contribution to our modest feast included a bottle of red wine, Italian or Spanish, that was not easy to find at a regular store.

Sevka also got back late, just soon enough to keep his mother from becoming hysterical. At the march, he had become separated from the Tryokhgorka Textiles column and fell in with workers marching under the banner of the Hammer and Sickle metalworking plant.

"I see," Urumov said. "It seems that you misled the leaders of the Party by marching in a column where you didn't belong."

On the way to Tosya's, Lenny and I had spotted San Vasilich, the local drunk, sleeping on a bench behind the elevator. San Vasilich was a famous character in the neighborhood. He used to say that he knew everyone in the neighborhood, but had no friends. Only drinking buddies.

Despite the warm weather, San Vasilich wore a pair of long johns and felt slippers. With every loud breath he took, his huge belly, over which a dirty undershirt was stretched tightly, inched closer to the edge of the bench. As we waited for the elevator, San Vasilich's belly finally outweighed the rest of his body and he tumbled to the unswept floor. Without opening his eyes, San Vasilich uttered a curse, burped, stood up on all fours and began climbing back on the bench. As we entered the elevator, his belly was once more looming over the floor, starting to inch lower.

San Vasilich was an electrician who worked for the building's maintenance department.

When, three hours later, Lyuda Polishchuk left Tosya's apartment and I went out to put her in a cab, San Vasilich was still asleep in the same position, his belly still hovering over the abyss.

In the meantime, Urumov had also managed to get completely drunk. Perhaps he had been undone by the long day and the fresh air. He fell asleep in the folding armchair where Sevka usually slept. Efforts to wake him were fruitless, and we decided to leave him alone. Sevka was small enough to share his mother's bed for one night, but barely.

Lyuda and I came out together and headed for Kirov Street. A taxi is not easy to find on an ordinary night, and on the Seventh of November it turned out to be impossible. The streets were still lively. Groups of boisterous young men walked along Kirov, sometimes holding up a companion too drunk to walk on his own. Every now and again someone would break out into a drunken song, and then fall silent after singing only a few bars.

We stood across from the main post office for a long time. No taxi came.

"It's late," Lyuda said at last. "You should go home. I'll walk. It'll take me half an hour to get home, no more than that."

"I'll walk you home, Lyudmila Antonovna," I said.

"No, seriously. I'll be all right. Go home."

We crossed Turgenev Square and entered Sretensky Boulevard, walking slowly and in silence.

"Go home, " Lyuda repeated. "It's getting late."

"It is late," I said. "That's why I should walk you home."

When we got to the end of the boulevard, we stopped under the blue neon sign of the lingerie shop on the corner. Suddenly, Lyuda kissed me on the mouth.

It felt strange. We stood there for a few moments, pressing hard against one another. Her lips edged down my cheek and I felt a love bite on my chin.

I could have stood there all night, kissing and caressing her, but unlike Urumov I was quite sober. I disregarded the throbbing in my head and pushed her away.

We were both breathless, as though we had been fighting. Perhaps we were.

"Go home," I said. I realized I was repeating the same thing she had been telling me, persistently, only few minutes before.

She didn't move.

"The emerald brooch you showed me," she said. "It's very dear to me. A long time ago, I had a fiancée. I was very much in love with him. He loved me too. That brooch was his favorite. I used to wear it every time we saw each other. He used to say that it made my eyes green. He was not a poet, but he often said tender, romantic things."

She paused. I waited for her to go on.

"That brooch is my memory of him. Our love is gone, it's finished and will never return. He was my first love, perhaps my only love. I won't be able to love anyone the way I used to love him. But I had this brooch, the only thing I had to remember him by. I was very upset when it was stolen. Please, be careful with it. Don't lose it."

"No, of course we won't," I said.

"He was wrongly convicted. I know that many women defend the men they love, but in my case it's true. He really did nothing wrong."

I shrugged.

"I know you don't believe me," she said. "Well, there is no need for me to hide the truth. That man, my fiancée, he fell in with the wrong sort of people. It was a mistake, a misstep. But what really was his downfall was that his case was handled by Vladislav Mironovich. We thought that Vladislav Mironovich would be able to help him. Mother thought so as well. But because that man and I were in love, Vladislav Mironovich went out of his way to get him convicted. He made sure that my fiancée got a very long sentence. Completely out of proportion to his guilt."

A blue letter on the neon sign over the lingerie shop began to blink, casting sickly pulsating light onto Lyuda's face. For the first time since she had kissed me, I looked at her and saw that she was crying.

"It's my fault," she said softly. "I destroyed him with my love."

Tosya waited for me in the courtyard, leaning against the fence around the Lenin bust. It was warm even at night and she wore a house dress and slippers.

"Did you walk her home?" she asked.

I nodded.

"Have you been waiting for me a long time?" I asked when we got inside my building.

"Not that long," she replied. "Sevka couldn't fall asleep and I had to sit with him. Your buddy Urumov snores like a fiend. I almost got a hernia turning him to his side, but it was no use. Wait a second, Matyushkin. Hold still."

I stopped on the landing. It was lit by three lightbulbs hanging from the ceiling. Tosya took out a handkerchief and rubbed my lower lip.

"She's a looker, that Lyuda Polishchuk," she said softly.

FIFTEEN

Zhorik and I reached the gate of the Dzerzhinsk Special Facility No. 14 in early afternoon. Fall was coming to a close. Dusk was arriving earlier with each passing day.

I had not called ahead. I had simply waited for the day when Budyonny could spare our beat-up military jeep and a driver. The driver, Zhorik, was at my door at five-thirty in the morning. The darkness outside was total.

We gassed up at a service station just beyond the Ring Road. I instructed Zhorik to make sure his two spare canisters were full as well. That told him that we were going a long way, but Zhorik didn't ask where. It was not his style.

While he pumped, I spread the road map on my lap and checked the route.

"Think we'll get there?" I asked him when he returned, pointing to our destination with the sharp end of a pencil.

Zhorik shrugged. He spoke little but had fierce professional pride. If he was told to get somewhere in a set amount of time, he did it. He never argued or complained that he was being asked to perform goddamn miracles, as Victor often did. He did his military service in Germany, as a driver for General Yakubovsky, commander-in-chief of Soviet forces in East Germany. That required driving from Berlin and

Moscow in one go, and then turning around and driving back. No distance was a serious obstacle to him.

He said nothing until we reached the city of Vladimir. He kept his eyes on the road and blew his cigarette smoke out the partially rolled down window. I was glad not to have to keep up a conversation. I was deep in thought, also chain-smoking into the window on my side.

The road passed through a monotonous landscape. The pine trees on the side of the road had faded to grey and the birch trunks stood white and straight in the leafless thicket. The woods alternated with collective farm fields long over-harvested, and wretched villages. Now and again Zhorik passed agricultural machinery and horse-drawn carts, swerving with panache into the oncoming lane.

Soon after the city of Vladimir we turned off the main road. After knocking on a couple of doors in a village, we finally purchased half a dozen boiled potatoes wrapped in a newspaper, two small onions, some hard-boiled eggs and an apple – large, sweet and worm-bored.

We picnicked on the side of the road just beyond the last house, settling on the slope of a roadside ditch, spreading a piece of oily tarp Zhorik pulled from the back of his jeep onto the wet grass. We dipped eggs and potatoes into a pinch of salt we had been given with our purchases. The salt was rough-cut and had the occasional pebble mixed in. I sliced one of the onions, setting the other aside for later. We had tea from my thermos, which Tosya had filled before I left.

The air was moist and heavy and it smelled of rotting leaves, mushrooms and approaching winter. The sky was overcast, November-like.

"Beautiful, isn't it?" I said.

Zhorik said nothing, surveyed the beet fields stretching around us in all directions and dipped his potato into the salt. He chewed on it, spat out a pebble and reached for his cigarettes.

"Let's get going," I said, when he finished one cigarette and before he had a chance to light another. "Save the rest of the food for later. Who knows when we'll get there."

"Two-thirty," Zhorik said curtly.

Alexei Bayer

The landscape didn't change after our breakfast stop. Zhorik went on driving in silence. He lit another cigarette the moment we got back into the jeep and continued blowing smoke out the window. We got lost a little in Gorky Region and drove around in circles for a bit before being pointed in the right direction by a none-too-sober local.

Around the city of Dzerzhinsk, named after the founder of the Soviet political police, the roads were unpaved, uneven and pockmarked, their deep puddles filled with orange rainwater. Our jeep kept slipping on them like slivers of soap in a public bath. But before we reached Special Facility No. 14, the pavement suddenly became excellent and the road straightened out. Zhorik floored the gas, bringing the vehicle to a stop in front of the gate with a flourish.

My watch showed 2:33.

The gate was tall and guarded by a pair of soldiers with Kalashnikovs at the ready. Above the wall, which was taller than the gate and topped with barbed wire, rose guard towers, manned by still more soldiers.

While camp officials went looking for Major Karbyshev, the head of the camp's investigation department, I waited in the office. The jeep had to be parked outside the gate and Zhorik, happy to be left alone for a bit, took a nap in the cab.

The camp office was no different than any other government office, with glass plaques affixed to doors, marking them as Bookkeeping, Buildings and Grounds, Supplies, Nurse Station, etc. The door marked Commanding Officer was shut, and from behind it came the sound of someone typing slowly with two fingers, making long pauses between taps to find the right key.

I had been shown into the library, which the glass plaque on the door advertised as the Lenin Propaganda Room. It was hung with banners, posters and similar stuff and contained a few out of date newspapers and magazines, mostly from the city of Gorky. Rather bored, I went so far as to read a clipping from a local newspaper preserved in a display case. It praised the achievements of the camp's administration and its success in labor competition with other collectives in the region.

Karbyshev came in with the unhurried gait of someone who did not expect his visitor to be an important person. His manner didn't change after he inspected my ID. Neither my rank, nor – especially – my position at Criminal Investigations made a strong impression on him.

"You've come a long way, Senior Lieutenant," he observed. "And yet you've given me no advance warning. What can I do for you?"

I decided to cut to the quick.

"We're investigating a case which has been of special interest to comrade colonel," I said, lowering my voice. "I believe you know what I'm talking about and understand the nature of this case. It involves a former inmate of your correctional institution, Daniel Frezin."

To say that I was fishing would be saying nothing. The chain of reasoning that had brought me to Special Facility No. 14 was tenuous and was based on three assumptions. First, was Colonel Nakazov's assertion that the Polishchuks' apartment could have been fingered to Frezin by a former accomplice with whom he had served time. That was how Special Facility No. 14 came up. Second, Senya Pavlov, the kid from a good family who got a long sentence and was now serving it at Special Facility No. 14, was Lyuda's fiancée. It all fit, suggesting that Nakazov had put Pavlov away and was now keen to get him another sentence. This led me to the third assumption, namely that Major Karbyshev, the man in charge of investigating criminal activity at the camp, had already been contacted by Nakazov.

I was bluffing, but I wasn't taking a very big risk. If Nakazov had contacted him, Karbyshev would now be busy building a case against Pavlov. If Karbyshev was out of the loop and knew nothing, I could always have affected surprise and said something like: "Well, I was under the impression that you had been informed."

In any case, the problems would arise later, when I would have to explain to Nakazov why I went to question Pavlov. For that, I would have the emerald brooch and the fact that Lyuda had identified it as one of her missing pieces of jewelry. It probably wouldn't have gotten me off the hook completely, but a conversation with Pavlov was worth the risk.

It became clear right away that Karbyshev had been informed. At the first mention of 'comrade colonel' his broad, slightly feminine face spread into a happy smile.

"Yes, of course," he waved his puffy hands about enthusiastically. "I've actually been just thinking that we haven't heard from comrade colonel for a long time. No new instructions and no signal to proceed. Otherwise, everything is ready. We're standing by."

He was at pains to demonstrate to me that he and Nakazov were thick as thieves. He even had me worried for a moment that he would rush to call Nakazov right away.

"I need to talk to Pavlov," I said coldly. "Comrade colonel has told me to expect all the necessary cooperation from you."

"Yes, of course. No question about it. I'm fully on board. Do we need to open a case right away? As I mentioned, we're chomping at the bit here."

"I'm not authorized to give you a go-ahead. You'll have to wait until comrade colonel contacts you."

"Comrade colonel told us to get ready almost a month ago. We did, but we've kept him on his construction crew for the time being, to make sure he didn't get suspicious before the time is right. Besides, it's been a busy time here, and we can always use an extra pair of hands. You see, we're building a new apartment complex for corrections personnel. Because, as matters now stand, unless you've got a family, you have to live in town and commute to the camp by bus. It's damn inconvenient, as you can imagine."

If he expected me to commiserate with him about his commute, he was disappointed. I listened to him patiently and said nothing. It was important to keep him at an arm's length. I looked at my watch demonstratively and that made him bite his tongue.

"They will have line-up and roll call in three and a half hours," he said, also glancing at his watch. "Then they'll be fed, then another line-up and roll call, the last one for the night. Then it's lock-up. Depending on your time constraints, we can call for him over now or wait until they're finished. I would prefer— "

"Thank you. Now would be the best time."

He went out to make the arrangements. When he returned I said, "You understand, Comrade Major, that there is no need to mention my arrival to Pavlov beforehand. It has been decided that this conversation has to come as a complete surprise to him."

This had been decided a couple of hours earlier, while I was riding in Zhorik's military jeep, but I didn't think this fact merited mentioning.

"Yes, of course," he said, a note of respect now creeping into his voice. "Let's use my office. We'll be more comfortable there."

While we walked down a long corridor, Karbyshev went on talking, still intent on showing me how friendly he and Nakazov were, and also on finding out some more about me. I had taken a cold and official tone with him, which would seem well above my lowly rank and position as a mere Criminal Investigations detective. He was now trying to worm out of me whether I was a more important person than my documents represented, and whether I was not with the Committee for State Security.

"How are things over in Moscow?" he asked cautiously. "How is comrade colonel doing?"

"Comrade colonel is doing very well," I replied tersely. "He's doing his duty as every State Security officer must. Just as we all do."

"Yes, of course, comrade."

He gave me a look of considerable respect. I didn't keep up the conversation and walked on silently, staring straight ahead.

In his office, he let me have his desk, which was covered with regulation green baize and contained a lamp and a glossy, last year's calendar with views of old Tallinn. He took up a position on a pink settee along the opposite wall. He placed a stack of typewriter paper and several carefully sharpened pencils on a coffee table in front of him.

"Comrade Major," I said when he finished his preparations. "We should be careful not to tip Pavlov off. I will have to conduct this conversation one on one, if you know what I mean. Without any witnesses."

If Karbyshev had been disappointed, he hid it well.

"I understand completely," he said hurriedly. "No one will disturb you here."

"Excellent. And, naturally, there is no way for anyone to listen in on our conversation without me being aware of it, I trust? I do not think that comrade colonel would take kindly..."

I let the sentence hang, making it sound a bit like a threat.

"Yes, of course, Comrade..." he hesitated and then stated my rank with a knowing smile, "Comrade Senior Lieutenant."

I had to be straight with Pavlov, to hit him over the head from the start. I couldn't be certain, of course, that Karbyshev wouldn't eavesdrop on us. After all, listening to other people's conversations and recruiting informers among inmates and free workers – who were themselves for the most part former inmates – was the essence of his job. But I had to take my chances.

"You're in deep trouble, Senya," I began without any introduction, "I don't have much time and I need you to trust me. That's point one."

Pavlov eyed me suspiciously. It was part of camp lore that whenever somebody wanted you to trust them, and claimed to be in such a hurry that you were required to make a quick decision, they were out to screw you.

Pavlov was a tall man with a slender, muscular body and a boney face. His eyes were dark, opaque and dead, like everyone else's inside. His head had been shaved, but the hair had started to grow along the edges of a quilted hat that he hadn't bothered removing. He scowled at me across Karbyshev's desk, baring a set of uneven, tobacco-stained, decaying teeth. His sharp Adam's apple moved up and down every time he swallowed.

His jaw was set and he had begun to harden under the influence of the camp, but I could see why Lyuda Polishchuk fell in love with him.

"Point two," I went on. "You're looking at a new sentence. Adding up what you have left from the Rokotov case, you might never come out. As you know, camp convictions are easy to obtain and sentences are long."

"Sure," he said.

"Point three. You should talk to me because your next interrogation will be conducted by an old friend of yours, Major Nakazov. "

"Really?" Pavlov said cautiously.

"He's a colonel now. He's been investigating a murder. Which it turns out you set up from here in the camp."

"What murder? What was it that I set up? I have no idea what you're talking about."

"Do you know Daniel Frezin?"

"Of course I do. We were both convicted in the Rokotov case. He was here until he was released a few months ago. He got a very short sentence. What of it?"

"Were you friendly with him?"

"Not particularly."

"But friendly enough for you to point him to a juicy place to rob?"

"What do you mean?"

"What I mean is that apparently you gave him the address of the Polishchuks' dacha," I said softly. "I don't believe you did, but Colonel Nakazov has a different view on this matter."

"It's bullshit," Pavlov said.

"It may be," I conceded. "But it still looks pretty suspicious, I must say. You and Frezin knew each other. You were accomplices, part of the same gang. You served time together. And you knew the Polishchuks."

"Bullshit," Pavlov repeated.

"The problem is that it didn't work out as a robbery, but ended up being a murder."

"Who got killed?" Pavlov asked quickly, but caught himself and added, trying to sound casual. "Somebody from the family?"

"Yes," I said. "Somebody from the family."

"Who?"

"Don't you already know?"

"No, I don't."

"Does it matter to you?"

"Not really. I'm just curious."

"Well, if you don't care..."

There was a long silence, which I eventually broke:

"The father."

He was relieved, even though he did his best not to show it.

"Too bad it wasn't the mother," he said. "Anton was a fairly nice guy. The mother's a nasty old bitch. Anyway, at least you can't pin this murder on me."

"Don't be so sure about that."

"What, for telling Frezin about the Polishchuks' dacha? Even if I did, which I didn't, I have nothing to do with any murder."

"Polishchuk was killed in September. One day later, before anybody knew that he was dead, somebody hit his apartment. Nakazov is sure that it was you who told Frezin about Polishchuk. His version is that some accomplice of Frezin's robbed the apartment after the robbery at the dacha went wrong. Frezin's trial was fast and furious. But for some reason your name was never mentioned. Why not, do you think? Any idea?"

While Pavlov pondered my question I thought of Karbyshev and how much I hoped that he was as good as his word. Otherwise, I could end up at the Special Facility No. 14 doing time with Pavlov. It was a flimsy ground to tread, relying on the integrity of a camp investigator.

"Enough bullshit," said Pavlov. "I didn't help anyone commit a crime. Least of all Frezin. We were never close, and here at the camp he had his own circle of friends and I had mine. That's the truth. But you guys don't give a damn about the truth. You and Nakazov can frame a saint if you put your mind to it. Was it Frezin who killed Anton?"

"Maybe. At least that's why they got him executed."

"They did?"

I nodded.

The news didn't upset Pavlov too much. On the contrary, he seemed amused. He gave a short, surprised wolf whistle.

"Good job," he said in a voice filled with admiration. "Comrade Major Nakazov finally got him. I take my hat off to him."

"He's a colonel now," I corrected.

Two hours later I came out of the gate of Special Facility No. 14 accompanied by Major Karbyshev.

"Can I give you a ride, Major?" I asked.

He clearly hadn't been listening in on my conversation with Pavlov, otherwise he would have acted very differently. I was sincerely grateful to him for that.

"Yes, I would appreciate it, Comrade Senior Lieutenant. It's not far, and it's not too much out of your way. We single officers still have to be housed in town while the new apartments are being built. I happen to be single. A bachelor by conviction, so to speak, a confirmed misogynist."

He gave a short, embarrassed laugh.

"It's pretty damn inconvenient. The town is a godforsaken rathole, a swamp of ignorance. No culture, no refinement, nothing. You won't believe some of the stories I could tell you. It's no place for an officer to be living. When the new buildings are finished, that will be true heaven on earth. There will be running water, toilets, central heating, all the comforts. And we'll be living here, behind the gates."

Zhorik was asleep in the jeep with the motor running. The windows had become thick with condensation and when I opened the door the bluish mix of tobacco smoke and the smell of sweaty human flesh hit me in the face.

"How do you manage to sleep and smoke at the same time," I asked. "A normal person would die in here."

Karbyshev had climbed in the back seat and, as if to confirm my words, began coughing violently.

"That's from going around with the windows down," Zhorik said. "That's how you catch a cold."

Karbyshev lived in an old red-brick building that rose alongside ramshackle peasant huts and free workers' barracks. The yellow squares of its five stories of windows glowed against the black sky overhead. I kept silent as Zhorik drove, ignoring Karbyshev's evident desire to talk about Pavlov. The line of subordination that had been established between us didn't allow him to ask. I could almost feel his impatience swelling in the back seat. His burning curiosity was further confirmation that he had taken to heart my warning against eavesdropping.

The jeep reached Karbyshev's door and I jumped out onto the unpaved, muddy ground to shake his hand.

"You're leaving, then," he said, clearly disappointed. "It's pitch dark and a long way to Moscow. As I said, you're more than welcome to stay. We'd have a glass or two as a nightcap. I've got pretty decent vodka that a colleague brings me from Gorky, and we could put your driver up at my deputy's place. He's a bachelor too, by the way."

I thanked him, shook my head and got back into the jeep.

Neither Zhorik nor I said much on the way back. At the end of the day, Zhorik was even more taciturn, and I had to go over what I'd learned from Pavlov. I was fighting the headache that the steady hum of the engine and the headlights of the oncoming traffic had given me. Every now and again, the red taillights of five-ton trucks heading to Moscow would light up in front of us. Methodically, relentlessly, Zhorik chased them down and overtook them.

It had taken some time for Pavlov to start talking. But when he did, there was a sudden gush of words and information. Perhaps he was finally convinced that I was not working with Nakazov, or else he just had a lot weighing on him and he was yearning for a sympathetic ear.

When he was arrested and Nakazov began interrogating him, Pavlov knew right away that he had met the State Security major before. Nakazov clearly recognized him as well.

The first session was short, and Pavlov kept tossing and turning in his cell, trying to figure out how he knew the major. The memory came in the morning. It had been at the Polishchuks' apartment. The major was a friend of Lyuda's parents. He had knocked on the door of Lyuda's room one evening, when she had some friends over and they were listening to jazz records. Lyuda had a sizeable collection of American LPs, which were a huge rarity in Moscow and very valuable, too. Despite the age difference, the major knew how to talk to young people and charmed everybody, especially the girls.

When he recognized the major, Pavlov was greatly relieved. Not that he had been too worried when he was arrested. He didn't think he was guilty of anything serious. Certainly he had never bought or sold foreign currency, and he hadn't even known that Rokotov did. And now, with a friend of the Polishchuks in charge of the investigation, he was certain that the whole incident would soon be swept under the rug. Pavlov had been a frequent guest at the Polishchuks' and knew Lyuda's parents. He and Lyuda were seeing each other and she was the apple of her old man's eye. And since Pavlov had played only a minor role in the Rokotov gang, it could easily be presented in an innocent light. True, he had made a mistake, his choice of friends had been unfortunate, but it was an error of judgement and not a crime. He would certainly be released soon.

But it didn't turn out that way at all.

The second interrogation by Major Nakazov was grueling. Nakazov began to pressure him, threatening him with a long sentence. And forget the hope of an early release or help from the Polishchuks. Pavlov's mother tried to get in touch with Anna Panteleyevna, but she refused point blank to meet. One time, Pavlov's mother waited for Anna Panteleyevna in front of her apartment building. It was humiliating when Madam Polishchuk pulled her sleeve from his mother's grasp and pushed past her, declaring that she wanted nothing to do with her.

"Lyuda tried to help," Pavlov said. "She pawned some of her jewels to pay for a lawyer. But there was no way a lawyer could stand up to Nakazov. When they heard that State Security was handling the case, they all ran the other way. "

Having first put the fear of God into Pavlov, Nakazov made him an unexpected offer. Pavlov had to testify against Frezin. Apparently, Frezin was to become the key figure in the Rokotov gang. It might even have become known as Frezin's gang, though in Pavlov's opinion Frezin lacked the character to be a top man. He could have been an enforcer, Pavlov thought, but as a mastermind he was not credible.

A typical career criminal, as Pavlov described him.

"No brains. Absolutely no brains. I've met a lot of guys in here, and I can tell you that even in an ordinary gang, say burglars or safe-crackers, he would never have risen above an enforcer. I didn't agree to Nakazov's terms right away, and asked him to give me a day or two to think it over. Of course, I had no desire to get a long sentence, which was what he was threatening me with, but I also didn't want to testify against Frezin. A rat's life at the camp is hard, you know that. You get gang raped for being a snitch. That's the kind of choice he gave me."

Pavlov got lucky. He didn't have to make a choice after all. Something had fallen through, because Nakazov soon called Pavlov in for a late-night interrogation session.

Nakazov was in a really foul mood, drawing little stick figures on a piece of paper in front of him.

"Look here, Pavlov," he said. "You never testified against Frezin. Remember, you said nothing about him and signed no statements. Got it? Even if you're shown your own testimony with your signature on it, tell them you lied because you were hoping to get a more lenient sentence if you fingered Frezin."

"But I didn't sign anything, anyway. You gave me time to think it over."

Nakazov suddenly flew into a rage and started to scream and stomp his feet.

"Do you understand what I'm telling you, you motherfucker? If you're shown anything you've signed, your job is not to stare at it with your mouth open like a virgin when she sees a dick for the first time, but to say nicely like, 'I'm a bastard and a fucking moron, I was trying to mislead the investigation and I fingered Frezin in the hope of a more lenient sentence for myself.' Got it, or you want me to stamp it all over your stupid face?"

I never heard the gentlemanly Colonel Nakazov use such crude language, but somehow I didn't doubt the accuracy of Pavlov's story.

In any case, Nakazov then left Pavlov alone and all interrogations stopped. But at the trial Nakazov suddenly declared that Pavlov had intended to mislead the investigation and had given false testimony against another suspect. State Security wanted the court to take a note of this while sentencing Pavlov, which the court did. Pavlov's ended up one of the lengthiest sentences; even those who were far more involved with the gang got four years or less.

"Frezin got only two years," Pavlov concluded. "He was lucky."

"Sure," I agreed. "He was lucky, for a while. You can say he got a gift of two years' of life."

As far as my investigation was concerned, the most important thing I learned from Pavlov was that Nakazov and Frezin had been old acquaintances. But Pavlov had more surprises in store.

"Actually," Pavlov said when I thought our conversation had come to an end. "Actually, that entire case, I mean the Rokotov case, had plenty of weird stuff in it. Things don't add up. At the trial, and even in the press, there were various accounts of Rokotov and his lavish lifestyle. How he was throwing money around, how he loved the high life, eating at expensive restaurants, and all kinds of lies like that. Then there were all those stories about a string of mistresses he kept, dressing them in expensive clothes and giving them fine jewelry."

"Why?" I asked. "It wasn't true?"

"I knew Rokotov pretty well. We were studying English, although for a different purpose. We also loved jazz. But these stories about him, it's just not him at all. He recruited people into his gang at the Foreign Languages Institute, and music fans who bought and sold records near record stores. Those were the kind of people who worked for him, but no one suspected him of being the leader of the entire organization, even though he collected all the money and seemed to be in charge. He, too, always used to say that he was just an employee, nothing more. Apparently, he had people above him who kept a close watch over him. When I first met Frezin at his house, Rokotov told me that Frezin was the one who was watching his every step. That was very likely, because that was the kind of job that Frezin could do."

Pavlov pulled another cigarette from the pack I'd left on the desk, rolled it between his thumb and forefinger and lit it. He drew in the smoke, and his Adam's apple went up and down. "Any chance you've got a Pall Mall on you?" he asked.

"What's that?"

"A brand of American cigarettes. Never heard of it?"

I shook my head.

"Good stuff. You've gotta try it some time. Better than your Red Presnya crap."

Pavlov waved dismissively at my pack and went on with his story.

"Whenever Rokotov had to pay for something, anything, he always used to say that he shouldn't be spending the money and that the boss would twist his neck if he found out. I don't know whether he was for real or just bullshitting people. What I do know is that Rokotov was as tightfisted as Shylock. He just hated spending money. For him, money was the beginning and the end of everything. He loved money for its own sake. He used to say: 'You've gotta respect money. When you treat it with respect, it comes to you. Money is just like women. If you love them, they love you back.' But he had no interest in women. 'I don't mind the whores,' he used to say. 'I respect them, because it's all on the up and up with them. You pay, you screw them and it's a done deal. It's true love that is a killer. It never costs you as much as when you get laid for free.' It's true, he seemed to get more satisfaction out of money than women. So, all that talk about the Big Boss could have been a way of getting out of spending money."

Pavlov drew on the cigarette again and leaned in closer.

"What I miss most is women," he said.

His eyes became dreamy as he stopped for a minute and reminisced.

"I had a confrontation with Frezin," he continued. "There was a woman involved. One night I was at Aragvi – a fancy Georgian place on Gorky Street, in case you don't know – with a guy from New Zealand. Nice guy, by the way, but that's beside the point. Rokotov used to ask me to take some of his foreign friends around. I guess you can say he hired me, because I took them to restaurants or the theater and Rokotov footed the bill. That was one thing he never begrudged the money for. I guess it was good for business. I knew that the New Zealander would be with his wife, so I asked a friend of mine to join us. Americans call it a double date."

Pavlov sneered.

"Funny thing was that the New Zealander's wife was ugly as sin, and a real shrew, too. As to my date, I'd taken a real looker along. The foreigner was so taken with her, I worried that even his missus would get wise to it."

"I see," I said.

"No, it's important," Pavlov said. "You'll see in a second. So, that's the scene. We're sitting around a table at Aragvi, drinking and chatting about R&B and the Russian ballet. All of a sudden, Frezin shows up at the restaurant and comes over to join us. The New Zealander was going home the next morning, and Rokotov needed to hand something off to him at the last moment. They couldn't have found a worse place to do it, because Aragvi is a hard-currency place and it's always crawling with State Security snitches. All the waiters and the maitre d's are paid informers, if not KGB employees. No one could have just come up to our table and handed something to a foreigner without getting busted right away. Frezin had come in with a group of friends, and then he sat at our table for a few minutes as though he had run into some acquaintance by accident. He pulled over a chair, poured himself some vodka and spent a few minutes chatting with me. Maybe the vodka went to his head, I don't know, but he too started to stare at my date. He was ogling her breasts and leering like a madman. Then he went as far as to wink at her, like she was a whore at the train station. If I hadn't been with the New Zealanders, I would've punched him in the face, I swear."

"Aragvi is not a good place to settle scores," I observed.

Pavlov nodded.

"I did have a score to settle with Frezin, but I still had no desire to testify against him the way Nakazov wanted me to."

He took another cigarette and changed the subject.

"Rokotov loved jewelry, though. Baubles were his one weakness. He always bought them, whenever he could lay his hands on pretty or expensive pieces. Especially if it was something unique. All his contacts among foreigners knew that he wanted jewelry, and he also dealt with appraisers at consignment shops. Whenever an old lady would bring in something valuable, he'd be the first one they'd show it to. And he always paid the highest price. That was another thing he didn't mind spending money on, jewelry. And the fences, of course, they always had the best pieces. A guy working for Rokotov once concealed a nice necklace from him, I suppose he wanted to give it to a girlfriend. That was probably the only time I saw Rokotov get really mad and really violent. He beat the guy senseless and afterwards never trusted him again. The poor sucker would've probably ended up being knifed, but luckily for him he got busted soon afterwards."

With the conversation taking a turn toward jewelry, I pulled out Lyuda's emerald peapod and showed it to him.

"Have you ever seen this?" I asked.

The peapod lit up, catching the light from Karbyshev's desk lamp and making his dingy office seem even uglier by contrast. It was like a reminder of a different life, one that had room for beautiful women, fine perfumes, mirrors, chandeliers and wine.

Pavlov glanced at the brooch and gave no sign of recognition. The camp is the best teacher when it comes to giving lessons in self-control and caution.

"No," he shrugged. "A nice bauble, though."

SIXTEEN

Uncle Nikolai died in the second half of November.

When city folks die like that, suddenly and in mid-stride, it's called a sudden, unexpected death. It doesn't happen much in the cities. In the country, suddenly is how people almost always die, especially the men: in fall, after the crops are gathered and before a long winter. Uncle Nikolai was old by rural standards, almost sixty-two, born on the day of the Feast of the Baptism. He was the same age as the century.

Aunt Ksenia had been proud not only because she still had a man in the house, but because Uncle Nikolai was still robust. Their kids were all dead, but at least the husband could chop firewood, pull a bucket of water from the well or fix the roof. It was all in theory, of course, because Aunt Ksenia did everything herself and she always used to say that if she had asked Uncle Nikolai to do anything, she would've died waiting.

But now Aunt Ksenia was a widow, too, like everyone else in their village. Many had been widows since the war.

Tosya and I went down for the funeral. Tosya wanted to go with me and took unpaid leave from work, even though she had met Nikolai only once. Tosya was not particularly social. It's hard for her to make new friends. She didn't open up easily. Even to me. Whenever I complain about her reticence, she laughs and says, "You'll stomp all over my soul, Matyushkin, with your muddy boots."

That's why I was surprised that Tosya had developed so much affection for Uncle Nikolai in such a short time.

The cemetery was in Serpukhov, the nearest town. There had been plans to build a cremation facility there and the authorities had shut down the cemetery's chapel in order to convert it into a furnace. No work was being done, but the chapel remained closed.

Cremation was a major topic of conversation as we trundled toward the cemetery in a ZIS bus provided by the collective farm office.

"That's the new authorities' idea," grumbled Aunt Ksenia's neighbor, a short, ancient woman lacking front teeth. The communist government had been in power for more than forty years, but for her it was still new.

"It's all done for the Jews," she went on. "That's the sort of religion they have. Their religion prescribes that they burn in an eternal fire after death."

The other women nodded in agreement. Or maybe their heads were just bobbing up and down on their wobbly necks as the bus trundled over the potholes. There were no men on the bus, but for me and a young, slow-witted peasant accompanying his mother. He turned his head right and left and smiled mysteriously, as though he knew something no one else did.

"We used to have a cemetery in Zyatkovo," Aunt Ksenia said. "Our first collective farm chairman, Comrade Parfyonov, plowed it under and planted potatoes. He used to joke that the burial ground had the richest soil. He was the devil, that one. A Ukrainian, and from city stock in the bargain. Had no idea how to farm. Couldn't tell a ram from a cow in plain daylight. He got killed in the war, too."

Aunt Ksenia sighed. Then she smiled, smoothing the web of wrinkles running across her cheeks and gathering them at the corners of her eyes. She looked younger.

"His death notice was sent to the entire village," she said giggling, as though it was a funny joke. "He'd never managed to get himself a proper wife. He liked dallying with young girls instead. And married women, too."

There was no official religious service over Uncle Nikolai's body, especially since the church was shut down and stood surrounded by scaffolding. But there was a prayer of sorts, said in the cemetery, at the edge of the open grave. A thickset man came, dressed in civilian clothes, wearing a broad-brimmed hat. When he unbuttoned his overcoat, it was revealed that he wore a gilded cross on his chest, suspended from a gilded chain. He took out his vestments, a large bible, a silver censer and other religious paraphernalia from a wooden suitcase he had brought along.

Tosya had never been to a religious service and watched everything eagerly, never taking her eyes off the priest.

By the grave, standing a bit apart from the old women and the slow-witted peasant, was Colonel Nakazov. He towered over them. He also stood out because of his quality leather overcoat. I had spotted him when we first pulled up to the gate and the gravediggers began unloading the casket through the back door.

I didn't want to bother Aunt Ksenia at such a time and turned to her neighbor instead, the one who had been talking about cremation.

"Who is that?" I asked.

She squinted at Nakazov, chewing on her toothless gums, and then lisped, "God knows. Some kind of writer. He owns a dacha somewhere around here. The late Nikolai, God save his soul, used to do work for him. Some carpentry, I gather. The guy paid him in vodka."

The gravediggers carried the casket to the graveside. It was hammered together roughly, from thick pine boards, but when I put a shoulder to it, as tradition required, it seemed very light, almost weightless. The mother of the slow-witted peasant pushed him forward to help us carry it. He grinned foolishly, rolled up his sleeves but stayed back. So did Nakazov. He brought up the rear of our small procession, walking at a leisurely pace along the weed-infested main pathway.

I expected him to leave at the start of the service, or at least to arrange his face into a condescending smile. A State Security officer by definition had to be an atheist, and Nakazov, with his cynical and sarcastic mind, would, I was sure, laugh at religious superstition. But Nakazov surprised me. He maintained a solemn expression throughout the service, standing with his hands clasped. His face was inscrutable.

When the service came to an end and old women began throwing clumps of clay onto the lid, Nakazov also approached, picked up a handful of earth and tossed it into the grave. Then, he sought me out in the crowd – Tosya and I stood out from the rest no less than he did – looked me straight in the eye and crossed himself. He put his fur hat back on and was the first to leave, heading toward the gate without turning to look back.

I also threw a bit of earth onto the casket. The gravediggers approached, spitting on their hands and taking up their shovels.

"Here we go, boys," one of them shouted cheerfully.

Clinking against the pebbles, the shovels flew through the air with astonishing speed and the dry graveyard soil began to thud against Uncle Nikolai.

"Rest in peace, " said Tosya under her breath.

She gave a sign of the cross, awkwardly and a little shamefacedly, and then repeated it more confidently. For my part, I don't believe in crossing myself.

The cemetery was quiet. A few crows circled silently over the group of men shoveling the earth and bent women in black huddled together under a white autumn sky.

Back at the village, the women immediately started to prepare the food. Tosya was not good at domestic tasks. She could neither cook well, nor serve a meal properly. She had not had anyone to learn from, since she didn't remember her mother and kids at the orphanage were not taught to keep house. Whenever she tried to help at other people's houses, women laughed at her and teased her because she acted more like a man in the kitchen, not knowing where to turn.

The cooking was done in Aunt Ksenia's house, but it was too small to fit all the guests. Every Zyatkovo resident was there, of course, and others as well – men in their forties, probably school friends of Uncle Nikolai's boys. They came by bus from Serpukhov, where they now lived in new, five-story apartment buildings on the outskirts and worked at the chemical plant. They kept arriving in tight-knit groups of three – mother, father and a child of twelve or thirteen – and walking down the main street in the gathering darkness.

The tables had been set up in the old church, which the first collective farm chairman, Comrade Parfyonov, had cleared of icons. Once the sacred images had been removed, Comrade Parfyonov turned the church into an education center and a house of culture, but it subsequently fell into disuse. A broken-down film projector stood in the corner, its lens turned toward the wall. Two long tables had been brought in and positioned at straight angles in the middle of the church, forming a T. The interior was dark, damp and cold, and the half-heartedly scraped fresco of the Last Judgement was partly hidden behind old political banners.

The women brought out bowls of marinated cabbage garnished with red cranberries and sugar, pickled cucumbers and tomatoes, boiled potatoes and marinated mushrooms, placing them on the two tables that had been densely filled with half-liter bottles of Moskovskaya vodka, resembling anti-aircraft rockets at the November 7 military parade.

Although there were no seating assignments, the arriving couples broke up and men headed to the smaller table, which had more vodka. As soon as they settled down, several callused hands reached across the table for the bottles. The first toast, to Uncle Nikolai's memory, was pronounced and drunk in silence and without clinking glasses. The glasses were hastily refilled and emptied, and only after that did the food begin making its rounds.

Nakazov sat across from me. He looked up and made a show of surprise, as though it was the first time he had seen me.

"Hello, Senior Lieutenant," he said. "I'm glad to see you honoring the memory of an honest Russian man. Have a drink with me."

"With pleasure, sir, Comrade Colonel."

"Don't you start, Senior Lieutenant. I'm getting tired of your 'Comrade Colonel.' You're being too formal."

We drank once to the deceased, and then twice more, without making any toasts. Nakazov's plate was empty and, following his example, I had yet to take any food.

The conversation around the table was picking up. The men discussed their work, criticized the shift manager and complained about overtime rates and bonuses. The old church somehow began to feel warmer and brighter. Nakazov and I drank glass after glass, smiling at each other across the table. Tosya came up to us from the women's table, holding a shot glass in one hand and a fork with a quarter of a boiled potato in the other. The potato had small pieces of onion sticking to its sides. She and I drank one more toast in Uncle Nikolai's memory.

"I want to drink to Aunt Ksenia," said Tosya. "Let's hope she won't be too lonely."

I refilled our glasses.

Suddenly, Nakazov got up, leaned across the table and said softly, "Don't think, creep, that your activities behind my back will go unpunished. You thought perhaps I would never find out. Well, I did."

I have no idea why he decided to do it. Perhaps it was the half-dozen shots we had drunk in quick succession without having any food.

I looked at him innocently.

"I'm not sure I understand what you're talking about, Comrade Colonel," I said.

"Don't play the fool, Senior Lieutenant. Keep in mind that none of your meddling in the investigation helped Freak avoid the death penalty. He kept his appointment as punctually as the Kremlin clock. I'm sure he's happy where he is right now. By which I mean the section of Hell reserved for murderers."

"God rest his soul," I said sadly. "Should we drink to his memory, too, Comrade Colonel?"

Nakazov gave me a dirty look and sat down. Pink blotches had started to spread across his clean-shaven face.

"If you're talking about my testimony at Frezin's trial, I don't understand why you are so angry with me, sir," I said. "Your instructions were clear. I was supposed to tell the truth. That is exactly what I did."

Before I had finished, Nakazov was on his feet again, pushing his sweaty face toward me.

"Are you a fucking idiot? Don't you understand when people are being nice to you?"

I was going to respond, but Tosya felt it was time for her to intervene.

"I swear to God, Matyushkin," she said. "Are the two of you nuts? Don't you see that it's not the time or place to start an argument? You're being disrespectful."

Nakazov took Tosya's measure, keeping his eyes for a few seconds on her breasts, and then turned to me.

"Who the hell is this, Senior Lieutenant?"

"My wife," I said, reluctantly.

"Your wife?"

Nakazov threw his head back and had a long, hearty laugh.

"You're a funny one, Senior Lieutenant," he said when he was finished. "So, this is your wife who's ordering you around? I don't care about that, of course, but how come she's telling other men what to do?"

He'd got his anger under control and went back to using his usual condescending tone.

"Listen to me, wife," he said, turning to Tosya. "First of all, I'll have you know that a funeral is exactly the time and place to settle scores. And, second of all, I don't know whether or not your husband likes to be pussy-whipped, but normal men don't allow their women to open their traps when they talk to other men."

The orphanage may not have taught Tosya to keep house, but it certainly had taught her to take care of herself. She could not only give a good tongue-lashing when she wanted to, but to use her fists, too, as well as any man. But this time she said nothing. She only sneered and turned away.

"You made a mistake, Colonel," I said, shaking my head. "Up until now, I didn't really give a damn what made you so eager to hang the Polishchuk murder on Frezin. The way I saw it, it's your business. But now I've got a personal interest in this business of yours. I may be shooting in the dark, and you merely wanted to win a general's star on your epaulets. But I have a suspicion that it's not that simple. I know that you had tried getting Frezin executed once before, but for some reason it didn't work out."

Nakazov had had enough. He stood up, tipping his oak stool over behind him. The impact, loud as a gunshot, sent a shudder around the room. The conversation stopped and everybody stared at him.

"Watch out, Senior Lieutenant," Nakazov said loudly. "You've gotta start minding your own business. Otherwise you'll come to regret it, I promise you."

As he turned to leave, his boots stomping across the stone floor sent an echo into the vaulted ceiling. He wanted to slam the door behind him, but the rusty hinges had a mind of their own. The door closed slowly, making a high-pitched, piteous sound.

Nakazov was right. The funeral *was* the place to settle accounts. Ten minutes after his dramatic exit a quarrel erupted at the other end of my table, promptly turning into a fist fight. At the other table, Aunt Ksenia and her toothless neighbor were having an argument of their own.

Several people rushed in to pull the fighting men apart, and soon they too were drawn into a fight amongst themselves. Tosya and I had no interest in seeing how it would end. People around us were rapidly becoming drunk and, besides, we had a bus to catch.

On our way home, fall suddenly came to an end and the weather took a sharp turn for the worse. Arriving in the city, we got caught in a nasty cold rain, driven violently into our faces by a fierce northern wind.

SEVENTEEN

"You shouldn't have messed with him," Tosya said. "He's the boss and in the end you'll be the one who loses out."

I shrugged. She was right and I shouldn't have let myself be provoked by Nakazov. What do I care about Frezin? What do I care about the Polishchuks, for that matter?

I knew I would get into trouble, but I didn't expect it to start quite so soon. The very next day, on Wednesday, I ran into Budyonny in the corridor outside my office. I saluted him according to regulations. He didn't reply, which was highly unusual for him, but stopped and stared at me until I entered my office, shutting the door behind myself.

Urumov was out. He was working on some minor case, chasing after pickpockets at the Savyolovsky train station.

During the past two months, Lenny had been walking around with a stupid smile on his face, somehow managing to turn nearly every conversation to Lyuda Polishchuk and her surreal beauty. After what happened on the night of the Seventh of November, I was reluctant to continue this line of conversation.

Lenny was still out later in the day when our office door opened without a warning knock and Budyonny walked in. He stood in the cramped space between our two desks and his bulk somehow sucked all the air out of the room. He looked pensively out the window for a long time and lit a cigarette. As a rule, he almost never did this, insisting that everyone smoke on the landing or in the special room. He believed that the commanding officer had to inspire his troops through personal example.

He drew on his cigarette once or twice and tossed it, unfinished, through the open transom.

"How are you doing on those apartment burglaries?" he asked.

"Well," I began vaguely. "I'm wrapping them up."

If I were completely truthful, I should have told him that the case was basically closed and that all the loose ends had been tied up. But there was the issue of the emerald peapod and the possibility, however slim, that my two suspects were connected to the burglary at the Polishchuks. I had not mentioned anything about the peapod to Budyonny and instead I began listing other break-ins that my two suspects had confessed about.

"Why don't you pass it all to Kostya Pirogov," Budyonny interrupted me, averting his eyes. "Fill him in. I'm sure he will be able to tidy everything up. He is an able investigator and, besides, you've already done all the detective work, anyway."

"I see," I said grimly. Taking somebody off a case just before it is completed was highly irregular. It was an even rarer occurrence than smoking in offices.

"What is it that you see?" Budyonny shouted, suddenly angry. "Look at your goddamn office. It's a pigsty. You've got nothing to do now, why don't you clean it up? How can you do any work in this chaos? I'm telling you, until you put your office in order you won't get any new cases. Is that understood?"

I nodded. I was glad that I had kept my notes on the Polishchuk burglary separately, and that the emerald peapod, being a valuable little thing, was not stored with the rest of the evidence. Kostya was a diligent guy, a solid employee and a hard-working detective, but he wasn't an especially imaginative fellow. He would not try to dig any deeper than the list of burglaries I had compiled, and for all of those he would have confessions and thorough descriptions provided by the stepson. And, what with the stepfather being a convicted felon, I was sure that any state prosecutor worthy of the name would have no difficulty getting them convicted. With Kostya on the case and going by the book, the boy, Peter, was doomed. I felt sorry for him, but there was nothing I could do about it. Maybe he would be more careful when he got out. If he got out.

Lenny listened to my account of Budyonny's visit and gave a long whistle. Then I told him about my encounter with Nakazov at the funeral.

"I can see a very clear cause-and-effect relationship, Pavel," he said, patting me sympathetically on the shoulder. "He made short work of you."

Lenny had convinced himself that he too had a personal score to settle with Nakazov. To my surprise, I discovered that Lenny was the jealous type, and Nakazov's courtship of Lyuda had stuck in his craw. When, in accordance with Budyonny's orders, I began clearing my desk, pulling out dog-eared folders swollen with yellowed papers and pale carbon-copy sheets, he sat astride his chair facing me, blew the dust from the corner of my desk and set down a clean sheet of paper.

"Let's do this properly," he stated. "Start from the beginning. What do we know about this case?"

What we knew was relatively little, and what we did know didn't add up. If Pavlov was to be believed, Nakazov's plan to have Frezin shot traced back to his investigation of the Rokotov case. Why he was so keen on getting rid of Frezin we had no idea, but he finally saw his chance when Polishchuk's body was found and I, coincidentally, arrested Frezin on the same train line.

But this version, if it could be called that, was full of holes. What did Nakazov have against Frezin? Pavlov had hinted that Rokotov might not have been the head of the gang of black market currency dealers and might have been chosen arbitrarily. State Security was under pressure to put an end to the problem of street-corner currency dealing, and they promptly found the guys who were responsible for all the black market activity. Rokotov and two others were presented to Khrushchev as gang leaders, tried, convicted, and shot.

Pavlov's version of events seemed correct. It was an open secret that the arrest and conviction of three hundred people in the Rokotov case didn't put an end to illegal currency dealing; it was still flourishing in front of the Bolshoi Theater and around hard currency hotels.

Lenny drew a number of circles and squares and connected them with arrows. He then inscribed the names of our main protagonists into the circles and squares.

"Let's say Nakazov initially intended to make Frezin the head of the gang, but for some reason he changed his mind or found a more suitable candidate," Lenny began. "According to Pavlov, Frezin made a very poor gang leader, in any case. But there must have been more to it, since Frezin's starring role was not just cancelled, but his name barely got a mention at the trial and he got a ridiculously lenient sentence."

Lenny put a fat question mark over the square that he had previously marked as Frezin.

"Here is another idea," I said. "We know that Nakazov was in love with Lyuda and probably tried to seduce her."

Lenny blushed and muttered, "So what? What does that have to do with Frezin?"

"Not with Frezin, no. But in their freshman year in college, Lyuda dated Pavlov. She seemed to be in love with him."

Lenny's face, already crimson, turned the color of boiled beets.

"Is that true? How do you know that?"

His lips, pale against his dark red face, barely moved.

"I do," I said. "Pavlov was a frequent visitor to the Polishchuks', where he even met Nakazov. Not surprisingly, given his connection to the family, Pavlov expected to be let off easily. But Nakazov, on the contrary, was especially harsh with him. He began to pressure Pavlov to testify against Frezin and to finger him as the gang leader. Then, having for some reason changed his mind about Frezin, he turned around and requested a harsher sentence for Pavlov, claiming that he had been trying to mislead the investigation with false testimony against an accomplice."

"Sure," Urumov said angrily, crossing out the diagram he had just drawn.

"But it doesn't explain why Nakazov changed his mind about Frezin and why Frezin got treated so leniently," I said.

Indeed, it explained nothing. Suppose there really was a highly organized gang in which Rokotov, rather than being the key man, played a less important role. Let's say he was in charge of personnel and recruitment and ran the network, collecting hard currency from dealers. Along the way, he informed on those in the gang whom he didn't like and could no longer trust. Rokotov had once told Pavlov that Frezin was his direct link to the true bosses and that Frezin's job was to watch over Rokotov. That made sense.

Lenny picked up another sheet and started to draw circles and arrows all over again.

"Everything is extremely simple," he declared. "The real boss of the gang was not Rokotov at all but someone else. Frezin knew who that was and was willing to make a deal with Nakazov. He would reveal the name of the actual leader and Nakazov in return would get him off the hook or, at most, would make sure that Frezin spent very little time behind bars. Frezin obviously lived up to his end of the bargain – otherwise his sentence would not have been so short – but Nakazov still managed to sink Pavlov, a successful rival for Lyuda's affection."

Urumov uttered the last couple of words with considerable difficulty.

"Now, we're getting somewhere," he continued. "We now have a direct connection between Nakazov and the currency trading gang. It's pretty clear he was dressing up relatively minor players to look like big bosses, while the real big bosses weren't even mentioned at the trial."

"Sure," I said. "Frezin obviously gave Nakazov their names but none were arrested. Why? Was Frezin the real boss and did he pay Nakazov off to leave him alone?"

"I doubt it," Lenny said.

"I do too. Pavlov thought that Frezin made a good enforcer, but didn't have the brains to be anything more than that."

"So, Nakazov knows who the real leaders of the gang are and he's probably using this information even as we speak," Lenny continued. "Is he still investigating this gang, gathering information in order to arrest the top leaders? It's possible but highly unlikely - and I'll tell you why. Two years ago, when Rokotov and his friends were arrested, it was the number one priority case in the entire Soviet Union. The order to crush the black market in currency and to put an end to speculative trading with foreigners had come directly from Khrushchev. Getting to the bottom of it and arresting the leaders was important then, when the Big Man's attention was on the case. For someone like Nakazov it would have been an extremely astute career move. Bringing the real leaders of the gang to justice now would invalidate that old investigation, the one they completed two years ago. It would mean admitting that they made a mistake and executed the wrong guys, while allowing the real culprits to carry on. If Nakazov comes out with a different result now, he would antagonize his superiors at State Security and would be demoted for his troubles, or worse." Urumov paused. What he was saying made a lot of sense. I waited for him to go on.

"This means that Nakazov is using whatever information he got from Frezin for personal gain," Lenny concluded triumphantly.

"It would seem so."

"What is he doing then? Blackmail?"

"Obviously."

Lenny stared at the sheet.

"We've got another important set of links here," he said and drew another square, marking it with a name. "What is the connection between Nakazov and Polishchuk? They are old friends, we know that. Suppose the timing here is not a coincidence. Frezin gets out of jail and Polishchuk turns up dead."

He drew an arrow connecting the two squares.

"No, it's too neat,," I said after a while. "Frezin strangles Polishchuk and later that same evening gets busted for harassing a woman on a suburban train, an act of hooliganism that is completely unrelated to the murder. Such things don't happen in real life. There has to be a logical connection between these events."

"Agreed," Lenny said. "Nevertheless, suppose that the two events, Frezin's release and Polishchuk's death, are connected. We don't know how, but let's assume this for the sake of argument. And let's assume that there is a further connection between the murder and the robbery at the Polishchuks."

"The murder and the robbery must be connected," I agreed. "That is also too much of a coincidence. But I don't see how all three events fit together."

"Neither do I," said Urumov and placed the sheet of paper in his desk drawer, having folded it with exaggerated care. "At least not yet. To be continued."

For the rest of the day he didn't mention Lyuda once, which was uncharacteristic of him.

EIGHTEEN

After observing Tosya for about ten minutes as she made herself up in front of the mirror, arranged a fashionable nylon head scarf over her freshly curlered hair, straightened out the line of lipstick at the corner of her mouth and put other finishing touches on her appearance, I asked casually, "Shouldn't we take my Zundapp? I'll be parking it for winter tomorrow, and so I figured..."

Tosya stared at me as though I had just escaped from an insane asylum.

"I wonder about you sometimes, Matyushkin. Have you looked out the window recently? It's raining cats and dogs. We'd get to the theater covered with mud."

Sometimes Tosya completely loses any sense of humor. This was, unquestionably, one of those times.

Lyuda had invited us to the theater. She had purchased tickets for Alexander Ostrovsky's *Poor Bride* at the Mayakovsky Theater.

"Everyone says it is a shockingly brilliant production," Lyuda said. "The critics are raving about it. I'm sure Tosya is going to like it."

Tosya was happy at first, and even clapped her hands for joy when Lyuda extended the invitation, just like a little girl. But then she turned sad.

"What's the matter, Antonina Ivanovna?" I asked.

At first I thought that she was jealous of Lyuda after what happened on the Seventh of November, but it turned out to be something else entirely. Eventually, she confessed that she had never been to a real theater. At the orphanage, the older kids had once put on a play, something about the Revolution and the Civil War. It was a long time ago, when Tosya was still very little. That was the only live theater production she had ever seen.

"I bet everyone is going to be dressed up and stuff," she said. "I have nothing nice to wear."

I don't know a more beautiful woman than Tosya when she puts on a plain cotton dress from her Tryokhgorka Textile Plant and arranges her auburn hair under a cotton kerchief. But when it came to attending a play at a real theater dressed like that, Tosya would not hear of it.

"Why don't you suggest I wear a house dress, Matyushkin," she snapped.

It was true, she had no fashionable clothes. Except perhaps for a dress for special occasions that she had worn exactly once. But she and Lyuda conferred over the phone a few times, and later Lyuda passed her a small care package, containing a glossy fashion magazine, a golden cylinder of bright red lipstick, a bottle of French perfume and a transparent nylon head scarf. The fashion magazine was in a foreign language but had plenty of pictures, the bottle of perfume was so tiny I was scared to hold it in my hand and the headscarf was light as a feather. Smiling condescendingly, Urumov handed me the package at work. Over the past several weeks he had been to the theater several times, attending not only tame Ostrovsky plays, but some really cutting-edge underground production at Moscow State University, where a persecuted director from Leningrad had put on an uncensored foreign play.

What the play was about, Lenny could not adequately explain, but he repeated several times, "Old man, it was awe-inspiring. Old man, the whole point was that you saw students, amateurs, normal people like you and me perform on stage. They are not deadened by formal training and can convey true, unspoiled human passions which your average Mastroianni can never fake, no matter how hard he tries."

Lenny had learned this nonsense from Lyuda and her friends and repeated it without, I suspect, fully understanding what he was talking about. But the mere fact that he could mouth something like this made him unique among Petrovka policemen.

Tosya spent a long time examining the pictures in the glossy magazine and consulting some more with Lyuda over the phone. Then, wrapping it carefully in a piece of newsprint so as not to damage it by accident, she took it to the bathroom and locked herself in. For two hours all her irate neighbors could hear in response to their insistent knocking was a low growl. She was focused on the task at hand.

When I too knocked on the door, she shouted that I should go home to get ready and come pick her up in an hour. My request to see the work in progress was met with a rebuke, "Fools shouldn't be shown the work before it's done."

When I finally got to see the result, it surpassed all expectations. Tosya was practically indistinguishable from one of those models whose pictures were in the fashion magazine, except she was not sickly skinny but the other way around: tall, strong and healthy.

On Tosya's insistence, we arrived well before the curtain and had to wait for Lyuda and Urumov in a stuffy hallway near the front entrance. By the time they emerged from Urumov's hatchback Moskvich – which was shortly after the first bell – Tosya had turned pale from nerves. Lyuda took some more time to review Tosya's outfit, making her turn this way and that and clicking her tongue appreciatively.

"You look stunning, my dear," she said. "Just stunning, Tosenka."

"Let's go in already," Tosya implored her. "Everybody is sitting down already. We won't find a seat."

"Oh, don't worry," Lyuda said, perfectly calm. "I can assure you that they are not going to start without us. Nor is anyone going to take our seats."

She was right. Until the moment we took up our seats, the theater was buzzing with hundreds of voices, the rustle of playbill pages, the humming, the coughing and the laughter. From the orchestra pit came the cacophony of instruments being tuned. The third bell rang just as we pushed past the well-dressed couples on our way to our seats, giving us just enough time to settle down before the enormous chandelier on the ceiling began to dim. Our seats were probably the best in the house, in the center of the fifth row of the orchestra.

At intermission, when the lights came on again, Tosya sat motionless, entranced by what she had seen. Urumov brought her back to reality by shaking her unceremoniously by the shoulder and announcing, "Come. Let's go. Otherwise there'll be a crash at the buffet."

Having a seat so close to the stage has another advantage. It is the closest to the buffet. While Lyuda and Tosya held a table, Urumov, looking very much at home, raced to the front of a rapidly forming line and discretely handed a three-ruble note to the man behind the counter, who promptly switched his attention to him.

"So," said Urumov winking at the man. "No sausage today?"

"Always in short supply," said the man, shaking his head compassionately. "Maybe tomorrow."

"Tomorrow will be too late. In that case, my good man, give me a white fish sandwich and two with ham. And a bottle of mineral water. And a beer. What about you and Tosya?"

I hesitated, uncertain what to order from the abundance displayed in the glass case in front of me. Urumov didn't allow me to make up my mind, especially since the line was pressing at us from behind.

"Give him two more ham sandwiches and one with lox, my good man," he said quickly. "And a bottle of orange soda, if you have it. If not, anything sweet with do. And yes, I almost forgot. Four fruit tarts."

Holding our loot aloft, we pushed our way back to our table. All the other tables had been taken, and the poorer theater-goers from the third row of the balcony had to lean against the walls as they chewed on sandwiches they had brought from home. While we were placing our orders, our two vacant chairs had attracted considerable attention, but Lyuda had mercilessly repelled all comers.

"How do you like the performance?" she asked Tosya.

"It's fantastic," Tosya replied enthusiastically.

"I agree," Lyuda said. "The director's interpretation is awe-inspiring. Plucky, even daring, I should say. And the acting is extraordinary. A few weeks ago, Lenny and I went to see some amateurs perform at the University. It was interesting, of course, and fresh, but they're no match for professionals."

Tosya kept nodding her head and smiling happily.

The first bell rang, but Lyuda had every intention of continuing to sit at the table and finish her fruit tart. Tosya, on the other hand, had finished her food long ago and shifted impatiently in her chair. After a while, Lyuda noticed her imploring glances and got up, and we began to make our way back to our seats. Lyuda was directly in front of me and she constantly greeting friends and acquaintances.

Suddenly, she rushed into the crowd and began hugging and kissing a young woman. The woman might have been pretty had she not been so ordinary. Her face was singularly unmemorable and she was certainly not dressed with the help of a glossy fashion magazine. I was a little surprised that she was Lyuda's friend and that Lyuda showed so much affection for her. I would rather have expected this young woman to be one of Tosya's friends from Tryokhgorka, not someone in Lyuda's circle.

The woman was with her mother, an invalid moving with difficulty and leaning on a walking stick. Despite Lyuda's affection toward her, she didn't seem to be too happy to see Lyuda. She drew back and blushed, and seemed ill at ease. Lyuda kept asking her various questions, none of which I could hear for the noise in the foyer. The young woman answered reluctantly, softly, in monosyllables, looking away. She almost literally breathed a sigh of relief when the second bell rang.

Tosya, who was standing next to me on pins and needles, was also happy to be going again.

"Please, Natasha, don't disappear," Lyuda called out to the young woman. "Come to see us sometime. You'll make Mother happy."

But the crowd had already swallowed the young woman. Everyone was now in a rush to get back to their seats. The woman's mother was hobbling along, trying to keep pace.

"Natasha was Daddy's secretary," Lyuda explained when she rejoined us. "I haven't seen her since he died."

She grew sad and shook her head as if to chase away unpleasant thoughts.

"Let's get back to our seats."

During the second act, I kept looking at Tosya. She was completely taken with the action. Paratov, the dashing merchant who seemed to think of nothing but parties, was clearly not her favorite. She had little sympathy with four-eyed Karandyshev, a clerk whom everybody treated like a piece of shit. But whenever Larisa, the heroine, stepped onto the stage, Tosya's eyes would light up with adoration.

After the curtain fell and the actors got their bouquets and finished coming out of the wings to take bows, Tosya continued clapping. She even turned down Urumov's offer to drive us home; it was as though she was afraid to spoil her emotions and wanted to walk in order to sort them out.

We walked side by side, and I knew better than to break the silence. Tosya ignored the thin, cold rain and stared straight ahead.

"You'll laugh at me, Matyushkin," she said when we reached the intersection with the Boulevard Ring. "I feel like that poor girl, Larisa. That's what I am, a poor bride."

"And what about me? Am I the fancy-pants seducer or the cowardly clerk?"

"You, Matyushkin?" Tosya gave it some thought. "You're a combination of the two."

"Neither fish nor fowl," I said.

By Nikitsky Gate we caught up with Natasha and her mother. They walked slowly, paced by the old woman. Natasha supported her tenderly from the side.

"A few more steps, Mother," she was saying. "We're almost there. Look, we only need to cross the street and the trolley stop is on the other side."

"My dear girl," sighed the older woman. "I'm good for nothing. Useless, really."

Natasha wore a shapeless winter coat trimmed with worn and faded rabbit fur. Her half-length boots were also old and shabby. The only nice thing she had on was a fashionable headscarf. An imported nylon headscarf with a pattern of large blue polka dots. I knew the headscarf very well; it had haunted me in my dreams for three months, and I stared at it as if I had seen a ghost.

NINETEEN

"Anton Pavlovich and I were in love," Natasha said.

I was beginning to like this woman. Her looks were not flashy, and she was just like her looks: plainspoken, honest, direct and completely without artifice. At the theater, she hadn't noticed me, but now, at the meat processing plant, she recognized me immediately.

"You're from the Serpukhov train," she exclaimed when I pulled a chair up to her table at the cafeteria. "You arrested that awful man. The one – the one who murdered Anton Pavlovich."

It was late and the place was almost empty. Natasha had come down after most of her colleagues had finished their lunch, in order to be alone, and had settled at the corner of a long cafeteria table with her bowl of soup and a piece of chicken.

"She always eats alone," I had been told earlier in the day by a lady at the personnel office as she pulled Natasha Polyakova's file from a fireproof safe. "She is not a gregarious member of the collective. There is nothing we haven't tried to draw her out. She's too old to be in the Young Communist League and she's shown no interest in joining the Party. Nor does she have much of a chance to pass all the checks required for party membership. She's a good girl and a solid worker, diligent and smart. The late Comrade Polishchuk, may he rest in peace, never complained about her and was happy with her work. But she's not active in social or political events. She does attend meetings and political information sessions whenever attendance is required, and she also volunteers for unpaid work on Saturdays, but without real enthusiasm. The Party secretary at the plant, Comrade Derzhavin, had a serious talk with her about her lack of political involvement, but it was no use."

Mouthing this official nonsense, she puffed up a little and her black suit jacket suddenly became too small. Her massive breasts seemed to be bursting out from beneath her silk blouse. But when she closed the file, she deflated to her normal size. Her voice also changed, becoming softer and more feminine.

"She's a shy one, Comrade Senior Lieutenant. And she's lonely. She lives with her mother, who can barely walk. Is this the way for a young woman to live? No husband, no family, and yet she's already pushing thirty. I do so hope that she finds her match one day soon. Every woman needs a little love in her life."

I had intended to park my Zundapp for the winter but changed my mind that morning. The weather was bad, but I put on my father's raincoat, which enclosed me in a huge waterproof bubble, threw its enormous hood over my head, and headed toward Taganka, to the giant Mikoyan Meat Processing Plant.

I know Moscow well, from the central district within the Boulevard Ring where I live, to the larger section enclosed by the concentric Garden Ring and on to the remote outskirts that have been added to the capital in recent expansions. However, to find the Mikoyan Meat Processing Plant you don't need any special knowledge of the city – nor a map, for that matter. All you need is a nose and a basic sense of smell.

They say that people who like sausage should never be allowed to see it being made. I would add to this that they shouldn't come anywhere near places where it is made. The smell is overpowering. It hangs heavily over the entire neighborhood, inspiring melancholy thoughts of eternal rest. But don't despair. Wait half an hour, and you'll get completely used to it. That's human nature for you. Man can get used to anything.

"Our love was unusual. It was very old-fashioned. People don't love like this any more."

Natasha turned away to gather her thoughts. Then she began her story.

She came to the Mikoyan Meat Processing Plant in the late fifties. She had a high school diploma, but she couldn't afford to go to college. She had been raised by her mother and didn't know her father. By the time she finished school, her mother, who had always been sickly, could no longer get out of bed. Natasha went to a technical school to learn typing and shorthand and took a number of short-term secretarial jobs. By the time she was hired as a third secretary in Polishchuk's secretarial pool, she had some work experience. In addition to his three secretaries, Polishchuk had a girl in the reception area of his office whose job it was to brew tea and to serve cookies and sandwiches at meetings.

There wasn't much work and the pay was good. In addition, at major holidays and before New Year's, the staff was given a bonus package of smoked meat, sausage and other delicacies that were rarely available in stores.

At first, her new boss made a very bad impression on her. He was a typical high-level bureaucrat. He was rude to his staff, but would turn into a sycophant in the presence of his superiors.

Natasha smiled sadly.

"It's strange to think that I once thought so badly of Anton Pavlovich. And so unfairly, too. My first impressions are so often wrong, I should have learned to distrust them."

The lunch break was at an end and work at the plant had resumed. Through the window of the cafeteria I saw workers dressed in once white, but now reddish-brown overcoats straining to push heavy carts. The carts were riding on narrow-gauge rails and had racks of metal hooks on which pig carcasses were strung up in purple and yellow rows. The carts were heavy, each requiring two workers to push them along. The workers aimed their carts into the gaping opening in a long, low, whitewashed structure that resembled a barn. From inside came the clang of heavy machinery and a sickening chewing sound, as though some steel monster were masticating those carcasses behind the whitewashed walls.

"Can you stay a little longer?" I asked Natasha.

"Yes, I can," she said, waving her hand as though to dismiss concern about having to go back to the office and giving me another one of her sad, shy smiles. "I have almost no work these days. We have not been given a new boss yet. Anyway, I'll probably be looking for another job."

In the first two years of working for Polishchuk, Natasha exchanged no more than a dozen words with her boss that didn't relate to work. He never seemed to notice her and he certainly never asked any personal questions.

"Actually, that was good," she added. "At other offices, the secretarial pool sometimes doubled as the boss's personal harem. It's better to be ignored by the high and mighty of this world than get too much of their attention."

Then, Natasha's mother took a turn for the worse. She had always suffered from a bad back, but now she couldn't even lie in bed without being in an excruciating pain. She couldn't sleep at night and her cries kept Natasha awake, too.

The local doctor told them that surgery was urgently required, but such complex procedures were performed by just one specialist in all of the Soviet Union, Professor Vyshegradsky at his world-renowned spinal cord clinic. The wait to see him stretched to three years or more, and even then you had to be well connected to be operated by him.

Natasha and her mother were in despair. Her mother could no longer live with constant pain and thought of suicide.

"I wasn't much better, either," Natasha admitted.

Then, one day out of the blue, they received a call from Professor Vyshegradsky's clinic. A very pleasant young woman, a nurse, told them that a spot on the doctor's schedule had unexpectedly opened and that the doctor would see Natasha's mother right away. "If comrade professor decides that she requires surgery," the nurse said, "he will operate on her the following week."

It was a miracle.

"I may sound dramatic," Natasha said, smiling, "but that phone call literally saved our lives."

After the surgery and during her mother's long rehabilitation, Natasha took many unpaid days off work to care for her. They had gone through their savings and had to borrow from friends. Natasha often had to go without food.

But then someone began sending her mother extraordinary food packages, including never-before-seen foreign tins, jars of orange juice, fresh tangerines and other exotic things. Sometimes there were bouquets of flowers and get-well notes, unsigned.

Natasha and her mother were at a loss as to who might be sending them all those nice things. They were very much alone in the world. When her mother came home from rehab and Natasha went back to work, the riddle was solved, and it had a completely unexpected answer. One day Natasha got a letter from her boss, Anton Pavlovich Polishchuk.

"I have kept it, of course, and even though I knew it by heart, I took it out and reread it a thousand times when Anton Pavlovich was killed. I've read it so often, the sheet is falling apart."

The first letter was long, running to six pages. Polishchuk began by apologizing for taking the liberty of arranging for Natasha's mother to be seen by Professor Vyshegradsky, with the help of his connections at the Moscow City Party Committee. He hadn't dared to offer his help openly for fear that Natasha, who he knew was a very private person, would turn it down.

Then he continued.

"Dear Natasha, I'm sure it has not escaped your notice that I'm unhappy in my personal live. Yes, I do have a wife and a beautiful daughter, but they don't understand me. All they care about is the material side of life: apartment, car, driver, fashionable clothes. I make a lot of money; the government and the Party reward me generously for my hard work, but money is not what I care about. I have been watching you in secret for a long time, and I feel that you are someone in whom I can confide. I'm asking you to allow me to be honest with you, to open up and to tell you what happens in the hidden depths of my soul..."

They began to correspond.

She waited for his every letter eagerly, snatching each one impulsively as it arrived and reading and re-reading it a dozen times. Then, she would sit down to write a reply right away. Polishchuk wrote infrequently, only when he had an opportunity. His letters came two or three weeks apart, and sometimes even longer.

They developed a deep feeling for one another and it continued to grow and strengthen with each letter.

It was not the kind of love that is common today, Natasha repeated. It was something very different, something straight out of a nineteenth century novel, or even from the Age of Chivalry, like Tristan and Isolde. It was a sweet, noble feeling, deeply tragic because it could never be consummated. But there was a lot of joy, too, in their love for one another. They were soulmates, they were as intimate and as honest with one another as two human beings could be. They understood each other perfectly, as though they were one.

They had their intense correspondence, but no more than that.

Early on, Polishchuk had written to her defining the limits of their relationship.

"I'm not a free man. I have a family, I'm tied to it and I will not be able to break my family ties in order to make my sweetest dream come true. I do so wish to spend the rest of my life with you. And yes, I'm disappointed in my daughter, I see her shortcomings only too well. Believe me, I don't have scales over my eyes. I know she is selfish, she loves only herself. Her interest in material possessions, in trinkets, cars, fashion magazines and harebrained young men verges on the pathological. But I still love her. I can't stop loving my own daughter. I have a responsibility to be a good father to her, and I will have to bear this cross to the end.

"And I have a wife, too. It may have been a mistake to marry her, but this mistake can no longer be corrected. I swore to be faithful to her and I must keep my word. You would not have been able to love me if I were dishonest, if I stooped so low as to break my word or deceive my wife.

"But what ultimately prevents me from being with you is not my responsibilities as a father or a husband. I do not want any common, ordinary, physical relationship between us. Physical intimacy would have brought our love down to the level of animal passion. Let's love one another, let's correspond, let's trust each other completely and preserve our intimacy. Let's reveal to one another every secret that we have. Let's not make writing letters a duty, a task, or a penance. Let's write only when our souls demand it, when we feel an irrepressible urge to write.

"And let's not give fodder for gossip. Even if it's untrue, gossip has a nasty way of smearing and destroying a relationship, even one that is as pure as ours. Let's hide our feelings for one another. Let's save it only for our letters and not debase it by contact with the harsh reality of life. You may not know it, but it is a cruel, unfeeling world, my dear Natasha."

Natasha knew all his letters by heart and even as she recited them to me, she was always moved by Polishchuk's words.

"He was able to control himself to the end," she said, and then added hastily. "Almost to the end. I could sense how difficult it was for him. He was a strong, healthy man. I felt a physical passion in his letters, a strong sensuous desire. We kept writing to each other, and in his letters he gradually began revealing the deepest secrets of his extraordinarily sweet, tender heart. He knew how to love. I too wrote to him about my love and I shared with him everything. Sometimes I wrote naive, childish things. I recounted to him my silly little-girl dreams and I was never embarrassed."

She was embarrassed now. She laughed, hiding her face in her hands and placing her elbows on the greasy oilcloth.

"It sounds silly, I know. He never once made fun of me. He took everything I wrote seriously, even my childish babbling. I have never met another man who could feel and care for another person so deeply. But he was also strong and reserved and in control of his emotions. He never so much as hinted at our secret when we saw each other at work, even when we were alone in his office. 'Sometimes I'm so desperate to hug you, to press you to my heart, or even just to take you by the hand. Just to feel your body next to mine. But I know that even a fleeting glance or a smile could spoil everything. We might be happy for a few days, a week or a month, but then we'd lose each other.' That's what he wrote and he was right a thousand times over. He was an amazing person."

Tears welled up in her eyes and began to roll down her cheeks. Natasha pulled out a handkerchief and dried them up carefully.

"Sometimes he sent me flowers, at other times nice things to wear. That headscarf was a present from him, too. He had such good taste. Everything he gave me was beautiful. He always wanted me to wear the things he gave me, even though he never acknowledged them when he saw me at the office. Only in his letters."

She paused and sat, sobbing.

"How did you end up on the train with Frezin?" I asked.

Natasha folded her tear-stained handkerchief and put it away.

"One moment," she said. "Let me get my thoughts together. I'm getting to it."

It took her a few minutes to pull herself together.

"At the end of August, when he came back to work after his summer vacation, Anton Pavlovich became very nervous and irritable. Something had clearly gone wrong. He became short-tempered with the staff. He even yelled at me several times, something he had never done before."

"You don't have any idea what it was about?"

"No. Not really. I kept writing to him, asking what was eating at him and expressing concern about his state of mind. But he completely stopped answering."

"But you must have observed something, Natasha. You knew him so well, better than even his wife and daughter. Was it a money problem? Was he having a difficult time at work? Did he get in trouble with the Ministry?"

Natasha shook her head.

"I don't know if it's relevant. He got a strange phone call in early September. It came over his direct line. Very few people knew the number, and it was usually the Ministry that called. I was sitting near his office and his door was opened a crack, so I couldn't help overhearing the conversation. Actually, there was no conversation. Anton Pavlovich threw down the receiver in disgust and swore, using nasty, low-life obscenities, which was very unusual for him. Then he muttered under his breath: 'I just don't understand it. It's beyond belief.'"

"Who was he talking to? What did he mean? Please, Natasha, give it some thought. It's very important."

Natasha shrugged.

"I've thought it over a million times. I still have no idea. It could be anyone. It could be completely irrelevant, a personal call, for instance."

"Yes, of course. What happened next?"

"In early September, on Friday, I finally got a letter from Anton. It was very urgent. When I saw the envelope, I knew it wasn't one of his usual letters and felt my heart sink. I think seeing that letter gave me some kind of premonition. The thing is that we had our special way of exchanging letters, to make sure no one discovered that Anton Pavlovich and I were in a correspondence. But that letter came the same way the very first one did. He left it in the reception area, simply lying on my chair. Like the first letter it was in a plain envelope, which wasn't addressed. I had gone out because his wife had come to see him. Whenever she came to the office, which she almost never did, they had arguments and there was a lot of screaming. Mostly she was screaming at Anton, and calling him names. It was no different that time. When she left, I came back and found his letter. Obviously, something terrible had happened and he couldn't wait to write to me. The letter was short, just a note to tell me that he had been under a lot of pressure, that it was a very difficult time for him, and that he asked me to come to his dacha the following Sunday. He also wrote that he couldn't live like this anymore and that he needed to see me urgently. He had to change something in his life. It was like a cry for help."

"Did you go?"

"Of course I did. How could I not, if my beloved was reaching out to me?"

The following week Polishchuk was out of the office and she was frantic with worry and premonitions. She kept thinking of him incessantly, day and night.

"I don't know how I got to the end of the week," she admitted.

She got a ride to Vesna from a trucker who happened to be going to Serpukhov. The trucker was very nice and took his time helping her find Anton Pavlovich's dacha.

The gate was unlocked, and so was the door of the house. Natasha was nervous, her hands shook. She had been anticipating a meeting with her lover, but now she was struck by a terrible thought. What if Anton Pavlovich's wife or daughter had come to the dacha unexpectedly and he had no way of warning her not to come?

There was no wife or daughter in the house. No sign of Polishchuk, either. Natasha called out a few times: "Anton Pavlovich, are you there?" but got no answer.

She didn't go upstairs. She would have felt uneasy wandering in a strange house. She stayed downstairs in the kitchen and waited.

Apparently, Anton Pavlovich had gone out for a walk and was due to return shortly. Polishchuk loved to take walks in the woods, especially in late fall, in the dark and in wet weather, when the dying nature exudes the sharp smell of decay consonant with emotions animating the deep recesses of his soul. Natasha had learned this from his letters.

Or else, he might have taken a stroll to the station to meet her at the train. That thought flattered her.

The house was cold. Natasha went out and got a few logs to light up the stove.

"What for?" I asked.

She blushed.

"I thought..." she said haltingly. "I wondered how we were going to make love in such a cold house."

Women are more practical than men, and also much more direct. Even romantic souls like Natasha.

However, when she brought the logs back into the house, she changed her mind and decided to make hot tea first. She put a kettle on the primus stove and brewed the tea to be ready for Polishchuk's return. It was getting cold outside and Natasha thought he would be chilled. It was getting dark, too, and Polishchuk was due to come back at any moment. While the tea was brewing, she decided to set the table and then saw a handwritten note.

"I still don't know why I read it," she noted guiltily. "I'm usually not in the habit of reading other people's mail. I know it's awful. But I realized that only when I finished reading it."

The note was from Valya Sokolova from Bookkeeping. Natasha knew her very little, or rather she knew who she was, that was all. In her opinion, Sokolova was not very intelligent and a piece of work. Reading her note made Natasha's flesh crawl with disgust. It was insolent, crude and obscene. "I don't care if you respect me after I spent a weekend here with you. I don't give a damn about it, either. I'm not going to lie to you and say how wonderful it was and how great you were in bed. It was pretty lousy, if you ask me, and certainly no fun. I'll be straight with you. I know why I didn't get a promotion last year, and now you owe it to me. Just you try and wriggle out of it this time."

"It's so vulgar," Natasha said. "She's so shameless, going into such intimate details, I still can't think of that note without shuddering. After reading it, I felt I couldn't stay there another minute. I couldn't bear to look at him. Now, of course, thinking back, I don't blame him. Whatever happened between them, it's not my business and it doesn't matter. He was a strong, healthy man and his desires were totally natural. When I got home, at first I was going to tear up all his letters, but when I took them out and started re-reading them, I couldn't stop. I cried, I was so hysterical that Mother was worried about me. In the morning the crisis passed and I made a decision: no matter what had happened between Anton Pavlovich and Sokolova, and even if he had had other women beside her, I wasn't going to care. The true Anton was in his letters to me."

I nodded.

"So, you left before he came back? You never saw him?"

"I left right away. At that moment, the thought of seeing him was unbearable."

"Did you ever go to his study?"

"I don't know which room it was."

"It's on the ground floor, straight down the hall from the kitchen."

"I knocked on several doors on the first floor. That one was locked."

"Are you sure?"

"Yes. I tried the handle. It was locked."

"Are you sure Comrade Polishchuk wasn't in his study?"

"Do you really think it's possible? Anton Pavlovich sitting quietly in a locked room while I was in his kitchen?"

I shrugged.

"Did you happen to see anyone on your way to the station?"

"Yes, I saw him, I mean Anton Pavlovich's murderer. When I left the house, I saw someone walking toward me in the street. At first I thought it was Anton returning from the station, but then it turned out to be that man, Frezin. I was in tears and I was almost running. He must have thought I was insane. Can you believe it? I was relieved that it was some other man, not my beloved. And yet, I could have stopped him and Anton would not have been killed."

"Are you sure it was Frezin? You were quite shaken when you saw him."

"I'm sure it was him."

"He was going to the Polishchuks' dacha?"

"That I don't really know. I didn't see where he went. I didn't turn around once we had passed each other. Where else would he have gone? Later, when I was waiting on the platform, he showed up there too. I mean Frezin did."

"Really? How much time had passed after you first saw him?"

"I don't know. I didn't pay attention to the time. It may have been fifteen or twenty minutes. I was wrapped up in my thoughts and I didn't see him arrive on the platform. He seemed very agitated. He kept waving his arms and trying to talk to me. I wouldn't have talked to him under any circumstances, and at that moment I wanted to be left alone. Fortunately, there were other people on the platform, three young kids. That man, Frezin, was crazy. If it weren't for those kids, I don't know what he might have done."

"I remember those three," I said.

"Then, the train arrived and we got on. He still wanted to talk to me, but you already know what happened next. When the two of you began fighting and no one was paying attention to me, I got up and moved to another car. I got off two stops before Kursk Station. It was closer to my house anyway."

TWENTY

"Bad business," Lenny admitted when I finished recounting what I had learned from Natasha. "No one ever contacted her about it? Nobody has any idea that it was Polishchuk's personal secretary that Frezin had a conversation with on the train?"

"Not to mention that she was his lover, more or less," I added.

"Quite a story. Did you have a chance to chat with the bookkeeper?"

"What do you think?"

"I'm not sure about you, Matyushkin. After all, you've been on desk duty, since Budyonny finally figured out that you lack investigative skills."

"Keep talking, Urumov."

Lenny guffawed. He always found his own jokes very funny.

"What did she tell you?" he asked, turning serious.

"Valentina Sokolova told me that Polishchuk was an old goat, that Bookkeeping was more or less his harem and that over the years he had taken every girl from her department to his dacha by turns. He was scared of his wife, and he liked to keep his escapades under wraps. Especially since the Party also frowns on this sort of thing. Still, tongues wagged, as they usually do. It was only because Natasha kept to herself that she knew nothing about it. Or maybe she had heard something here and there, but I would imagine she considers gossip to be beneath her."

"I see," said Lenny. "What else?"

"She also told me that Polishchuk was pathologically stingy and that, besides jumping in the sack with pretty bookkeepers, the only thing he cared about was how to avoid giving his next paramour an expensive gift. The girls in Bookkeeping held a contest once, comparing who had received the cheapest gift."

"Who won?" asked Urumov.

I ignored his question.

"But he did hand out promotions," I continued. "In her note to him, Sokolova demanded to be promoted to senior bookkeeper, and she was. This created all sorts of problems in Bookkeeping. They have two of the least experienced employees as senior bookkeepers, while the older ones, who have been at the plant for decades, now work for Sokolova and her friend."

"I see," Lenny sighed. "Polishchuk was a true romantic. True romantics are all the same. They whisper romantic things into a young girl's ear, but all they really care about is getting them into bed."

"He didn't seem to want to get Natasha into bed," I objected. "At least not until the last moment. He was being romantic with her without any ulterior motive. What if he did love her? You have a very negative view of humanity, Lenny."

"What did you expect, Matyushkin? Criminal Investigations is not the sort of place that instills a love of humanity. You're lucky. You're probably marking your last days here. You can allow yourself the luxury of thinking well of people."

"Well, I did ask Sokolova about Natasha, our little romantic. Not directly, of course. I asked whether Polishchuk had been known to have his fun with young women from other departments, outside of Bookkeeping. She pretty much laughed at me. 'The girls in Meat Processing,' she said, "all stink of rotten meat. It's like screwing a dead body. Some people might like it, but I don't think Polishchuk was the type.' When I asked her about his secretarial pool, she was even more dismissive. 'He likes his secretaries to be Plain Janes. They are either weird or ugly. Or both. He was extra cautious with them, because he was scared of his wife.'"

"She's not half as dumb as Natasha thinks she is, that Sokolova," Urumov said. "Were I not so much in love with Lyuda, I'd ask you for her phone number."

"I don't have it," I said curtly. "It's all pretty interesting, but the most interesting thing she told me was this. She visited Polishchuk's dacha and she wrote that note, but that happened more than a year ago. She was there in July of last year. Do you think the note had been sitting on the table for fourteen months without anyone finding it?"

Lenny choked. When his coughing fit passed, he shook his head.

"That *is* the most interesting thing, you're right."

We were deep in thought and Lenny was drumming his fingers on the surface of his desk.

"Know what I'm thinking?" he said. "It turns out that you were wrong when you argued with Nakazov about Frezin. Whatever happened there, it is now clear that Frezin went to Polishchuk's dacha. I think you should apologize to Nakazov. You now have a reason to, and it's a perfect way for you to get back into his good graces and to be reinstated here."

"I've already thought of that," I said.

A long time ago, during the brief moment I was in charge of the Polishchuk murder investigation, Nakazov had given me the number of his direct line. I dialed it the following morning.

TWENTY-ONE

Nakazov picked up the call after the first ring. His "Hello?" conveyed a barely concealed irritation, as though he had been disturbed in the middle of an extremely important task. But when he recognized me his voice grew warmer, switching to the same good-natured, patronizing tone he always affected when talking to me. That is, whenever he wasn't yelling or threatening.

"Oh, my. I didn't expect to hear from you, Senior Lieutenant. But I'm glad you called. Honestly. I wish you'd stop that 'Yes, sir, Comrade Colonel' already. Do me a very large personal favor, as they say in Odessa."

"I'll do my best, Comrade Colonel, sir."

The warmth in his voice made me think for a moment that there was no bad blood between us. That there had been a funeral for Uncle Nikolai and no ugly scene at the old church.

"How's that foxcub of yours?" he asked. "Is he still rooting for Torpedo?"

"Yes, sir. He's a stubborn kid. There is nothing anyone can do to change his mind."

"Unfortunately, young men have become stubborn these days. They've got a mind of their own and pay no attention to us."

I wasn't quite sure whether he meant us adults in general or just the ones at the Committee for State Security.

"Am I correct in thinking that he's your wife's son," Nakazov asked, and by the way he put the question I knew instantly that it had all happened – the funeral and the ugly scene – and that none of it had been forgotten. There was bad blood between us. And then some.

"Yes, sir, Comrade Colonel," I replied. "You're correct."

"There we go again with the 'Comrade Colonel, sir,'" Nakazov said. "As you wish, Comrade Senior Lieutenant. But if I were you, I mean if she were my wife, I would have taught her a lesson on how to behave in the presence of other men. They need it every now and then, women do, you take my word for it. Otherwise they forget who wears the pants in the family and start ordering their men around She's got no business telling you what to do, and certainly not talking like she did to other men. You've gotta explain this to her. It's for her own good. Because if you don't do it, someone else might, one of these days."

Nakazov was dreaming if he really thought that anyone could teach Tosya "a lesson," as he put it. Especially if he thought that lesson ought involve any physical means of persuasion. I wouldn't want to tangle with Tosya.

"I'll try, sir," I said. "I'll do my best. She can be difficult sometimes, you know."

"If you don't think you're man enough for the job, don't hesitate to ask for help. I can send you a couple of good helpers."

I laughed as though it was really funny, but I got the message.

"Anyway, what are you calling about, Senior Lieutenant?" Nakazov asked, suddenly getting down to business. "Not to discuss your family life, I assume."

"Actually, I'm calling to apologize, Comrade Colonel."

I paused. There was silence on the line. Nakazov waited for me to continue.

"I mean, I'm trying, " I stumbled. "I have to apologize to you for saying all those things about you framing Daniel Frezin. I mean, for accusing you of hanging the Polishchuk murder on him."

On the other end of the line, Nakazov weighed my words for a few seconds.

"How come you've seen the light all of a sudden?" he asked cautiously.

"Because, sir," I began and stopped. I had run through this conversation in my head several times, but I still couldn't get it out properly. I took a deep breath and tried again.

"I found out that Daniel Frezin was in fact at the Polishchuks' dacha on the day of the murder. I was wrong when I testified at the trial and I was wrong saying all those things to you at the funeral."

I felt like an underclassman at the principal's office.

"Really, Senior Lieutenant?" Nakazov said, the note of irony returning into his voice. "How did you manage to find this out?"

"I had a conversation with Polishchuk's secretary, Natasha Polyakova. I should also fill you in on this conversation, because you were supervising the investigation into Polishchuk's murder. She was also at the Polishchuks' dacha that day. I will write an official report on the new information I received from Comrade Polyakova, and I will send it to you. You can expect—"

"Know what, Senior Lieutenant?" Nakazov interrupted. "Forget the official report. It'll take too long. Why don't you come see me at Lubyanka at 1300 hours sharp? Want me to send a car for you? What? Under your own steam? Very well then. Don't be late. We'll have lunch in our cafeteria. There'll be a security pass waiting for you at the main entrance."

At the security desk, a middle-aged guard wearing the single star of a State Security major demanded to see my passport, copied the information into a thick log on the desk and, instead of returning my passport to me, locked it in his desk drawer. He then wrote out a pass, validated it with a purple stamp that included the date and time, but didn't hand it to me. Instead, he picked up the handset of one of several phones lined up in front of him and mouthed something unintelligible into it. Having listened to the reply, he turned around and barked into an open door, "Stolypin!"

He then pressed a button under his desk, the lock clicked and I stepped through a set of metal doors to be met by a young junior lieutenant in a peaked cap with a pistol holster attached to his belt. He held my pass as he walked me through the twisting corridor, where we had to stop at two or three other checkpoints. The junior lieutenant showed them my pass and we were allowed to proceed.

Eventually, we took the elevator to the fifth floor, where my guard told me to wait. He waited with me in silence.

The tags on the junior lieutenant's lapels and the trimming of his peaked cap were green, the color worn by border guards. The border guard service was part of the Committee for State Security and it made sense to have their troops guarding headquarters. The KGB was a state within a state and its borders had to be protected.

When Nakazov came out, the guard saluted, handed him my pass, saluted again and was gone.

"Let's have a bite to eat," Nakazov said to me by way of a greeting.

The cafeteria in Lubyanka was a cut above the one at the meat processing plant. Or maybe two or three cuts. It was, to be sure, far superior to any cafeteria or fancy restaurant that I had ever been to.

"Grab a tray, Senior Lieutenant," Nakazov told me. "It's self-service."

I grabbed a tray and loaded it with a bowl of borshch, its iceberg of sour cream floating in the purple thickness, a plate piled high with Siberian *pelmeni*, with butter and vinegar on the side, and a dish of herring with boiled potatoes, swimming in golden sunflower oil and garnished with chopped scallions.

"Don't be shy," Nakazov said, egging me on. "Here, take a cucumber and tomato salad. It's dressed with Italian olive oil. Have you ever had fresh cucumbers and tomatoes in late November? I seriously doubt it. This is why you shouldn't be rooting for Torpedo, my friend. Dinamo all the way."

I tried to explain to him that I had been a Dinamo fan since the age of three, when my father, a Moscow city patrolman, took me to my first game, but Nakazov wasn't listening. He picked up a bowl of salad and placed it on my tray, nearly spilling the borshch on my pants.

"Eat, Senior Lieutenant, do yourself a favor. I'll bet you won't get another chance to taste fresh vegetables until next spring."

He turned and added softly, as an aside, "If ever."

The cafeteria was located in the old section of the building that had been built before the Revolution by the All-Russia Insurance Company and was subsequently adapted by State Security for its own needs. The room was vast, with ornate molding on its high ceiling and heavy draperies over its windows. We took a table by a window that faced Dzerzhinsky Square, where an endless line of traffic circled the bronze statue of the founder of the KGB. It stood with its back to the organization he had founded, looking instead at the Kremlin, as though keeping watch over it. For some reason, one of Dzerzhinsky's bronze hands was thrust deep into the pocket of his long, shabby military overcoat.

Nakazov had taken a bowl of fish stew and a pork cutlet. He swallowed a few spoonfuls of the stew and pushed it aside, then cubed the cutlet with surgical precision and ate it swiftly. After chasing it all down with a glass of homemade cranberry drink, he lit a cigarette.

"Don't mind me, Senior Lieutenant. Keep eating. No rush. When you're done, try one of these."

He pushed a pack of cigarettes toward me. The brand name was written in foreign letters: Pall Mall. Despite his advice to eat slowly, I wolfed down my *pelmeni*, leaving the cucumber and tomato salad untouched. I pulled out my own cigarettes, the Red Presnyas, and lit one up with a match, ignoring the massive gold lighter Nakazov had pushed toward me.

He caught a whiff of a Presnya's acrid smoke, grimaced and waited for me to talk.

"To make a long story short, sir, Comrade Colonel—"

Nakazov grimaced again.

"Polyakova Natalia Nikolayevna, born 1933. Unmarried, not a party member, shares a room with her ailing mother. Employed as the director's secretary at the Mikoyan Meat Processing Plant. She has been there for about three years. Approximately two years ago, she and Comrade Polishchuk began a relationship..."

"A workplace romance?" Nakazov asked quickly.

"Yes, a workplace romance, but an epistolary one, if I may use this term, Comrade Colonel."

"Do you mean they had an affair," Nakazov guffawed, "by correspondence? I don't know what you're talking about. I can understand when some eggheads play chess by mail, but sex by mail? How is that possible?"

"It was an intimate relationship, sir, an erotic friendship perhaps, but it was not a physical relationship. They were not physically involved."

"How about that? I didn't think it was possible in this day and age."

"Polyakova says that they shared their secrets and wrote of their love for one another. But they never had any kind of sexual relationship. They never even met outside the office."

"Who would've thought," Nakazov said, grinning lewdly. "Is it possible that my good friend Anton was a secret romantic? I was convinced that I knew him better than anyone. And I'm no amateur in judging people's character. And yet, I never would've guessed that he was involved in this kind of thing. You never know what goes on inside people's heads. Go ahead. What other surprises do you have in store for me?"

He rubbed his hands together.

"Polyakova says that approximately a week before his death Polishchuk became nervous and irritable. She doesn't know what was bothering him, but early in the week of the murder she received a letter, inviting her to visit him at his dacha on Sunday – actually, on the day of the murder. When Polyakova got to the dacha, she didn't find Polishchuk. Apparently he had gone out. While she waited for him, she noticed a letter addressed to him and written by another employee of the meat processing plant. When she read the letter, she realized that

Polishchuk had been involved in a relationship with that woman and that she had also visited him at the dacha some time before. Polyakova immediately left the dacha and on her way to the station she ran into Frezin, who was apparently on his way to meet with Polishchuk."

"Did she recognize him? Had she known him before?"

"No, sir, it was the first time she saw him, but then Frezin came to the station and accosted her on the platform."

Nakazov shook his head. He tossed his cigarette into his glass, where it fizzled in the remnants of the cranberry drink.

"An interesting bit of information," he said, lighting another of his long Pall Malls. "What a double life he led, my late friend."

He went on smoking. I began thinking about those three kids who had bummed a cigarette from me on the train that same night. I wondered whether they couldn't be the same trio whom Natasha had seen on the Vesna platform, and why they were there. They didn't look like Moscow Region hoodlums but big city delinquents on a trip out of town. The way they behaved, I was sure they were up to no good.

"I'll tell you what, Senior Lieutenant," Nakazov said. "It's not right for this story to get to Anton's widow and daughter. I'm connected to them by the ties of a close friendship. Comrade Polishchuk and I were old friends. Now that he's gone, I must take his place. Not literally, mind you, but I must be there to protect them. It was my duty to avenge Comrade Polishchuk's murder, and I did. Not like some barbarian, but acting strictly within the law. Even you have admitted that Comrade Polishchuk's murderer has been brought to justice."

"Yes, Comrade Colonel. I'm sorry I ever doubted it."

Nakazov nodded a few times, acknowledging my apology.

"I also have to do everything in my power to protect Comrade Polishchuk's reputation and to shield his wife and daughter from malicious gossip. I hope you understand what I'm trying to tell you."

"Yes, sir. Of course I do."

"This information must not go any further than this room. If circumstances change and we have to reopen this case, it's a different matter. By all means, we'll make use of what you have found out. But for now, Senior Lieutenant, I'm asking you to do me a personal favor. It's also an order, of course, from your superior officer and from an officer of the Committee for State Security."

"Yes, sir, Comrade Colonel."

Nakazov lit another cigarette.

The State Security building was a massive anthill that occupied an entire side of Dzerzhinsky Square. Hundreds if not thousands of people worked there, but the cafeteria was almost empty. There were very few people taking advantage of the assortment of excellent food, the rare delicacies and out-of-season fruit and vegetables this state within a state offered its card-carrying citizens.

"I do wonder sometimes," Nakazov said, exhaling the smoke to the ceiling. "I'm getting a little tired of this job. Naturally, I'm a born and bred Chekist, a loyal officer of the Committee for State Security, and I'm devoted to our cause heart and soul, but I too wonder sometimes whether we're on the right track. Occasionally, I fear we might go too far."

He looked out the window at the bony bronze back of Comrade Dzerzhinsky and at the distant watchtowers of the Kremlin, their red stars looming through the fog.

"Sometimes I just want to drop it all and go to my place on the Oka," he continued. "To live like a hermit, to see no one, to turn off the radio and to read no newspapers. There is no better fishing than at my place on the river."

I nodded, but I was hardly listening. I was still thinking about those three punks.

"But let's not indulge in futile dreaming," Nakazov said. "You're a good man and a top-notch detective. I'm impressed with your work. It's remarkable that you were able to find Anton's secretary and to get all this information about their relationship. Besides, my sources tell me that you have been taken off all investigations. How did you come across her, by the way? Were you freelancing, despite your commanding officer's orders?"

"No, sir," I replied, still thinking how I could get a lead on those kids. "It happened by accident. I saw her on the train when I arrested Frezin."

"Did you already know she was Anton's secretary?"

"No, of course I didn't. Lyuda Polishchuk pointed her out to me at the theater."

Nakazov sat up abruptly.

"I see," he said, his voice suddenly changing and his eyes narrowing. "Lyuda Polishchuk, you say? This is getting more and more interesting. Do you know Lyuda Polishchuk so well that you go to the theater with her? I know that she loves the theater."

I knew I had made a mistake.

"No, of course not, Comrade Colonel." I tried to laugh it off, but my laughter sounded a little hollow. "We have some mutual friends. We're casual acquaintances, no more than that."

"I see," Nakazov said, still eyeing me suspiciously. "No big deal, if it's just mutual friends and casual acquaintances. Because if you go around introducing people to your wife who bosses you around, it wouldn't do to take young good-looking students to the theater at the same time. Especially if those students happen to be the daughters of murder victims. It would have been a good way to get kicked out of Criminal Investigations altogether, or worse."

TWENTY-TWO

My expectations of being reinstated had been based on less than solid ground, even though I apologized to Nakazov and submitted a full report on my investigation – well, a nearly full report, not counting glossing over or concealing such unimportant details as my interview with Pavlov, the discovery of the emerald peapod, the existence of three young delinquents who had prevented Frezin from getting rid of Natasha, the only witness who could tie him to the Polishchuks' dacha, and several conversations with Lyuda Polishchuk. Tosya, frank as ever, dashed my remaining hopes.

"I told you, Matyushkin, don't stick your nose into other people's business. And don't stick your neck out, either. If you were taken off all cases and made to sit at your desk with nothing to do, it means that you crossed someone with the power to make trouble. Had you been doing your job, it wouldn't have happened."

"I *was* doing my job," I objected indignantly. "I had to investigate a crime. That's what I do, Tosya. I investigate crimes. Is it really my fault that, no matter where I turn, I bump into Nakazov?"

"Don't talk nonsense, Matyushkin. There is no way your job description included crossing your superiors."

"Why not?"

Tosya shook her head, exasperated.

"Think it over, Matyushkin. Your boss gives you a job. You have to do it as best you can. Nothing spectacular, mind you, just according to your abilities. If you're good at it, you get praised. You get all kinds of raises, bonuses and promotions. If you fail, you get yelled and screamed at. Right?"

"Well, that's obvious enough. What are you driving at?"

"The system is the same everywhere. At the Tryokhgorka Textile Factory, at the meat processing plant, at Criminal Investigations and even in the Kremlin."

"So what? Get to the point, Tosya."

"I am getting to the point. Be patient. What boss will ever give you a job that includes digging up dirt on him or on other bosses? Think about it."

That was Tosya's philosophy of life, a philosophy that she'd picked up at the orphanage. There, they divided the world up along very strict lines: "us" and "them." "Us" were kids at the orphanage. The rest were "them," and "them" were the enemy. "Them" colluded with one another, and especially with their teachers against "us," the kids.

It was a ridiculous philosophy.

"You've gotta understand, Tosya," I started to explain, "that there are different bosses. Nakazov is not my boss. I have my own boss, actually an entire chain of command, who have nothing to do with Nakazov and his chain of command. As to Polishchuk, he was another kind of boss, who had nothing to do with the other two."

Tosya stared at me as though I had a screw loose. "Do you really think so?"

I nodded several times, emphatically.

"Remember, Matyushkin, silly boy, all bosses are in league with one another. If, for example, one boss offers to you an alliance against another boss, don't even think of taking him up on his offer. The bosses will ultimately make peace with each other and turn on you, and you'll end up taking the blame for everything. Every boss is your mortal enemy, by definition."

That's what Tosya really thought. And yet, her own boss, head bookkeeper at the Tryokhgorka, was an extremely nice person. She liked Tosya and respected her for her hard work and professionalism. She even, I'm sure, considered Tosya a friend, or at least not a mortal enemy. I wonder what she would have said, had she heard Tosya.

"To make a long story short," Tosya concluded, "don't get your hopes up. You're not going to get your job back. If anything, things will get even worse for you."

I recounted this conversation to Lenny. He grinned and winked at me.

"She's right. You haven't got your job back."

"It's early," I said. "Let's wait and see."

I wanted to ask Budyonny what I was supposed to do now that my desk was all neat and orderly, and its drawers were as empty as a beggar's pantry, but Della barred me from getting in to see him.

"You're to wait, Senior Lieutenant," she told me coldly. "Comrade Lieutenant Colonel will let you know when he has a job for you."

Della might not be a boss, but as a secretary to the boss she was not one of "us" either. Secretaries and bosses are thick as thieves. Worse. Secretaries are like attack dogs that the bosses employ against regular folks.

Goddamn it. I'd been infected by Tosya's philosophy and had started dividing people into "us" and "them." Even though I didn't grow up in an orphanage.

But Lenny was even worse. It turned out that he fully shared Tosya's philosophy.

"Know what else she got right?" he said when I came back from my attempt to see Budyonny. "There is a hidden connection between all bosses. Just think of the Polishchuk case. The question on which this case hinges is whether the late boss of the meat processing plant and our friend the boss at State Security were allies or adversaries."

Lenny pulled out the sheet of paper on which he had drawn circles and squares a few days before, stared at it for a while to refresh his memory and began to add more circles and squares and to connect them with arrows.

"Suppose Pavlov was right and Rokotov was made to play the role of the leader of the currency gang strictly for the purposes of the show trial, while the real leaders were allowed to escape. Suppose that Frezin knew exactly who those real leaders were."

Lenny printed Frezin's name in one of the squares and drew an arrow pointing up, to another square that he marked with a letter X.

"Aha," I said sarcastically. "Mr. X. The Big Boss. *Capo dei tutti capi.*"

Lenny ignored me.

"Frezin violated the conditions of his release and took a substantial risk coming to see Polishchuk. But even before that, about the time Frezin got out, Polishchuk had started to get jittery. The conclusion is clear. Our Mr. X is none other than Anton Polishchuk. He lived high on the hog, had a nice apartment, a large dacha, a personal driver, a bunch of mistresses. He bought plenty of expensive jewelry for his daughter. All along he had a perfect cover. He was a high-level manager, he had a very good salary. Unlike the average Joe, no one would suspect him just because he lived well."

"That's the glitch in your logic, Lenny," I said. "He was already making a lot of money. Why would he want to take a huge risk by getting involved with hard currency dealing if he had all the money he wanted?"

"Pavel, you've never had money, so you don't understand those who do. Money is a special thing. No matter how much you have, you can never have enough. Everybody wants more. Those who have no money want more, and those who have plenty want even more. It's what makes the world tick, and it's the main reason why you and I have jobs. To think that a suspect couldn't have stolen the money because he already had more than enough is a rookie error for a sleuth."

"I see," I said.

Lenny always loved to lecture and explain everything.

"And one more thing. You don't know when Polishchuk began to dabble in hard currencies and jewelry, and what helped him build a successful career. Maybe there is a cause-and-effect relationship here, and, in fact, his career was an outgrowth of his currency dealing. What do you think, if you gave your boss's wife a really nice piece of jewelry for her birthday, would it not make your boss like you just a little bit more?"

I had to admit that he was right.

"I get it, Lenny," I said. "Go on."

"If we accept Polishchuk as the leader of the gang, we have the following question," Lenny continued, drawing a circle and marking it with an N. "How does Colonel Nakazov fit in?"

Lenny wrinkled his forehead. His dark face grew tense and his features somehow came into sharper relief.

"I've been asking Lyuda about Nakazov," he said. "He and Polishchuk go way back. I mean way back. She was very young when he first appeared. Even back then, he immediately started to show an unhealthy interest in her. He kept telling her how beautiful she was and patting her on the head while asking her about school and her piano lessons. She thought he was creepy, and she was afraid of him. Back then, more than ten years ago, Nakazov was already a major. He had risen fast through the ranks and he was expected to make a brilliant career at State Security. He was assigned to a group investigating the most important crimes against the state, such as terrorism, sabotage and espionage. When Stalin died, the group was disbanded and its commanding officers were expelled from State Security. Those whose ranks were major or below were luckier; they merely saw their career advancement frozen. Yet after Stalin died Polishchuk began his rapid climb up the bureaucratic ladder. At the time, the family lived in Izhevsk, a small town and the capital of the Udmurt Autonomous Republic, but he was soon transferred to Moscow."

Lenny's information was interesting, but it explained little and even made matters more complicated.

"If Nakazov had known Polishchuk for so long," I said, "then it's very likely that they worked together and that Nakazov was providing protection for Polishchuk and his currency dealers. It stands to reason, because dealers have to be protected. Otherwise the KGB would have rounded them up long ago, way before Khrushchev got wind of black market activities around Moscow hotels. Nakazov, after he fell from grace at State Security, was put in charge of hard currency hotels, recruiting spies for State Security among prostitutes and taxi drivers. When Khrushchev demanded that black marketeers be arrested, Nakazov would have been at the right place at the right time. But it also would have given Nakazov an opportunity to warn Polishchuk and to make sure that Polishchuk would not also be caught in the net. Nakazov then framed Rokotov and declared that all street trading had been rooted out, and got himself promoted straight to colonel, skipping a rank."

"It all fits," Urumov said, drawing a line from the square marked X to the circle marked N.

"Nakazov's own lifestyle is pretty rich, too," I said. "He has a dacha on the Oka, a military jeep not sold to civilians, which he uses for off-road driving when he goes hunting or fishing. He has a very expensive gold watch, a fancy foreign lighter, also solid gold, and he has given Lyuda Polishchuk expensive jewelry as presents."

Lenny nodded.

"Very well. Let's say that at first Nakazov wanted to frame Frezin as the leader of the gang and get him executed. This would kill two birds with one stone, because Frezin was the only guy in the gang who knew not only that there was a Mr. X whose name was not mentioned at the trial, but also, what was even more dangerous, who that Mr. X was. Suppose Frezin told Nakazov that he knew that Polishchuk was the true brains behind the currency operation. Nakazov already knew that. It was not the kind of information for which he would get Frezin off the hook."

"Right," I said. "But the danger then was that Frezin could finger Polishchuk to other investigators, not just Nakazov. It was a high-profile case, party brass and State Security generals were hanging around and looking over Nakazov's shoulder. Someone else could have questioned Frezin. It would have been even more likely if Frezin had been playing the role of the leader and was one of the main culprits, which must be why Nakazov decided to replace Frezin with another suspect. Nakazov pushed Frezin to the sidelines, so that his name was hardly mentioned at the trial, and so that he would get a very short sentence. The condition of the deal must have been that Frezin keep silent about Polishchuk."

Lenny put aside his sheet and we began to develop this line of reasoning, shouting and interrupting one another. Everything was starting to fit together nicely.

"Frezin gets out and begins to blackmail Polishchuk. That's the downside of putting Frezin away for such a short time, something that Polishchuk and Nakazov had not considered."

"Or else, they had considered it but didn't have enough time to prevent his release. Or else, Nakazov might have already had a plan for dealing with Frezin, but Frezin beat him to it by showing up unexpectedly at Polishchuk's dacha."

"Yes, by the way—" Lenny said.

"Yes, by the way," I interrupted. "I need to find those kids."

"What kids?"

"The ones who were on the Vesna platform when Frezin came back from Polishchuk's dacha and accosted Natasha. Natasha says that because they were there, Frezin had no chance to get rid of her as a witness."

Lenny shrugged, lost in his own thoughts.

"This is how I see it," I went on. "Frezin gets to the house, where Polishchuk had just returned from a walk. Or maybe Polishchuk was hiding in the house while Natasha was there, hoping that she would find Sokolova's note on the table and leave. Frezin shows up, they talk, they argue, and Frezin kills him. Then he remembers that he was seen by a young woman walking toward the station. If he could catch her there, he still had a chance to eliminate a witness. She's still there, but so are the other three. He gets on the train and tries to chat her up."

Urumov listened, then asked, "What if it was the other way around? What if it wasn't the punks who prevented Frezin from getting rid of Natasha, but it was Natasha who prevented them from getting rid Frezin?"

I hadn't thought of it and it was clearly a very likely scenario.

"In other words, you think that they might have been hired by Nakazov and Polishchuk to kill Frezin when he went to see Polishchuk?"

Lenny nodded.

"On the other hand," he mused. "Why the hell would he invite Natasha to see him if he expected Frezin?"

"I don't know. The meeting with Frezin could have been fixed later, and Polishchuk had no way of warning Natasha not to come. That's why he would leave that note for her to find, while staying quietly in the house, waiting for her to leave before Frezin arrived."

"There's one more thing," Lenny said slowly. "I also need to check something about the Polishchuk murder."

"What?"

"Remember the day you came back from testifying at Frezin's trial? You passed by the smoking area and I asked you how it had gone. Grigoriev from Forensics was also there smoking. When you left, he said, 'The problem with this country is not that we don't have smart people, but that nobody bothers to listen to us.' It's the same thing he always says, so I wasn't paying much attention. But he went on, mumbling something about Frezin taking the rap for a murder he, Grigoriev, knew he had no way of committing. I think I should ask him what he meant."

"You should," I agreed.

TWENTY-THREE

Tosya came to my room late and stayed overnight. When she fell asleep at last, I groped in the dark to find my watch on the night table. The fading phosphorescence of my old Omega showed nearly five o'clock.

The city was dark, there was a dusting of snow on the ground and cold radiated through the double-paned window. Tosya's hair scattered across the pillows and my shoulder smelled sweetly of her and of her room in the next building. The smell tickled my nostrils, making me feel safe and comfortable under the pile of wool blankets.

I curled up close to Tosya and fell asleep.

And I had a nasty dream. I saw the late Polishchuk. I knew it was Polishchuk even though he looked nothing like the portrait in his apartment or the snapshots I had seen in his file. Still, the man in my dream had a slightly porky face, which was how I knew it was Polishchuk.

He sat next to his daughter on an enormous divan covered with a Persian rug. The room was richly appointed, like the living room of a nineteenth century merchant, but in my dream it was Nakazov's office. Suddenly, Polishchuk turned toward Lyuda and started to kiss her. He stuck one hand brazenly under her shirt and began fondling her breasts. Lyuda, instead of pushing him away, responded greedily to his kisses, and her long, pliable fingers, with their large gold rings and blood-red nail polish, began undoing his trousers. As she did so, she stared right at me.

Watching them was both nauseating and exciting, but I also knew that Nakazov might return to his office at any moment. I felt a cold sweat break out on my forehead and I shouted to Lyuda, "Go home! Please, go home!"

She swatted at me with her hand as though I were a fly, and continued kissing her father. Her lips left a glistening trail of saliva around his mouth.

Tosya has an uncanny ability to wake up without an alarm. I felt her slip out from under the blankets and then the bedside lamp turned on, waking me up. Squinting at the yellow semicircle on the wall, I blinked several times, trying to chase away the disgusting dream.

"I'm sorry I woke you, Matyushkin," Tosya said wincing in the cold and collecting pieces of her clothing from the floor. "I wouldn't have found my things in the dark. Go back to sleep. It's not even seven."

I had no reason to get up early. At work, no one seemed to care what time I came in – or, for that matter, whether I showed up at all. I had no desire to go out and battle the cold, not to mention the rush-hour crowd storming the tram at Kirov's Gate. But I did suddenly have a desire for Tosya. Repulsive though they were, Lyuda's forbidden kisses had aroused me in a queer way that I didn't want to spend too much time thinking about.

I stuck my hands out.

"Come. Let's have another quick one."

"Matyushkin, you'll make me late for work," Tosya said reproachfully, as she climbed back into bed, joining me under the blankets in the warmth of our thick nighttime smells.

I was half-asleep again when Tosya turned off the light, tucked me in to make sure I stayed warm, and tiptoed out.

The next time I awoke was when the telephone started ringing outside my room.

It was late in the morning and the feeble November sun shone into my room through dusty windowpanes. The rings echoed insistently down the hall.

I wrapped the blanket around my shoulders, found my slippers under the bed and hurried to answer the phone.

"Hello."

Raisa, Lenny's wife, was very much unlike other women, especially other police detectives' wives. She hated gossip, and she never criticized other people behind their backs or complained about her husband. She wasn't considered conventionally good-looking and it may have been for that reason that she had a kind of fierce pride. Raisa was determined to ignore Lenny's numerous extramarital affairs. She felt it was beneath her dignity to admit that they even existed.

It may sound strange, but Lenny was faithful to her in his own weird way. Maybe faithful is the wrong word. Maybe the right word is loyal. When Lenny left them and went to live at his brother's place, I expected her to call me. I thought she would ask me to talk to him as his best friend and I dreaded getting that call. In her situation, any other woman would've called. But she never did.

Some time passed and I called her myself. I cautiously asked her how she was doing and inquired after the girls. I wanted to make sure she didn't feel abandoned. The problem with Lenny was that he had so few male friends. Whatever free time he had from work and family was taken up by philandering. Except for me, all his real friends were women, his former lovers. He had this strange ability to stay on good terms with them. Naturally, none of them would have been expected to call Raisa.

When I called her, she and I chatted about her work and about the girls' school, but we never mentioned Lenny. I sensed that she was glad to hear from me.

Now, she was calling me. She was trying to tell me something, but I was still half asleep and that may have been why I couldn't make out what she was going on about. Or perhaps we had a bad connection and, in any case, she sounded like she was choking. To make matters worse, at that very moment the lock on the front door clicked and my neighbor, Yevdokia Filippovna, her hands weighted down with shopping bags, struggled in through the front door. I was standing by the phone, trying to keep my blanket from sliding to the floor and revealing my complete nudity.

This was why I couldn't figure out what Raisa was trying to tell me.

"I've told him a thousand times," she sobbed into the receiver. "He's not a race car driver. Why the hell was he so goddamn reckless?"

For Tosya and me, Lenny's funeral was the second in a month.

This time, Tosya brought Sevka along, pulling him out of school late in the morning.

There was a sizeable crowd of mourners. Lenny's parents were surrounded by relatives from Odessa and from somewhere outside Poltava. His high-security physicist brother left his top-secret lab for the occasion, then left immediately after the funeral, heading for the gate of the cemetery, where a driver in a grey Volga was waiting for him. Our entire department came, of course, headed by Budyonny. Della wore a long black dress. Her eyes were red and had dark circles. Several other women were there, as well, some of whom I knew.

Budyonny provided two buses, both loaded with wreaths, as well as his beat-up official Pobeda for Lenny's parents and Raisa.

Raisa was holding up well. She didn't cry, but her dark eyes, even darker in the expanse of her deathly pale face, were fixed somewhere in the distance. She held her two small girls by the hand. They were seven and eight, pale, skinny and huddled together like wet seagull chicks.

Lenny's resting place was the crematorium at the New Don Cemetery. Unlike Uncle Nikolai, Lenny was part of the new government, according to Aunt Ksenia's toothless neighbor. Besides, he was Jewish and, in her view, his religion prescribed that he burn in hell. Actually, Jewish or not, Lenny rarely, if ever, thought of such complicated matters as God or religion. He used to claim that they made his head spin.

The core of the crematorium was a cheerless concrete structure with a smokestack belching black smoke. Large flakes of ash flew skyward, settling in the yellow grass alongside the headstones, on the fresh dusting of snow, on gaudy paper flowers and wreaths. The air held the sour smell of disaster.

We huddled together next to our buses and the pile of wreaths that someone had unloaded ahead of time. We were waiting for Lenny's turn in the oven. Two groups of mourners were ahead of us. They too stood in tight groups in the traffic circle, two black blots against the white snow. They too stomped their feet to keep warm, blowing on frozen fingers.

While we waited, Lenny's youngest daughter, Raisa, pulled her hand from her mother's grasp and ran off. She crossed the asphalt path and stopped in front of a stone relief on the wall. It showed a grieving family standing over a body that lay beneath the earth. The body was naked but for a loincloth, and its face was averted. The widow was shown with a young boy nestled into her shoulder. The boy was reaching up toward forbidden fruit hanging off a nearby tree. The message, as far as I could make it out, was that the man is dead and this is how the young come to know the bitter truth about life and death.

The art was appropriate for the crematorium, perhaps, but not for a seven year-old girl who had just lost her father.

Raisa called out to her. Her voice was harsh in the tense silence. The girl ignored her and continued to stare wide-eyed at the sculpture.

I crossed the path on a run and approached her, placing my hand upon her shoulder. She started, turned, recognized me, then asked, "Is Daddy going to be like this?"

I didn't answer and just gave her frail shoulder a gentle squeeze.

This piece of sculpture could be looked at in different ways. I was like that little boy. I may not look like him, but I too was seeking knowledge. In fact, I'd been seeking it for a long time. It now seemed just within my grasp. Yet, because I was getting too close to the truth, people had started dying. I was sure that Lenny – my friend, partner and the father of this little girl – had not simply had an accident. So

I had a choice. I could continue to seek knowledge, which meant that others might die as a result, or I could let go of the forbidden fruit.

The boy in the stone relief was holding on to his fruit as if his life depended on it. His tiny fingers seemed fused to it.

Lenny's family had a plot at the New Don Cemetery, to the left of the main building. It was marked by a large polished slab of granite, under which lay Lenny's cousin on his father's side and the cousin's wife. Or rather, whatever was left of them after cremation. Lenny's ashes were to be released to the family in two weeks.

After the ceremony, we went to Lenny's future resting place and stood over it in silence. Eventually, Raisa would have a photograph of him transferred onto a ceramic oval and get his name chiseled into the granite in gold letters.

Nearby yawned a huge, open yellow grave, dusted with snow. It had been dug in preparation for the burial of the crew of a passenger airliner that had recently crashed at Vnukovo Airport. There had been no information about the disaster in the press, since such things were never reported, but at Criminal Investigations everyone knew about it, and the city was swirling with rumors and gory, largely inaccurate details and figures. A small crowd of onlookers stood at the edge of the abyss, staring down with a mixture of horror and morbid curiosity.

Lyuda Polishchuk came to the cemetery late and stood behind a row of tombstones, waiting for us to leave. She was holding a bunch of carnations, which were out of season and extremely expensive. I turned around when we passed the main building, in time to see her approach Lenny's future grave and lay – or rather toss – the red blooms onto it. They scattered over the stone like drops of blood.

Raisa and the girls, along with Lenny's parents, left in the Pobeda, our colleagues from Criminal Investigations were shuttled back to the office on the two buses. The three of us, Tosya, Sevka and I, headed for the exit. We were going to take the tram to Raisa's apartment. Lyuda caught up with us on the main path and walked alongside us in silence.

"A sad business," I said.

There was nothing else to be said. Tosya turned to Lyuda and squeezed her hand. Lyuda stopped, turned her face away from us and burst into tears. Tosya hugged her. They stood there, motionless, Tosya also now weeping.

Slightly ahead of us, I saw the familiar, tall and slightly hunched figure of Sasha Grigoriev from Forensics. He had not gone back with the others and was slowly making his way toward the exit.

"Sevka, go stand there with your Mom," I said quickly and hurried after Grigoriev.

I caught up with him just outside the gate. We stopped and lit up our cigarettes.

"A sad business," Grigoriev said. "Are you going to Raisa's?"

I nodded.

We were silent for about a minute. Grigoriev had a habit of talking slowly, often pausing and pondering his next sentence. He also liked to draw deeply on his cigarette and expel perfectly rounded rings of smoke.

But my patience was running out.

"Listen, Grigoriev," I said. "Lenny told me just before he died that you had doubts about Daniel Frezin being responsible for Polishchuk's murder."

"Of course I did," said Grigoriev. "Huge doubts, as a matter of fact. What of it?"

By then, Tosya and Lyuda had also exited the cemetery. Tosya had her hand around Lyuda's shoulders. They were followed by a sad-looking Sevka, who was also on the brink of tears.

"Tell me about your doubts, Grigoriev," I said. "And be quick, please."

"Well," Grigoriev replied slowly, eyeing Tosya and Lyuda who were coming toward us. "My doubts are of the following nature: Frezin couldn't have killed that guy."

"Why not?" I asked him, lowering my voice.

"Because he's a man."

"Who's a man?"

"Frezin. The fellow executed for Polishchuk's murder. He was a man."

"Of course he was a man. What of it? Be a little more specific, Grigoriev, please."

"You see? We don't deny that he was a man. Which means that he didn't kill Polishchuk."

"Who did, then?"

"I have no idea. That's your job to find out. What I do know is that whoever killed him was a woman."

Grigoriev had been speaking a little faster. My sense of urgency may have been starting to rub off on him. But he still wasn't fast enough for me.

"How do you know that?"

"It's my job to know those kinds of things, Pavel. I have a degree in forensics, remember? At first I thought Polishchuk had been strangled slowly, like he was being tortured, because if a reasonably strong man had wanted to strangle him with a fishing line he would have cut his head off. But the line on Polishchuk's neck wasn't even that deep. It might have been consistent with a version that he was strangled slowly or tortured."

"That's possible," I said, glancing at Tosya and trying to signal to her not to come any closer. "Frezin might have tortured him or tried to scare him. He could have misjudged his own strength."

Tosya understood my frantic signals and stopped. Lyuda also stopped, put her head on Tosya's shoulder and began to cry again. Sevka, standing next to them, sniffled.

"You may be right," Grigoriev agreed readily. "But Polishchuk was still strangled by a woman."

"What makes you so sure?"

"He was strangled by someone who wasn't very strong. Whoever strangled him snuck up behind him unexpectedly, yet even so, he struggled for a minute or two. What I saw at the scene of the crime were signs of struggle, not torture. A brief struggle, yes, because the line cut into his throat, but it was fairly intense all the same."

Grigoriev fell silent and I thought he was done.

"I'm pretty sure," he added, "that a fishing line was chosen precisely because it was a woman who was strangling the victim. A silk cord wouldn't do, a strong man could overpower a woman attempting to strangle him with it. But a fishing line not only cuts the flow of oxygen to the lungs, but stops blood from flowing to the brain, and it also cuts through the tissue, being so thin and strong.

"I see," I said. "Thanks, Grigoriev. You've been great help."

"Besides," added Grigoriev after I had already started toward Tosya and Lyuda, "the body had a small scratch near the left ear made by a long, sharp fingernail. It was probably inflicted when the murderer threw the line over Polishchuk's head. Fingernail scratches are very distinctive."

I suddenly remembered what Frezin had said when he was being interrogated by my Moscow Region colleagues, two days after I arrested him. He had shouted something about me pinning a crime on him.

It didn't make a lot of sense at the time, but now it did.

"Why didn't you say anything?" I asked Grigoriev.

"To whom? I put it all in a report. First they told me that you were in charge of the case, and then suddenly you weren't. There was plenty of other work, so I put my report aside. At one point, I tried telling this to Lenny, but he was too busy with more important matters."

Grigoriev tossed away his cigarette, glanced meaningfully at Lyuda and grinned.

TWENTY-FOUR

Natasha Polyakova's fingernails were short and raw, practically cutting into the flesh of her fingers. I had noticed this during our first meeting. Nervous people with low self-esteem tend to bite their fingernails. I had no idea whether or not she had already been biting her nails when she and Frezin were on the Serpukhov train together. But I do know that people who bite their fingernails often have nails with sharp and uneven edges.

A few days later, Budyonny unexpectedly called me into his office to explain what had happened to Lenny. Apparently, it was the first frosty morning of the season and there was black ice on the road. Plus, the black ice was covered by a thin layer of snow that had fallen overnight. Lenny should have long since parked his Moskvich for the winter. Instead, he decided to go for a drive. The devil only knows where he was going so early in the morning.

Budyonny's accent was so strong I could barely make out what he was saying.

"Do you know where he was going?" he asked. "He was all the way out at New Cheremushki. His wife has no idea why."

I knew very well that he had been headed to Sukharevka, to pick up Lyuda and drive her to school. It had become something of a daily routine for him. But Budyonny didn't know that Lenny was living at his brother's apartment at New Cheremushki. I shrugged and shook my head.

"Bad business," he concluded. "So tragic, so unexpected. He was a pretty good driver, wasn't he? So completely out of the blue."

Budyonny droned on, explaining to me how the brakes on Lenny's Moskvich locked and he skidded while executing a sharp turn, but I had stopped listening. I was watching Budyonny's face and especially his eyes, which doggedly avoided mine.

Yes, it had all been very unexpected, and Lenny, of all people, was so full of life. It was hard to imagine him dead. He liked to poke fun at Budyonny and to imitate his accent behind his back.

And yet, when four days ago Raisa called me and was sobbing into the receiver, I examined my reaction to what I had just heard and realized that I wasn't at all surprised. It was as though I had known that it was going to happen. Maybe not when or how, but I had known that one day soon I would hear that Lenny was dead. I hadn't been aware of it, but that knowledge had been stuck in my heart like a splinter. I had learned to live with it before I understood what it was.

I felt guilty now whenever I thought of Lenny. I also thought of Lyuda, how she had stood motionless at the gate of the New Don cemetery, letting herself be hugged by Tosya and weeping. And before that, how she had spilled those expensive carnations, so fresh and so red, onto the granite of Lenny's grave. Was she also feeling guilty?

Budyonny droned on. In the courtyard of our building a man dressed in dirty overalls was filling a wheelbarrow with coal from a snow-covered pile.

"Bad business," Budyonny repeated.

I turned and our eyes met. I knew immediately that he didn't believe a word of what he had been saying.

"I need to check on something, Ashot Modestovich," I said. "I'll need access to the archives."

Budyonny didn't reply, and I continued.

"I want to find three young men who might know something about the Polishchuk murder."

He probably should have asked me what the Polishchuk murder had to do with Lenny's death, but he didn't.

"Sure," he said, his accent becoming even thicker. "Whatever you have to do."

TWENTY-FIVE

It was a Sunday afternoon, and I knew that my three subjects would be together. And they were, hanging out in the courtyard of their apartment building, towards the back, where other tenants didn't normally venture. I had been on their tail for a few days and by now knew their routine. They were pretty regular in their habits, for a trio of street punks.

I trailed two of them to their trade school near Paveletsk train station, keeping a safe distance to ensure they didn't spot me. If they did, they might recognize me, and I didn't want that to happen.

The third member of the gang – their apparent leader, the one who had been wearing the windbreaker with a hole in it on the Serpukhov train – no longer attended trade school, having been expelled a few months before. He was now awaiting his draft summons for military service, which was why the local police didn't bother him.

Back in September I had gotten a good look at him. So even when I saw his smeared, out-of-focus mug shot in the Petrovka archive, I had no difficulty recognizing him. And once I had him, finding the other two took less than a minute. They were neighbors and lived across the river on Yakimanka Street.

In fact, all three had police records full of bookings for various petty offenses, hooliganism and bullying going back to before they had entered their teens. On a recent occasion, there had been a more serious charge of assault and robbery, but the case was dropped. The mother of the ringleader, it turned out, was a secretary at the district party committee. His file contained a letter from her boss describing him as a decent kid from good, proletarian stock, as well as an anonymous report from a neighbor informing the authorities that he was a troublemaker who drank, used obscenities in public, and terrorized his neighbors. But the recommendation by a party boss trumped a report by a police informer.

It was a rough neighborhood, despite being a stone's throw from the Kremlin. It had once been settled by merchants and artisans and numerous churches remained from that era, though the municipal government was gradually tearing them down or converting them into offices, factories and storage facilities. There were also several large tenements – never particularly luxurious, spacious or comfortable – now broken into overcrowded communal apartments. The apartments were a rich breeding ground for both bedbugs and juvenile delinquents, the latter growing up to become thugs.

The courtyard was dominated by a gloomy six-story building constructed, like those around it, of sooty red brick and pock-marked by small, square, closely-spaced windows. In a desperate attempt at middle-class decency, some of the windows had lace curtains and houseplants on windowsills, with the odd birdcage hanging just in sight. The roof sported a forest of TV aerials that pierced the dismal, low-hanging clouds.

To get to where my three targets were spending their Sunday afternoon, I walked through a dark, low archway, crossed a squalid little garden and a kids' playground, rounded a wooden shed, and climbed through a hole in the fence. The asphalt courtyard was neglected and unkempt. A door behind a chimney led to the basement boiler room. The chimney, built taller than the building, was made of the same sooty red brick. Long ago, someone had painted a hopscotch grid near the boiler room door, but over time the green oil paint had faded and flaked off. Further back, next to the blind wall of another building, ancient poplar trees, now leafless, loomed over the ruins of a gazebo.

Despite the relatively early hour, it had already begun to get dark. I stopped, took a deep breath of the cold, rotten Moscow air, and looked around.

The punks' three silhouettes were visible inside the gazebo as three identical, hunched-over shapes, resting their feet on the bench. They wore cheap earflap hats pushed high up on top of their heads – the prevailing fashion among street hoodlums. On the benches surrounding them sat five or six school kids, none older than eleven or twelve. They were passing around a lit cigarette.

The moment I emerged from behind the building, everyone in the gazebo turned and watched. I crossed the cracked asphalt slowly and deliberately and stopped in front of the gazebo, lighting my own cigarette. That gave the three punks time to take a good look at me.

"Go take a walk," I told the little ones.

They didn't move.

"Why should they?" asked one of the older punks.

"Because I said so," I replied and turned to the kids again. "Go ahead, scram."

"Scram yourself," one of them piped up, emboldened by the support of their older comrades.

"Yeah, get lost, mister," added another.

Physical means of persuasion should not, as a rule, be used, especially with minors, but there are exceptions. I was about to snatch up one of the little ones by the scruff of his neck – I had my sights on the cheeky one who was talking back – and toss him out of the gazebo to encourage the others, when one of the three older punks suddenly intervened.

"Didn't you hear what he told you?" he said to the kids. "Get lost."

They looked at him, uncertain what to do. His two buddies turned to him in surprise. He had a pimply, round face and bleached eyelashes.

He jerked his head in my direction.

"Remember the cop on the Serpukhov train? It's him."

The ringleader nodded and turned to the underage smokers.

"Get moving."

Reluctantly, they got up and made their way to the exit. I didn't wait for them to get out of the earshot. I was becoming impatient.

"Is this the way to do serious business?" I asked, faking anger. "You were told to do a job."

At first, I had considered waylaying each of them in turn and putting their feet to the fire individually. One of the three would have cracked. But that would have been labor-intensive and would have taken more time than I had at my disposal. I was bluffing now, but I thought I knew what they were going to tell me. I was looking for confirmation, not new information.

"What's the matter?" I continued when they didn't reply. "Lost the ability to speak?"

"It's not our fault," the ringleader said. "Everything went wrong from the beginning. We did everything just as we were told. We waited on the platform the whole time. The trains came and went and no one got off."

It was a direct hit and an encouraging start. I had guessed correctly. I could just coast from here.

"Then, when we figured out what was going on, it was too late," he continued. "We didn't screw up. We got bad instructions."

"It was the same on the train," the pimply one added. "You were there and you saw what happened. How were we supposed to know that we were all on the same team? We didn't think we had an opportunity, and it was your fault."

"Right. It was because of you," the ringleader added.

"Don't you talk to me like that," I warned. "I did what I had to do because you screwed up."

"We didn't screw up, I told you," he said. "We had no idea what to do when he showed up on the platform. When it didn't work out the first time, we thought we'd get another chance on the train. And then you showed up."

"In other words, you got money for nothing."

"What are you talking about? We didn't get any money."

Their surprise was too strong and too instant to be anything but genuine.

"You didn't?"

"Are you nuts, mister? Who was supposed to pay us?"

"The same guy who ordered the hit."

"How were we going to find him?"

That called for a time out.

"Right," I said. "Let's start from the beginning. Were you paid an advance?"

They looked at each other.

"No, we weren't."

"When were you supposed to get paid?"

"After the job was done."

"And how were you going to find him?"

The ringleader shrugged.

"How would I know? It doesn't matter now, does it? Since nobody showed up, we figured, the deal's off."

"I get it," I said sarcastically. "You were hired to do a job, but you have no idea by whom. Is that right?"

"Should he have given us his address?"

"Don't you get smart with me," I said. "He was supposed to pay you an advance. Did he?"

The ringleader shook his head. I looked at the other two.

"Really?" I asked. "He didn't?"

They were now acting respectful with me, the way young punks like them are supposed to act with those who have standing in the criminal hierarchy. That was a good sign.

"Interesting," I continued. "I'll have to get to the bottom of this. How much were you supposed to get for the whole thing?"

"A thousand," the ringleader said.

"Actually, you were supposed to get twice as much. A thousand up front and a thousand after you do the job. You'll have to pay back the first thousand since you failed. Do you have the money?"

They stared.

"We were never paid anything," said the pimply punk.

"Someone's not telling the truth," I said. "I suspect it's you three."

I waited.

"We didn't get any money," the ringleader said.

"And what if you just pocketed the cash without telling your two friends? How would I know?"

"I didn't. I swear."

"I won't take your word for it. Who was the guy who approached you? Medium height, leather coat, salt and pepper hair? Looks like a cop? Or maybe State Security?"

"What?"

I had a fifty-fifty chance of missing, and miss I did. Clearly, it wasn't Nakazov. The ringleader suddenly became suspicious.

"A fat older guy then? Pig-faced?" I persisted.

The three of them exchanged a look and didn't reply. Apparently, it was another miss, and that was pretty strange. I didn't think Nakazov and Polishchuk would outsource such a sensitive job to a third person. On the other hand...

An ominous silence settled over the gazebo. I had to continue talking and not let them see that I had hit a dead end. At least, given the amount of money they had been promised, one thousand rubles, which would have been a huge sum to these punks, I was sure I was on the right track with my next question.

"What was your job exactly? Were you to wait for him to show up at Vesna, knife him and throw him on the tracks?"

I stopped talking and the silence around me deepened.

"I don't know what your game is, but I'm sure you've made a mistake," the ringleader said slowly. "We had no job to do. We know no one who looks like a pig or a cop. Why don't you go on a fishing expedition somewhere else, copper?"

The respect with which they treated me before was now gone and his manner had turned menacing. I didn't give a damn about that, but

I must confess I was dismayed. All my theories had crumbled before my very eyes.

"Sure," I shrugged, trying to hide my disappointment. "I'm going to leave now, but the way it looks is that you were paid a thousand rubles as an advance on a job you didn't do and are giving me the runaround. There's no way you'll get to keep the money, and whether you want to talk to me or wait until other people come to sort the situation out is up to you. Let me just warn you that the longer it takes, the worse it is for you."

"I told you already, we didn't get any money. The big guy said we'll be paid later, a thousand rubles, not two thousand. It wasn't our fault. If anything, it was his. He told us she was going to get off the train at two in the afternoon at the latest, but there were three trains, just as he said, and she wasn't on any of them."

"She?"

As I stood there with my mouth open, the pimply punk broke in, talking nervously and rapidly, "It's true. And later, too. When she showed up on the platform, we couldn't do anything. That guy popped up out of the blue and started talking to her on the platform. We were supposed to make it look like she jumped, but we couldn't even come near her with him talking to her. It was even worse on the train. You were there. And then, after you took him off the train, she was nowhere to be found. Where were we supposed to look for her?"

That didn't fit at all. "She" must have been Natasha Polyakova, that much was clear. But why on earth would Nakazov and Polishchuk want her killed? It was completely mystifying, but I didn't have time to ponder it for too long. I had to salvage the situation with my three punks.

"Let's quit pulling each other's leg," I said. "The guy who approached you was huge, about twenty-five, dark curly hair. Is that right?"

The ringleader nodded. Third time was a charm. He was less apprehensive now.

"Then, let's start from the beginning," I said. "Tell me how it all happened. The huge guy shows up one day and—"

The pimply punk jumped in immediately.

"It wasn't like that. He checked us out before." He turned to his companions. "Remember, I spotted him at the movie theater?"

"Right," the ringleader picked up the narrative. "We were working the Udarnik movie theater and that was when we saw him for the first time. He was easy to spot, him being so huge. Then he came over here, the same way you did, and said that if we wanted to quit wasting our time picking pockets and cutting purses, he could help us make some real dough. He showed us a picture of a woman. Not very pretty, about thirty years old. Our job was to take a suburban train to Vesna station, on the Kursk line, and hang around until we saw her get off the train. There were three trains stopping at Vesna between noon and two, and she was going to be on one of them. We would let her go and wait for her to come back. She wouldn't be long, he told us. She'd be alone and she'd be pretty upset. The station should be deserted at that hour and it would already be dark. With express trains passing by all the time, our job was to sneak up behind her and push her off the edge of the platform."

"And you?"

The ringleader shrugged, "It didn't seem like a difficult job, and we wouldn't be caught if it was done right."

"And a thousand rubles is a lot of dough," his pimply friend added.

I sneered. "Especially since you were supposed to get twice as much."

"Well, we didn't know," said the ringleader.

"And he didn't offer you any advance, is that right?"

All three of them shook their heads energetically.

"You should've asked him for an advance," I insisted. "Next time you'll know. What happened at the station?"

"We got to the station early, like he told us. Except there were three trains one after the other, and she wasn't on any of them, as I said. But we kept waiting."

"How long?" I asked.

"I don't know. There were two more trains from the city after the first three. It must have been two more hours."

"Why did you wait so long?"

"Why not? We had gone all the way out to the boonies and there was nothing else to do."

"Go on."

"Then that other guy, the one you took off the train, showed up. But he came from the other direction. He gave us a nasty look and started walking toward the dacha settlement. By then we'd already decided to head back. We had no smokes left, we were cold and hungry and we figured that something must have gone wrong in the big guy's plan. And that was when the woman finally showed up. Except she didn't get off any train. She just came from the dacha settlement. What the big guy had been right about was that she was really upset. She was crying and pretty much talking to herself. We must have missed her somehow on the platform, but I don't think so. She seemed completely crazy and there was no way we wouldn't have noticed her if we'd seen her. Maybe she came earlier or got there some other way."

"She did," I said.

"It would've been easy to get rid of her. It was dark, and there was no one around, and she stood right by the edge of the platform. Had there been an express or a freight at that moment, we would have done it right away. The weird thing was that she almost looked like she was going to jump under the train on her own, without our help. But then, almost immediately after she arrived, that guy came back to the station, almost running. He went right over to her and they began talking."

"What were they talking about?" I asked.

"They weren't, really. He was touched in the head, like her. She wouldn't answer him, like she was trying to get away from him. At first I thought he had also been sent there by the big guy. Like he had hired us to get rid of her, and sent him too, as insurance. But he wasn't trying to push her or anything, and soon it became clear that they were just a couple of nuts meeting on the platform. While we stood there wondering what to do, a train pulled up and they both got on. We did too. There was no point hanging out there any longer."

"What happened when I took the guy off the train?" I asked. "I gave you another opportunity, didn't I?"

"She was gone. When you got off, we looked for her all over the train."

"You're a fine bunch," I said, becoming really angry now. "No idea who ordered the hit, no idea how to find your client, no idea who the victim was, nothing. Some creep promises you a thousand rubles, and you're ready to kill for it. It's a good way to end up in jail, or worse. You know, getting executed is not a lot of fun, just ask the guy I took off the train back in September. Then again, I don't think he's in any position to answer."

"Don't you come 'round here trying to lecture," the third punk suddenly piped in. "We've heard enough."

He had been silent the entire time. He was bigger than the other two and probably slower on the uptake.

"I don't give a damn how you end up," I said. "The sooner you get yourself behind bars, the better it is for everyone."

"You're a cop then," said the ringleader.

"I am, actually."

I had no more time to waste on them.

"See you around." I said. "Think next time before you act."

I turned and walked away.

"Hey," they called out.

I stopped and pivoted around.

"What, you gonna jump me?" I asked. "I think you had that idea back in September, on the Serpukhov train, but wisely changed your mind."

They stayed where they were.

I was riding up in the elevator in my building when it finally hit me. I slapped myself on the forehead, it was so simple. All this time, the solution had been staring me straight in the face.

"Damn," I yelled as the elevator stopped on my fourth floor. "Who would have thought it was all so simple?!"

I was in no hurry to get out. I had an idea. It was absurd, but it required thinking through And if it was correct...

That was when I missed Lenny most. Him and his brain. But his brain had been smeared all over the cracked windshield of his Moskvich, and whatever had not spilled out of his cracked skull as the Moskvich was flipping down the icy New Cheremushki road was now floating around Moscow as weightless molecules of black ash.

My God. It was so damn simple.

TWENTY-SIX

Budyonny is too cautious. There is never any point in explaining anything to him. The less he knows, the more chance there is to get his go-ahead. If you overload him with details and explanations, he'll have more reasons to worry about ways it could go wrong.

That's why all I told him was that I wanted to question a suspect and to have the victim's family present. Nor did I bother mentioning what case I was working on, who the victim was, or whom I was going to invite to be present. Budyonny gave me a doomed look, like that of a man condemned to be hanged in the morning, and then gave me the green light.

But then again, the kind of show I was about to put on, there was no way in hell any boss, not just Budyonny, would have allowed it.

Since Lenny's death he had grown older, his back had somehow become more hunched, and he seemed to have lost weight. He had even neglected to fire Della, so that with each passing day she was setting a new endurance record in the anteroom of his office.

"I'm sorry, Ashot Modestovich," I said to myself as I left his office. "I'm afraid I'll be shaking you from your apathy. Please try to forgive me, even though you probably won't."

Oh, well. Budyonny never trusted me and always expected me to pull off some strange trick or other, but I'm sure nothing could have prepared him to what he was about to see.

I picked up Natasha Polyakova and brought her to Petrovka. We drove in Victor's Pobeda, riding in silence. I sent a colleague, Sasha Slantsev, to deliver the summons to the Polishchuks, both the mother and daughter. Slantsev was a remarkably well-mannered young man with an unruly head of blond curls that made him look more like a poetry student at the Gorky Literary Institute than a policeman. But beneath his soft exterior there was a serious, diligent and highly reliable cop. He was tactful and polite, but could also be tough when the situation required.

"What do you mean, we have to appear at Criminal Investigations headquarters?" Anna Panteleyevna demanded, working herself into a rage. "When are you going to leave us alone? Don't make the mistake of thinking that, because we no longer have Anton Pavlovich, Lyuda and I have no one to protect us. Make sure to write your name and rank on a piece of paper and leave it on my desk."

"They have quite a collection of writing implements," Slantsev subsequently told me. "At least a dozen gold fountain pens. Her desk looks like the fancy stationery counter at GUM."

Slantsev liked pens and pencils so much that he really ought to have attended the Literary Institute.

I found Hera at the meat processing plant. He was still working there, even though, as Natasha told me, the new director, who had been transferred from a large machine tool factory in the Urals, no longer used him as a driver. The new director had brought along his own driver from Nizhny Tagil. And not only the driver but five young secretaries, as well. She and Hera, Natasha said, giving me her trademark shy smile, were both underemployed. Besides, the new director had been given a brand new personal car, leaving Hera with Polishchuk's old Volga.

"How's life, Heracles?" I said in greeting when the receptionist at the plant finally put me through to the garage and the gruff person who answered the phone located Hera.

"Eh? What?" Hera asked cautiously. "Who is this?"

"Don't you recognize me? Senior Lieutenant Matyushkin, Criminal Investigations."

"What do you want?"

"I want to give you an opportunity to relive the old days. Would you like to bring Anna Panteleyevna and Lyudmila Antonovna to Petrovka?"

"What for?"

"That's none of your business. They've received a summons. You know where we're located? When you get here, leave the car somewhere for a couple of hours and come on up with them. Make sure you're on time."

"Do I have to?" he grumbled.

"If you don't want to come on your own accord, I can of course send you an official summons."

Despite my warning, they came half an hour late. I waited at the security desk downstairs. From my vantage point, I was able to see Hera drive the Volga to our building, find an empty space in a row of official vehicles, and park it under a sign forbidding anyone not connected to Criminal Investigations from parking there, not even bothering to glance at it.

I had not seen Lyuda since the day of Lenny's funeral. She looked at me and blushed when I greeted her in a cold, official manner, giving no sign of recognition. Anna Panteleyevna probably recognized me, she had seen me at least three times before, but if she did, she kept it to herself. As a result, my only official acquaintance in the group was Hera. We shook hands.

They were issued security passes and we headed upstairs.

I had left Natasha in a room adjacent to Budyonny's office, which we use for interrogations and police lineups. The room is small and narrow and can be observed through a one-way mirror from an even smaller, airless room on the side. The mirror is old and of poor quality, so that while you interrogate a suspect you can see the silhouettes of those who are observing you alongside your own reflection. The effect is disconcerting. But it was the best we could do.

When I left Polyakova, I closed the door and turned the key twice in the keyhole. Then I went into the adjacent room as quietly as I could. The moment I left, she got up and silently, quickly walked to the door. She tried the handle, to check whether I indeed had locked her in, then shrugged and returned to her seat.

Then I stepped into Budyonny's office.

"I asked the Polishchuks to come," I said. "Both the widow and the daughter. They'll be observing an interrogation. Perhaps you should be there with them. During the interrogation, please keep an eye on Gnatyuk. He's Polishchuk's former driver. He's a pretty big guy, rather intimidating, but he's harmless. Just watch him while I ask Polyakova questions."

"Should I maybe call in an armed guard?" Budyonny asked sarcastically. He had been a champion wrestler in his younger days and the idea that he couldn't handle someone, even a much bigger man, was preposterous to him.

"It would be a good idea," I said gravely.

Budyonny looked up from his desk suspiciously. He had already started to regret giving me permission for whatever it was I was about to do. And, indeed, I had quite a surprise in store for him.

All four of us – mother and daughter Polishchuk, Hera and I – left the elevator and were greeted by Budyonny, who had stood there awaiting their arrival. As soon as I introduced them to each other, Anna Panteleyevna announced that she was not going to take it lying down and that she would certainly lodge a complaint.

"Anton Pavlovich's murder has been solved and the person responsible has been brought to justice. My daughter and I dearly wish to be left alone. Senior Lieutenant Matyushkin," she pointed at me, "was taken off Anton Pavlovich's murder case by State Security Colonel Nakazov because he was getting nowhere with his inquiries. I think that this low comedy is the result of Comrade Matyushkin's personal grievances. Why do we have to be punished because of this man's ambitions?"

"Oh, please." Budyonny was all smiles. "Please. No. What grievances? Madam Polishchuk, it's a mere formality, nothing more than that. Am I right, Comrade Senior Lieutenant? The person responsible for the murder of your husband confessed, he was tried and got his just reward, so to speak. The case is closed."

"Do not think that we have lost all of our influential friends," Anna Panteleyevna continued, disregarding his attempts to calm her down. "Do not make this mistake, I'm warning you."

That was not the kind of mistake Budyonny was likely to make. His fear, readily visible on his face, was rather the opposite: that all of their influential friends were still supporting them. He continued to smile broadly, like a hospitable innkeeper, but his eyes were cold and watchful. He was not taking her threats lightly. While shaking Anna Panteleyevna's hand, he managed to give me a quick look over her shoulder, which contained a not-so-veiled threat if anything went wrong.

Little did he know.

"Of course, Anna Panteleyevna," I interrupted her. "We'll definitely keep your concerns in mind. Please follow me. I would ask you to remain silent. These walls are not as soundproof as they should be. You'll hear everything that goes on in the interrogation room, but we can also hear you."

Della had set the little table on the side, placing upon it a modest choice of refreshments: a bottle of mineral water, four cups of weak office tea, and a bowl of cookies and chocolate candy. Anna Panteleyevna cast an eye over the spread and gave it a dismissive shrug. I don't know what she had expected to find at Criminal Investigations headquarters.

Through the one-way mirror we could see Natasha still sitting in her chair, hands folded in her lap and head turned toward the window. She didn't seem to have moved since I left her and didn't react now to the sounds coming from the adjoining room.

My interrogation took longer than I expected. To begin with, I asked Natasha to repeat the history of her relationship with Polishchuk, starting with her mother's illness and the anonymous assistance they received from him. She went on to describe how they started to write to one another, and continued to exchange love letters while maintaining a chaste relationship in real life – or rather, avoiding a real-life relationship altogether. She concluded by recounting how she received an unexpected request from him to come to Vesna on that fateful Sunday.

Natasha was shy and hesitant at first, knowing no doubt that she was being heard and even guessing, perhaps, by whom. She spoke slowly, in a drawn-out monotone, but she was still providing a detailed description without any inconsistencies compared to her previous version.

There was a deep silence behind the one-way mirror.

Natasha, meanwhile, reached the point in her story where she found the letter on the kitchen table at the Polishchuks' dacha. I interrupted her.

"Please tell us what they letter said, as accurately as you can remember."

Natasha hesitated, giving me a questioning look. I nodded, encouraging her to go ahead.

"You seem to have memorized it by heart," I said when she finished.

"Naturally," she replied softly. "No woman could forget such a thing."

"Was the letter signed?"

"No, it was not."

"But you knew who had written it.

"I recognized the handwriting. It had been written by Valentina Sokolova from Bookkeeping."

"Did you know about their relationship?"

"No, I did not. I hate gossip and never pay any attention to what people say."

Natasha went on to describe how she left the dacha, ran into Frezin on the way to the station and saw Frezin again on the platform some time later.

"In your estimation, how long was it from when you left the Polishchuks' house until when Frezin appeared at the station?"

"I have no idea, which is not surprising given my emotional state. It could have been ten minutes, twenty minutes or longer."

"When you left the dacha, were you certain that there was no one else in the house?"

"Yes, I'm sure of it. There couldn't have been anyone else."

"You were at the house for a long time, forty-five minutes to an hour. Did you go out for any reason?"

"I did. I went out several times. I went to get firewood because the house was very cold. I also went out because I thought that Anton Pavlovich might have been working in the garden or walking around the property."

"Did you go into the other rooms? Did you look into the dead man's study, for instance?"

She shook her head.

"You didn't even try?"

"I didn't know where his study was. I knocked on one of the doors on the first floor and turned the handle. It was locked."

"Can you be certain that Comrade Polishchuk wasn't elsewhere in the house while you were there?"

"If he was, he would have had to be very quiet."

"Did Frezin behave strangely when he came to the station?"

"He tried to talk to me. I thought he was drunk or something. But I wasn't myself. I needed to be alone and I didn't want to see or talk to anyone. I had no idea then that he had just killed Anton Pavlovich."

Natasha had been talking for a long time and, to my surprise, no sound came from behind the mirror. I glanced at the four silhouettes showing through my own foggy reflection. The two female figures kept still while the two male ones, Hera's enormous form and a smaller one with a head of hair resembling Zeus's crown, fidgeted nervously in their chairs.

"Why do you think Frezin came up to you on the platform?"

"I have no idea. He could have realized that I had seen him go into Anton Pavlovich's dacha. I was a witness."

"An interesting version," I said. "Frezin goes into the house, strangles Polishchuk and then remembers that he had been seen. It fits very well, and I commend you for it. The only glitch is that we know for a fact that Polishchuk was killed by a woman. Or at least by someone who was not strong enough to strangle him quickly, even with a sharp fishing line."

Natasha stared at me.

"Listen to me, Comrade Polyakova," I continued, switching to a cold, official tone. "Polishchuk was attacked unexpectedly, from behind. He was sitting at his desk, with his back to the door. Most likely, the attacker was someone whom he knew and, moreover, he knew that person was in the house and might come into his study. There was a mark on his neck that was left by a sharp fingernail. Whoever murdered him accidentally scratched him while slipping the line over his head."

Polyakova had her eyes fixed on me and they were now filled with horror. She said nothing, waiting for me to go on.

"Let's consider a different scenario," I said. "You arrive at the dacha to meet your lover. He's there, he is happy to see you and everything is as you two had planned. Then, when he goes to get something in his study, you spot a letter on the table that is addressed to him and written by another woman. You read it and discover that your lover had been visited by another employee of the meat processing plant. The letter was written more than a year before, but you don't know that. Perhaps you don't even care. Blinded by jealousy, you rush into Polishchuk's study and strangle him with whatever you can lay your hands on, which happens to be a fishing line. Your momentary madness is perfectly consistent with your personality, your romantic bent and the highly emotional relationship you had with your boss. When your rage passes and you realize what you have done, your only thought is to get away from the house. Lucky for you, you see another man going into the Polishchuks' dacha right after you leave it, and that allows you to cover your tracks by throwing suspicion on him. Even more luckily, he turns out to be recently released convict."

I paused to catch my breath and to check on the four silhouettes behind the glass.

"Tell me, Comrade Polyakova," I continued. "Do you always bite your fingernails or did you only start doing it recently?"

I had been concerned that Natasha would become hysterical, but nervous tension and outrage showed themselves in a strange, eerie, otherworldly calm.

"No," she said tersely. "I've been biting my nails as far back as I can remember. Nothing of what you have just said could have happened."

"Why not?"

"Because it didn't happen. I told you the truth."

Because there had been no explosion from behind the mirror when I expected it, I no longer expected it to come. But I was mistaken.

"Let's talk some more about the time you were alone in the house. Did you hear any strange noises?"

A noise – very loud one – suddenly came from behind the mirror.

It was a kind of suppressed moan and the screech of a chair on the linoleum as it was pushed forcefully backward. Then came several loud cries and the mumbling of my boss.

"Why?" Anna Panteleyevna shouted. "Why on earth do we have to listen to this nonsense? Why do we have to tolerate this malicious slander of Anton Pavlovich, the defamation of his character?"

I hurried into the next room. Anna Panteleyevna was in hysterics. Her face had turned red and her lips were twisted unnaturally. Saliva flew out of her mouth with every word. When she caught sight of me, she jumped up and began to pound on the refreshments table with both fists, sending the cookies and candies flying onto the floor. They were followed by a loud thud as the mineral water bottle tumbled down after them.

"You should be ashamed of yourself," she wailed, ignoring me and addressing Budyonny. "How dare you allow your employees to make such insinuations about my late husband? In the presence of his poor daughter, as well! My dear Anton, my sweetheart. They have soiled your memory with lies. You are no longer here to answer them. You can't punch them in the face. They know that and they think that they can do so with impunity."

"Why?" Budyonny bellowed after her, rising to his feet and, coming close to me, leaning on me with his considerable bulk. "Why did you stage this farce? Are you trying to get me fired? After thirty years of service? Is this what you're trying to do?"

"Very well then," I said, adopting a conciliatory tone. "You may be right and Polyakova has absolutely nothing to do with Comrade Polishchuk's murder. She may even be lying about her alleged relationship with your late husband, Anna Panteleyevna."

Anna Panteleyevna let out a howl. I continued.

"I'm a detective, and every detective worth his title always has a number of hypotheses for any case. Here's a different one, see if you like it better. Have you ever heard the name Urumov, Anna Panteleyevna? Lenny Urumov? He used to work here, before he died in a car crash."

While her mother was convulsing in hysterics, Lyuda sat motionless facing the wall. Now, hearing me say Lenny's name, she turned abruptly to face me.

"As I mentioned," I said, "your husband was murdered by a woman. Our forensics expert initially informed Lenny Urumov of his conclusion and Lenny started to work on it. It so happened that Lyudmila Antonovna had first hand knowledge of what Lenny was working on and exactly how far he was getting. Let's not discuss why or how. Let's just say that she did. When it became clear to her that Lenny was getting somewhere in his investigation, he suddenly died. A tragic accident. His car brakes failed. Now this seems like a strange coincidence, especially since it is Lyudmila Antonovna who was in a perfect position to doctor the brakes on Lenny's Moskvich. The Moskvich was parked in front of a New Cheremushki apartment building where Lenny was temporarily staying. That too was known to Lyudmila Antonovna. Do you know automobiles, Lyudmila Antonovna? Do you have a driver's license?"

While I spoke, all four of them – Anna Panteleyevna, Lyuda and Hera, to say nothing of Budyonny – maintained a stupefied silence. Even after I stopped, they could say nothing and continued gasping for air.

"There is one other important detail," I added, using the extra time their stunned condition afforded me. "Someone else was aware of the correspondence between Comrade Polishchuk and his secretary, and that someone obviously wanted to make sure that suspicion would fall on Natasha. Then there was the matter of certain young punks, who appeared at Vesna station when Polyakova left Anton Pavlovich's dacha, and who she thought had saved her from Frezin. In reality, they had been hired to push her under a train and to make it look as though she had murdered her lover and then committed suicide. And that explains why no letter was found on the kitchen table. That same somebody removed it."

Still nobody moved. It was getting eerie.

"To continue along the same lines," I continued, feeling that I should now strike the iron while it was hot. "Hera, my friend. Do you perhaps know who it was who hired those three punks?"

That was when the dam finally broke. It was Lyuda's turn to have a fit of hysterics. She hid her face in her hands and began weeping. Anna Panteleyevna opened her mouth and a single, loud, unbearable note came out of it. She raised her index finger like a dagger and pointed it straight at my heart. Budyonny also tried to say something but was unable to utter a single word. The moron Hera rose from his chair to the fullness of his extraordinary height and, the top of his pompadour scraping the ceiling as he roared like a wild beast, advanced toward me.

Anna Panteleyevna stopped screeching long enough to try to stop him, "No, Hera. Don't!"

It was no use. White with rage, he was coming closer, raising both arms over his head as though he was about to split wood. Had

I waited for the blow to fall, I would have certainly been dead. But I didn't. I punched him in just the right place in the lower part of his big belly, which was looming menacingly over me, and the giant, bug-eyed, began gasping for air. He sat on the floor, his rage almost visibly steaming from his ears.

It could have seemed comical, but no one was laughing.

Anna Panteleyevna grabbed the weeping Lyuda like a rag doll and pulled her toward the door. Budyonny, bowing incessantly and backing down the hall like a waiter at a hard-currency restaurant, wrung his hands, pressing them to the medal ribbons on his uniform jacket. He let them by, dancing and hopping in place, and followed them down the hall. Sometimes he cast hate-filled glances back at me, gnashing his teeth. Lyuda, who was being supported by her mother, also kept staring at me. Large teardrops welled tragically in her green eyes, rolling down her cheeks.

The procession headed toward the elevator. As they waited for it to arrive, the widow's indignant screams and Budyonny's pitiful replies reached me from the other end of the corridor.

"You can consider him fired, Ma'am. Please, Anna Panteleyevna. He will not soon forget this day."

"No," shouted Anna Panteleyevna. "None of you will ever forget this day. You, in particular. I'll destroy you. You'll weep bitter tears. Everyone in this circus which you call Criminal Investigations."

I had nearly forgotten all about Natasha. She was still in the interrogation room, sitting in the same chair where I had left her. Her eyes were fixed on the one-way mirror. Hera had gotten to his feet and began breathing more or less normally.

"Should I sock you one more time?" I asked, affecting a solicitous tone.

Hera spat out some nasty oaths.

"Well, if you've had enough, I don't insist," I said. "Go home. The show is over."

Hera took a step toward the door.

"But don't think I'm done with you," I added before he had a chance to get away. "I have half a mind to give your address to those punks from Yakimanka. Let's see if they push you under a tram if I promise to pay them a thousand rubles."

Hera was gone in a hurry, passing Budyonny who was on his way back. I thought he was going to yell at me and stomp his feet, but yet again, for the umpteenth time that day, I was wrong. He was calm. He walked into the room quietly. After all the noise, it would have been refreshing, had it not been for the red blotches on his face and the sharp angle at which his uniform necktie hung on his neck. Speaking so softly that I had to strain to hear him, he said, "That's it. You no longer work here. Gather your stuff and get out. Get the hell out of here, please."

TWENTY-SEVEN

I hate waiting. Waiting is an exhausting task. When you wait, nothing ever happens.

"Don't stand there staring at the tea kettle, Matyushkin," Tosya always says. "Don't you know that a watched kettle never boils?"

That winter I didn't seem to be able to bring anything to a boil.

There were delays with getting my discharge from Criminal Investigations. For one reason or another, the process dragged on for weeks, then months. After that fateful interrogation, I was no longer allowed into the building, but Personnel was also not releasing my work papers and, as long as they held on to them, they weren't officially allowed to take back my police ID or my service Makarov. That is the bureaucratic procedure and it cannot be altered.

It suited me well.

Being still officially employed, I couldn't look for a new job and my future was uncertain. On the positive side of things, I was still getting paid, though I was embarrassed to collect the money. No one should be paid for a no-show job.

But then again, I was working. Waiting was my new job.

Guys from work talked to me reluctantly, carefully weighing every word, like walking on eggshells. But they didn't cut me off completely, which was a good thing. From them I found out that Budyonny had plenty of trouble on my account, that he had been called up to the fifth floor five times, to Internal Investigations, and had to submit reports explaining my conduct and his failure to properly supervise me. It all nearly gave him a heart attack, but in the end he was neither removed from his position nor demoted, just reprimanded.

Kostya Pirogov got my job, and Lenny had been replaced by my old friend Ryumin, who had been brought in from Moscow Region and promoted.

"As for you," Sasha Slantsev told me in a conspiratorial whisper over a beer at some dive near Kuznetsky Most, "they may soon be bringing charges. Ryumin has been asking around about you. He's been badgering Kostya about your relationship with Lenny."

"I hope Pirogov told him that we were intimate." I said angrily.

Slantsev didn't smile.

"It's not funny," he said. "Ryumin is really pressing him, and Kostya thinks he has support in some pretty high places."

"I'm sure he does," I said.

Waiting is hard work. Watching one's back is hard work, too. It gets on your nerves, all that turning around and being scared of your own shadow.

The worst was that I had to stop seeing Tosya. I had a lot of respect for Colonel Nakazov and I knew better than to ignore his threats. His remark about helping me set Tosya straight bothered me so much that right after that disastrous interrogation, I told her I didn't want to see her any more. I had to do it, even though it might have been too late.

Tosya and I live in the same courtyard. Our buildings have the same street address. We couldn't help running into each other all the time. She would turn away and we would pass each other without exchanging a word, and each time I would feel a lump in my throat. It was clear that she missed me too, but was too proud to show it.

Her face was angry as hell.

Her Sevka was also angry at me. He was a tough little kid, and I was proud of him. That winter he showed he was a man, though still a small one.

I missed her terribly. I missed the feeling of her hands caressing me, the brush of her lips, the touch of her fingers, forever soiled with purple accountant's ink.

Waiting was how I spent the winter. I knew what I was waiting for, but I didn't know when it would come.

In late December, I got a phone call.

"I need to talk to you. You must give me a few minutes of your time. I can't talk over the phone."

She was middle-aged and overweight, but once upon a time she was probably very attractive. Her husband, a high-level government official, had been arrested after the war. When he came back from the camps in the mid-1950s, he was an invalid, bed-ridden most of the time.

"He wasn't an enemy or a traitor. He was innocent. He has been exonerated; the Party apologized to him and reinstated him in its ranks. He's an old Bolshevik. He knew Comrade Sverdlov before the Revolution."

When he was very young, their son had had a privileged upbringing. There were special schools for the nomenklatura and special food stores with an unlimited selection of food and clothing. They spent summers at the Black Sea. Then, when his father was declared an enemy of the people, there followed the daily humiliations that befell a son of the repressed. He had to change his name, taking his mother's maiden name, Pavlov, and he had to renounce his father as a traitor. Nevertheless, he grew up a good kid. He did well in school and had a special talent for foreign languages. He spoke English like a native.

She smiled and dabbed a tear in the corner of her eye.

Then, in his first year of college, he was arrested as part of the infamous Rokotov hard currency case. He was more like an innocent bystander, all he had done was help out an old friend once or twice. He knew nothing about any hard currency deals. He thought he was showing foreign visitors the achievements of Soviet culture by taking them to the Bolshoi Theater or the Tretyakov Gallery.

"Before the trial, he reassured me that everything would turn out fine, that he might even get off without doing any jail time. Instead, he was treated very harshly. We thought this was because of my husband, even though my husband had been exonerated and the Party had acknowledged its mistake. But now Senya has been brought to Moscow. He may be facing another sentence."

Before the arrest, her husband had been friends with a few ranking officers at State Security and, when his record was cleared, some, though by no means all, of those old friendships had been revived. Through these connections, they had learned that Senya Pavlov was being held at the Lubyanka. She could not get an acknowledgement of this from the authorities, much less permission to see him. The case was political, they told her.

"Is it true?" she asked.

I said that I didn't know.

"But you interrogated him in the fall. Was it in connection with this case?"

"I can't help you," I said. "I don't have any information. There is nothing I can do for you or for your son."

"Please," she implored. "I assure you, there is absolutely no way he could have been involved in any political activities. He was a member of the Young Communist League."

"I really don't know anything," I repeated. "In any case, I don't think it would be a good idea for us to continue to meet."

As she was leaving, she stopped and turned.

"If it's a question of—" she said. "If it's a question of, you know, money..."

Waiting was boring and so, to break the monotony, I devised a game of tailing the giant Hera. I didn't expect to discover anything new, but it might speed up events a bit.

I didn't try too hard to hide from him, and at last he confronted me by the entrance to his apartment building.

"What do you want?" he asked.

"Nothing," I said. "But maybe you and I should have a friendly chat, Heracles. You know, bury our differences."

His lips trembled slightly, but he screwed up his courage.

"Get lost, will you?" he said.

"Watch your manners, Hera, " I said. "If you don't want me to punch you again."

We were talking tough, like a pair of third-graders in a schoolyard.

"Don't you threaten me," he said.

He had pulled himself together sufficiently to talk back to me.

"Anyway, you're living on borrowed time," he said. "Enjoy it while you can."

"I see. You don't think I'm long for this world, do you? Is this what you're trying to tell me? How do you know that?"

"I've heard a rumor," Hera said darkly.

That was exactly what I wanted to hear.

Another way for me to dispel my boredom was to hang around near the entrance of the Forum Cinema and stare at the Polishchuks' apartment building from the opposite side of the Garden Ring. I saw Lyuda several times, but I don't believe she ever noticed me. Her mother was another matter. Every now and again, I would notice their window curtain move ever so slightly and a shadow would pass across the window. This always happened when Anna Panteleyevna was at home.

Hera continued to drive Anna Panteleyevna around in the official Volga. That was, as far as I could make out, his only job.

When I told Pavlov's mother that we must no longer meet, it was more for her protection than for mine. I made an effort to find her son. No one knew anything about him at Criminal Investigations and he was not in Butyrka prison. As long as he remained at the Lubyanka no information would seep out. But at least I tried and my conscience was clear.

Soon after New Year's I took a three-day trip to Izhevsk. The cold spell that usually comes in mid-January was especially severe that year. The Urals and the Upper Volga suffered particularly hard, with temperatures falling to record lows. The hotel in Izhevsk had no hot water, but it was no use complaining, because the hotel had no vacancies and, were it not for my Criminal Investigations ID, I would not have gotten a bed there. My five roommates and I were all in Izhevsk on business, coming from every corner of this vast country. The only thing we had in common was that we were all male. The sheets on the six narrow beds lined up against the walls of a long narrow room had yellowed with age and bore the telltale blood spots of squashed bedbugs – some things just don't come out in the wash. The restaurant offered an assortment of Udmurt national dishes, each heavier than the next. Given such amenities, the lack of hot water in the floor's single shower was but a minor inconvenience.

Fortunately, the building of the Udmurt National Archives, the object of my trip to Izhevsk, was located downtown and could be reached in a five-minute trot through the unbearable cold – a chill that constricted one's breathing and tightened the flesh on one's face. The Archives building, on the other hand, was so well heated that it was more like a steam bath. The cast-iron radiators crackled and all but melted; the faces of the young attendants behind the main desk glistened with perspiration.

Izhevsk was a hard slog, but I found what I had been looking for.

The information I gleaned from the Udmurt National Archives was a little unexpected but it filled in the square that Lenny had drawn around a certain "Mr. X" not long before his death.

TWENTY-EIGHT

During my long winter of waiting, our local drunk, San Vasilich, became my best friend.

"There is nothing stronger in this world than the ties of friendship steeped in a strong drink," San Vasilich claimed. He had a philosophical bent, particularly after a strong drink or two.

The ties of our friendship were especially strong since I was the one paying for the drinks.

His only complaint was that we didn't drink as often as he would have liked. Twice a week and no more was my rule. Typically, we drank in the comfort of my room. Even though it would have been to his advantage to share a half-liter bottle between just the two of us, he always brought along a companion. He was used to sharing a bottle three ways, as drunks do, and that was how he preferred it.

Eventually, one of San Vasilich's friends tried to steal my father's Omega wristwatch. He almost succeeded, too, had it not fallen onto the landing through a hole in his pocket while I, as was my other rule, was seeing them off immediately upon finishing the bottle.

"Look at that," San Vasilich said to his friend. "That's a vile thing to do, stealing from friends. You need to be taught a lesson."

The two of them began fighting right there on the landing. I didn't care who won, so I slammed the door.

One evening, as I entered the courtyard, I found San Vasilich sprawled on a snow-covered bench. Spring was in the air, but the air still turned cold and frosty when darkness fell, and San Vasilich was trembling in his threadbare overcoat.

"I've been waiting for you, Pavel," he whispered, hardly able to move his frozen lips

"Oh yeah?" I said. "Why?"

After the incident with my watch, there had been a bit of an estrangement between us.

"Remember you asked me to warn you if something unusual turned up?" he said in the same conspiratorial whisper. "You have a visitor."

"What kind of a visitor?"

"A kid. An athletic kid, in a pretty good shape. Dark hair. Not a Russian. I wouldn't be surprised if he turned out to be a Tartar."

"I see," I said. "A colleague of mine?"

"Oh, no. The other way around. One of those who make your life hell."

"How can you tell?"

"He dresses too good for a cop. He's got a lot of respect for himself. You know what wise guys say? If you don't respect yourself, others won't respect you, either. I used to have a buddy, a real made man. He didn't even drink vodka. He used to say to me: 'You should be embarrassed getting soused like a pig.' I should have listened to him. It's too late now, I guess. What do you think?"

"Yeah," I said. "It's too late now."

San Vasilich seemed relieved. I thanked him and headed for my building.

"Are you going in?" he asked. "On your own?"

"Why not?"

"Well, you know better, Pavel," San Vasilich said, rather disappointed. "Otherwise, let me gather a couple of guys from around the neighborhood. We could jump him when he isn't expecting it and pull a few buttons off his fancy coat."

"Let's not, San Vasilich," I said. "I've lost faith in your guys. Besides, why start pulling buttons off a guy's coat right away? Let me find out what he wants. Maybe he's just paying me a friendly visit."

I went inside, rode the elevator up and pulled my keys from my pocket. My visitor seemed to be shy, making himself known only when I went to put my key into the keyhole. He was also unusually light on his feet, because I had been listening for him and yet he still got right up next to me without making a sound.

"Come with me," he said softly in my ear, poking something sharp into my ribs.

I turned around slowly, showing him that I was holding in my hand my service Makarov, and not a bunch of keys.

"Was this how Arkady Matveyevich told you to come get me?" I asked. "Or did he tell you to ask nicely first?"

It was, as I had guessed from San Vasilich's description, Shamil, Arkady Matveyevich's protege.

"Nicely first," he admitted reluctantly.

"In that case, drop the knife. Gently. I don't want you to frighten my neighbors."

He let the knife fall onto the landing. It made a sound barely louder than when my Omega had fallen there a few days before.

"Take three steps back."

He took the three steps back and stood there, eyeing me.

"Now, let's talk nicely," I said, still pointing the Makarov at him. "What does he want?"

It turned out that Arkady Matveyevich wanted to see me urgently. I knew that he'd miss me sooner or later. We hadn't seen each other since September, and so much had happened in those few months. I didn't necessarily want to see him, but I had no reason to turn down his invitation. It would have been rude, and besides, he was an invalid.

"How do we get there?" I asked.

"I have a taxi waiting."

"Come on," I said. "You've been waiting for over three hours. Your cabbie must have left long ago."

"He hasn't," Shamil said. "Not if he knows what's good for him."

He bent down and, picking up his knife on the fly, pocketed it as we went down the stairs. The driver was indeed still there, waiting for us by the courtyard's Kirov Street entrance. He wanted to say something to Shamil, but then took one look at him and bit his tongue.

Shamil took the passenger seat next to the driver and gave him curt instructions. The cab's meter showed an astronomical sum. When we arrived, Shamil pulled out a wad of red ten-ruble notes. Judging by his reaction, the driver did not leave unsatisfied.

Arkady Matveyevich greeted me in his wheelchair. As usual, he got straight to the point.

"Do you know why Anton Polishchuk was killed?"

"I don't," I replied, falling in with his businesslike manner.

"Really? Are you hiding something from me?"

"No, Arkady Matveyevich, I am not. Why are you interested in this case, anyway?"

"Because I don't understand it."

"What is it exactly that you don't understand?"

"What confuses me is that no one had any motive for killing Polishchuk. I mean the only ones who wanted him dead were my clients. They didn't kill him, even though they surely thought about it. Aside from them, there wasn't anyone on earth who had the slightest reason for getting rid of him."

"Well, you and your clients should be happy then," I said brightly. "They wanted Polishchuk dead and he turned up dead. Someone must have done them a favor, completely free of charge. What's bad about that? Unless, of course, they wanted the satisfaction of killing him themselves."

"Not funny," Arkady Matveyevich said. "I always like to know exactly what happens in my world. If there is something I don't understand, it means that I wasn't told, and this is something I can't afford. The cops are the ones who are never told anything. That's why you have to use your noggin to figure everything out. You're not very good at it, and so

Alexei Bayer

you always end up with the short end of the stick. But I don't have this luxury. So, why was Polishchuk killed?"

"I can't help you," I said. "I certainly can make a few guesses, but I don't know for sure."

"That's your job, to guess. My job is to know."

He waited for me to say something, but I kept silent.

"Why don't you share some of your guesses with me?" he suggested.

"No, Arkady Matveyevich, There is no point in sharing guesses. When I know something for sure, you'll be the first with whom I'll share my knowledge."

He sneered.

"I hope you mean it," he said.

"Who are they, these clients of yours," I asked.

He gave me look of mock amazement and shook his head.

"I see," I said. "Not something that I should know. But you understand, unless I know, I won't be able to confirm or disprove any of my theories. It will take much longer to find out, which means that I will only be able to inform you later, rather than sooner."

Arkady Matveyevich gave it some thought. In the end, he seemed to agree with my reasoning.

"My clients are a group of very wealthy men," he said. "Polishchuk knew a thing or two about them, and Frezin wanted him to share this knowledge."

He fell silent again.

"Arkady Matveyevich," I said, sighing deeply. "You obviously don't trust me. I still have no idea who your clients are, what kind of knowledge Frezin wanted, and why he was so keen on getting it. It's all smoke and mirrors to me."

His face reddened and he gave me a sharp look. He was not used to being talked to like this and he hated having his hand forced.

"Fine," he said angrily. "There is a group of people who specialize in shaking down underground entrepreneurs. Those entrepreneurs, my clients, own secret factories that make good quality clothing and other stuff not available in stores. They sell their output at flea markets all over the country and make a lot of money. A whole lot of money. All illegally – the government doesn't know about them, and the law is busy trying to catch them. When they are shaken down or blackmailed, the entrepreneurs, for understandable reasons, can't go to your colleagues, the cops, for protection. This is what those doing the shake-downs are counting on. They are serious people and when they engage in blackmail they don't stop halfway. Let's just say that they don't faint when they do a little bloodletting on the entrepreneurs' wives and kids."

He paused.

"Got it so far?"

I nodded.

"While doing time, Frezin made these blackmailers' acquaintance, because your colleagues had been able to put several of their key players behind bars. Frezin told them lots of interesting stories about Polishchuk. Specifically, he claimed that Polishchuk could lead them to extremely wealthy underground entrepreneurs. The crème de la crème of the Soviet black market, so to speak. The moment Frezin was out, he got in touch with Polishchuk and offered him a partnership. Polishchuk would give Frezin the names of my clients in exchange for a share of the proceeds when the blackmailers did their thing. It was an offer Polishchuk couldn't really refuse. If he did, he himself would have gotten the shake-down. After all, Polishchuk was no pauper, and Frezin had reasons to suspect that, despite being a high and mighty manager, Polishchuk would not run to the police, because Frezin had incriminating information about Polishchuk and his own black market dealings. Besides, Polishchuk also had a wife and a daughter, and they could be taken to some quiet place outside the city, where no one can hear your screams."

"Nevertheless, despite Frezin's threats, Polishchuk refused to cooperate, is that right?" I asked.

"He did, on the spot. He refused to talk to him."

"Did he know Frezin?"

"Frezin claimed that he did. He certainly went around telling people stories about Polishchuk."

"Interesting," I said. "And what's your role in all of this?"

"I happen to have connections on both sides of the barricades, so to speak. Among the underground entrepreneurs, as well as among Frezin's friends, currently in jail. I'm helping the sides come to an amicable agreement."

"How is it going, so far?"

"So far, not very well. I don't like it when there are no results. I'm not some lousy collective farmer, toiling all day long without getting anywhere. Polishchuk refused to talk to Frezin, and Frezin started threatening him. But threatening is one thing and killing is another. Frezin had no reason to kill Polishchuk. My clients had a reason to kill him, but they didn't. That's the strange thing about this case."

"Couldn't Frezin have killed him accidentally?" I suggested. "Maybe he decided to get physical and miscalculated?"

"Maybe. Everything is possible. But still, it doesn't add up. It doesn't look like an accident, and there is no way the murder could have been premeditated. Frezin was no fool, he knew that if he murdered Polishchuk he would lose both Polishchuk and Polishchuk's contacts. That would put him in an awkward position vis-a-vis his prison friends. They're not the kind of people who let somebody lead them on and waste their time. They don't take to bullshitters."

"Are you sure it wasn't your clients who did it, Arkady Matveyevich?" I asked after a long pause. "Could they have hired you to seek a peaceful solution, then got someone else to make war behind your back?"

"By someone else you mean a woman, right?" Arkady Matveyevich asked. "You know that Polishchuk was killed by a woman, don't you? Why are you bullshitting me?"

He was well informed, I had to hand it to him. And he was getting mad. But I'd had enough of him, too.

"Are your clients really as wealthy as all that?" I asked.

"They are. I never deal with little fish."

"In this case, why did they get so scared of Frezin? Let him find out who they are, what of it? The blackmailers are in jail, there's nothing to worry about for a long time. Plus, there's always the possibility that the blackmailers would be rehabilitated, see the error of their ways, and come out as honest citizens."

Arkady Matveyevich looked at me suspiciously and said, "Don't play the buffoon."

"But it's you who's bullshitting me, Arkady Matveyevich," I said. "Why would the black market entrepreneurs hire you as an intermediary? Being what they are, wealthy underground businessmen, they have powerful people protecting them. They would've made short work of any Frezin who came around, sniffing for their names."

"Maybe you're right," he said. "What of it?"

"I'll tell you what I think," I said. "I suspect that it was the blackmailers who hired you. They don't need the names of the entrepreneurs just now. They are in jail. This is a much more clever deal: you and Frezin working together and from opposite directions. Frezin's job was to approach Polishchuk and to give them a reason to be worried. Then, suddenly, you appear and offer to take care of the blackmailers for a not-so-small sum. It would be smaller, of course, than if the gang were out of prison and the black marketeers could be shaken down, but enough to tide all of you over."

"Those wise guys, they think they're smarter than everyone else," I thought on my way home.

I was mad, but it hadn't been a total waste of my time. I didn't give out any important information, and got something useful out of him. It wasn't a big deal, of course, just a few minor details to add finishing touches to the overall picture.

TWENTY-NINE

When I removed the tarp that had swaddled my Zundapp all winter, a thought flashed through my head: "It won't be long now."

I headed to the Oka, to the same spot I had taken Tosya and Sevka the previous fall. Except now it was spring. Or almost spring, very early in the season. The snow still lay in the ravines, in deep ditches alongside the road and in the shade under the thick fir trees, where it had become compressed and blackened. The woods were still grey and brown, bristling with bare limbs. They were dotted light green and yellow by catkins of willow trees that grew along the banks of the river. The sun had dried the top layer of half-rotten leaves, but underneath the ground was still soggy with melted snow and felt soft underfoot. The river was fast, dark and swollen and full of melting ice floes, broken branches and bits of trash. The southern wind was moist and heavy with springtime warmth.

I sat on the banks of the Oka and drank vodka directly from the bottle. As winter drew to a close, I began drinking alone, which was better and more cheerful than in the company of San Vasilich and his thieving friends. I drank to Uncle Nikolai's memory and then to Lenny's.

"It won't be long now, buddy," I said out loud.

I had fallen into the habit of talking to Lenny as if he were right beside me. I asked his advice and discussed various aspects of the case with him. I also tried to see things through his eyes. It might have been a little crazy, but it was useful and sometimes his advice was good.

Then I rode my Zundapp into the village and knocked on Aunt Ksenia's gate. Her dog didn't recognize me; it had been a while since I had last visited. The woodpile by the door was low, even though the spring nights were still cold and Aunt Ksenia would have to stoke the stove for several more weeks yet.

In the house, I pulled out my half-empty bottle of vodka.

"Look at you, how skinny you've gotten," Aunt Ksenia said, squinting at me.

She pulled up the trap door and was going to go down to the cellar to get some pickled cabbage and cucumbers to go with the vodka.

"Don't worry about it," I said. "There's hardly any vodka left."

She sat down on the bench by the kitchen table.

Aunt Ksenia had aged. Or rather, she had grown into her age. Before, when Uncle Nikolai was still alive, the sun-tanned, hardened skin of her face was deeply lined and her hair was all grey, but she was strong and energetic. Most importantly, she was still very much a woman. She loved to flirt and tell dirty jokes, and there was something young and girlish in her eyes. Her hands were muscular and her full breasts protruded almost aggressively from beneath her cotton blouses. Now she was no different from the other widows in Zyatkovo.

We drank to Uncle Nikolai's memory.

"May you rest in peace, old man."

Aunt Ksenia crossed herself.

"As I was saying," she said. "We're all widows here. I got used to it over the winter."

I spent no more than half an hour in her house, until we finished the vodka.

"Will you leave the bottle?" Aunt Ksenia asked hopefully. "The deposit is twelve kopeks. A lot of money."

As I had planned, I started back before dark. My rearview mirror is marred with black spots and spiderwebbed with cracks, but it's original. I didn't have the heart to replace it, because you could never get an original part. The German who years ago rode this bike across my land used it to look in the mirror to see what was happening behind him. I sometimes wondered whether all the reflections weren't still there somewhere, retained like a movie or a bunch of still photos. That German might have seen the reflection of his death in this mirror.

Soon after I turned onto the road to Moscow, I checked the mirror. The road stretched straight and empty behind me, except for in the deep, dark distance, where there was a tiny black spec, a familiar jeep not available for civilian purchase. Seeing it there, keeping a safe distance, was a nice surprise. I smiled and gave my Zundapp some speed, getting up to around eighty kilometers per hour.

The jeep accelerated, too, so as not to let me out of its sight, but still staying well behind. I pushed the gas to reach a hundred. Busy as I was watching the jeep in the mirror, I nearly slammed head-on into a lumber truck after a sharp turn, then narrowly missed the three cars that were on its tail.

"Watch out, buddy," I said to myself. "No need to make it easy for him."

But I had no fear of crashing. I knew I wouldn't, and I had no doubt in my mind that I would live to see this case through to the end. Watching the jeep behind me, I knew exactly how it would come out. I felt so happy, I could have sung for joy.

First my Zundapp and then the jeep zoomed past a small settlement at full speed, and then the road was empty again, with trees closing in on both sides. I checked the mirror again and saw that the jeep had fallen back. Could I have been mistaken? Could the anticipation I had felt all morning have been deceiving me? I slowed down and looked behind me. The jeep was still there, no closer and no further back.

After a bit longer, I slowed to let him catch up. He was picking up speed, too, so the next time I checked my mirror he was on my tail. We rode like that for a minute or two. I slowed and moved to the side of the road, to let him pass if he wished. He didn't. He slowed too, to stay behind me.

Suddenly I felt a slight bump against my bike. Once, twice, three times. There was a crunch of metal hitting metal. But the Zundapp is a heavy and stable machine, especially with its sidecar attached. It's not easy to push it off the road. The front wheel hit a pothole, but I held on and accelerated. This time, however, I stayed below sixty.

A van passed us going in the opposite direction and he fell back. But then, as soon as the van disappeared around a bend, the jeep moved into the oncoming lane, accelerated, passed me and then turned the wheel sharply into my path.

Crash.

I had a lucky fall. There was a more or less gradual descent off the highway, and a deviation onto a dirt road. Besides, the deep ditches were still filled with soft, half-melted snow. I hit the brakes, letting the jeep get ahead, and steered the bike to the right, rolling with its natural, rightward vector. The bike listed and fell onto its side, screeching as the metal skin on the sidecar was torn off by the asphalt rushing beneath it at fifty kilometers per hour.

Making sure my foot wouldn't get caught under the falling bike, I released the handles and rolled down the slope. The snow under the brittle crust was soft, sticky and heavy. As I dove into it head first, I checked the right pocket of my leather jacket to make sure it was still zipped. The last thing I needed was for it to get stuffed with wet snow.

Inside the pocket, beneath the zipper, I felt a reassuring heft.

The Zundapp continued to slide forward for a moment longer, then turned upside down and tumbled into the ditch. The sidecar cracked and fell off. The front wheel twisted awkwardly and continued to spin in the air, its spokes catching the orange rays of the setting sun.

The sounds of the crash died down and silence fell over the road.

I had readied myself for the fall, relaxing my body and folding into a compact ball, as we had been taught at the academy. Going with the grain made it a lot easier. Still, I hit my head on something hard – perhaps a piece of wood under the snow or a lump of ice. The pain was sharp enough for my cry to be authentic, and I felt something warm seep out of my skull. A bloodstain on the snow would be a particular stroke of luck, I thought. Despite the pain, I stayed conscious. I rolled over and lay motionless, the warm blood melting the snow around my head.

The blood, actually, might have even been too much, I thought, but there was nothing I could do. The good thing was that it had melted the snow around my face and I could see the road, although it was tinged with red.

The jeep stopped, then reversed.

He could have driven down the dirt road, which would have placed him right where I was lying. The jeep was an off-road vehicle and it would have easily negotiated the few remaining patches of snow. He could have then finished the job without getting out or getting his feet wet. But I suppose he didn't want to leave any tracks.

Instead, he parked the jeep by the side of the road and got out. He was dressed in civilian clothes, wearing the same leather coat he had worn when he came to Uncle Nikolai's funeral last year. I automatically made a mental note of it, as though fixing the scene with a camera lens.

He stood on the road looking at me for a few seconds. Helping me was clearly not part of his plan. I shifted slightly and groaned through clenched teeth. He waited to see whether I would move again. Then, he lifted his right hand, in which he had been holding a gun all that time, and began to aim. He was going to do a thorough job of it and he was surely a crack shot. He bent his left arm at the elbow and used his left hand to steady the barrel of the gun while keeping his feet apart. As he froze in that position, holding his breath and getting ready to squeeze the trigger, I couldn't help admiring his form.

Everything was working out exceptionally well for him. He had me where he wanted me and he had all the time in the world. The road was empty and he would have heard any approaching car long before it swung into view.

Confidence can be its own worst enemy. While he was aiming for the kill, I raised my hand from the snowdrift and took a shot without aiming.

My first shot wasn't very good, but it did the job. It hit him in the thigh, sending up a tiny spray of blood. He reeled and lost his aim. He managed to get off a shot, but the bullet whistled through the pine tree branches above my head. I squeezed the trigger three more times, this time taking aim. Now that he was bent in pain, holding his wounded thigh, I found myself with plenty of time on my hands. My fourth shot missed him completely, but it made no difference. The second slug had hit him in the shoulder, turning him sideways, and the third had pierced his head. He stumbled and fell. It was even a bit anticlimactic. I expected the impact of the shot to throw him backwards, but instead his body tumbled down the slope toward me. It continued sliding into the ditch until it was halted by my Zundapp, the front wheel of which was still spinning. Nakazov lay against the edge of the sidecar, oozing a greyish, purplish mass from where a second ago had been his fur hat and a head of thick, salt-and-pepper hair.

"There we go, Lenny," I said aloud when the woods around me stopped echoing with the sound of gunshots and a frightened flock of crows settled back onto the electric wires. "I told you it wasn't going to be long."

That was when I made one of the worst mistakes of my life. Perhaps the end to my winter of waiting made me stupid. I have no other excuse.

Nakazov's body was far enough down the slope that it could no longer be seen from the road, especially in the approaching darkness. He had dropped his gun and it had disappeared under the snow. I did not have time to look for it, and there was no certainty that I would find it. His jeep was idling on the shoulder. He hadn't expected to linger.

I stopped at my place and changed. I put on my uniform, for the first time in many months, because I was going to see Budyonny, getting him out of bed if need be. What I should've done was go straight to Sukharevka, even if I were frozen stiff.

Now dry and dressed, I looked up from the Forum Cinema, in front of which I had parked the jeep. The windows of the Polishchuks' apartment shone brightly over the city. It seemed like a good sign.

The door was opened almost immediately. Anna Panteleyevna wore slippers and a pink terry cloth bathrobe. Her hair was in curlers.

"Oh, it's you," she said, not even trying to conceal the disappointment in her voice. "I thought it might have been Lyuda returning."

"Did Lyudmila Antonovna leave?"

"Yes, she did. No more than quarter of an hour ago. Half an hour at the most. It's late, young man."

"That's strange," I said.

"Yes," the widow admitted. "I too was a little surprised, because she left so suddenly."

"Do you know where she went?"

Anna Panteleyevna shook her head.

"I have no idea, to be honest with you. She never tells me anything. Hera came about an hour ago. She packed an overnight bag, took some clothes and a toothbrush, and the two of them left. I asked her where she was going, but she didn't bother to reply. I'm used to it. She sometimes leaves like that, suddenly, and she never tells me where she's going. It was so different when Anton Pavlovich was alive."

Anna Panteleyevna sighed. She stood in the doorway, blocking my way. She seemed to have no intention of letting me in. Yet she also did not show any of the rancor of our previous meeting at the Criminal Investigations headquarters. Apparently it had been forgotten.

Suddenly, I thought of something. About an hour before, when I climbed out of Nakazov's jeep in my courtyard, I had seen a shadow lurking in the archway leading to Kirov Street. Just as I spotted it, the shadow moved swiftly away.

"Let me in," I said with sudden urgency.

"It's too late, young man," she said. "I'm about to go to bed."

I stepped forward, pushing her unceremoniously toward the wall.

"Where is she?" I asked once I was in the apartment.

"I told you," she said indignantly. "Lyuda is not here. She has left. You're being insolent."

The living room looked much poorer. Gone were the portraits of Khrushchev and Anna Panteleyevna with her late husband. The expensive furniture was still there, but there were no plates on the wall and the selection of porcelain in glass display cases was far less splendid. But I had no time to look at her antiques.

The living room was empty.

Ignoring Anna Panteleyevna's protests, I headed down the hall. It was a vast apartment, with a number of intersecting hallways and many closed doors. I opened them all, one after the other, looking in. There was no sign of Lyuda in the master bedroom or in her own room. I then checked the bathroom, pulling back the shower curtain.

"Who are you looking for?" Anna Panteleyevna kept asking as she followed me around. "I told you. Lyuda packed an overnight bag and left. She and Hera are gone. There is no one else here, I assure you. You're being insufferable."

She was telling the truth. There was no one else in the apartment. She was quite alone.

Having finished looking into all the rooms, I rushed to the kitchen, putting some distance between myself and the widow. It was also empty, but in the sink there were two cups. I took them out and sniffed at them.

The kitchen turned black before my eyes. I had been thrown off my Zundapp, I had been shot at and I had killed a man – all in a day's work. But now, for the first time that day, I was truly scared.

Scared or not, I had to act, and act fast.

"I see you found what you have been looking for," came an eerily calm voice behind my back.

Anna Panteleyevna stood by the door of the kitchen, her hand in the pocket of her terry cloth bathrobe. She looked a bit like the statue of Dzerzhinsky, the founder of the Secret Police, in front of Colonel Nakazov's headquarters.

But unlike the statue, Anna Panteleyevna could move. She began to take her hand out of her pocket, pulling out some sort of heavy object. I didn't wait to see what it was. Taking two rapid steps toward her and putting my entire weight behind my fist, I hit her squarely in the face. I would normally have thought twice before hitting a man like that, much less a middle-aged woman. But this was far from a normal situation. She didn't make a sound. The force of the blow threw her backwards. She hit her head on a doorjamb and began to slide, lifeless, to the floor.

I turned her onto her stomach, pulled her hands together behind her back and cuffed her wrists with a pair of brand-new, shiny East German handcuffs. Then, leaving the front door wide open and not bothering to wait for the elevator, I headed downstairs, bounding down three steps at a time.

Praskovia, the concierge, was sitting at her desk. She was listening to folk songs on the radio and knitting. Seeing me in front of her, she pulled back and glanced at the front door, as though intending to bolt. At the moment, I would have frightened a dead person.

"Where the hell is she?" I roared.

"Who are you looking for?" she squeaked.

I grabbed the front of her dress and shook her like a rag doll. Her head bobbing from side to side, her dentures popped loose and clattered onto the tiled floor.

"You know who, you old bitch."

Had she continued playing the innocent, I would've murdered her, and given the look in her eyes, she realized that.

"I have nothing to do with it," she began to mutter toothlessly. "It's the Polishchuk woman. She said she'd give me as much money as I wanted. She said she'd support me till the day I die."

"Where is she?"

I was close to losing it. I pushed my face into hers and shouted with all the strength of my lungs.

The pupils of her crafty green eyes were dilated and her toothless mouth twitched. She could no longer speak and pointed to the door behind my back. I threw her to the floor and rushed toward the door. It was locked. Taking two steps backwards, I burst it open with my heel. The plywood gave way and the door flew off its hinges. The force of the blow propelled me through the door and I nearly fell.

The crammed storage room was lit by a bare lightbulb. On the floor, in a puddle of her own vomit, lay Lyuda Polishchuk. She wore the same terry cloth robe as her mother, except hers was blue. The robe was open at the front, exposing a naked body that seemed to be made of wax. Her fingers were twisted, as if convulsed and then frozen, clinging to her throat. Her once beautiful features were contorted. Around her lips, which I had so passionately kissed at Sretenka Gate a few months ago, was a crust of white foam. Her body was still warm and rigor mortis was only just starting to set in.

"Lord in heaven, Holy Mother of God and Virgin Theotokos," wailed the concierge, sending an ominous echo up the stairwell.

THIRTY

I had to explain everything to Tosya and Sevka. From the beginning.

But first I had to report to Budyonny, and then, with him at my side, give my full account of events to the very serious-looking top brass at State Security on Dzerzhinsky Square. Recounting everything that happened took a long time, and by the time I finished a new day had dawned. At that point, the top brass got into several official Volgas and our long cortege sped out of Moscow in the direction of Serpukhov, accompanied by a truck full of Internal Ministry troops. The top brass remained in their Volgas while the soldiers searched the woods for Nakazov's body, which had been dragged away during the night and gnawed on by feral dogs. There was some justice in that, but it was an inconvenience.

A pair of police dogs were dispatched to the Polishchuks' dacha at Vesna, where, after they had sniffed around for a few minutes, Hera's enormous and not-yet decomposing body was dug up from a flower bed. He had been shot in the head.

Forensics later discovered that Hera's palms and hands were scratched and covered with blisters. Apparently, he had dug his own grave, convinced by Nakazov that it would be mine. I could imagine how hard he had labored, fighting against his aversion to work. Hera's official Volga, still registered to the meat processing plant, was found parked by the train station of a small town on the other side of Moscow, in the direction of Leningrad.

Once all this unpleasant but necessary business had been taken care of, I could go to see Tosya and Sevka. With all due respect, neither Budyonny nor the top brass at State Security asked me as good and relevant questions as did Tosya. She's a smart one, my girl.

To begin with, she realized how lucky I had been that Nakazov had decided to deal with me personally. Had he sent Hera or someone else entirely, a paid killer, everything would've turned out differently. Nakazov would have still been at State Security and he would have been able to arrange a cover-up, even if I had been lucky enough to shoot the killer.

"He must have been itching to wring your neck with his own hands, Matyushkin," Tosya said, laughing. "You'd gotten to him over the past few months, never letting go and continuing to pop up in unexpected places like a Jack-in-the-box."

"I don't think so," I replied. "It was all part of the plan. Nakazov had opened a case against me. It was going to be a big frame-up involving Lenny and Senya Pavlov. The idea was that Lenny and I had decided to shake down the Polishchuk widow by threatening to charge Lyuda Polishchuk with her father's murder. That was the real reason I had gone to see Pavlov. Under the guise of interrogating him, I wanted to get some dirt on Lyuda, in order to blackmail her mother more effectively. Pavlov had confirmed that, after Nakazov brought him to the Lubyanka and offered him a deal. But then Lenny and I had a falling out, and I murdered Lenny by tampering with his car brakes."

"But none of that is true, Uncle Pavel," Sevka exclaimed.

"But it would have stuck. Nakazov's plan was to shoot me and then claim that I had figured out he was on to me and had tried to murder him in the woods. He had planned the whole thing pretty thoroughly."

Tosya shrugged. She liked her own explanation better.

I then recounted my cowboy shootout with Nakazov and announced, "That was the Prologue. Now, Act One, Scene One."

Tosya had become addicted to the theater over the winter. She and her colleagues from the textile factory had gone to several performances. That was why I set up my presentation as a play.

"What did we know about the Rokotov Affair? Lenny had told us that it went back a couple of years, when Khrushchev took a trip abroad and, on his return, demanded that State Security put an end to all black market activities around Moscow hotels.

"Major Nakazov was thought to be the right man to head this investigation, because his job had been to spy on foreign tourists staying at those hotels. For a few months his investigation was spinning its wheels, but at last the gang was busted and its leaders were put behind bars. The head of the whole operation, Nakazov reported, was one Ian Rokotov.

"But we also now know that, when the gang was arrested, Frezin was supposed to play the leading role at the trial, even though he was not the boss of the criminal organization. He seemed like a perfect candidate for a frame-up, what with his prison record and lifestyle consistent with the popular image of the career criminal. Khrushchev would have appreciated this casting decision. But at the last minute not only was Frezin's role in the gang suddenly reduced, but he practically disappeared from the case, receiving only a very short prison sentence. Instead, Rokotov became the star of the show, even though he didn't look much like a gang leader.

"Two questions arise, therefore. If Rokotov was not the real leader of the criminal organization, who was? And why did Frezin get off so lightly?

"When Khrushchev was abroad and somebody pointed out to him that all that black market activity was taking place around Moscow hotels, it came as a complete surprise to him. But State Security could not have been in the dark about this. State Security always worked with illegal money changers and black marketeers, just as it did with hotel staff and hard currency prostitutes."

"Matyushkin," Tosya interrupted, jerking her head toward Sevka. Meaning I shouldn't be talking about prostitutes in his presence, Sevka being an innocent little kid.

"Yes, of course," I said, clapping my palm over my mouth and winking at Sevka. "I meant to say young students who come to hard currency bars to practice foreign languages."

Sevka guffawed, and Tosya frowned at both of us. I continued.

"Nakazov, who had been recruiting snitches for State Security and placing spies at hotels for years, had to know about all the black market dealings around the hotels. The facts that so outraged Khrushchev were part of Nakazov's daily routine. Therefore, Nakazov was in a position to bust the gang on the same day he was appointed to handle the investigation.

"But he didn't. He delayed making arrests as long as he could, until there was a real risk that he would be replaced by someone else. The question is why?"

"He must have been protecting someone," Tosya said.

"Absolutely. But if Nakazov was protecting the gang, why didn't Rokotov and Frezin know about it?"

"Maybe they weren't really that high up in the organization and Nakazov worked for the real leaders?" Tosya suggested. "And, in order to protect those real leaders, Nakazov turned the investigation in such a way that Rokotov was presented as the leader, even though he wasn't."

"Something like that," I said. "In reality, the story was far more complicated. Rokotov didn't become a scapegoat out of the blue. He had been carefully groomed to play this role for a very long time. Frezin, too, had been groomed for his role. From the start, there had been a fallback plan that, if the gang was busted, these two would be arrested and put on trial as criminal bosses."

"Why would they have agreed to that?" asked Tosya.

"I doubt they knew about their assigned roles. In this case, there were many roles that different people were made to play. They played them very well, never for a moment suspecting that they were on stage."

"I don't get it," Sevka said.

"Wait and see, young man. It will all become clear in a moment.

"Rokotov was the gang's manager. He was the only person who understood how it worked from top to bottom. It was an extensive organization broken into independent cells. Small groups bought hard currency without knowing about any of the other groups. Sometimes they even competed with each other at larger hotels. They passed the currency to higher-level buyers, who also knew only their own cells and no one else. The buyers then passed the currency up another layer and then another, and finally to Rokotov. If a cell got busted, it could be easily isolated before it could pull down the entire gang.

"Eventually, all the proceeds were gathered by Rokotov. He was known to many in the gang, but very few people suspected that he was both recruiter and the final buyer. The reason why he wasn't busted, however, was that he snitched to the authorities. He provided information about the gang to Nakazov."

"Wow," Sevka said.

"Nakazov always knew what was going on inside the gang, which allowed him to provide it with highly effective protection. He was like the internal police. Whenever Rokotov complained about some low-level buyer who was ineffective or traded on the side or talked too much, Nakazov promptly arrested him. But Rokotov, for his part, was convinced that he was snitching to State Security and not to the gang's own internal security officer.

"Whenever Rokotov accumulated a certain amount of hard currency, he would place it in a suitcase and take it to the left luggage service at one of Moscow's railroad stations. The suitcase was a special one, it had American locks that couldn't be picked. He would've been very surprised if he knew that his suitcase was ending up in the hands of the same State Security major to whom he was snitching.

"For his part, Rokotov thought that the suitcase was being retrieved by Frezin. Rokotov had been told that Frezin was his link with the operation's top leaders. Frezin, on the other hand, thought that he, Rokotov, was either the leader or a close associate of the leader. If both of them were busted, they would have fingered each other. With Nakazov in a key position at State Security, there was a very good chance that this would be the end of the investigation."

"What did Nakazov get out of it?" asked Tosya. "Why would he protect the gang?"

"I'll get to that in a moment," I said.

"Frezin's role in the organization included protecting Rokotov's money-changers and making sure that no other gang infringed on their territory. But that was something that Nakazov could do even more effectively. If a competitor emerged, Rokotov would first try to bring them under the gang's umbrella. If he failed, Nakazov would put them away for a few years.

"So, Frezin wasn't a real enforcer, he just played the role of one. More importantly, his job was to find rare and valuable jewelry. The real leaders of the gang – who were, I repeat, unknown to either Rokotov or Frezin – were very interested in jewelry. Not just any pieces, but anything of museum quality. Such pieces were sometimes smuggled into the country by foreigners, who exchanged them for icons, which were even more valuable in the West. But more often the pieces were bought from fences. Frezin, who had connections in the criminal underworld, spent most of his time looking for rare jewelry. When he got hold of something very valuable, he would pass it on to Rokotov or directly to the leaders of the gang – probably using something similar to Rokotov's suitcase.

"The fact that some pieces of jewelry passed through Frezin's hands is pivotal for this entire case," I said.

Tosya and Sevka no longer asked any questions. They sat glued to their chairs, waiting for me to continue.

"So, when he was put in charge of the investigation into illegal currency dealing, Nakazov began preparing the ground for his phony case and making sure that the real leaders would not be implicated. Finally, when he could wait no longer without risking dismissal – which could have been catastrophic for the real leaders of the gang – he announced that he had broken the case.

"Nakazov then arrested Rokotov and Frezin and began to mop up the rest of the gang while interrogating the two presumed leaders. Rokotov was easy, falling into his assigned role, but Frezin proved a harder nut to crack. In the course of the interrogation he revealed to Nakazov that he knew who the real leader of the gang was. He wasn't supposed to, but he somehow had found out. He went as far as to name him: Anton Polishchuk, director of the Mikoyan Meat Processing Plant.

"Note that Nakazov didn't pass this information on. Nowhere in the documents related to the Rokotov case was the name Polishchuk ever mentioned. Instead, he struck a deal with Frezin: Frezin would keep mum about Polishchuk, and in exchange he would get a very short, almost symbolic sentence. Meanwhile, Rokotov and two others were found guilty and eventually shot.

"Let's sum up what we have so far," I said.

"The putative leaders of the gang of black marketeers are executed, Frezin is in jail, and the real leader, Polishchuk, is not only free but has escaped all suspicion. But we still have lots of unanswered questions. What happened to all the hard currency? Some was found in Rokotov's suitcase when it was retrieved from left luggage at the Yaroslavl train station. But even though it was stuffed full of dollars, German marks and pounds sterling, it was a miniscule portion of the volume of black market trading.

"Another question: Why would Rokotov need so much foreign currency? Moscow is not New York City, after all. You can't just go out and buy cars, yachts and chateaux full of servants on the Riviera. You can't even buy a lousy private plane here.

"Act Two. Let's go back a few months before the gang was busted. One evening, Frezin finds himself at Aragvi, the finest Georgian restaurant in Moscow, sitting at the same table as young Senya Pavlov and Lyuda Polishchuk. Pavlov is having dinner with a visitor from New Zealand. The foreigner is leaving Moscow early the next morning and

Rokotov had sent Frezin to pass something on to the foreigner. Lyuda is there as Pavlov's date.

"During this short meeting, Frezin stares at Lyuda and something about her makes a very strong impression on him. That something is not Lyuda's extraordinary beauty, but rather an emerald brooch. It's a very distinctive piece of jewelry, in the shape of a pea pod. There is no possibility that another such brooch could exist in Moscow. And just the day before, Frezin had passed this brooch on to the leader of their gang.

"Frezin then quickly established that Lyuda was Polishchuk's daughter and that she had received the brooch as a birthday gift from her father. Frezin did not have a formal education, but he was pretty smart. He began to spy on Polishchuk and probably watched the Sukharevka apartment. That told him what kind of people the Polishchuks associated with."

"What kind?" Sevka asked.

"Frezin figured out right away that the people who visited Polishchuk were wealthy. Some extremely wealthy. And none belonged to the party or government elites. They were wealthy people of the kind Frezin knew during his time behind bars, because this kind often get in trouble with the law. They are underground entrepreneurs, people who set up illegal private businesses.

"Frezin didn't have enough time to get to the bottom of it and figure out everything. But when Nakazov hauled him in, he had formed a pretty good idea of how the gang functioned and where the hard currency it was buying in such quantities went."

"Yes, where?" Tosya interrupted me. "Who would need so much currency?"

"Those underground businessmen, that's who. They earn huge illegal profits making consumer goods and clothing. Keeping their wealth in rubles is risky. At the start of 1961, the government had a currency reform, exchanging old ruble notes for new ones. Those who had hundreds of thousands and even millions of rubles hidden under their mattress ended up with wads of colored paper that had no value. Hard currency is far more secure. Besides, many of those underground entrepreneurs harbor hopes that they will one day go abroad, as tourists, for example, and live it up. And then there are some who are convinced that Communism will one day collapse and they will be able to spend their money openly."

"They are nothing but a bunch of traitors," Sevka exclaimed, incensed.

"No," said Tosya. "They are all crazy. It'll never happen, Sevka. Communism is here forever. Right, Matyushkin?"

"They should be shot," Sevka insisted.

"We're trying," I said. "Or at least Nakazov's people are."

But we had digressed.

"In the labor camp, where he was serving his short two-year sentence, Frezin met blackmailers specializing in shaking down underground millionaires. Frezin told them about Polishchuk and Polishchuk's connections among rich entrepreneurs. When he came out, he contacted Polishchuk and tried to propose a deal on behalf of his new friends. Polishchuk would either give him the names of the entrepreneurs or else he would be shaken down. The blackmailers had a scary reputation, they had been known to kidnap members of businessmen's families and torture them until they had been paid.

"The plan was a bit more complicated, because the most important blackmailers were still doing time, but it doesn't matter. What does matter is that Polishchuk refused to talk to Frezin. Worse, he insisted that he didn't understand what Frezin was talking about. He claimed to have no knowledge of Frezin, Rokotov, or, for that matter, any underground entrepreneurs."

"Curtain. End of Act Two."

"Oh, my God," Sevka said.

He was listening intently and finding that making a concentrated mental effort was very difficult.

"Should we take a break?" I asked.

"No," Sevka objected. "Go on."

"Act Three.

"A weird thing happens. Unexpectedly for everyone, Polishchuk turns up dead.

"Unexpectedly, because Frezin had no interest in killing Polishchuk and, moreover, he couldn't have been the murderer in any case. Why? Because everything around the murder had been set up so as to point to a different person. Just as Rokotov and Frezin had been groomed for the roles of gang leaders, so Natasha Polyakova had been carefully prepared to be Polishchuk's killer. As with the other two, the preparation had started a long time ago.

"Actually, Natasha had been groomed to play some kind of a role, but which one exactly was to be determined at a later date.

"Her grooming began when the Rokotov affair was still being investigated, as soon as Frezin told Nakazov that he knew the identity of the true leader of the gang. Natasha and her mother started to get anonymous assistance that, as she subsequently found out, was coming from Polishchuk. Soon thereafter, she received her first romantic letter and she and her boss started corresponding. But Polishchuk refused to talk to her in person or to become involved in any way except in their letters. Furthermore, he insisted that they kept their love a secret. A secret from everyone – and, first and foremost, from Polishchuk himself.

"Natasha is a loner. She's a romantic soul who has never known real love. She was raised in poverty by an invalid single mother. But she has read a lot of books and longed for her Prince Charming. Whoever chose her was a brilliant psychologist. She fell desperately in love with Polishchuk and he, to judge by his letters, returned her love. Still, Natasha scrupulously carried out his wishes and never in his presence hinted at their secret relationship. She admired him for his strength of character and for his ability to separate work from love. Imagine, he forced himself to ignore her when she came into his office, even to be rude, to yell at her. What a hero.

"The author of this brilliant play didn't risk too much. If Natasha's correspondence with her boss came out, it could have been easily shown that an impressionable young woman had simply lost her mind.

She was imagining a love affair with her boss and even had written the letters herself. She would be packed away to a nuthouse and the story would end there.

"But when it was decided that Polishchuk had to be killed, the role of the murderer went to Natasha. She got a letter inviting her to visit him at his dacha. She didn't hesitate for a moment. At the dacha, meanwhile, everything had been set up. She would not find Polishchuk in the house, but while waiting for him she would come across a letter from another one of his paramours. The letter – which was authentic, by the way, but written about a year before – would open her eyes, revealing Polishchuk not as the romantic hero of her dreams, but as a dirty old goat.

"The plan called for Polyakova to be so shocked and devastated by the discovery that she would immediately leave and rush to the train station. At the train station, three young punks hired to push her under a passing train were waiting. Her murder would be dressed up as a suicide. Once Polishchuk's body was found, the explanation would be obvious. An emotionally disturbed secretary murdered her boss in a fit of jealousy and then committed suicide. Her letters to him would then be conveniently discovered.

"But the plan didn't work.

"Natasha didn't come by train but hitched a ride from a trucker. The punks didn't see her arrive and were confused. Then there was Frezin. No one had expected him to pop up like that at the Polishchuks' dacha.

"Frezin saw Natasha leave Polishchuk's house in haste and in a state of agitation. Unlike her, he made a thorough search of the house when he got in, breaking into the study and finding Polishchuk's body, which had been lying there all along.

"Polishchuk's death was a severe blow to Frezin. He had come to have it out with him, to put the fear of God into him and to get him to cooperate. And there he was, Polishchuk, dead as a doornail.

"Confused, Frezin returns to the train station and sees the young woman he saw rushing out of Polishchuk's house. Convinced that she might know something about Polishchuk's murder – why else would she have rushed out of the house like that – he tries to talk to her. He is agitated, but he also doesn't want to ask her about the murder directly. After all, the study door was locked. Is she the murderer or an innocent bystander? Did she see the body? Who is she? Why is she acting so strangely?

"This becomes his undoing. His behavior, his persistence in trying to talk to Natasha and his overall appearance attract the unwelcome attention of other passengers. A quarrel erupts and I end up arresting Frezin."

I grinned.

"Frezin was certainly a piece of work," I said. "But he didn't kill Polishchuk. And, although he never intended it, he did a good deed. He saved Natasha."

"She was framed pretty well," Tosya said. "Whoever came up with this plan didn't leave much to chance."

"They thought of every detail," Sevka added, impressed. "They even made sure that it would look like Polishchuk was killed by a woman."

Spring, still in its early stages, had arrived. The evening was unusually warm, with a soft breeze blowing in through the open window. In the courtyard, Sevka's friends were playing soccer and their shouts and the sounds of a leather ball being kicked about filled Tosya's room.

"The truth is," I said after a long pause, "Polishchuk *was* killed by a woman."

THIRTY-ONE

Tosya gasped and Sevka almost jumped out of his chair. I waited for my audience to settle down and announced a little more solemnly than I probably should have, "Act Four. The final act."

"Who then needed to kill Polishchuk?

"Clearly, underground businessmen might have wanted to kill him if they feared that he was going to expose them to blackmailers. But they didn't. Besides, they couldn't have set up the entire complicated scenario involving Natasha. That could have been done only by someone who knew Polishchuk exceptionally well and, moreover, was close to him at all times. It had to be someone who could copy his handwriting well enough to fool his own secretary. It had to be someone who was aware of his amorous escapades with other women. And someone who could access the dacha. In other words, it had to be a member of his immediate family.

"But that's all beside the point. The underground entrepreneurs had no reason on earth to fear Polishchuk. Polishchuk couldn't have given out their names even if he wanted to. The truth is that he didn't know any of them. When he seemed flabbergasted by Frezin's proposal, it was because he had no idea what Frezin was talking about. He knew nothing about underground millionaires or, for that matter, about hard currency speculation.

"However, since he refused to cooperate with Frezin, the gang of blackmailers was threatening to attack Polishchuk's wife and daughter. That wouldn't do at all. Polishchuk had to be eliminated, and it was done skillfully and swiftly.

"The first glitch happened when the punks at Vesna station failed to push Natasha under the train. That made her unfit for the role of the murderer. The plan was changed in mid-flight. Thanks to me, or rather the happy coincidence that I arrested Frezin, a new killer was promptly found and substituted for the original one.

"Frezin's problem was that, during the Rokotov trial, Nakazov had offered him a deal – silence about Polishchuk in return for a short sentence – and he had held to his end of the bargain. So Frezin was convinced that Nakazov would not deceive him the second time around, as well.

"What Frezin didn't know was that the situation had changed completely," I said.

"How so?" Tosya asked.

"Nakazov wanted Frezin alive after the Rokotov trial, but once Polishchuk was dead, he no longer had any use for Frezin."

Tosya and Sevka tried to puzzle that one out.

"If Frezin didn't kill the plant director, and his secretary didn't either, who did and why?" Sevka asked.

I took my time before answering.

"He was killed by the real leader of the hard currency gang."

Tosya and Sevka stared back at me. I waited a bit longer, then continued. "Frezin was mistaken. He got close to identifying the real boss of the criminal organization. But he didn't really get to the bottom of it. What he had was a scrap of paper, a torn front portion of an envelope addressed to the boss. It probably contained that emerald brooch that Frezin then saw Lyuda wearing. Frezin was convinced that it pointed to Polishchuk as a gang leader.

"Captain Zapekayev found the scrap of paper in Frezin's pocket. But Frezin didn't need to hold on to it for the address of Polishchuk's dacha. It wouldn't have been hard to memorize the address. Frezin was going to confront Polishchuk with that scrap of paper as proof, which was going to convince Polishchuk that he, Frezin, knew his real position in the hard currency gang.

"The envelope was addressed to A.P. Polishchuk. The last name and the initials. Frezin naturally assumed that the initials stood for Anton Pavlovich. It was an obvious mistake."

"But in reality..." Tosya gasped.

"Yes. In reality the initials stood for Anna Panteleyevna Polishchuk."

Once more the room was plunged into deep silence. I waited and then began to recount to them a story from the distant past that had a direct bearing on the tragic events we had recently witnessed.

"The story began in the early days of the Great Patriotic War. In the fall of 1941, a certain Anya Serafimovskaya met one Vladislav Nakazov in Izhevsk, her hometown. The handsome young junior lieutenant of State Security had been evacuated there from Minsk. He was posted in Izhevsk for just a few months, but it was enough for them to have an affair and for Anya to get pregnant. Nakazov had no desire to tie himself down to some provincial girl. He had had plenty of others, and in the ensuing years he would have hundreds more."

"Those were difficult years," Tosya said. "Officers were moved from one place to another all the time."

Tosya didn't like me to say bad things about anyone, even Nakazov.

"By the time Anya gave birth to a baby girl, Nakazov was long gone from Izhevsk, but she didn't bother shedding tears for him. In fact, she was already married to a factory manager. At 34, he must have seemed to her an old man. His factory had been evacuated from Kiev and he had spent the war in Izhevsk."

"Does that mean that Lyuda was Nakazov's daughter?"

"She was."

"Did Polishchuk know?"

"I don't think so. Neither Anton nor Lyuda Polishchuk knew who her real father was. Lyuda actually thought that Nakazov had a perverted interest in her. Indeed, for an adult friend of the family, he acted rather strangely. On the other hand, he knew that Lyuda was his daughter, and in his own way he truly loved her. During the war he had a bout of measles, which in adult men can cause sterility. He never had any other children.

"When Nakazov found out that Lyuda was in love with Pavlov, his anger was not jealousy. He was probably just being overprotective. Besides, he surely knew the bit part Pavlov was playing in his black market gang. And Pavlov's father had been in jail under Stalin. Which was why Nakazov got Pavlov put away for such a long time."

"Sure," said Tosya. "He must have liked Lenny even less."

"Yes, a married man nearly twice her age and a Jew. He hated him, there can be no doubt about that. He got suspicious when I let it slip that I knew Lyuda. At first he thought that I was running around with her, but then he must have put a tail on her and discovered that she was seeing Lenny.

"To return to my story, Anya Serafimovskaya turned out to be no ordinary girl. She took it upon herself to advance her husband's career, and for this purpose she used the true father of her daughter, with whom she reconnected soon after the war. At that time, Nakazov was at the height of his power, working on a team assigned to the notorious Doctors' Plot and other high profile investigations involving cooked-up conspiracies against the Soviet State. In the early 1950s, largely thanks to Nakazov's influence, Polishchuk was transferred to Moscow and promoted to an important managerial position. His wife and beautiful daughter, who was ten or eleven at the time, accompanied him to the capital.

"Soon, however, Stalin died and Nakazov lost his exalted position and was given a far less prestigious job: keeping an eye on foreign visitors to the Soviet Union. But for Anna Panteleyevna his new job was a godsend. It became a turning point in her life. With Nakazov in charge of surveillance over foreigners at hard currency hotels, she saw a fantastic business opportunity. Once her husband became the director of the meat processing plant, he began to meet rich underground wheeler-dealers, probably because fresh meat was in short supply after the war. She also figured out that these wheeler-dealers would be glad to buy hard currency if offered the opportunity.

"Gradually, Anna Panteleyevna created an organization. At first, the deals were small, then the volume of transactions began to grow and soon they became enormous. This was at the end of the 1950s, when foreigners began coming to Moscow in large numbers and controls were loosened."

"Why did they let those foreigners in?" Sevka asked. "They're all spies. No good has ever come from those damn foreigners."

"Everything was working out well for Anna Panteleyevna," I continued, ignoring his outburst. "Her lifestyle was luxurious, she had a beautiful apartment in the center of Moscow, modern furniture and beautiful clothes. A dacha bought for a considerable sum from the widow of a hero test pilot. A young, good-looking driver who tooled her around in a brand-new Volga and could be relied upon to perform other sorts of services while her husband was at work. She began to collect antiques and porcelain, and amassed a jewelry collection that was unique throughout Moscow. And, unlike so many secret millionaires, she could enjoy it in the open, even flaunt it, because her husband had a high-level job and was paid a nomenklatura salary.

"Polishchuk's position served to hide the true sources of her wealth and to camouflage its extent, but the money also helped advance his career. What minister could resist favoring an employee who gives his wife or daughter a priceless bracelet as a birthday gift, or who finds some never-before-seen lingerie for a mistress? Money can buy everything.

"But Anna Panteleyevna never let down her guard and remained cautious to a fault. No one in the gang had any idea that she even existed. Underground entrepreneurs who bought hard currency from her at a steep markup knew her more as a naive intermediary and not the true seller. And, when he was needed, there was always Nakazov, who could defuse any dangerous situation and eliminate inconvenient witnesses.

"Nevertheless, when Khrushchev demanded that illegal currency trading be stopped, Anna Panteleyevna realized that she was walking on a knife's edge. Had Nakazov not been appointed to lead the investigation, she could have been looking at a long prison sentence or even a firing squad. When Frezin, being interrogated by Nakazov, mistakenly identified her husband as the real leader of the gang, she had a brilliant idea. Why not make him the fallback leader? When push came to shove, Frezin would confirm it, and convincingly so, since he believed it to be true. Meanwhile, clues could be scattered here and there implicating Anton Pavlovich in the gang's activities. She invented an affair with Natasha, which could be eventually used for the same purpose. She must have been quite amused writing those love letters. She even included certain hidden clues in the letters that she knew would mean nothing to Natasha but which would finger Polishchuk as the leader of a hard currency gang if read by people who knew about its existence. Of course, that would only be the last resort, if investigators got too close to discovering her own role in the business."

"But then she killed her husband, right?" Sevka asked.

"She did. With Frezin and his con friends on Anton Pavlovich's tail, she realized that she had made a serious mistake and would now have to get rid of her husband."

"How did she do it?"

"That was the most straightforward part of the entire plot," I said. "She arranged for workers to repair the roof, so that her husband would have to stay at the dacha on Sunday. Hera came to pick them up and she and Lyuda went back to the city. They got into the car, said goodbye to Polishchuk and drove off. Hera was in cahoots with Anna Panteleyevna, but Lyuda knew nothing about what was going to happen. In a few minutes, Anna Panteleyevna said she had forgotten something and that they had to go back. They returned to the dacha and Hera stayed in the car with Lyuda, to make sure she would not follow her mother into the house. Anna Panteleyevna, meanwhile, snuck into her husband's study, where she knew he would be, and strangled him with a fishing line. She then locked the door and arranged Valya Sokolova's letter on the kitchen table, to be discovered later by Natasha. She also left the front door unlocked. An elegant and easy murder. Could her daughter have imagined that, in the five minutes her mother had been in the house, she had strangled her father?"

"Who was not even her real father," Sevka said.

"What about the burglary at their apartment?" Tosya asked.

"Anna Panteleyevna herself removed their most valuable jewels, fearing that the police might search the apartment after the murder. She might have also wanted to convince blackmailers that, after the death of her husband, she had no more money left."

Tosya shook her head.

"Of course, Anna Panteleyevna told the concierge at the apartment building what to say to the police about the burglars. She came up with the story of the three painters. And then she made sure that the police discovered the emerald brooch, to make the theft appear more convincing."

I fell silent. I thought of Lyuda and how she begged me to be careful with the brooch, to make sure we didn't lose it.

"After Polishchuk's death, Anna Panteleyevna furnished her apartment far more modestly. She obviously expected a visit from Frezin's associates. She must have thought that, after she was finished with me, the blackmailers were her only remaining problem."

"But then Matyushkin came along and reshuffled her deck."

"I guess so," I said modestly.

"Anna Panteleyevna didn't like Lenny and me from the start. When I started to question witnesses at the dacha, she got alarmed. Maybe not really scared, but enough to tell Nakazov to take me off the case.

"But I didn't let go and she watched with growing alarm as I started getting somewhere. I was still far from discovering the truth, and even of suspecting her of being in some way involved, but I had dug out enough information to dismiss Frezin's trial as a complete sham. When I interrogated Natasha and had the three of them witness it, Anna

Panteleyevna realized that I had found the three punks and knew that they had been hired by Hera.

"While I was interrogating Natasha, I talked nonsense on purpose, and Anna saw it. But she couldn't figure out what my game was. She and Nakazov chose to get rid of me, making it look like I had attacked Nakazov. That was exactly what I was hoping they would do. Because with Nakazov protecting her at State Security and me essentially fired from Criminal Investigations, I wouldn't have been able to make any charges against her stick.

"Nakazov was supposed to get rid of me, but Anna Panteleyevna wouldn't have been Anna Panteleyevna had she relied exclusively on Nakazov. She trusted only herself and therefore had a Plan B, to be put into effect if Nakazov failed. In the last desperate move, she tried to make it seem like her daughter, and not her husband, was the putative head of the gang.

"When I arrived at my apartment in Nakazov's jeep, Anna Panteleyevna knew I had killed Nakazov and she put her Plan B into operation. With Nakazov alive, she would never have dared to kill Lyuda. He wouldn't have forgiven her."

"How could she do it?" Tosya exclaimed.

"She put a sleeping draft and a poison in her tea. Lyuda first grew drowsy but was conscious long enough for her mother to lead her downstairs and lock her in the storage space. The poison was slow-acting and it didn't kick in until later. The concierge didn't know that Lyuda would die. Later, Anna Panteleyevna would have claimed it was an accident, or simply told the concierge that she was in it to her neck and she would have to shut up."

"She's a monster," Tosya said.

I nodded.

"Well, Matyushkin," she added a few minutes later. "I forgive you for dropping us like you did. I believe you when you say you were only protecting us. But in future, you should know that Sevka and I can take care of ourselves. Am I right, Sevka?"

"You were going to get me a pair of skates," Sevka said, changing the subject. "You promised."

"I will, Sevka," I said. "But it will have to wait until next winter."

"Next winter won't come for another year."

THIRTY TWO

Sevka was disappointed about the skates, but otherwise he looked at me with eyes glowing with admiration. Just having him look at me like that was enough to convince me that I would go through it all over again if I had to. But I also wanted Tosya and me to have a kid of our own. Not that I didn't love Sevka or didn't think of him almost like my own son. But I would've loved to have one of my own all the same. Mine and Tosya's.

"Go to bed, Sevka," Tosya commanded in a voice that brooked no objections, and then added more gently. "Tomorrow is a school day."

ABOUT THE AUTHOR

Alexei Bayer is a New York-based author, translator and, by economic necessity, an economist. He writes in English and in Russian, his native tongue, and translates into both languages.

His short stories have been published in *New England Review*, *Kenyon Review*, and *Chtenia*. His translations have appeared in *Chtenia* and *Words Without Borders*, as well as in such collections as *The Wall in My Head*, a book dedicated to the 20th anniversary of the fall of the Berlin Wall, and *Life Stories*, a bilingual literary anthology to benefit hospice care in Russia.

Murder at the Dacha is also being published in Russian, in Russia, in 2013.